O Beulah Land

Books by Mary Lee Settle

The Love Eaters
The Kiss of Kin
O Beulah Land
Know Nothing
Fight Night on a Sweet Saturday
All the Brave Promises
The Story of Flight
The Clam Shell
The Scopes Trial
Prisons
Blood Tie
The Scapegoat
The Killing Ground
Water World
Celebration
Charley Bland
Turkish Reflections
Choices

O Beulah Land

by Mary Lee Settle
with a new introduction by the author

UNIVERSITY OF SOUTH CAROLINA PRESS

Copyright © 1956 by Mary Lee Settle
Introduction to the USC Press edition © 1996 by Mary Lee Settle

Published in Columbia, South Carolina, by the
University of South Carolina Press

First published by Viking Press, 1956
University of South Carolina Press edition published in 1996 by
arrangement with the author

Manufactured in the United States of America

00 99 98 97 96   5 4 3 2 1

Library of Congress Cataloging-in-Publication Data

Settle, Mary Lee.
    O Beulah land / by Mary Lee Settle ; with a new introduction by
the author. —University of South Carolina Press ed.
        p.   cm.
    ISBN 1-57003-115-0 (pbk. : alk. paper)
        1. Virginia—History—Colonial period, ca. 1600–1775—Fiction.
I. Title.
PS3569.E8402   1996
813'.54—dc20   98–2226

The Beulah Quintet

In 1954, I began a third novel before my first two, *The Kiss of Kin* and *The Love Eaters*, had been published. It grew from a questioned image. A man hit a stranger in a drunk tank on a hot, summer night in a small town in America. "Why?" was the question about one act of violence that would draw me away from the present—how far away I had no idea then. I began to learn a past and a language. I found fears, dreams, and hatreds that once had reason, frozen into prejudice. I began to see people at the time of these reasons, these hopes, these illusions. I found not only what was happening but what they thought was happening, a change and flow of belief that reflected the time as a mirror. The search would grow into *O Beulah Land*, the first written but the second volume of a quintet I never intended. It would take twenty-eight years to finish. The five volumes cover more than three hundred years.

Prisons, volume one, is about the source of our American democratic language. I found the event that gave me the earliest answers I sought—where our language began—in a churchyard in Burford, England. All that was left of the execution of Corporal Perkins and Corporal Church were bullet holes in a wall. The time of their execution was May 17, 1649.

O Beulah Land, volume two, begins with the image of a woman stripped down to survival, lost and mindless with fear, moving toward the east through the Endless Mountains. Her name is Hannah Bridewell. The time is 1754. She glimpses a small valley that she never forgets. It is the first sight of Beulah. Hunger for land of one's own, safe from exile, is the guiding force of the time. The land would be always a little farther west, a little out of reach, over the next mountain, down the next river. *O Beulah Land* ends in 1774.

Know Nothing, volume three, begins in 1837, with a boy thrown into the Great Kanawha River to learn to swim. The eighteenth-century log house has been replaced by the mansion of Beulah. The past has already rusted into the shapes of legend. Heroic legend and the deep-stressed imitation of gentility have gagged simplicity. The place is Virginia, and the end of *Know Nothing*, the first shots of the Civil War.

The Scapegoat, volume four, is the story of the mine wars in the Valley of Beulah. I found its language and its deaths buried in the report of an investigation into a massacre during a coal strike in the Kanawha Valley in 1912. Railroad lines follow the creeks into the hills. Coal dust stains the white dresses of the girls. On a pretty front porch, carved like white lace, sits a Gatling gun.

The Killing Ground, volume five, is the story of *The Beulah Quintet* itself, how a death in a drunk tank that I had envisioned so long ago became the last Hannah's own search for a reason for the death of her brother. She returns finally in 1980 to a changed valley, recovering from the disasters of the coal fields, which have been a phase, no more permanent than the hungers before them. *The Beulah Quintet* ends as it began, with Johnny Church riding into Burford.

Introduction
The Lost Land of Beulah

I did not have the luxury of looking back on the years of *O Beulah Land* from the present with all the arrogance and future knowledge of a past time. That is the privilege of historians. I had to become contemporary, think as they thought, fear what they had feared, use their own language with its yet unchanged meanings, face a blank and fearful future. I had to forget what I already knew.

I was living in England in 1951, far, I thought, from the place and time I sought. I was wrong. I went to the British Museum, and there, all around the walls, in the huge catalogues that had been kept so carefully for so long, I found an Aladdin's cave of memory. The eighteenth-century *Gentlemen's Magazine* was in the shelves near my favorite seat in the great round reading room. I began with that. In the back of each issue were the book reviews. They were my first source, long-forgotten books about the new, feared, fascinating land of Virginia, which was a generic name for a wild place beyond a terrifying sea. They were all there, still in the stacks—the books about battles, about discoveries, about laws, about captivities, told by the people who had experienced them, in their time and in their language.

Our memories are long. We are the children of our grandparents' childhoods, their memories of their parents and grandparents, what they have cleaned, deleted, forgotten, denied. But nothing in my own historic memory seemed to reach into the mid eighteenth century. To inform my book I had to create an eighteenth-century past of my own. I read for ten months without taking a note, let the past become a present, let it fall beyond intelligence into reliving, which is true sensuous recall, where dreams come from with all their fears and future hopes of things long past.

Then, one night, I dreamed that I was building a log cabin in a clearing in the woods. It had to be at least four feet high so that I could claim occupancy and get my deed for the land by paying a quitrent to the colonial government. I still remember the smell of buckskins long worn, the wind in trees gashed by my ax to claim tomahawk rights, the gaunt, naked trees that had been girdled so that they would die and be easier to clear for planting. Memory had entered dream and I was ready to write.

I began to find everything I needed, there and in England—American brown bears at the zoo, a puma, Tower muskets at the ancient arsenal, the Tower of London. A former guardsman who was one of the librarians at the British Museum taught me the order of drill of the Guards' regiments that had not changed since the eighteenth century, whispering commands as we stood in the corridor between the North Library, where some of the rarest books in the world are kept, and the reading room, porting arms with imaginary muskets that were higher than our heads.

I measured how far I could see across a wild unknown river by pacing the Roman façade of the Museum. I found out how to call a hog from a Shakespeare scholar in the North Library, reading first folios at the great leather-covered table across from me. He was so surprised at my question that he lifted his head as if he were still in Iowa, and called "Sooey!" across the silent company of scholars and people staying warm in one of the coldest winters in England who read, wrote, and slept all around us.

I took a bus to New Forest, what is left of the royal hunting forest of the Saxon kings, and found more huge virgin trees than there are in all of the modern surviving forests of what once was the wilderness of Virginia.

I was taken into the storage vaults below the British Museum, and there were Indian artifacts that had come from the valley that I would call Beulah. In the corner of the vaulted cave were two tea chests full of what I thought were furs. There were stretched circles of leather painted with designs. I lifted one of them and found that the leather circle was attached to a long hank of blond hair. I had found the scalps of our own ancestors.

A review in the *Gentlemen's Magazine* led me to the story of an engineer attached to Braddock's army who had been captured while building the Braddock Road (now route 40 through Virginia and Pennsylvania). He was a prisoner in Fort Duquesne. He was there when the battle took place a few miles upstream from the fort. After the battle a French soldier brought him a book found on a body. It was

Russell's Seven Sermons. I went to the catalogue, heaved it out, and found the entry that I had learned to expect, the early 1750s edition . The only secondary reference I used was a reprint of primary documents that covered the true events, long misted over by contemporary self-protecting excuses and our own romantic illusions about Braddock's defeat at Fort Duquesne, a battle fought in the wrong place and at the wrong time of day, a real battle where everybody was late.

One day I came on a painting in the Tate Gallery and began to cry, and I think of it now, of all it tells, however covered by legend, of the sadness of having to leave home. It is called *The Last View of England.* The sad faces of a young couple and their small baby, standing on the deck of an immigrant ship, haunt me, and should haunt us all—not intrepid pioneers, but poor young people leaving home forever for a strange place of hope and fear.

One evening I found the title and the impassioned theme of my book. I had brought back to London from a visit to my family in West Virginia a recording of old hymns sung by Burl Ives. I listened to the hymn "O Beulah Land" for the first time.

> *O Beulah Land, sweet Beulah Land,*
> *As on the highest mount I stand,*
> *I look away across the sea,*
> *Where mansions are prepared for me,*
> *And view the shining glory shore,*
> *My heaven, my home for evermore.*

I still stand in that room in England, and still hear that hunger for a land hoped for, fought over, and never quite found— what we think of as the American Dream, lost, defiled, complicated and used by the cynical, and still so deeply sought by the rest of us—to own your own home, shrunk from a claim in the great woods to a lot in a suburb, a place nobody can make you leave.

Over and over it happened. I stumbled over, walked into, sought out, found my book *O Beulah Land,* beginning with Hannah, lost in the Endless Mountains, and ending with the last colonial year before the American Revolution.

O Beulah Land

To Christopher
for Albion and Beulah

CONTENTS

. . . his dream must have seemed so close that he could hardly fail to grasp it. He did not know that it was already behind him, somewhere back in that vast obscurity beyond the city, where the dark fields of the republic rolled on under the night.

Gatsby believed in the green light, the orgiastic future that year by year recedes before us. It eluded us then, but that's no matter—tomorrow we will run faster, stretch out our arms farther. . . . And one fine morning—

So we beat on, boats against the current, borne back ceaselessly into the past.

F. Scott Fitzgerald, *The Great Gatsby*

PROLOGUE

O Beulah Land, sweet Beulah Land,
As on thy highest mount I stand . . .

Chapter One

A SINGLE footprint lay alone. It seemed dropped from nowhere onto the underbrush between the black, muscular roots of the high tree which dominated the ragged, lonesome hollow. But a small hand, human, on a thin, rootlike white arm, wavered over the indent, fluttered the leaves, and the print was gone.

At twilight a raccoon licked along the dry ground, sniffing the trail made by stains of blood which had fallen as the foot had fallen, lightly; smelled and scratched like a dog, and ambled away, the color of the shadows, disappearing through a world its own color.

The night came down, and the trees were ghostly under a full moon. Tiny settlements of double lights defined their branches. Some appeared and disappeared like stars; some were as constant as planets, blinking out only as eyes blink after staring. The night stretched on, and even sleep could not blot out the universe of watchers.

Inside the tree, huddled among the brush, plumped up the way a woman would plump a pillow, a small something alive could be heard from time to time, though not seen even by the wildcats, the wolverines, the panthers that crouched on the sea of branches. That it was a woman was certain from the thin arm, from the small footprint, and now, in the lowest time of heavy night, from the catch of her breath and the wary, light way she turned as quickly on the leaves as she could, careful of disturbing the pressing nothing of the outside night—turned and listened; turned again, stopped, and listened; waited still in the black tree for the sound of moving, a footfall, the startled crack of a twig; waited for the rhythm of breathing.

She lay near sleep, staring back at the twin stars up the other side of the cut, which from time to time moved, dropped, went out like lamps, and were replaced by others. She tried to form her fear into an image: the huge, rough nose pressed against her side; the harsh grab of a human hunter; the moving shape filling the waist-high opening of the tree and blotting out the hungry watchers—forced herself to wait even for the slow kneading of the muscles of the snake across her tense, cold stomach, around her legs, or violating her thighs and crawling, as familiar as the serpent with Eve; forced herself to make these images of terror to deaden the wider fear of the silence, of the tall trees, of the blank, left-alone nothing—until the unholy scream of an animal pierced the night, when twin stars swooped down from the branches.

The morning came early still in August. The eyes of the night animals went out, fading with the first paleness which the thick trees let filter down. The whole wilderness seemed as quiet as the holding of a huge breath. The dim shapes across the gap sprang nearer, began to color from their first grayness. Suddenly the sun pierced once, from high above, a thin watery line, and the air was filled with the shrieking of birds. The woman thrashed awake and screamed as if her head itself had burst into great jostling morning noise. But she had slept.

[4]

Where there is a cut, there will be a freshet; beyond the freshet, a spring branch; beyond the branch, a creek; beyond the creek, a river, flowing and interflowing like the capillaries, the arteries, the veins of a man. Where the water flows down, sooner or later there will be men. But where it flows from, only the underbrush, the high trees, the silence, and in the midst of the silence the mountains, the Endless Mountains.

No balance here, no leveling, plumbline, measuring intelligence; just the old convulsions, making the earth's shape. The water followed, and the animals found it, tracing the roads; and the first men, the color of forest clay, followed the animals and the water until they claimed the traces for themselves. So a single papaw falling, rolling down the banks of the forest was Newton's law— unmeasured, undiscussed, unheard; the woods arranging themselves, like a thousand-mile-wide surrender to the law which is so inevitable that it can crush the will and mind of a man.

When the papaw fell the woman crept out of the tree, watching where her stiffened limbs set her feet, and grabbed it from the ground so fiercely with her cold hand that the smoky blue skin broke and yellow pulp squished between her fingers. Where she had come from there had been not even sweet papaws, only a choking mass of tangled and insidious laurel hugging at her dress; rhododendron run wild over and under, making a strong mat which rose almost to tree height, mile upon mile of thick snaking roots, like the unkempt head of some insane giant. For two days she had stumbled, fought, thrust her body against the unyielding mass, without food, without water, in a maze of God, leaving a thin trail of linsey behind her in the selfish, high undergrowth, while above her head and out of sight the wild moving tops of the plants lifted their handsome black-green swirls of leaves and tried to charm the sun.

Fifteen feet below the sunlight, in the darkness, for the first time a little beside herself with horror at the tunneled labyrinth, she had heard the scurry of thousands of creatures, and could not see them, except as shadows like the fear she ran from. She had fallen among the waiting coils. They had held her while she slept and woke in fits and pushed and inched painfully on through a tunnel dug with her own body against the massive spider web. Thirty-six hours later she had felt rather than seen the cut, the clearer bank, and crept into the tree exhausted, still wild with fear, covering her tracks by the habit of survival rather than because she thought any more.

If she had been going to die she would have died that night, but her natural will churned on, irresponsible to any consciousness she could muster, making her live. The will decided, and she slept, the panic dying down finally, like the last of a fever.

The woman who woke up, weak as she was, was new, made free for a time of haunting memory by shock, a different woman from the one who had blundered into the thicket. She had been a haunted, chased creature, mindless with panic, in the two weeks she had been driven east by her own fear, kept alive only by some boundless miracle that lets the nervous fawns live, or the silly, vulnerable fish. Now she was no longer running from the west, too scared to scream, with the devil at her heels. She was headed east, ready to meet the sun as it rose to guide her. But to do it, her will demanded first calmness, then food, and rest.

So after two days the papaw was welcome, and she licked its pulp from her fingers and found another and another under the glossy, heavy-bearing bush. Not thinking, she slid some of the fruit to her pocket, but where that had been was a long tear, and the soft fruit felt cool against her bare leg before she realized what she was doing.

She looked down, following her own hand, and burst into a sob, feeling up and down her body where the thicket had torn her dress into rents until it was like the garment of some mourning widow in a desert of the Bible. But no one heard the sob; like the papaw, the tears obeyed the law of God and fell among the dry leaves and the thick dust at her feet. There was no one to hear—no one but many living things who pricked their ears and rolled to sleep again, or deer who lowered their heads delicately back into the high river meadow just beyond the tree she stood by. No one to listen for two hundred miles that she knew of—except something behind her that she was aware of but could not call to mind, something tracking, inevitable as the law around her. Remembering only as the deer had remembered, conditioned to danger, she too pricked her human ears, listened, holding her sobs with her breath, and dropped down out of sight behind the papaw tree.

At last, hearing the wind sky-high above her head as it shuffled through the leaves of the forest roof, she crawled forward, for she had parted from the noise of the wind another sound, the moving river. She rose up on her knees and let her head come slowly above the high grass in front of the papaw tree, and saw that she was at last back to the river highway and on her trail.

She was kneeling on a small hill that sloped in front of her into a long, narrow meadow. Its grass was heavy and brushed with yellow by the heat of August, tall enough to ripple in waves as the wind caught it. It covered a valley broken by mounds, some so low they seemed only natural hummocks in the grass, some as high as houses. It was as if the valley had been lived in once, and died in, the dead abandoned there so long ago that a few trees, like the tree she had slept in, had taken root in the mounds and had grown huge and spread their virgin branches in great dark pools of summer shade.

Away in the distance, near a wide river bend, protected by a circle of hills like ancient earthworks, she saw deer and elk feeding and knew they had not scented the devil who stalked her, that as long as they moved and munched the meadow of the bottomland without dropping dead in their tracks she too was safe from all but the silence, which, when the day protected her, seemed to retreat high in the sunny sky above her and not to swoop near until the long shadows of evening would pull it down, a smothering blanket.

She rolled gratefully in the harsh grass and, safe in the sun, fell asleep again, not meaning to. She slept until the sun turned the shadow of the papaw tree and covered her, and she woke up shivering, not knowing where she was, and came alive to the present fear again. She was conscious only of the lost time her nap had cost, time running without carrying her nearer the misty rim of mountains in the distance. The deer flies hung about her, humming, but she had been too exhausted to know. Now, fighting them away from her face and her dirt-streaked gray legs, she got up from the grass, where her body had flattened a cradle. The animals were farther off up the river; nothing had disturbed them. It was still too early for them to skitter to their own secret night shelters. Down along the river the cane-brake shuffled in the stronger wind, which slapped her black hair against her face as she rose into it.

She ran, using the higher mounds to hide herself, watching her footing to keep from falling on those that had been so eroded by time that they were only stumbling blocks in the valley floor. She seemed to be playing hide and seek with the silence itself, hiding from something she did not bother to think about or name, as instinctive as an animal. She waded along the swampy bank to gather into a bundle what canes she could reach without falling into the water.

If she had panicked before, if she had cried, now she had forgotten. The present contained work, quick work. She snapped stalk after stalk of the high, sweet harvest, and when she trudged back two hours had passed and it was long evening. Her hands shook and bled from the sharp sticks she had dragged, painfully dropping, retrieving, in a frustrating snail's pace across the great meadow and back into the shelter of the papaw tree. In front of it, facing the bend of the river, she built herself a cane-shelter for the night, so low that from any distance the high grass obscured it, so near to the color of the grass that it was camouflaged as carefully as the wood-colored raccoon or the shadow-dappled snake. But she respected the nameless thing she hid from. From the formless papaw she took branches, tearing from under the tree's main branches to hide the scars, and covered her shelter with the beautiful slick leaves so that the great bush seemed only to spread a little more. Because she had slept or worked the whole day near its protecting bulk, it was familiar, and she felt safe against the strangeness around her.

[8]

She sat down now, halfway inside her shelter, for the wind had grown cooler, and stared away across the meadow, the way a woman rests between demands, dreaming beyond her work—never done, anyway. Such dreams are dangerous. Before she could stop herself she began to dream of meat, to be possessed by biting, demanding hunger which made her ears roar and her stomach contract, demanding, demanding, rejecting in a rush of yellow vomit the papaw she'd gathered for her evening meal.

She fell, half in and half out of the little shelter, not flat, for she had rolled forward from her hips and her legs were still under her, and waited until the squeezing of her stomach stopped. She whispered then, without knowing she did it; she had been alone for so long she was no longer aware of where thought left off and turned to sound from her mouth.

"Gawd, but I'm hongry."

But she went on lying there, too weak to move. Up-river of her the deer stirred, but they might as well have been the shiftings of her worked imagination, growing wilder in the woods, for all the good they did her. Like the grapes of hell, they tantalized as they nuzzled in the grass.

Just as they had many times before during the two weeks, the twitching squirrels moved from where her sudden movement had frozen them, whisked and frisked down the trees behind her, nearer and nearer, to investigate the new thing that lay there, finally quiet, across the vomit of the papaw. This time she knew they were coming and stayed still, all her soul concentrated on her right hand, which she had flung beyond her head as she fell. The hand lay as still as a trap. A fly landed on one of her fingers, and, triggerlike, the finger nearly responded, but she kept it from moving, now peeking along the ground through her hair as an inquisitive squirrel came nearer, stopped and listened for nothing, like a fool, twitched its lovely tail, came still nearer. Now she sighted along her bare arm; her hand waited, waited; watching with a terrible patience, took in the details of the squirrel's thick mat of delicate fur as it moved and

[9]

parted and then was still again, took in its sloe eyes intent on the new white, rootlike thing across the ground; watched as it sat, tail hoisted like a flag, then moved over, almost touching the hand waiting as still as a stone. The squirrel sniffed; still the hand waited—sniffed again, and still it was too soon; sniffed again, now at the center of her palm. The finger and thumb snapped like a vise and trapped the squirrel by its tiny doll hand as it sprang back.

They screamed together—fine, weak, almost silent screams. Her other hand darted out, choking, choking until the tiny animal hung limp and let go her right hand where its little rodent teeth had bitten through the soft flesh of her thumb-pad until they met.

She did not remember what happened then. She sank back inside the shelter and slept again, not even remembering to set the canes in front of it to cage herself safely against the wild animals. When she woke, the sun up again, she felt better than she had for many days, and when she could find only tufts of torn fur instead of the squirrel skin she'd reckoned on to lay over her scratched leg, she thought the animals had been there in the night and torn it so savagely. Not even the blood, and her swollen, bitten hand, made her remember that she herself had done it.

So on the sunny morning of the first of September, 1755, having eaten a raw squirrel and slept, off and on, for all but two or three of the last twenty-four hours, she was strong enough in her body and in her driven mind to take some stock of herself and begin to plan.

Where she was she had no idea. It might have been, as far as she could remember, one of the valleys of the moon. She might have been born in this vast place—miles on miles of deserted wilderness, with its deep rivers, twisted creek beds, hills, its tree after tree after tree, its cold heights, its streaming lowland, and its vast, tangled, murderous rhododendron thickets. She could remember, at last, her own name—Hannah. Behind that, nothing but shadows, shifting and changing before she could turn her attention full on them. Her mind, then, seemed as vast and as deep as the forest itself, stretching away eternally on all sides, engulfing, dark, and full of things she could not see; but her memory seemed only like the long wire of sunlight that lights so little, one thing, one group of things at a time, resting on them until they are familiar, the rest—the vast rest—unknown and unexplorable; for she could no more guide her own memory than she could catch and tame the fleeting sunbeams.

She was Hannah; she was here. One thing, one startling thing more, flashed to light. Here she was as vulnerable as any beast—more so. For she had neither fleetness nor teeth nor perfect eyes nor warning nose to protect her; she had only her will to go east, and her brain—poor unlit wilderness—and the thumbed hands that lay in her lap. She knew that she must never light a fire, any more than the perpetually warring animals did; that she must not follow the side of the river where the buffalo highway ran, but must keep to the narrower valley, where there were no beaten roads to draw man on. She had realized long since, from watching the wide, deep river wind out toward the sunset, that if she went on against its current, used it like a map until it was shallow enough to cross toward the high mountains far yonder to the east, she would, if she survived, find some kind of safety. But what that safety would be she did not know; she would go on toward the mountains as we go toward death, inevitably moving, driven without choice.

Sighing, having finished her survey of herself, her needs, and the bend of the river—the near meadow still in the dawn shadow from the hills across the river—she got up and said again.

"I wisht I hadn't of et that whole crittur."

So, putting dreams away, she set about her business. She tore long strips of cane with her teeth, chewed along them until they were moister than the dew had made them, preoccupied as a woman knitting by the fire. Two basket-like soles grew in her hands while she watched the sun rise full over the hills beyond, and had to turn as it hit her eyes, and watch down-river, with the vacant look of a craftsman who lets his eyes float without focus until he needs them.

There was a new taste when she chewed, a juice from the stalks, sweet and pleasant. It stilled her hunger as she worked, and she forgot it for a time in the dear excitement of the shoes she'd planned. She sat until the sun was high and hot on her shoulders, then was ready to slip her feet into the shoes, which she had lined thick with soft grass; they were so tightly caned that they made a seven-inch-wide flat print scented with grass stain instead of her own sweat and blood. She put them on and tied them with braided grass, telling herself she must watch out for leather bark along her way, or the ungiving grass braids would cut into her tender scratched legs. She looked down critically at her two huge feet, making up her mind by habit, as if she had some choice in the matter; made up her mind, got up and walked, then almost danced, all alone there, holding the tatters of linsey aside with her hands, pleased and satisfied at the comfort. Then she laid the tall grass in layers around her legs and strapped them on as carefully as she had made her shoes—two great yellow-green hay-legs, with a little body on top.

"Sweetheart, I do look a sight!" Hannah grinned, embarrassed, at the papaw tree. Seeing it reminded her, and she shook herself and went to work again, made a new large pocket of cane, and strapped it to herself with a grass-braid belt. This took until noon, and she had still not eaten or been to the river to drink. Sadly she filled the pocket with papaws, meaning to tip them out when she had a chance, and went on her way down to drink at the river, hoping with all the pain of ambition fed too long on hope that she would find a little something along the way.

The summer wind was still blowing down-river, full in her face, growing hotter as she walked through the grass toward the herd of deer, which had returned to graze. They did not scent her until she was nearly on them, and even when they did the old ones only raised their heads inquiringly, then bent to food again. One great regal elk with a heavy Stuart face, and antlers like two high diagrams of the rivers of his kingdom standing against the sky, reviewed her tiny figure as she passed, disinterested but watchful as he fed, kneeling on his foreknees. A few of the fawns, which had grown big through the summer, skittered sideways and then went still and lowered heads toward their food again. That was all; they were aware but not gun-shy, as placid as cows, the bucks far gentler in the sun than any farmyard bull. Hannah noticed none of this as strange. She noticed only, measuring with her eyes, how far from the mother the silliest fawn had strayed, noticed and felt the grass along her leg, and resolved to look for sharp stones in the next creek. She stepped high through the grass on her new great booted legs, watching at every step for the snakes, as all eyes and ears as an animal; but, being a woman, she had to rest over and over as she walked the great five-mile bend to the next creek at the end of the meadow. It was only when she leaned down to put her face in the creek to drink that she found food and tools.

It took an hour to catch two little fish in a creek alive with them. But hunger has wits of its own. After trying and trying, watching and learning, Hannah dug with one of her rocks, improving on the smooth creek bank where the fish glided under little eaves in the fast falling water, half-asleep there but always out of reach. She made a small inlet of water in the bank, then, with a large stone at the inlet's narrow mouth, pinned the fish as the current spilled them in.

To celebrate when the first fish came into the trap, she threw the papaws into the creek and watched them bobble quickly down stream. This time she had learned enough to keep a part of the second fish. She kept it back from her raw feast, wrapped it in leaves, and put it in her pocket with the few sharp flints she had gathered.

These were the activities, the slight dramas. In between them she walked, stumbled, crawled, automatically, hour after hour, changing her way without thinking as the sun wore down on her till her legs ran with sweat under the grass and she tanned a harsh brown over the gray of fatigue. She wandered blindly along the river meadows and down the restful game tracks that ran between them in halls of trees where the woods grew down to the

[13]

river bank. At first she walked tentatively, with the steps of a woman used to a busy street and lost among the crowds. But, as the days passed, her stride changed in keeping with the space, the terrible freedom of being entirely, hopelessly alone. But always she seemed still to be wandering, although the direction never changed, and always she faced up the unplotted, rolling river.

She had learned finally to swim the wide mouths of the deeper creeks, like a deer, holding her water-panicked head high and strutting wildly with her hard, thin, now brown hands across the water, holding in her mouth the precious cane pocket, or its successor—for the flints cut, and she had to make the pocket and the shoes over and over, damning the time lost as she worked frantically.

This way she trudged through the first days of September, insane with monotony, fear, and sometimes forgetfulness, walking the now rarer, smaller valleys of buffalo grass, the track of time lost completely, only automatic will making her move on.

Of that time she could call to mind later only one separate scene. The bottomlands had run so long in strips between the hills and river that she stopped in her tracks at the sight of a deeper valley lying like an upturned hand between two hills across the river. The gentle place rested, with a creek like a lifeline running through it, as if God, sickened by the magnificence of the huge trees and the mountains, had lain down in mid-Creation, flung out His lovely hand, and gone to sleep awhile. She could see from the river bank the grass-thick bottom near the creek; the flat, trodden yellow ground where the animals had come so long for water; the grove of cedars on the hill behind it; the first turning maple on the hillsides beyond. She stood with her arms crossed, measuring from a distance in her mind's eye, and frowned a little calculating frown. But the wide, calm river was between them; like Moses, she had to gaze from far off.

Even as she watched she saw upright figures move in single file down the light, sandy game track, which widened toward the

[14]

creek. The glimmer of a copper pot caught the sun, and Hannah, two hundred yards away, across the river, dropped into the underbrush and lay without a sound, as if the flash of light had been a gunshot, until the wind changed and fanned her face, and she felt safe to crawl away among the trees. So she went on, more wary for a while after seeing the other human beings, then lapsed into her automatic trudge again, past the long semicircle of rock that formed a rampart of perpetually sighing falls which fanned a halo of spray across the river, past the wide basin above it where the water flowed in two great strips, one green from a long, gentle mountain valley, one brown from tearing away the mountain soil in its rush from the miles of gorge to its present peace, where it lay round high islands of rock like a wide moat combining many castles. But Hannah saw nothing of this to remember. She was too tired to do more than put one thick, grass-packed column of leg in front of the other. Sometimes what rambling thoughts she had took on a rhythm, and she would hum a little or sing the only words that ever came—

"With a ruffdom, ruffdom, fizzledom madge . . ."

—over and over again until she cried to get the silly words washed out of her head. So she'd go on, her face streaked with sweaty tears, for miles, with a ruffdom, ruffdom, fizzledom madge, keeping step with her song though she begged herself not to, until only sleep could release her, and for a few days she would forget, until the merciless song sneaked in again and whipped her to a march.

Every day the high mountains came nearer; she found herself climbing up and down the spurs of the hills as the water cut gently through between them, the bed not yet narrow enough for the water to slip its lead.

Once she had to climb a high cliff that jutted out over the water. It took the whole day's light, climbing, catching, stumbling, to get across the ridge and down again. She had covered two hundred yards to the east when the night finally came, and she poked a long stick into a huge hollow fallen tree to flush the smaller animals and crawled to sleep at last.

The mountains thrust gradually higher and higher until it was only the sun of the hours around noon that she felt directly. The bare cliffs towered, reminders that the mountains were convulsions of stone, that their green trees grew hard, fought for the earth. The narrow river roared over steep falls, or past single grand table rocks, which forced the water to sing around their keels like ships striking upstream. Then, at the shoals, trout jumped high and the nervous spray jumped after them and rampaged among the rocks. The louder roar of the river meant another thing. There were no more papaw trees in the now tiny, room-sized plateaus too high to be taken at that time of year by the raging water, and the fish were too wary in the perpetual motion of their existence to float lazily into the traps Hannah made from time to time in the bank. Once in a while she found a few blackberry bushes that had not been stripped by the bears, and chestnuts half-hidden in the ground from the season before, left over by the squirrels. But not enough—never enough. She was possessed again by hunger, hag-ridden with it, at the mercy of her daydreams.

September, before the new harvest, was a cruel time to be in the mountains. Millions of animals had cleaned the ground and bushes. Once hunger drove her to a berry-packed shrub, but feeding on the bitter sleek fruit made her stomach gripe and melted her bowels. It was two days after the blank, shivering sickness before she was able to crawl on.

The mountains were turning slowly from summer green and as high as she was a snap of frost was already in the air. Here and there the sumac lay like drops of blood along the banks, and the maples blushed bright scarlet in groves, ripening in huge patches high on the south front of the mountains. But they could not be eaten; Hannah ignored their brightness and searched for food, as tenacious and single-minded as the tree-roots themselves.

At dawn one morning, on a rock table jutting above the rushing river two hundred yards upstream, two tiny figures moved, became one, moved apart again, in the early mist. What they were she could not be certain. Then a sound rose above the loud roar of the river, reverberated down the gorge against the mountainsides, caught her with the stroke of the wind. She began to move up-river herself, warily, nearer to the dancing tiny figures. The sound rushed at her again, the scream torn from an animal in pain. But, apart from the two howls, the figures seemed to be dancing silently by the noisy river; as she came near enough she saw they were bears.

Even nearer, they seemed, from across the river, to be playing. One was obviously caught by something on the rock's surface; the other danced back and forth, out of the reach of the caught bear's slapping paws. They could, from the movement, have been flirting, vast and affectionate. But, nearer, she saw the caught bear begin to flag, slump sideways, its neck broken by a final slap; saw, too, that down its fat belly a wide bib of blood ran. The other bear closed into the gushing chest; the blood was obviously a red signal for its greed. She stood, entranced, watching the bear feed for a while across the narrow river, then, satiated at last, wander slowly away into the woods.

She began to plan a way across the dashing water, here over shoals, shallow but swift. She went far upstream and entered where it lay in a deep pool—plunged in and fought her way across it, pulled by the heavy current, rolling, grabbing, as she let the water tumble and bruise her, carrying her downstream, but to the bank where the table-rock stood, blood-covered now, like some vast altar.

The bear had caught its foot in a fissure of the rock. Its chest was nearly gone; its guts lay in the sun. Hannah ate until her head swam, the strong fat running down her skinny body— gorged her fill as the other had. But, being more provident than the killer, she bound the liver and heart with the animal's sinews

[17]

to carry with her. Then, full, her work finished, she began to drowse, drunk with meat, until the sun struck her sprawled body, and heated the blood on the littered rock. The dangerous clarion smell of the fresh kill rising in the heat made her jump up, sober with fright, and run to the river to wash and wash the blood from herself, her hands shaking. She buried what slivers of meat were left, with the liver and the heart, covered them with a mound of rocks to protect them from the animals, and finally, clean and full, she crawled onto a low thick nest of branches and slept through the night carelessly and deeply.

Next day, from the new vantage point of the north bank, she saw that the river was bending dangerously toward the south, and that to go east she would have to leave it and steer only by the sun—leave the river and climb the ridge behind her, where the sun had risen.

It was a vast, rising corridor through a grove of thick black trees, cedar and spruce, clinging to the ascent and reaching to the sky. Under them nothing grew; only the rock showed, or the ground, brackish brown with damp needles, slick underfoot and dark. Not so much as a leaf, a vine, disturbed the mountainside. She began to climb through the black woods when she had strapped the meat to her shoulders. Twice she saw branches move, turn into long black snakes, and slip to the ground and away—as shy as she was.

At the top, hours later, she fell. Most of the meat, which had loosened from its bundle without her knowing it, worked free and, before she could catch it, bounded out of sight down the steep, slick grade. She kept on looking dumbly at the path it had taken, then rested, said nothing, bowed her shoulders a little at the inevitable and turned to what she had left. What she had clutched and held was the liver, and on part of that she made her meal.

When she dragged herself over the last slope in the evening, the melancholy black grove ended, and the comfortable sycamores,

[18]

with their leaves like flat, dependable hands, stood over her in a little grove as she climbed a high flat rock which jutted over the cedars below and made a natural lookout.

The sun had almost set. Before her, casting long shadows on each slope in turn, rolling as far as she could see into the distance, stretched the vast virgin mountain range, nowhere high enough to be above the tree-line—the Endless Mountains, turning blue in the shadows of the distance. The first valley lay giddily deep below her, and among the shadows in the distance the promise of thousands more seemed the furrows in some field hell-high and hell-wide. Nothing but forest, as far as she could imagine, a maniac scale of endless, endless trees.

For two weeks she climbed and slipped, sprawling up and down the mountainsides, finding here and there a game trail to walk, but too fearful of being followed—though the danger was long past—to do it for long. Still the mountains seemed a vast repetitive puzzle, meant to drive her insane, her movements as useful as treading a day-long treadmill.

The places where she rested at night became familiar and, being familiar, were enough different from one another to keep her from going mad enough to lie down and die.

In the hollows she found creeks again for fish. In one her eye caught a stone the size of her thumb. It was almost black on the creek bed, but it gleamed as red as a jewel for a king's crown when she fished it out of the running stream, where the water had caressed it as smooth as a pigeon's egg. She held it for a long time, letting the sun play with it in her hand, finding it so beautiful that she laughed aloud. There was not an hour after that when she didn't feel in her cane pocket to see if it was still there, or bring it out and smile to see it still so bright and pretty in her hand.

Then one night the owls hooted, freezing her with fear. No other wild animal had scared her so much. The little animals investigated her when she sat, so that in her weary loneliness she came to cherish them and could make herself catch them to eat only when she had nothing else. They seemed pathetic to her, as much at her mercy as she was at the mercy of the mountains' inhuman laws, which she was learning by crushing experience to obey. Even the wildcats, she soon learned, padded away from her. The deer and the elk she saw seemed to have no fear of her.

Although she never lost her horror of the snakes, she learned to avoid the rocks they homed in, the cups of grass they'd like to sun in, the fresh dung they'd curl around—being naturally so cold that they crawled to warmth wherever they could find it. She learned to listen for the whirr of warning nervous bones of the rattlesnake, to see the copperhead imitating the brightness of the sun—but cold as all the rest—and to slip aside as branches melted swiftly into great black snakes. As for other bears she saw, they were too fat with fall, too drowsy, or too cowardly to bother her. She had learned to detour for miles rather than be caught in the terrible thickets. So there were only the loneliness, the hunger, the bone-tired nagging of her body, to make her steps flag and hone down her spirits.

Now, with the owls' hoots, never ceasing through the night, the fear returned and froze her back.

When, in the morning, the calling stopped, and no figures rose and rushed out of the forest toward her, she was sick with relief that they had really been owls that hooted and not some painted devils. The morning was as undisturbed as if it held its breath. The birds were still. All the sounds she had got used to and now called silence had ceased. It was as if she had gone deaf. When she was halfway up the next slope the trees began to move. They whispered. They seemed to sway from the top rhythmically in the yellow air.

Then the rain came, first in cooling, long drops, then in sharp rods that nailed her, clinging, to the running, roaring mountainside—a September storm that wracked and wrenched the huge trees, set boulders moving in the thousand muddy rills. It was as dark as night; then lightning brightened the opposite hill; the trees sprang out, sick yellow, and disappeared again. The near thunder so ripped the air that it seemed to push against her when it howled and cracked. She managed to get uphill of a huge tree-trunk and was pinned against it, hurt and howling to be let loose by the lashing wind, without knowing, in the wild whooping air, that she made any sound at all. How long it lasted she could not know; she was aware and left exhausted by it when at last it calmed to a steady rain, leaving the mountainside a watershed littered with treacherous dead branches. Long after dark she found a rock ledge that had protected the leaves below from the rain, and crawled under it, exhausted.

She woke, hearing the rain in the pitch-darkness of night, hearing more heavy breathing by her leaf bed, which she had banked high in the luxury of finding such a good place to rest. The smell which permeated the cave was not the fetid smell of bear, but the musty smell of a great cat. She saw no eyes shining and realized that the beast had not yet found her. Then almost at once she knew that the breathing was beyond breathing, had slipped over into being the satisfied purr of a cat in dry comfort, and that as long as the noise went on she was safe. The presence of the animal was taking the chill off the rain-laden air, and, stiff with fright as she was, she began to drowse; her body was battered too much by the long storm and the falling on the wet slopes to let her stay completely awake. But she woke, frozen, when she felt movement, felt the great, living, damp, soft pelt beside her, and knew that whatever beast it was, tired to death too, had crept close to her for her pathetic warmth, and still purred, drifting to sleep, meaning no harm.

In the first glimmer of dawn she saw it pause at the cave's mouth, look back once at her, with eyes as gray as stones, and pick its way gently into the morning on light buff feet, disappearing

[21]

even as she became conscious. It was a huge tawny cat that faded into the dawn like part of a dream.

There was rain again.

It rained for still another day—no sun to steer by, only the wet slate-sided mountains, only worse hunger. The whole world ran with cold water. When she found an overhanging rock to shelter under, she stayed there, shivering, huddled, no longer hoping that the rain would ever stop but still waiting, listening to it, too tired to move. When she did move it was for a whole day over the flat top of the mountain she had climbed. In the sun it would have been a green savannah; here and there limestone rocks had forced themselves to the earth's surface, and around them stout grass, nearly blue in the wet, would have attracted herds of animals. Now the deer sheltered under the trees while they ate, their coats brackish with wet. The wind was freer and blew the rain against her face in gusts. She moved away from the meadows and trudged along the edge of the forest.

All day she knew she was being followed. Once, down a long running avenue, she saw a great cat squat, piss, scratch the pine needles and earth up, smell carefully, then trot away out of sight again. Toward evening she knew where it was by a raw scream that seemed to knife through the dark twilight.

Night fell before she could find any dry place to sleep. The slight wind had swerved and carried the rain into the farthest corners of the few rock-caves on the east side of the great mountain.

By the time the night was black she was hot with fever, shaking, too sore to move, and had to rest under a hanging rock on wet leaves. She fell into a deep, deadened sleep, and when from time to time her changing fever woke her she imagined great dancing shadows; the crackling of a huge, hot fire; the soft, wet surface of a great pelt nestling closer to her; the great satisfied purr; and, in her dream, the constant roar of water, beating everything down.

[22]

In the daylight, when she woke, or stopped dreaming, the sun was shining. The wet woods around her gleamed and sounded with the last slow dripping of water from the leaves. She was too weak to care that the rain had stopped. Her body seemed no longer to obey any wishes or will she might have remembered. There was only habit left. She turned as the sun slipped slightly to the west, and made her way down the long decline on legs as tentative as a fawn's.

In the tiny round valley at its foot she found that the creek, instead of curling round the level, disappeared into a great wide black mouth, which lifted at one side like a half-smile in the side of the mountain opposite. Over it the mountain-side rose, a huge rock-face, bloody with red hanging creeper. It rose as high above her in the distance as she could see by tipping her head back. In crevices she could see bright leaves, a few stunted, grasping shrubs; far in the high distance, a rim of evergreens. It was as if, having run a kind of natural gantlet for over five weeks, she realized that it was all a cosmic joke, with herself as the tiny bait; that that black high mouth laughed; that the wall it sat in was the high wall of a prison, to cage her, no matter what her will was, beyond strength, beyond hope. She sank down against a tree in the little warm, pleasant valley at its foot and wished, way beyond praying, that she could die.

But she could not die; she could only be lashed up again by her own puny, flickering will, grub the tiny valley for roots to chew, for a handful of rain-laden berries. The storm had swelled the creek and brought down dirt from the mountain so that the fish were hidden. She could only go, unsatisfied, into the cave-mouth far enough to find dry leaves in the gloom, and try to sleep and gather strength. Even there she had to find a ledge to protect her against the cold air that breathed from miles inside the mountain, far colder than the outside air. But at least the sandy cave-floor was dry. The cave sloped down behind her, seemed to stretch in an echoing black space forever, full of sound

[23]

all night: the swish of wings, air whispers, shadows swooping low over her head, small bone nails scuttering across the rock floor; here and there, far away, the breathing and lowing of other larger animals who'd found the cave a shelter from the rain. Outside, in the moonlit night, eyes shone and came nearer, passed beyond her into the cave. There were a rush of running, the raw scream which slapped the sides of the vast tunnel and made the birds fly out, a huge darker cloud against the moonlight—then silence.

After her nerves, dulled almost dead, had got attuned to the returned uneasy whispers, she felt once again the huge soft pelt against her and knew that part of the fever-dream had been true, that the great mountain cat had warmed her, had eaten, and had returned again for a third night to have her company. She put out her hand and touched its back, left her arm lying against the living body, and went to sleep, warm at last.

In the morning it was gone, and she was rested. For a second as she woke she forgot where she was and found the tiny valley peacefully familiar. Then she remembered and turned away from the deceptive pleasure into the cave. She knew the great cat had made a kill and that she might find some of it left, so she closed her eyes, opened them again to see against the darkness, and stumbled down the sloping cave floor. In the dark, inching into the blackness to keep from falling into pits, she heard instead of seeing. She found, on its side, half-eaten, the body of a deer; she could see only its shadow as her eyes got used to the deep dark. But she ate her first meat since before the rain and knew she was going to try to climb the mountain wall.

She began in the early morning to work up one side, which looked more sloping, more broken, than the rest of the rock, which sheered for two hundred feet before it sloped at all. She rose, then, step by step, pulling herself up by the rooted shrubs, lying flat to rest against the barely sloping rock—rose, slipped giddily, caught herself, went on. When the sun found her she was a tattered speck clinging against the cliffside, not daring to let her

[24]

strength run out in crying, not daring to look down for fear of plunging after what she saw, level with the top of the highest valley tree. It was nearly noon.

When her voice came at all, it was to gasp only. She climbed on silently, carefully, having often to rest against the rock to still her head, finding each safe step a separate miracle. When she heard her voice finally in the late afternoon, it said, using breath against her will, "Oh, pray Gawd pray Gawd pray Gawd, pray . . ." as repetitive as breathing in her dry cracked mouth. When she rested, laying her sweat-covered cheek against a dirt cranny of the rock, she could see the drops of sweat slide from her forehead and fall, like tears, out into space.

The sun had gone over the mountain and the evening wind had begun to gather when she came within clutching distance of the tree-roots which curled over the cliff-top like great handles, finding their way back into the safe earth above. Her hands made their own red tracks, groping upward in a last tiny ecstasy of care, for fear of grabbing too quickly at safety and plummeting down past the now distant treetops to the ground.

She pulled herself finally over into the trees, but could no longer walk to find shelter. Her last effort had been the rock-face; her last prayer had already been said; her last weak struggle had been made against the law. Now she crawled up the gentler slope by habit—as a snake moves till the sun sets, even after it is dead. She crawled, fell, crawled again, up and down the camel back of the mountain. She fell and slept without shelter for a time, hardly knowing she rested; she never knew when night came and covered her.

⋆   ⋆

It was high sunlight of the next day. She had been forty days and forty nights in the wilderness of the Endless Mountains. Ahead of her, down a steep slope, a green savannah stretched like Eden. Surrounding it, like houses around a green, the now brilliantly

[25]

colored fall mountains seemed to stand guard. It was a little kingdom of grass, where the trees grew gently in little groves as if the hand of man had somehow modified the terrible natural law with a little tenderer mercy of his own. There was a delicate cat's-paw of a breeze. A pretty creek ran through the valley, winding, not rushing, like a little road.

It was the last mirage. Even as she crawled to the edge of it the grass began to move, to grow into crouching figures, to creep toward her in the little morning wind. The trees came now, each black branch undulating, the camouflage a failure, each a snake dropping nearer and nearer. The wind began to touch, to tug her hair, even as the horde of moving shadows under the grass came nearer. All the fears she'd run from in forty days broke against her eyes, and it was as if the wild beasts, the human devils, had waited at this green meeting-place until she came. They formed from the grass, more and more, were the color of grass and were no shape but grass, but still were there, moving like an army in the wind. Over her head in the trees the wind gathered. She heard the raw wild shriek of triumph come out of it, high in the branches.

Then she passed beyond hearing and lay still.

Chapter Two

JEREMIAH was worried.

He hadn't seen Hagar for nearly three days, and it was near her time. So he stood in the narrow door of the log hut he'd built, looking squint-eyed over the savannah, which undulated in the fall wind, and wondered. It wasn't only that Jeremiah needed Hagar, though she was to him a pearl of great price. It was more than that. He understood her whims. Sometimes she'd listen for hours while he talked. She was intelligent in her own stubborn way. But still, she couldn't carry stubbornness to the point of bearing secretly in the woods, where the wild beasts might find her in labor.

Jeremiah wrinkled up his forehead, sniffed, and listened. The steady weaving of the wind made hearing more difficult. But it was a wind he needed. He had planted his first wheat in the savannah —the first which had survived, anyway. Now the last of it was drying and waving among the other grass, where he had cleared, made a snake-fence, and planted his tender grain in a patch of gold a quarter-acre big among the yellow-green buffalo grass. The logs of the fence made a drunken zigzag, which was almost hidden by the green and the gold slapping back and forth as the wind blew it up into waves.

Behind the shack the protecting woods stretched—to the end of the continent, as far as Jeremiah was concerned. He was hardly interested. He had known he was home the moment he'd stepped into the high valley from the Eastern Trace. The trees made a protective background for his hut, hid his smoke, kept the savannah buffalo and elk from stampeding into his fencing, and left the whole east to wake him in the morning. For he had made the front of his shack to face the savannah down a slight slope through the last of the trees, as if the thousand waving, tree-studded acres were his own front garden.

Jeremiah walked around to the back of the hut and listened. The morning sun was higher now, and threw down dappled light onto the hard, new-cleared ground, where several barren trees stood, forlorn of leaves, in the turning fall forest. They seemed to draw a cold of dying to them, for Jeremiah had "girdled" them, stripped them of bark in a circle a foot wide, and was leaving them to die of hunger and thirst and be ready for felling and firewood in the winter.

Once he thought he heard something, but whatever it was didn't call again. He waited, not even stepping across the crackling surface of the hard ground for fear he'd drown the sound of the call when it came again. But whatever it was, was in the ear of his mind. He went on slowly around the hut.

The panther shrieked.

Jeremiah acted without stopping to think, automatically and correctly, his senses schooled to the danger of that sound. He grabbed his old musket from inside the door, stepped high through the grass, out across the savannah, straight toward the sound he had heard from the edge of the woods half a mile away. High in a tree he saw a buzzard, and in another a great bald eagle, resting dignified and patient in the moving air. They acted as pointers.

Now he went more slowly, nearing the trees, saw the great tawny cat up in the branches, dropped, scuttled as silently as he could, nearer and nearer, until he could rest his elbow on his knee to steady the gun. He knew his shot had to kill, for, wounded, the panther could tear at him before he could reload.

The shot did kill. The panther crashed out of the tree into the underbrush—in one second the most aware, light, and electric even of cats, in the next as dead and heavy as a bag of sand.

The buzzard lit out and flew in a great circle. The eagle never moved, just tipped on the branch against the sky, not afraid of the puny man below. Jeremiah got up and leaned his gun against his own protecting tree. The panther lay, shrunken and heavy, in the crushed underbrush, its hind legs with their swelling, strong muscles flung out behind it like the legs of a man, its forelegs seeming to stretch to catch the shot, and its great head lowered between its shoulders as if it had died of grief. Out of the hollow where a great gray eye had been, the blood poured. Jeremiah had not destroyed the fine tawny pelt. He made a horn of both his hands, shaping them like curved shells around his mouth.

"Soooo-KEEEEEE! Suke, suke, suke, suke, sooo-keeee!" he called into the waiting forest. The trees caught the sound and spun it round among themselves. It bounced on and on, reverberated, and died out. It had moved the eagle, which now circled as the buzzard had and came back to its roost. The air settled again after the noise, and Jeremiah listened as he had done back at the hut, patiently.

It was when he was turning, disappointed, to get his gun that the edge of his eye caught the flick of a rag being tugged at by the wind. He went on turning in the grass and looked again. The gray rag—no, not rag, but something else—flicked behind the grass ten yards away. At first he walked, then, seeing what it was, ran toward the bundle, which was shrunken and gray, looking deader than the panther; for it was no longer heavy but looked light and dusty, ready to be borne into the air in fragments before he reached it. Now the wind played with a strand of gray hair, now tittuped a gray shred of linsey. It was only when Jeremiah laid his hands along the skeletal figure and turned its shrunken skull-like head to him that he saw that it was a woman, and that the woman was still barely alive.

Jeremiah looked down at Hannah for a little while, too shocked to pick her up. His great worried eyes took in the ludicrous remains of clothing, the bag clutched in her hand—a woman, a white woman, and alive. The realization did a strange thing to him. He put his face into his hands for a minute, and when he looked at her again his eyes were wet.

He said, "Amen," and gathered Hannah up into his arms.

She wasn't much to carry. She weighed, he judged, somewhere around seventy pounds. When he cut away the bound grass and tenderly took off the shoes her legs were like dead sticks. He cut off the tatters of linsey and laid her on his own soft deerskins in the corner of the hut. Then he began to take handfuls of grease from a wooden drum, and to rub her body carefully, to rub life back in with the grease—along her pitiful high ridge of pelvis; along the bowed thighs, the emaciated arms, the chest where there were no breasts but only dark smudges of her teats, the rest a rib-cage, every bone jutting; along her neck that seemed no longer capable of holding up her head, where her closed eyes sank in hopeless, shadowed pools; even along her skull and hair. Her right hand seemed frozen into a fist. When Jeremiah finally eased it open a red stone fell from it. The hand twitched twice when the stone was gone, then gave up. Jeremiah put her little prize beside her so she could see it if she waked. Then he wrapped her warmly in deerskins, as one might a papoose, set water over his fire, and went into the woods.

He searched now along the ground as he had searched an hour before among the trees. Hagar forgotten, he searched with herb eyes, hunter's eyes—in which everything fades from the trained vision but a certain kind of leaf, a certain tendril, or the quick flick of the squirrel or scawmed animal in the fragmentary sun. What he wanted was a root, and when he had been led to it by its bright fall berries he went as familiarly toward the part of the woods where it might be found as if he had himself planted it in his garden, and brought an armful of it back, running with it, its great roots swinging like dirty pendula, not even watching for snakes in his shock and hurry.

So Hannah's first fragment of consciousness was of an interior, of soft skins and luxurious warmth around her, and of a bitter, strong herbal drink that was being spooned into her mouth. Jeremiah sat beside her, watching, through the rest of the day, and on through the night by the light of his fire. When the frustration of watching was too great he would rub her again and again with the grease, and, when her eyelids fluttered, would tip up her weightless head and shoulders and make her drink, now the bitter brew, now one that tasted of strong meat.

And when that failed to soothe him or bring her round, he prayed aloud by the light of the fire, and his moving shadow, as he prayed, jumped and danced like a huge monster over the ceiling— in the day only the underside of the bark shingles that made his roof; now, by deepest night, vaulted and high in the firelight as a church.

Hannah opened her eyes and saw the giant black, dancing shadow-figure stretching up the wall, gesticulating along the eaves, and knew she had been caught, but felt physically so much safer, so much warmer, that her fears could not take hold enough to make her move. She lay there listening to the first human voice she could remember after so long.

"Dear Lord and Father in Heaven, hark unto me, a miserable sinner!" The great shadow seemed to be groaning. "O heavenly Father, spare me and spare this lone crittur that thou hast led down unto Goshen."

The fire flickered; the shadow quivered; the voice intoned. "Lord, let me have her as Thou hast sint her to me." The voice paused to search for the right praying words, then went on, growing stronger.

"O Gawd, have mercy on me. I'm as lonesome as Adam in this hyar Paradise. You done led her hyar, Lord—don't jest take her from me. She ain't much, O Lord; she ain't no Eve, Gawd knows; but I pray Ye save this pore leetle lean thing. O Lord, save her. I ain't talked to nuthin but a hawg for eight-ten months. O Lord, see fitten to let her live. It ain't that I complain of my cross, Lord. It ain't that I ain't aimin to carry my load. I'll sing hosannas same as ever, but pray Lord leave me somebody. Ye done brought me out hyar to do your works—ain't I made myself vile for Ye? Ain't I been vile in the sight of men Lord knows how many times? Hyear me a-beggin, O Lord, hyear my prayer. Spare me this hyar woman to live, O Lord. She may turn out a deival—Lord Gawd A-mighty, right now I'd rather live with a deival than nuthin but a damned cantankerous hawg.

"O Gawd, I'm humble for the hawg; I'm dust for her; but 'tis not much to keep the life in that thar pore crittur in the corner. O Lord, look down on Goshen. O heavenly Father, see clear over Goshen. Warsh me in the blood of Your pity, O blessed Lamb, hide me in the fountain of Your precious blood. Take pity on a pore pukin mourner, for I'm sick. Lord Gawd, I'm anxious—oh, anxious, how anxious . . ."

The shadow had begun to sway rhythmically over Hannah's head, and the words got through to her—"Gawd . . . Goshen . . . pity"—so when Jeremiah got up from the floor later, when the fire had gone low and the first faint fringe of dawn was dividing the long black meadow from the black, high bowl of the sky, he found that she had fallen into a calmer sleep. She was no longer unconscious now but really asleep, with the faintest dawn of color coming back to her cheeks. He saw that the red stone was gone, and Hannah's hand lay fisted over it, close to her cheek.

[32]

Jeremiah felt too happy at the sight of her to be contained by the small hut. He threw open the narrow door and walked out to thank God in the first pale morning for answering his prayer. There, beside the path, he almost stumbled over a huge female form. Contented grunts were coming from it, and an unmistakable aroma. He dropped beside her and counted along the struggling wall of lives at her side, counted ten squealing, glugging forms hanging to her. Hagar had come home to litter.

"Pore old Hagar," Jeremiah told her. "Ye come home and I niver even hyeared ye—let ye lay hyar in the wilderness while I's in thar a-prayin for Rebecca. 'Tis the way of the Bible, sweetheart —the way it always did go." As it got lighter, while he squatted there, scratching the hog's head behind her ear, he counted the valuable piglets, damp pink sausages of greed beside her, over and over again.

For once in his life, after the events of the day and the night, Jeremiah was too happy even to pray. He spoke then to God familiarly, squinting across Hagar at Him as if He walked toward him in the edge of rising sun.

"Lord, I reckon this is what they meant when they said, 'My cup runneth over.'" And he went on scratching Hagar behind the ear.

When Hannah really waked for the first time, late that morning, her visions and half-delirious memories of the night slipped into focus; she began to take in the real size and the real shapes of the place around her—first, of the tall, stooped man who sat beside her, watching her so anxiously.

He was dressed from head to foot in skins, without linen or tanned leather anywhere about him. His buckskin shirt and breeches were cut in some semblance of the white man's garments she had seen before—except that they had no buttons or laces, but only tied hide thongs to hold them over him. But there the resemblance to any white man—indeed, to any other man in the

[33]

world—ended, unless she counted as Indian the familiar herbal and clay colors rubbed into his clothes, because they were from the same materials the Indians used.

It was the designs that held her eyes, before she could look up into his face.

For he had daubed on the buckskin over his heart a white clay lamb, with legs like sticks, and a kitten's face, and its head cocked a little sideways so that it looked up at Jeremiah's chin. It had around its friendly head a yellow halo, and along its chest, big enough to reach to its stomach, a red heart like the heart on a valentine. Down from the heart red dots dripped in lines running to the edge of the shirt, starting again at the belt, and going on down the buckskin trouser leg. On the right side of the shirt there was a single large, stern eye with a pupil the size of a buckeye. Instead of lashes it shot out streams of yellow, the color of the halo. Here and there the yellow had worn off where his right arm had rubbed against it, as if the actions had dimmed the light from the heavenly buckeye.

Then she looked for the first time at his face. As people will unconsciously make portraits of themselves when they draw, Jeremiah had drawn his own eye on his shirt—except that the eye on the shirt was calm almost to the point of being entirely without expression. Jeremiah's round eyes were as anxious as a man's can be. They looked at her from under heavy black brows, and thick black hair hung over his forehead and down behind his ears to the neck of his shirt. The most astonishing thing about his face was that from middle cheek up he was as brown and seasoned as the puncheon surfaces of his shack—but below that his face was white; his mouth formed a curiously delicate pink O of concentration; the skin around it had the pallor of the black-haired Celt. As he felt her eyes on his chin he let one of his brown hands fly up to stroke and hide the whiteness.

"I jest reckoned I'd shave"—murmured, apologetic, came the first words Jeremiah ever spoke consciously to Hannah. But he

[34]

doubted that she heard him at all, for she never wavered, just kept on looking up into his eyes, as if she were trying to read what she saw there. Because they were black, and because he had round dark circles under them, he had a sad expression on his thin, brown, weatherbeaten face—sad and patient. Across his face the patience seemed to stand up to the anxious eyes and win, except that, when the wind slapped a branch over and over against the log wall just beyond his head, his eyes would dart the way of the sound, aware as a hunter, worried as sin, then back to Hannah, lying on the bed, slowly coming to life while he waited and didn't dare speak again for fear of frightening her, even though they'd seemed to go on watching each other for a full two or three minutes.

As it was, Hannah spoke before he broke the silence again.

She said, "I'm hongry"—and even to herself her voice was curiously small and windy, but Jeremiah's heart leaped when he heard her speak at last.

"I reckoned on it," he said simply. "Ye done et plenty of broth. 'Tain't no use tryin to give ye nuthin more'n that for a day or two. Ye'd jest puke." He went to the hob, where a copper pan smoked, and poured her a gourdful of hot meat broth. "Now ye jest hist up thar and I'll feed ye, mawm. I been doin this off and on for a day now. Don't ye call to mind how I fed ye off and on? Though ye niver said nuthin," he added sadly as he hoisted her up to drink from the gourd.

She shook her head at the question, hardly trying to remember, she was so intent on the broth.

"Now I'm goin to lay ye a piece of jerk hyar for ye to chew on," Jeremiah told her when she had finished drinking and seemed already so drowsy again that her head nodded against his arm. "Hit's nuthin but deer, but if ye git hongry hit's best. I'm a-comin back."

Whether it was the emotion of finally making contact with her and knowing that she would live, or whether it was sudden ter-

[35]

rible shyness at her being something besides a pore crittur to be nursed—all bones, piss, and bear grease—Jeremiah got up. He did not even then stand quite upright, for he was six feet tall at least, and although his thin body was as straight as an Indian's he tended to jut his head forward so that he looked as if he were peeking from under his eyebrows during a prayer. He almost stumbled out of the door. But Hannah never noticed. She was already asleep.

It was the softest time of evening when she woke again. Out through the open door she could see the sky, purple over the dark grass, as if it were hesitating, quiet and peaceful, before it plunged to black for another night. The fire in the big rock fireplace, which stretched eight feet across the whole opposite end of the shack and dominated the room, dimmed, flickered, put forth tongues of flame now just turning bright in the twilight from their blue obscurity in the bright day.

But the heat that blessed the tiny ten-by-fifteen-foot room was not all from the fire. By the long wall, opposite the open door, lay a great, contented, sand-colored sow, whose eyes, like Jeremiah's but with infinitely more content, gazed at Hannah's pallet. But the sow, being on the floor, seemed to look straight into Hannah's eyes. Lined along in front of her, the piglets squealed and sucked, crawling, tugging, trying to push their weak way straight into Hagar's Gothic line of teats. Besides Hagar and the fire, there was only a low stool pushed near the hearth, within reaching distance of a hob made of two crutched sticks pushed down into the dirt floor of the deep fireplace, with a green stick between them. From the cross-stick a copper bucket hung, blackened by the fire, steaming gently. On one side of the fireplace Jeremiah had built a tiny rock cave with its entrance, eight inches square, facing into the fire. Inside it Hannah could see a small brown knob, half-buried in hot ashes that had been shoveled into the space. On the other side of the fireplace logs were piled. But

[36]

it was the hearth she watched. The fire chased over a large stone embedded with fossil bones of tiny animals like cornucopias, springs, and fobs. They lay inside the hearthstone like ghosts of jewels. From time to time, through the gaps between the logs of the wall, the evening breeze stirred the fire so that it danced over the fossils and seemed to die away. On the other side of the door the wall was covered, up to the pitch of the roof, with a thick, head-high pile of skins.

Hannah reached out her hand and let it fall beside her onto the earth floor, which was beaten hard by Jeremiah's feet and Hagar's great rolling body, as if she had to catch and hold this vision of contentment and warm luxury before the mirage disappeared and left her again to the terrible silence of the great indifferent woods. As she slipped into the reality of her comfort, she began to recall where she had come from, not as a thing of so much time passing, but as a separate existence. She was there in the cold—the whole experience remembered in that word. Now she was here, warm, and it was all that mattered. She sighed.

The rhythmic sound of an ax, a hollow thunk against wood somewhere on the other side of the wall by her head, told her where the man was. She waited, suspended but still awake, as quiet and peaceful in her own way as Hagar was in hers, for him to come back.

It was almost dark when he did. On his arm he carried a great beautiful tawny skin, which he spread over her. "Now this hyar's for your own, mawm, kind of a prize. 'Tis raw—I done dried it two days in the sun. Work it a bit with your hands. Hit'll come soft, thin." He tucked it round her.

"I'm aimin to calk thim holes in the mornin that's lettin the wind in. Hit don't bother me none, but it would you, ye bein so peaked. Now I'm fixin to rub ye right now. 'Tain't no use for ye to carry on. If Gawd hadn't of meant me to look after ye He'd wouldna brung ye. I'm a doctor anyhow—seventh son. All seventh

[37]

sons is doctors by birth, as ye've no doubt hyeared." He had reached for the tub of bear grease, and then pulled over the stool before he stopped to look at Hannah.

Something was wrong. Both her hands were buried deep, grasping the huge pelt she had felt before and remembered only by touch and by dream. Her red face was screwed into a wide grin of sorrow, and her eyes were tight closed in an effort not to cry—but she was crying anyway; the tears came in two streams down her temples and into the greased tendrils of her hair. She held her breath, but when she had to expel it a sob came with it and shook her, brought on another and another, making Hagar raise her hog's head from the ground, listen, and lay it down again.

Jeremiah had dropped the stool and the bear-grease bucket and knelt beside her, misunderstanding as tenderly as he knew how—the gentleness of a man with animals, not of a woman with children. "Now, don't ye take on so." He smoothed her hair from her face and tried to lift her hands. When he saw they were clasped to the pelt he tried to shake, to slap them loose. "Ye'll make yourself bad," he kept saying. "Why, I undressed ye and laid ye hyar. Ye're too bad to be timid, mawm. Do ye think Gawd would of taught us about greasin a pore tard body'ts been layin out thar in the woods efn he niver meant us to . . ." But when she didn't seem to hear him, he apologized for misunderstanding and tried again. "I concluded 'twas because ye was timid of your pore body, sister. Is it because this hyar painter skeered ye in the woods? He wouldn't of laid for ye; he's after my crittur thar, Hagar. You needn't to of been skeered. I shot him when I found ye. Ye're all right." But he saw it wasn't fear but sorrow that twisted her face so—the face of a little girl who has lost her pet and learned about death—and, being a man who had to depend on his instinct for his life, began to sense what had happened.

"Hark, mawm," he told her calmly, as if he were telling a story—quietly, to make her stop the awful sobbing so she could hear his voice. "That thar's the pelt of the painter—ye'll travel fur and wide before ye'll find another varmint who lives a life as sad as the painter's. His shriek is like a woman in hard labor. He strikes your heart cold when ye hyear him. Thin he hongers for the same meats as a man—his beeves, his hawgs, all his dear critturs. Thin, more, he gathers in his great limbs turble strength and can kill thim great dumb beasts three times his size. So that would make the painter the natural enemy of man in all his ways. Thin thar's the pity, for the Lord niver willed no man-hate into the lovely crittur. He jest niver willed none to him. So when the painter sees a campfire he'll crawl right up to it and purr himself to death while the hunter holds the gun to his ear so's not to spoil his pelt. He'll sneak beside ye to sleep, likin your warmth, and niver hurt a hair of your blessed head."

Jeremiah reached out and stroked the great skin, where Hannah's hands now lay lightly. "Yet I'd shoot him and I'd shoot another and all, for, love like he do, his life means our death, for he'll wipe out our critturs—and that means he wipe us out, like as not." He looked over his shoulder at Hagar, who had got used to the sound and now lay fast asleep, no eyes, all snout. "The nights I've waited humble before the Lord that Hagar thar warn't a-layin out from home whar the painter had lit and rid her screamin back while he bit the life from her."

She was quiet now, and he picked up the bear grease and started massaging her arm. "Thar's some that'll tell ye painters is hateful. They have to figure that to be able to do what they've got to. They'll make out like they's fine and brave, bein downright ashamed what they do. They ain't nary a bit of use to act so. When Jehovah brought His children into the Land of Canaan, He told thim to take the land. He niver said nuthin about thim bein deep in hate, about thim as had to be cleared out. I'll swear ye're gittin some meat on your bones already. I can tell it under my fingers. That thar rib-cage don't look so stark as it did even a day ago."

He turned her gently over and began to rub the thick grease

[39]

into her back. "I'm goin to leave ye some tea, and I want ye to drink it. 'Tis called sang tea, and hit'll give your life back. They do say doctors from all over the world use this hyar same sang from right out of the mountains. 'Tis a root of life—bitter, but like a miracle of God what it does to your pore tard body. They pay any amount for it back yonder, too. I used to hunt it afore I come out this fur. Any amount."

He finished and tucked the deer skins and tawny pelt around her again. "Now ye can eat. Don't mourn about the painter. 'Tis hyar to keep ye warm." As he finished he gazed down at Hannah's face. The grief over the great cat seemed to have broken the floodgates of her horror, and she had sobbed out all her troubles, had lanced her fear and let it flow clean—blessed, clean tears— and now the ravages which had kept the tiny muscles drawn tight around her eyes and her mouth and had made her face gray seemed to have been melted by the tears. The blood flowed gently back, lighting her cheeks again; her eyes lay under peaceful, flickering blue lids. Her mouth, bitten and creased with exposure as it was, seemed released and wider, and faintly the rims of her lips showed, curved and a little opened, a sweeter pink.

She was so changed he stared and had to turn away, murmuring as he did, "I ain't niver even hyeared your name."

"Hannah," she told him, and the strength of her voice surprised them and woke Hagar again. It was light and clear and young.

"Have ye no second name?" he asked her.

"I've no memory o' one." She stared at him until he had to walk away. Behind him, he thought he heard her giggle.

"And how old are ye, Hannah?" He watched the fire, standing with his back to her.

"Goin on nineteen," she told him. "Unless 'tis October. Perhaps I'm already nineteen."

He knelt by the fire. "I've baked ye a pone. Y'ain't too pore to eat a pone," was all he could find to say.

Chapter Three

Bᴜᴛ ᴡʜᴇɴ Jeremiah found his voice he talked for three days. He talked like a flood, as if a dam had been broken. He talked close to her, just staring at the wall above her head, or tending to her or to Hagar or to the fire. He talked out the door and into the woods on his chores, his voice fading clear away into the wind and sigh of the woods, or being only a soft mutter behind the ax, then swelling into recognizable words again as he came back to the cabin, his arms full of firewood, so that she could pick up the general drift of the perpetual hungry talk. He talked as Hannah ate, with the childish gluttony of starvation. Sometimes during the time of his great talk his long, skinny form would rage up and down the hut like an angry jackknife, making the light of the fire wave through the room, and would preach to her, whether she watched him in fear or closed her eyes as if she slept. She never knew whether he left off the talking to sleep or not, for she slept so much herself, but she did from time to time see him throw himself down on the hard dirt hearth and sigh and pause for breath, so she supposed he slept there.

"Now, let's see," he told her. "I's born into this world, near as I can say and what my pore brother done told me, along about May of the year seventeen-thirty, or so he told me, though sometimes I do feel younger, and sometimes I do feel older—Gawd be blessed, that ain't much, so I don't gwye much upon what he told me, Gawd rest his pore soul. That was my first birth—ye understand, Hannah? Hit took place in Liverpool—leastways I was told so." At this point he had disappeared out of the shack door, and his voice floated for a while behind him as he went off to harvest.

"Who knows what my pore paw's temptations was, to leave us go like he done? I ain't one to jedge. For it was bad times, and I don't reckon ye say no more about it. Leastways, he did sell usn—for seven pounds apiece. I's five, and my pore brother ten—two strappin boys to a ship's captain. 'Twoulda been all right efn that thar captain had of lived. . . ." His voice faded out altogether, and he was gone, harvesting, for three hours.

In the evening he came back, carried in the rest of the grain, and flailed it in front of the door, so he couldn't see her as he talked through the dun cloud of chaff. "That was when my brother, Gawd rest him, was thirteen, and we'd been in the colony along about three years. It had broke his pore heart, that's what I reckoned—and they was hard on him. They cut him down, and they did bring his cold corpse up afore a court of law in Williamsburg, and me thar beside him, too skeered to mourn. And they was wise, so what could I of said?" The chaff flew so hard that Hannah could not see even his outline, but she could still hear.

"So they sentenced him a bloody corpse for the crime of self-murder, and our master told me 'twas sech a sin for him to do, and not finish his time, which had been bought and paid for, that 'twas right for me, as his brother, to sarve the four years left of his time as well as my own." He began to sweep the freed grain up from the great flat rock he had maneuvered in front of his door. "It was after that I met the Reverend Mr. Stone, me bein as near about—oh—sixteen years as I can reckon, big, mean, awk'ard . . ." He was out of earshot again, and Hannah went to sleep.

"I didn't niver larn to read or write or nuthin," he said, sitting beside her, as soon as she opened her eyes. She almost screamed before she recognized his voice, for he was like a ghost, covered from head to foot with chaff, only his eyes—looking like burned holes in a white blanket—and his voice were like Jeremiah instead of those of some Lazarus risen from the dusty grave. He had a blackened pone in his hand, and her gourd of broth, and he waited wisely this time to see if she had strength to lift herself up. She did, without realizing that it was the first time she'd moved herself; shifted onto her elbow and took the broth in her hand. He laid the pone down beside her and went back to the bright fire for his own food.

"But he's as good to me as I ever remembered a man to be, for I reckon I'd felt more the rough edge of the world, situated as I was. I was lyin deep when He brought our paths to cross. 'Twas the beginnin of my second birth—I's born in Christ. Have you been born again, Hannah?" He looked up at her from the fire, but she was bending over her broth, dipping the pone in it so carefully that he didn't wait to have an answer but just went on.

"I'll niver forget that first meetin. Thar I set, no more than wallowin in the mire. I only went because all those hyar people was goin down thar, and what else was thar to do?—not readin or writin or nuthin and as for the wenches, not that they'd of looked at me, I's no more than somethin been bought and sold. Anyhow, I's a-settin thar in the back of Mr. Stone's meetin and Hannah, I'll swear to Gawd he spoke right to me as clear as I'm a-settin hyar a-talkin to ye. 'O Lord God have mercy,' he said Mr. Stone said. 'I can see into the hearts of these hyar sinners, black as pitch, full of ugly hate'—and I'll tell ye, Hannah, when he said that I damn near jumped up and hollered. I could feel the sweat in the palms of my hands and a chill down my back as efn I'da

[43]

been seized onto by some shiverin thing. Thar's some down front, mostly women, was already cryin, 'Yes, yes!' ever'thin Mr. Stone said. I'll tell ye, it wasn't long afore he's a-standin up thar a-beggin the deival to leave go of thim as warn't saved. Hannah, I'll swear afore Gawd, I felt claws on my back. I felt claws on my back, Hannah, and I jest knowed I was lost. With my hatin my master like I done . . ."

He forgot his pone, which lay on the stone beside the fire, for his voice seemed to lift him to his feet as he told her the story. "Thin he hollered these hyar words and let—me—tell—you, I's struck to my shiverin lonesome soul. *'Thou, Gawd, seest me!'* " He stood there, still, watching the wall above her, as if the words struck a deep fear in him that even in the full spate of his talk he could not tell her.

He stared so long at the wall that when he did speak it was as if he'd read the words there and now read them out to her, slowly. "I quit shiverin as I had been. I's too skeered to shiver. I seed the full majesty of His powerful grace as efn it was a turble yaller vision. That justice—imagine that justice!" He fell silent for the longest time since he had started his talking, and when he started again his voice was lower, and he made no pretense for a minute of speaking to her.

"I felt no more thin a wood-chip a-floatin like they say on the face of the water, that God in His turble justice could give movement to, or jam up tight and not allow to float no more, and me without the power in my limbs to no more'n half crawl into a cornfield opposite the cabin old Miz Coleman had give over to Mr. Stone for the meetin."

Hagar shook the piglets from her as she got up, and they began to paw blindly at one another and squeal, but the mother had seen the pone and smelled it. She lifted her huge body, walked quite delicately a few steps, and grubbed along the warm stone until she had the pone in her mouth.

"Hannah, 'twas in that thar cornfield, the October night around me, that I wrastled with the Lord, and me on the side of the deivals that had a-holt of me. Finally they let go. I never seed thim, mind ye. I won't say that. But I felt thim holdin me rigid, hate in my belly like Mr. Stone had seed. For believe me, the man who'd bought me and my brother was a turble man, and someday I know Gawd'll give me strength in my arm to pay him for my pore brother. Well, layin thar in that field I prayed and I begged to be saved from hell. 'Twarn't no use. The Lord wouldn't have me. I jest lay thar not hyearin no blessed voice or nuthin. Thim people commenced a-comin out of the meetin, and I hyeared thim goin on about how Miz Coleman's brother-in-law was saved, and they's a-gloryin that, and thin some other people I didn't know; they was new people. Three out of four of thim got saved that night—and the fourth was no more'n a ten-year-old, so they wasn't seemin to worry too much. The other three, maw and paw and gal, was hosanna-in down the road, and everybody was a-shakin hands with thim and welcomin thim as efn they had come from a long way away. I could hyear a-laughin and a-cryin together as I's a-layin thar behind that corn, not darin to show my black soul in the town. But when they'd all gone I crep home —efn that's what ye'd call it, though Lord Gawd, I'm better off now and that's sayin somethin, to what I was thin. Oh, I's lonesome—I couldn't figure out how that triflin brother-in-law of Miz Coleman's got saved that night and I niver. He seed things and all—"

One of the piglets began to scream as Hagar settled her great weight down again. Jeremiah bent down, freed the piglet, and held it to a nipple, still talking.

"I'll tell ye that night I's a-layin thar, and I had somethin— visions, dreams, somethin. Gawd or the deival alone knows what thim things was, but I wrastled. Lord, I wrastled for to save my wretched soul. Two of thim big blackened deivals had a-layed holt on me and they's gittin ready to throw me in a big damned pit of everlastin blue blazes whar I'll swear I could hyear them pore

souls—and over all I hyeared the voice of my brother, a-beggin
me to ask for mercy afore they flung me in like he was, for he
done wrong accordin to the Bible and the Colony of Virginia.
Even efn he was hard-pressed he still done wrong and had to be
punished."

He let himself slip down from squatting until he was sitting on
the floor beside the now contented pigs. "Holy Lamb, I know he
done wrong and I still can't allow that Gawd niver pitied him
a-tall. He do have pity, don't He? Well anyhow, 'twas only a
dream, a veesion to teach me, so Mr. Stone said, for I sneaked
off the next day and caught up with him jest as he was fordin his
horse over the crick to go on somewheres else to take the Word.

"I said, 'Mr. Stone, what am I a-goin to do?'

"He's bendin down, tryin to shorten a stirrup on his old sheepskin saddle. I said I'd fix it for him. He niver answered what I
ast him—not right thin. I reckoned he niver hyeared me, so I
said, 'Mr. Stone, I been wrastlin ever since the meetin last night.
Why don't Gawd want me?'

"He's up in the saddle by thin, and he looked at me so starn.
'Are ye ready to take the redemption road?' That's what he ast me.
I jest stood thar a-lookin at the ground. 'Ye jest take your first
step along that road—take up your cross and carry it along that
road. 'Tis the only way to Jesus' bosom.' He put his horse to the
crick, and halfway across he leaned around and hollered, 'Thanks,
brother, for fixin my saddle.'

"Well, I jest stood thar lookin across to where he's disappearin
up one of thim narry roads way deep in the trees, and I reckoned
to myself one redemption road's as good as another, so I set foot
in the crick and started out to follerin. It was pretty clear what
cross I had to carry, once I set foot in the crick, for I's a redemptioner already, but in sin, not like Mr. Stone meant. I's bound for
fourteen years and I'd done no more thin eleven years of my sarvice, and with my brother's time I had seven more years afore I's
redeemed. But I knowed that warn't what Mr. Stone meant. So

I histed up my cross and I went across that crick and struck out up the other redemption road. I knowed efn I got caught I'd pretty near git beat to death to pay for it, but Gawd took care of me. It begun to rainin."

He saw then that Hannah was holding out her gourd, not daring to interrupt, so he filled it for her, still talking on, still forgetting to eat.

"I follered that Mr. Stone three-four days, slippin into the back of these hyar meetins. I's sleepin in cornfields and the Lord was providin. I sure did git sick of raw corn, though. Ever'time I took a drink of water I blowed up turble—jest blowed out and couldn't hardly even fart," he said, explaining to Hannah. "Well, Mr. Stone got kinda used to seein me standin up thar in the back, and he come and talked to me. I's pretty proud, gittin singled out, when I hadn't even been saved and nary a one of thim people had shook hands with me. I said I's follerin like he said, and he said, 'So long as ye're a-follerin ye might as well make yourself useful and git somethin to eat, son,' he said. He called me 'son.' That very night the Lord come to me like they said, and I was saved. I's speakin in unknown tongues, they tell me, and I don't recollect none of that. But I do recollect a great light broke over me, and the voice of Jesus come to me in my mind like they say. He said, 'Jeremiah Catlett, ye ain't niver belonged afore to any but that deival Mr. Oakley, but now ye're Mine. Y'ain't hisn no more. I got ye.' Well, He had me. I set out to git His Word in my mind because I couldn't read it or nuthin, and Mr. Stone ridin and me a-walkin, we lit out all through the outlyin woods, up and down cricks, takin the Word, and him quotin and me gittin it all as we went. Mr. Stone reckoned I knowed as much chapter and verse as he done."

Hannah had gone to sleep again. The empty gourd rolled from her hand as she lay, and Jeremiah knelt by the pallet and covered her over where the skins had fallen and left her sharp shoulder bare. What happened to Mr. Stone she didn't know for a long time, for Jeremiah had obviously told that part of it to the fire and to Hagar in the night. By the next morning he was as quiet again as ever, the story over. Only, from time to time, he referred to things as if he took for granted that she knew them.

"Course I don't for a minute believe he meant to turn me in," he said once and disappeared out the door. Later in the afternoon, when he was grinding grain in a hollowed stone, he looked up at her. "Mr. Stone wouldn't of done nuthin like that, but I couldn't take no chance, could I?"

Chapter Four

THREE WEEKS later the first snow of winter came. The trees had not even lost their last leaves. The mountainside was still ripe with the fall, and the grass of the great meadow still had green about it. For a few mornings before, the dew had shown like gray hair, frosty in the dawn, when Jeremiah went down to get water at the creek. The high days of the Indian summer had passed without the killer shadows of creeping men. It had been a lucky year. Now as Jeremiah stood where he had nearly a month before, worried about Hagar, the Indian summer, gray frost, stubble field, scarlet and yellow leaves, and the grass—all were blotted out. The world he saw was as white as a shroud, and he thought for a while of the problems of winter.

His small stock of grain was in. The rock and log crib, full to its bark roof, showed its treasure through the air spaces between the logs, made fatter by the white, clinging snow. Behind him, in the cabin, the skins were rising higher, and he knew before he felt the snow, by the way it lay, that it was soft, hunter's snow; that tracks would guide him to the animals, with their coats thickened for winter, for the gun, and finally for the English ladies and gentlemen, who wore for luxury the beaver which had in life been possessed by work.

Jeremiah had had a good breakfast; light smoke from its cooking still curled up from the chimney to linger under the snow-laden trees as his own breath was doing while he stood there and sighed. He bent his head from habit and started down the obscured path through the virgin snow, making a new pattern as he went, breaking the winter path. He did not say a word, or look back. By the set of his head, by his sad eyes, which watched without noticing the ground in front of him, he showed that something was wrong as loudly as if he had bawled at the black trees. But he did not make a sound to disturb the white stillness of the first snow. He only disappeared slowly through the trees, as quietly as if he were walking in the air, and reappeared beyond them in a few minutes, a much smaller figure, black against the white of the meadow.

Now there was another figure in the doorway, with her hand out to close it more tightly after him, for the wind had swung it open again and was lifting tufts of snow over the log at the doorsill. She watched his figure leave a trail in the distance that looked as if it had been drawn with a pencil by some great baby. The track was not straight. It seemed to curve, to lose its direction, to find it again, to sway down the white savannah, past the snake fence, showing sharp against the snow—down toward the creek. She stood for a second, then made a small movement that could almost have been a shrug—a tiny shift of her shoulders —closed the door, and sat down before the warm fire again. The light from the snow was cold and white, filtering in through the spaces between the logs which Jeremiah had not finished calking. Its paleness made her shiver, although the fire was warm, and she drew toward her the log that Jeremiah had shaped and hollowed into a hominy block. She dragged herself up and stood, legs bent, beside it, lifted the heavy log pestle in her hands, then let it carry itself down by its own weight. She soon got into the rhythm of the corn-grinding, of the hollow sound of the pestle thumping against the wood, sending the breaking kernels up in a little contained cloud. The pestle churned faster and faster; the rhythm quickened. Just to hear it was evidence enough that the woman who guided it up and down with such an edge of ferocity was not only busy but also very angry.

Even with her mouth set in that woman's line of wordless resistance, Hannah had changed so much in the last weeks that no one but Jeremiah would have recognized her as the emaciated flotsam he had brought in and dumped down so tenderly to keep its bones from rattling like a shaman's medicine bundle. Not that Jeremiah had thought of her in the first weeks as any bundle of magic at all. But now her round face was the youngest-looking face he believed he'd ever seen. She had a habit of holding on to her lower lip (which had been so weather-burned it was like a wound, and now was full and pink), of holding it tight in her teeth when she thought, as if to keep it from pouting out like a child's and betraying her youth. Because she had regained weight so quickly, her body had little beauty except when she moved, as she now did, lithely but with a sturdy kind of animal strength. She had certainly never seen herself before with these podgy rolls of new fat. Jeremiah found her crying once, but she didn't tell him that time that she'd lost her body along with her memories, and wanted at least her body back.

The pestle lifted and plunged through her loose hands. Hannah's forehead showed little jewels of sweat, which caught the firelight and glittered. She stopped long enough to take off the buckskin shirt she had made for herself out of Jeremiah's softest skins. He had picked them for her and had sat, watching proudly, while she plunged the bone sliver again and again and sewed herself the shirt and a buckskin skirt.

She stood, stripped to the waist, her breasts, which were round and full but small, lifting and lowering in rhythm with the pestle.

[51]

Jeremiah came in from the creek, where he had had to break a thin film of ice to get his wooden buckets full. He set them down, glanced at Hannah, then went on watching her as she worked.

"Ye do that pretty good, Hannah," he told her, and reached into the fireplace for his stone pipe and began to smoke.

"Lord a-mercy, I ought to!" She stopped long enough to wipe her forehead with her arms, and took up the pestle again.

Jeremiah was silent for a long time; then he spoke, so casually that it made her start and stare at him, frozen, with the pestle lifted high. He said, "Ought ye, now?"

The pestle plunged down for an answer, but Hannah herself was as still as a stone.

After a few minutes Jeremiah went out again, gun in hand, and slammed the door behind him.

It was later, loping bent-kneed through the woods with his flintlock balanced casually in his right hand, as ready as an extension of his fist, that he remembered that Hannah had indeed looked like a shaman's bundle of bones and rags when he'd first seen her and begged God to keep her alive. Now, after he had cared for her without any temptation but pity, had cleansed her weak body all over, relieved her, and nursed her, something terrible had happened. Something had changed. He was so aware of the magic of the bundle now, instead of its ugliness —the heat of her in his cabin, the times he had chanced on her when she stood working in the cabin, as her habit was, naked to the waist. Suddenly he could see again her gently moving pink breasts as she pounded the mortar. He stopped, faint for a second, stroking his buckskin trousers with the same movement, hardly knowing he was doing it. Then he was hotly more and more aware of the magic he'd brought in, of the obsessive magic. He remembered his plea—"She may be a deival"—and was certain, certain, his left hand moving faster and faster, now grabbing at his trousers to get them open, that she was a deival, a deival, a deival. He leaned against the tree with a sense of falling, and knew

[52]

at once that he was possessed of her—and she was a deival, with moving breasts, pink lips, and young as a ripe apple. "Ooooh!" he moaned, meaning to start to say his prayers but not getting to it. For his terrible sin splattered the snow in front of him, sinking through it in a hundred hot melted tiny holes, as if the sparks from a children's sparkler had fallen.

Jeremiah looked down at his gun, which he had not let fall from his right hand, and listened for some kind of wisdom to come to him in his temptation—prayed without saying a word, lest he interrupt and lose the text that might spring to mind; prayed to be free of the deival woman who'd taken his mind off God, who was carnal and wicked just by being alive and being there and driving him out to the woods to commit the sin of Onan and scatter stars in the snow.

"If thine eye offend thee, pluck it out!" His memory had spoken in his own ear, and he knew he had the means to save himself from the woman, the Jezebel who ground the corn, if he only had the strength.

If God indeed meant him to have Hannah, instead of resisting her as a temptation, then why had He left him so lonely, why had his life been so hard? Jeremiah had understood that he had to work his salvation, and had known himself, had spoken in tongues as one of the saved, even as Mrs. Coleman's brother-in-law had done before him. He knew what he had to do and turned back to the cabin, gripping his rifle so that his knuckles stood out white against it, and if he had had a "yaller vision" before, now he had another, but this one evil, pulsing and beckoning him with a plump woman's arm, beckoning him through the black trees over the white, soft snow.

It was a long way back to the cabin. More snow began; huge wet flakes clung to his hair, to his fur winter apron. The whole still forest around him was as empty as a hollow shell; all life seemed gone from it, dead with the summer. Jeremiah walked straighter this time. There was in his walk the sense that the time

[53]

of wandering, of indecision, was over. He had applied his poor heart as best he knew how to seek out wisdom and the reason of things and to know the wickedness of folly; and he accepted as gospel the lamentations of a rich, wise old Jew in a decaying kingdom, a man full of sorrow, who had fallen in love in his youth and had found the words that possessed Jeremiah—"More bitter than death the woman, whose heart is snares and nets, and her hands as fetters." Unhappily, neither the heat, the desert, the luxury, nor the hard-bought imperial wisdom which brought forth the Ecclesiastes was there—only the cold words and the snow, and a twenty-five-year-old man alone.

Inside the cabin, Hannah was nearly asleep. The work she had to do early in the morning was finished. Jeremiah had gone hunting; the day of snow was the first day when a woman alone in a hut could relax without having to be as wary as an animal. The whole white day was ahead; Hannah put off her beckoning chores and, staring at the now white-scrubbed hearthstone as Jeremiah had stared early in the morning, she reached for the dry tobacco. Using her palms to crush the leaf, she made it into powder and began to rub her gums, drowse, and spit into the fire. She had passed from the stage of wishing to the place where wishes take shape and become animated as dreams, where the walls of the cabin were disappearing, and Jeremiah was there, near her—a different Jeremiah, the dream-wish widening the cabin and making a bigger man of him.

Jeremiah pushed open the door with a loud creak that cut the morning stillness, and walked in. Hannah jumped up, still half asleep, wiping the tobacco dust from her hands and her mouth, still not knowing whether he had come back or whether the dream was vivid.

But it was not a dream Jeremiah who muttered, "I reckoned I'd come on back. Hit's fixin to snow pretty hard." He set his gun against the wall and came to the fire, not ever looking at her.

"Ye want some broth?" She reached forward in front of him,

[54]

and he saw that she had put her shirt on again, and that the soft curve of her arm was already shaping the garment into her mold of ownership.

"Hannah!" The word came before Jeremiah expected to say it, and she stopped, her arm a bare six inches from his face.

He said nothing more, so she put her hand on his shoulder gently and said, "What, Jeremiah?" Then, when he said nothing— he was so deep in her nearness, and as frightened of her temptation and his own strength as Eve herself had once been, who was tempted by the great snake—she said again, a little petulantly, "Jeremiah!" to wake him up, and shook his shoulder slightly.

"I've got to take ye someplace, gal. Ye belong somewhar, don't ye?" And, after the visions of Jezebel torn by hounds, that was all the admonishing he could do, and that not even looking at her, but staring at the fire.

"Why?" she asked him then, and squatted in front of him to see his face. So when he did look at her, close to him, and smelled the sweet smell of her sweat of the morning, and the fresh crushed tobacco dust which still clung to her face and hair; when he saw that her position was the same, with her knees in the air, as she would take to receive him or help out a child; he could only tip her back onto the floor—both of them fumbling, tearing at their clothes—and drive into her again and again, not speaking but groaning loudly, while Hagar slept and the piglets suckled, the fire became coals and the snow thickened to a veil of white, hiding the cabin from the nearest tree—until her passion and then his, his twenty-five years, the energy held down by the lid of guilt and loneliness, were finally slaked, and they both lay on the rug exhausted, his arm across her stomach, above her navel. Later, as her sweat dried and the outside cold sneaked nearer, she got up and stoked the dying fire while Jeremiah slept; then lay down again and watched it catch and build and make the walls of her new home dance, drowsing, as full of peace as Hagar.

[55]

BOOK ONE

July 16, 1754 – July 12, 1755

I look away across the sea
Where mansions are prepared for me . . .

Chapter One

Hᴀɴɴᴀʜ flicked awake and shot to her feet at the same time, poised to go on running through the winter streets, her heart shaking. Then, remembering that she was safe after the sickening danger of the afternoon's chase, she leaned with a sigh against the doorjamb where she had hidden, and stroked her stolen wool shawl. She wiped the fear sweat off her hand, then went on stroking, with her whole straightened fingers enjoying the softness and the solid pressure even of her own hand against the creeping London cold.

Now through Downing Street a few house flambeaux were already flaring in their sconces against the dusty twilight. Down the street, near the park, a shadow man came shuffling out of a doorway and sniffed the air as if he had to make any real decision about whether he should join the evening promenade. He finally stepped into the quiet street. Hannah had to grin. She rolled herself out of the doorway, still as sleepy as a kitten, and yawned widely, then shook herself to get back to work.

Hannah was a Londoner, its streets her cradle, its magistrates her parents; she took to the evening promenade up and down the crushed shells of the Mall as naturally as she had taken the shawl several hours before, to be chased for it through courts, over cobbles, brick, mud, slip-slapping along the city drains, following the nerves of London until she had fallen to rest in the deserted door at last. She slowed down a little as the man she was stalking for her dinner seemed to float ahead of her in the mist, disappearing and reappearing closer than she intended him to be.

She stopped for a pause. Now in the park, near the white ribbon of the Mall, Hannah began to see the cold. A single officer sadly wheeled his mount as he practiced alone in front of the rubble pile of the half-finished Horse Guards' Palace. His scarlet coat seemed blue in the winter dusk. Hannah leaned against a stone balustrade and watched the lonely show as the rider careened his ballet horse across the Parade and then seemed to freeze in motion, brought his mount, as docile and delicate as a girl, to a halt, and then began again. The precision made Hannah forget the shadow man and her dinner. She could only drum the balustrade, wishing that she were wrapped in the morning crowd instead of being so lonely, and that the fine officer were inspecting a dead straight line of scarlet soldiers and would notice her.

Hannah was not given to daydreams. She sniffed an overdue long winter sniff and patiently scratched her nose as she walked on, now sadder, to the beginning of the arrow-straight Mall with its round, symmetric trees. They floated over her head in the purple beginning of evening. Here and there an early link-boy, passing, shot light up into their nude branches and made the black stumps left from the formal clipping jump as if they had been touched.

Her pause had cost something. Her shadow man was nowhere to be seen; he had disappeared among the strollers, fat and half-asleep, walking off their four-o'clock dinners. Like a gardener judging a ripe crop, Hannah was sure she could fork her dinner from the rich silk garden without any trouble. She judged coolly, professional at the only thing she had ever in her life been taught to do, as a jungle cat is taught to kill neatly by its provident mother. She read the people as she rubbed past, biding her time —the fat culls, the coxcombs, the solemn old men in their square shoulder wigs, the panniered city women in the flat milkmaid hats, and here and there a budding tuft-hunter, tentatively imitating them all, tiptoe on thin legs.

Over under the trees, watching, sullen with some kind of longing, she saw a dark boy standing. He was not looking at any single face, but through the crowd as if they were ghosts, isolated in some trouble of his own. He was handsome. He was also, by the signs, broke to the wide, even dressed as he was, with a good bag wig, and red court heels, leaning on a gold-headed cane. His suit was good broadcloth, but so thin that his shoulders hunched a little in the cold. Hannah went on staring, wondering if he had popped his greatcoat or had put his fortune on his back one day in summer and could never have afforded the winter anyway. She pulled her new shawl tighter. It was then that she saw the angry eyes stop and focus on one man. It was her shadow man, now reared back with pleasure, holding his hands under his heavy coat behind him, exposing his fob. She saw that, like an awkward swimmer who fears the current, the dark boy's hand seemed to waver under his lace too long, far too long, over the fob-pocket. The hand was huge, shaking. Hannah whispered a silent warning as she saw it fumble at the pocket, its fingers awkwardly forked.

The crowd eddied, full of noise. He was hidden under it. Hannah ran by habit to watch the fun of an arrest. Already behind her she could hear the call, "Thief," singing away from the bunched group around the boy, who now lay on the ground. Hannah pushed through, on the ready. As she got near the front of the crowd the boy sat up, his hands covering his face, his bag wig hanging drunkenly over his shoulder.

Hannah saw with the horror of the Bridewall-bred and -toughened that he was crying. The sight made her own hand shake as she automatically forked the nearest pocket. Someone slapped her wrist against the pocket and held it there, hurting. Then, too late, she heard behind her the familiar runners.

Squire Raglan did not notice the arrest of the girl. He was too intent on controlling himself in the nightmare he had waked to. He stumbled to his feet, trying to brush the dead leaves from his threadbare coat.

Squire, one of that army of self-appointed arbiters, the apes, the hangers-on, those who stood on the edge of literature, in constant expectation of miracles, took his last walk, frog-marched down the Mall, where now no rich patron waited, no comfortable widow, only the crowd, mostly as broke as he was, making a path of jokes and laughter.

He hardly listened when the magistrate committed him to Newgate Prison. As a matter of fact, standing huddled in the evening raggle-taggle of arrests jostling and protesting at the bar, he didn't know it was himself until the runner grabbed his arm again, leaving four deep-dug dirt marks on his fresh-scoured sleeve.

The next morning he was taken through the white vapors of winter down Fleet Street toward Temple Bar. Now the famous coffee houses and the brilliant taverns were closed and shuttered. At first he was able to see the shapes of buildings through the freezing mist; then only sounds came through it—the tinkle of thin ice cracking under the tumbril's wheels, the wheeze and groan of a forest of hanging signs over his head. An early workman stumbled near enough the tumbril for Squire to see a shape, but backed away again like a frightened ghost, not because the tumbril was dangerous but because it was threading a careful way over the open sewer in the road's center to keep from getting lost. It was too cold for the smell to hang in the air.

With the close-packed shapes around him, Squire could manage to keep a little warmer than he had through the night. The miseries of the watch-house and of the cold had not yet left his mind free for a more philosophical despair.

Now the wheel sounds changed as the tumbril went from the dirt road to cobble. They stopped, and Squire could hear the huge gate of Newgate being pushed open. Inside the press yard the mist was thinner. Two tumbrils for the day's executions were pulled up beside a studded door, and a freezing family huddled against the wall by one of them, waiting.

"They come to say their fond farewells," a voice croaked behind him. "This hyar blood will have the whole of the king's court, eh?" The speaker banged Squire's arm.

"Arrr!" Another sound came from behind Squire. He was too full of a sudden inner shower of cold fear to pay attention to the laugh.

The old lags knew better than to let new prisoners near the tiny fires they'd managed to build on the stone floor of the open inner court. The fires were so small that Squire could only tell there were any at all because of the huddles of people. High around him rose the indifferent cold stone walls of Newgate. Here and there he could see at a window the face of a prisoner who had bribed the turnkey to let him stay inside the cell, out of the bitter winter day. If it had been calculated for it, the prisoners' side of the great building could not have been better designed to teach the dead truth of the reality of mercy and the size of one soul and body against the Portland stone juggernaut of the law. No one paid any attention to him. None of the bleak, caught company even spoke.

It was the Janus face of London, and, as it is for one who has been too much in love, it was easy for Squire to slip into hatred— easy to stay there, too, since hatred is a more fitting emotion for a criminal innocent than love. He sank down on a corner of a stone bench and hugged himself, knees up, head down, hiding, making himself as small as he could, almost asleep from shock. He couldn't drop all the way into sleep because by the middle of the morning Newgate was having its own promenade—the prisoners rioting, drinking, quarreling, howling in a ghastly travesty of the world outside. From time to time someone jostled against him, and once, when he was nearly asleep, he felt his stick being drawn carefully from his hand. He woke and clutched it, suddenly wild with fury, ready to lash out at whoever he could find to hit.

But there was nobody there. Only a young girl stood near him, watching him, leaning easily against the stone wall.

"How old are ye?" she asked, staring at him.

"Today is my birthday," Squire answered, surprised. "I am—twenty."

"Ye're no more nor nineteen, if that. For shame of yourself, a fine gintleman like you in such a place as this! Hyar, give me your stick. Ye'll need some food."

"Demme, what would I lean on?" Squire leaned now beside her, slipping without knowing it into a fashionable pose because Hannah Bridewell had said he was a gentleman.

"Lor'!" Hannah whispered, impressed—not at his speech. By now she was fingering his ruffles. She held her hand out for the stick.

"How do I know ye'll bring me the money?" Squire teased.

She was a soft, pretty girl, and she had a thick country shawl over her shoulders, which he needed, he was sure, worse than she did. Squire smiled at Hannah.

For some reason Hannah did bring back the money. From that time on until both their trials it was considered in Newgate that Squire was hers because of the strange thing Hannah had done. No one bothered him; no one stripped him when he lay asleep in the men's cell; Hannah could even hang up his shirt and shams to dry while he lay in a corner on a pallet she had commandeered, wrapped in a blanket she had managed to steal when an old woman died in the night, before the others found the body.

But to Squire, lying there, Hannah Bridewell was the devil's joke on him. True, she was better-looking than the rest, and had not whored, so was clean. The shameful, pressing need to couple with her in the cold yard, with the locked bodies of London slum women for a love-tent, was too horrible to remember—except

[64]

when the need flowered again, persistent, curing his terror, the icy injustice of it all for a little while. But to have had dreams up to a day in December of— What were the dreams? He closed his eyes and tried to stop shivering. Anyway, they were not Hannah Bridewell—called that because she had been born in Bridewell.

One evening she brought him news, along with his clean clothes, two Indian garters to replace the ones he'd had stolen by another newcomer who didn't know he was Hannah's, and his shoes, which had been repaired by an old shoemaker who'd fallen into the gin habit and from there into stealing, and now sat in a corner, happy again when he couldn't get a dram, repairing the sorry shoes of the whole prison just to pass the time. He had taken special trouble with Squire's. They were the only ones with red court heels.

"Squar, your trial's tomorrow. Now I've decked ye out like a gintleman. Ye hold your tongue and don't be bitter and boastful. Ye play the bashful gintleman, for it will help to save your life." She reached forward then and stroked his hair, which now, without powder, lay silky and dark across the pallet. "Pore thing," she muttered. "Niver mind. 'Tis a good thing to have some fever. Thank Gawd hit ain't the jailbird fever, that's all. Hit makes ye look pale and is a help with the jury. Some stands by the stone wall for hours afore they go into the dock, so's to git like you. Remember all I told ye. Plead not guilty." She straightened her thick shawl around his shoulders.

"I'm not guilty." Squire was sullen. "I never meant—"

"Oh, Jesus, listen to the boy! Ye're guilty as the deival himself." Hannah laughed. "But ye mustn't say so. Now I told ye . . ."

When she had finished giving him his instructions for the last of so many times, Squire took her hand.

"Oh, Hannah, how can I ever thank ye? Ye have seen me at my darkest hour. Someday—" He was beginning to cry with the sentiment of fever and fear.

"Oh, listen to yourself!" Hannah said roundly and slapped his

[65]

hand. "Ye'll not want to see me again for many a long day. I'm
Hannah Bridewell to enough. Now I reckon myself to be Hannah
Newgate to you." She slapped his hand again and almost ran away
to keep from showing him that his words had touched her at all.

An old lace thief, groaning and mumbling her way through the
women's cell, found Hannah behind a huge stone pillar. "What's
up, baby-face?" she asked, grinning.

"Oh shut your gob, ye old hedge-whore." Hannah turned her
face to the stone to hide.

"I do believe Miss Hannah's fell in love with a gintleman."

"Oh go tuck yourself up, ye bitch," Hannah muttered at the
wall.

"I'll see you tucked up and sell apples to the mob," the old
woman teased. "As for him, he'll show a fine pair of heels on
Tyburn Tree!"

Hannah didn't answer. She couldn't. Her shoulders were shaking.

"Oh, Weasel," she wailed finally, "the watch was worth quids.
They'll tuck him up sure." And she fell against the old woman's
fat shoulder.

"Listen, ye fool sop," the woman told the girl gently, "ye've got
your own worries, with your own trial tomorry. I'll lay ye honest
money ye ain't even told the pretty namby-pamby thar." She patted
Hannah's back rhythmically, not daring to say any more.

"They'll niver tuck me up nohow." Hannah's sobbing turned
into a little giggle. "I can plead my belly."

"Ye're not!" The Weasel clawed Hannah off her shoulder and
held the girl back to look at her, delighted.

"I am too." Hannah grinned shyly.

"Well, damn your bloody peepee eyes!" the Weasel said, con-
gratulating Hannah with great affection.

*   *

Whether it was dawn or not, Squire couldn't tell. He was shaken up long before the late winter day by the turnkey, and, with fifty dead-quiet men, shuffled along a vaulted underground corridor, thickly whitewashed so that there were not even the telltale rubbings of human bodies. High above, through the stone, he could hear the faintest rumble of tumbril wheels and knew they were passing under the press yard. From somewhere high in the prison he could hear the thin wail of a baby. But no light ever came to this underground passage to the Old Bailey. Only the flambeau of a warder fluttered up ahead and made the shadows of the prisoners dance against the white wall as if they were already hanged.

It seemed hours in the cell. Men came and went and came back again, their faces ghastly pale or relieved, according to the sentence. One boy of sixteen was carried back into the cell and dropped into a corner in a dead faint. He had coshed a man who had too soft a skull. No one went near him. Huddled there together, they were finished with bravado. Squire could not remember how long it was since the last word had been said. Like people waiting in some deadly fever hospital of the soul, they waited with dim patience, isolated completely in the crowded cell.

"Josiah Devotion Raglan, come into court." The turnkey wheezed and sighed as he opened the door and repeated the words in a steady mumble.

"That's you." A boy beside Squire pulled at his arm to dislodge him from the frozen stand his body had taken on its own when he heard the name. He moved out of the cell, in front of the man, in a dream. A warder closed in behind him. Without a word they marched through another dark, damp-smelling corridor, where only their footsteps on the stone floor steadily tolled under them.

Squire was conscious, for a second, of where he was. They had stopped but were still in the whitewashed cellar. There was no court, nothing but silence—no, not quite silence, a scurry, as of rats, high above. Before him the turnkey was opening a narrow door. The warder shoved him through it. It slammed behind

[67]

them. He could feel, in the dark, the warder breathing behind him on a flight of narrow steps, which twisted ahead of him. For a moment he was blinded by the thick darkness of the staircase. The warder dug into his back with his stick and jollied him forward. He could feel both shoulders sliding up the slick walls of the staircase. Then he felt, more than saw, a turn. Now the sounds were louder, defined as voices. Squire stopped, afraid he was going to vomit. The warder pushed again; this time there was a beam of light to climb toward. Squire rushed up the last few steps, goaded now at every step by the warder. He was flung into light which seemed to break over him from every side. He fell forward a little and, to save himself, clutched at spikes in front of him on a balustrade.

He had risen from the black tomb below into the center of the courtroom, where the dock faced the judgment seat.

Somewhere below him a bored voice recited, "Set"—it paused as a man in a black robe consulted a paper—"Josiah Devotion Raglan to the bar."

Squire's protecting stun was passing. The light, after hours of near-darkness, was the light of a pale winter London day, which poured in from three huge, bleak, naked windows, showing only the sky and the side of Newgate Prison. He could sense the eyes behind him, in front of him, beside him, and could not move for being pinned by eyes.

The dock of the Old Bailey stood isolated in the center of the court. The prisoner, Raglan, faced a very old man, who crouched in a chair too big for him, shrunken inside a blue fur-trimmed robe, his sharp face receding into a huge wig, under the high carved canopy of the judge's dais, where the velvet curtains fell, dignified, warm and soft, framing him. The only cold about him seemed to come from his eyes. Squire found that he could not look away, and felt unlocked from them only when the old man lowered his head to consult a paper.

[68]

The clerk below was mumbling something, but it was the old man Squire heard.

"The prisoner will have to pay attention and speak up. We have too many cases to try." The judge's voice was petulant. Turning to someone at his side, he managed to sweep the sheet of paper to the floor inside the dais, and a sprig of rue after it.

In the ensuing, complaining scramble, Squire heard the voice of the clerk, saying by rote, indifferent to the words, while he fumbled at some paper he was preparing on the table in front of him, "How sayest thou"—here he paused again for the name— "Josiah Devotion Raglan, art thou guilty of the felony whereof thou standest indicted, or not guilty?"

"Not guilty," Squire whispered, but thought he spoke.

"The prisoner must speak up." The judge sounded so indignant that Squire felt he ought to apologize to the old man.

"How the devil they expect me to hear evidence when . . ." The old man had turned and was mumbling to another robed figure at his side.

The clerk spoke louder now, seeming to take the judge's complaints personally. "Culprit, how wilt thou be tried?"

"By God and my country." Squire's voice scared him, but he had obeyed the judge.

"God send thee a good deliverance," the clerk mumbled as he started to sit down, fumbling in his heavy robe for a handkerchief to blow his nose.

A Bible, kissed black by thousands of culprit lips, was handed to Squire. He kissed it in his turn, but through a ruffle of his sleeve, as Hannah had warned him to do, lest he go to hell for lying under oath to God. He did it only to please her, since she had begged so through his bitter laughter. For indeed, if ever God had forsaken a man— The eyes on his back were too much. It was all he could do, then more than he could do, to keep from turning around.

His father, a green-black mournful figure, was standing at the back of the courtroom, high up the tiered seats of the gallery. Sure enough, he was in an attitude of prayer that Squire well knew. He had looked that way too many times after beating his soul cleaner in his filthy body.

"Will the prisoner face the court?" the aggrieved voice of the judge drew Squire around again. This time he was able to take in the figure who sat on the other side of the dais. She had raven-black hair; her white skin seemed polished after the drab gray-brown of the prisoners. She sat easily, flanked by huge flat-fronted panniers, which had taken so much room that one of the council had had to move close to another and was able to put his head on his colleague's shoulder and drift into sleep. Over her shoulders the young lady had thrown a fur-edged cape, and in her hand she held a delicate glass bottle, which she sniffed, then smiled over, self-assured to be so pretty in such a drab place. She leaned over and whispered to the judge, and the old, creased face seemed for a second to smile.

Then he motioned her aside and turned toward the witness box, where an old man was being sworn. Squire looked too. The man had some edge of familiarity about him.

". . . the watch cost every penny of five pounds." The man seemed angry over something.

"Will the witness consider the value of the watch again?" the judge commanded, annoyed.

The lady whispered over her shoulder to a gentleman behind her, and they both laughed.

"Five pounds." The man was certain.

"Four shillings and elevenpence value." The judge pounded his gavel at a murmur in the court. The witness was called down, fuming at the injustice of having his watch considered so cheap.

Squire hardly knew what he was saying when he was questioned. He was far more worried about controlling his voice in front of the lady so that it wouldn't squeak and betray him.

[70]

He was jerked back into awareness when the foreman of the jury got to his feet. The word "Guilty" hung for a minute in the bleak room.

The judge sighed and picked up a paper. "The judgment therefore of this court"—he put the paper down and looked at Squire, never taking the cold eyes from him as he finished—"is that you should be imprisoned in the jail of Newgate for one month; and after the expiration of your imprisonment, you should be transported to some of His Majesty's colonies or plantations in America for the term of seven years; and if within that term you return, and are found at large in any of His Majesty's dominions of Great Britain or Ireland, you shall suffer death as a felon within the benefit of clergy."

A hand on his arm spun him around, but not too quickly for him to see the young lady smile more widely, amused that she had had some say in court. Squire had had his one contact with the *ton*. He never knew that by persuading her father to set the value below the death price of five shillings because Squire was so much prettier than the others with his pale face and fine ruffles, she had saved his life.

*   *

Squire caught a glimpse of Hannah on the road from Newgate to Blackfriars as they moved at a snail's pace through the street crowd to be put aboard the lighter for the *Lucy Gay* at Blackwell. She was walking, chained in a double line of convict felons bound for Virginia. The shoving crowd was treating the convict line a little as if it were a parade, finding it a diversion to jeer and throw mud.

"See them Toryrories! Wampum and stinkibus!" a young boy bellowed, almost insane with the joy of his own noise as he darted through the crowd, keeping up with them. "Wahoo!" he Indian-yelled, full of bloody visions, half performing for the growing crowd, half in a wild world of his own.

[71]

Squire could not ignore the boy, and this was the one figure in a sea of faces, racing there, always beside them, that stood out—Squire's last view of a Londoner, the ugly, pockmarked, adolescent, cruel face. Here and there in the jostling crowd they had to push through, Squire could see a head come forward, bend close to whisper, a bundle pressed into a convict's hand.

He could not see much more, because he was traveling in a closed hackney with the curtains nearly drawn. His only company was one other gentleman convict, a young man who showed by the raise of one shoulder, more developed than the other—which made him seem to crouch a little in the corner of the carriage— that he had been trained as a printer. He sat coolly, watching the crowd past an edge of the curtain, his head turned away from Squire.

★   ★

The captain, a softhearted man, unchained the women when they were five days out to sea, although it was more than he dared do to free the men. He was lucky for a winter voyage. He lost only thirty of the men.

Fear grew in the ship as the Atlantic changed from blue to gray to the alien flat gray-green that was the American ocean. The convicts could not imagine the hot sun, never having felt it in their London hutches of cobble and damp. They knew only that picking tobacco leaves in the fields, after the uneasy pleasures of the London streets, was in their world one of the familiar ways of dying. Virginia. The name was enough to shoot horror into the backbone of every convict aboard. Virginia, transportation to the plantations—next to death, the final punishment.

A dim gray line was sighted on the horizon in forty-three days, but an offshore wind kept them at bay, like a vicious dog, for two days more. The convicts were forced out onto the swaying deck and made to sit in the pale February sun, some of them too sea-

[72]

sick to move. The captain hoped the air would give the cargo a little better color before the sale. It was hard enough for him— the usual cargo of seven-year felons. A few wheelwrights, carpenters, smiths, cartwrights, and masons were in the batch, which cheered him. They were badly needed, easy to sell.

"Sarvants are at a high premium here, they tell me." Squire was leaning in the doorway of the captain's cabin, where, as gentlemen, he and the printer had been allowed to travel unchained. "They do say I won't have much trouble." He picked a tooth and watched coolly as Hannah walked up and down the deck below. "The provincials have a yen for being learned the *bon ton*. They'll pay a thousand pound for a sarvant of my . . ."

"By Judas, why can't ye call yourself what ye'll be?" the young printer yelled at him and made Hannah look up for a second. It was the first time on the voyage that anyone had heard him raise his voice. "You look at most of those wretches down there." He pointed to the long rows in the dim sun. "Every last one of them will be sold as a bonded slave, owned by a master, probably for their wretched lives. They'll work in the tobacco fields until they drop. They—"

"Now, you been told wrong, young fellow. 'Tis only the blacks is called slaves. The whites is more called sarvants." The captain put his head out of the cabin door. "More like apprentices. Think of it more like that," he added as he wrapped himself in his greatcoat to go and inspect the prisoners.

"There's not a legal difference between a white slave and a black one. They work side by side. They—"

"Now there ye got it wrong." The captain laughed. "Whatever the whites is, they ain't black. They can say to theirselves, I'm an Englishman or a Scotsman or what have ye—all Christians of a kind. Them blacks is heathen. 'Tis fellows like you gets it wrong and stirs up trouble. 'Tis not the best foot to put forward in the colonies, I can tell ye." He shook his head as he stared at the

[73]

young man, judging the thin pale face with its still eyes, its gentle, slightly bitter mouth, as if he were trying to guess his age for the market.

"No, Jarcey Pentacost," he finished sadly. "I won't say ye're a republican, but ye've too free a mouth and nary enough muscle, though leetle fellows can be mighty wiry. Ye'll go cheap. Ye're worth naught." And he went away, still shaking his head, to inspect the cargo.

They landed on a cold March day which seemed to bluster outward from the whole continent behind Alexandria, rejecting the *Lucy Gay* from the quay so that she had to fight her way into her berth. Squire could see the buyers, most of them in the high collars worn ten years before in England, some huddled in little groups, some blowing and stamping to keep out the cold. In the distance the red coats of two English officers stood out like winter birds against the drabness. Squire began to shiver and could not stop himself as the gangplank clattered on the dock and the sound of chains running out roared over the loud babble ashore.

" 'Tis better to have a knave who can write your letters and dress your hair than an honest clodhopper," the English lieutenant was advising his companion, an ensign who looked like a tall pale child, as Squire stepped off the gangplank onto the wooden dock. He sidled near them, wondering how to make them notice him.

Jarcey Pentacost was bought first, by a man who obviously knew him. He was stunned with surprise when the man came up to him and greeted him sourly.

"Mr. Pentacost, I have heared from thy father," Squire heard him say as he motioned to a servant to take Jarcey's valise from his hand. The sale was made so quickly by the smiling captain that the two of them had disappeared into a carriage and Squire watched it clatter away before anyone noticed him at all.

The rest were being made to run, flex their muscles, lift, bend. In the distance, Squire caught a glimpse of Hannah, bravely giving a smile to a huge sutler in a leather apron, who was feeling the size of her arm without any expression at all on his heavy face.

The captain looked over at Squire, worried. He had made a mistake, and he knew it. The fact that Squire's advertisement read "lawyer or schoolmaster" had ruined his value; it kept the local planters from bidding. An old planter, thin as a rake and stained tobacco-color, walked close to Squire and seemed to be trying to smell him.

"Ever' last thief who can write his damned name calls himself a damn lawyer. What good's a lawyer for plantin nohow? One up Brewster planted a youngin in old Joe Leftwich's daughter, run off with ever' damn thing." He turned to the man next to him. "Give me blacks ever' time. These whites are triflin."

"Oh I don't know. German whites are good. It's English white —jailbirds . . ." the other man was saying.

"Irish whites are turble." The old man passed out of Squire's hearing, mumbling to himself, worried about something—Squire didn't give a damn what. He had worries of his own. Finally, in desperation, he jogged the young ensign's arm, his heart beating like a hammer.

"A thousand pardons, sar." He bowed and drawled; hairdressing, wig-combing, wit, heart, the fashion, the *ton,* went into one sentence to save his soul.

"What about this one?" the ensign said to his companion as if he had thought of it himself.

The captain was delighted. He managed to sell Squire at a far higher price than he had expected, mostly because the young ensign didn't want to seem mean in front of the older lieutenant.

At last it was done. Squire climbed weakly up behind the carriage. He had been so shocked, so full of horrible stage-fright —even at the dismal auction, so fearful of being left out—that he had hardly registered what either of the officers looked like. They jumped inside, and the carriage was off as if the furies were following, through the scattered little town of Alexandria, where here and there Squire could see a few surprisingly elegant small brick town houses rise up, wall to wall with the cabins and the long tobacco warehouses.

Squire's last sight of Hannah was as she sat, huddled with cold, in the back of the sutler's wagon, which had drawn up in the square opposite the ordinary. She seemed to be trying to keep her thin bones rigid, as a barrier against the harsh wind. Squire was sorry for a minute that he had no time to speak and cheer her a little.

Now the only movement on the quay, half river bank of gray winter mud, half naked wooden dock, empty and dead quiet, was of a few gulls battering the wind, high in the air.

★   ★

Squire's had not been the only dream dashed by the winter. Inside the carriage, as it rattled along the wide country street, fifteen-year-old Peregrine Cockburn, Ensign of Colonel Halkett's 44th Regiment of Foot, fell into a sulk. Beside him young Lieutenant Halkett, the colonel's son, half dead with the memory in his body of the previous night, had already gone to sleep.

Peregrine had some reason for sulking. This dismal frontier, this crashing wind, had not been part of his vision at all when his father had bought him into a good line regiment which was said to be smiled on by the Duke of Cumberland. The carriage lurched; Peregrine fell against Lieutenant Halkett, who moaned and stretched himself awake and began staring out of the window without a word. For eight years the 44th had lazed down Mary Street, Limerick, until they had grown into its stones. Three months after Peregrine's arrival to take his commission, full of high, peaceful hopes, he had sailed again, with an under-strength, taciturn regiment, which had not given a thought to action in years. They tore themselves away from English Town, Limerick, as a limb is torn from a man.

A new set of field officers came from London to sail with them. Colonel Halkett was upset; his son was enraged; but they

[76]

bowed to the way of the Army. General Braddock was a favorite of the Duke of Cumberland; his official family was made up of London soldiers from the Guards, eyed for preferment by a little easy campaigning, as young thoroughbreds are broken gently.

They landed at Alexandria in Virginia on February 8, 1755, still four hundred men under strength, hoping to reap the war fever in Virginia. All but a few Virginians received them with indifference, hid their best workhorses, and drove a hard bargain for their worst. Who cared if a dying Frenchman sat in a wooden stockade on the dangerous Ohio while his men committed suicide from the cold, wet despair caught of the forest winter? Perhaps a few speculators in high places, or squatters, those children of God fit only for the wilderness. Who wanted a regular Virginia Regiment in Provincial blue with fine silver lace, to lord it over their own militia first cousins who did their shooting in their own clothes and were content to run their farms and beat tobacco from the sandy bottom? It all cost too much, as the exhausted Eastern leaf got smaller, the hungry root reached desolately, having gorged the topsoil in a hundred years of orgy in Canaan.

One rumor had it that the French had come down the Ohio anyway only because Contrecœur had tried to take his wife back from the new governor after it was understood that she was to be his mistress. Other people swore the British regiments were there only to clean up the mess the young fanfaron Washington and his ragged Falstaffian recruits had made at Fort Necessity while he played soldier. Most people agreed it was because the rich Quaker merchant Hanbury had formed a company called the Ohio Company, and it had the ear of the Duke of Newcastle.

All this made little difference to Peregrine as he rode disconsolately in the bumpy carriage—or, for that matter, to the rest of the regiment. They were concerned with trying to learn to keep their skins. Neither Peregrine nor any member of his company had ever fired a live shot from a gun.

[77]

Chapter Two

This man could not be of the New World, this thin, sour man who fidgeted opposite Jarcey Pentacost at the tavern table. The shock of the landing and of his rescue at the ship still hung onto Jarcey and made him blank. Even the raw toddy the man had slammed down in front of him seemed to warm nothing; he drank it without flowering, his nerves twitching, still dry. He sat, isolated in the strange dirty room that smelled of damp pine and heady ripened tobacco, and tried to pull his mind together to listen to the man. He could hear the hollow wind flutter the roof shingles, swoop along the wide dirt road outside.

"I have done what thy father asked"—the man was complaining—"but I have no business with convicts. I am an honest Quaker."

"I can only thankee," Jarcey murmured, listening to the wind.

"Thank me no thanks, sar. I have done it for thy father. I have no more duties with thee."

". . . in four years." Jarcey found himself finishing his new thought aloud.

"In four years"—the man put down his toddy angrily—"I will do the rest. Thy father has wrote a bill in my care when thee has redeemed thyself and know the country. Not much, but when thee has earned it by thy industry I'll turn it to thee. I know my duty. 'Taint but a mite," he finished, satisfied.

Having nothing in common but disapproval and Jarcey's stake, they fell silent, out of words.

The silence weighed on the nervous man. "Has thee considered—" he began, to break the stillness.

But Jarcey had begun at the same time. "I reckon to bind out to a printer; 'tis my trade, that and—"

"Thee'd better to learn the lay of the land. We've little call for such-like fellows," the man interrupted.

The silence grew between them again. A haunch of drying tobacco scuttered in the draft.

The door was flung open, letting in a surge of pale sun, the wind, and several officers. It swung shut behind them, and they walked in a ragged group to the bar, where one of them began to rattle the wooden cage for service. Two of them, in red coats with buff facings and linen already a little dirty from the whipping dust, Jarcey had seen before at the quay, when the younger one of them was buying Squire. They stood with the other officers in red. Two in blue wandered a little apart from the others and stood talking together earnestly.

The Quaker was getting up. "I'll leave thee now. I have no likin for such tavern company," he was saying. The subject was obviously dear to him, for he sat back down again almost in the same gesture. "The lobsterbacks there think they own us, and as for the blue Provincials there, they ain't nary but a passel of rakes, spendthrifts, and bankrupts—a lot of useless lumber I tell thee, who has proved dolts in the management of their own affairs and has sold out to the Ohio Company. Bounty officers! Most of them are so landless they ain't even got a vote. As for the men, every rag, tag, and bobtail . . ."

[79]

The thin man had warmed to his subject; his voice had risen a little, and he leaned forward on the scarred, dirty board, his face so close that Jarcey could see the grains in his blackened wooden peg of a false tooth. Jarcey was staring, so fascinated at the wet wooden stump that he did not see a shadow fall across their heads until a young voice interrupted the man's venom.

"A chimney-corner politician, a Tom Tobacco Cuff, as I live!" The young man laughed.

There was complete silence.

"I cannot have the honor of callin ye out, as I see by your dress ye are naught but a Quaker and a coward." The tall young man in blue laughed again, his hard, handsome, sunburned face stretched over its square, heavy bones; then he lowered his head as his black eyes watched insolently for signs of fear in the man huddled below him.

Jarcey was impelled to his feet by the arrogance. His hand was clenched to keep from tearing the ruffle from the soldier's neck. All the morning, all the months of trouble, all the comforting illusion that he had left such faces behind him forever, the explosions of dreams, the dread certainty of the future, the raw whisky he had drunk, gathered in his hand. He could feel his face grow hot with rage.

A calm voice came from the bar. "Jamie, Jamie, be quiet. For shame of yourself!" If the voice had a hint of amusement, it had sense and authority enough to make both men, straining at each other, relax a little. Jarcey, feeling his nails bite his palm, began to smile to himself.

It broke the tension—except for the gaunt Quaker, who finally got up in the silence as if the world had jumped on his back. He began to argue, embarrassed, as he struggled into his thick black greatcoat.

"I've done my best for thee, young fellow; thee can't say I have not. I'm an honest man, which is not to be sneezed at in this

[80]

colony, not be sneezed at." His coat had lost the struggle. Crookedly, it was on.

"My eternal thanks to ye, sar." Jarcey began to come around the table. The young Provincial sneezed loudly as he passed. Jarcey couldn't finish. He showed the Quaker out, his face growing pinker and pinker with suppression. Then, when the door had been fumbled open and shut, he turned back to the table.

Jamie Stuart, watching the clenched mouth, thought the fight had started at last. He began to move toward Jarcey lightly.

Jarcey sank down by the board without noticing him and began to laugh, the laughter growing to a roar. He beat the board instead of all the faces of his anger. Even the red-coated officers in the corner stopped and stared. Jamie Stuart was watching him with his mouth hanging open. Somebody's hand was beating his back.

"A thousand pardons, gentlemen. I would have welcomed your rescue from that righteous fool had ye knocked all my teeth down my cowardly Quaker throat. Take a drink with me, sar." He grinned at Jamie.

"Well, I'll be blasted and damned. Are ye a Quaker?" Jamie sank down opposite him. "Come, Johnny," he said over Jarcey's head. "Here's a goddam Quaker with a mite spit!"

"I was bred up a Quaker," Jarcey explained.

"And what are ye now?"

Jarcey answered carefully, "Scholar and printer; Jarcey Pentacost, at your sarvice, sar."

Jamie couldn't stop watching him. He even yelled for drink without taking his snap-black eyes from Jarcey's face. "Well, I'll be damned," he whispered softly. "I'll be blistered and damned!"

"Lieutenant Jamie Stuart, Captain Johnny Lacey, at your sarvice, sar." The man with the soft voice spoke at last as he pulled a chair back and sat down beside Jarcey.

Jarcey turned and looked at him for the first time. Jonathan

Lacey was tall but neat. He held his head slightly forward as if he had a habit of walking for long distances, watching the ground. His face was not calm, but still, still as a portrait which watches quietly from the canvas because the subject has sat, waiting, until all action has drained from his face and only the memory of action is left. It was not until Jarcey had seen this stillness in Jonathan Lacey's face that he realized more. Jonathan's eyes looked exhausted, troubled, but his mouth hinted amusement.

"I reckon a coward and a Quaker can take a drink with a rake and a bankrupt. Allow me to pay, sar; the spendthrift has not arrived." Jonathan leaned forward at the board and rested on his arms. In the gesture, Jarcey saw that he was young, little past twenty. He still moved without fear of space, but with the opposite, an animal sense of capacity.

"Ye are new to the country?" Jonathan went on. His voice and accent were those of any English gentleman, but he spoke more slowly, as if in the raw world Jarcey had glimpsed outside and now heard banging, trying to get in, words were spare and precious. He did not use them as a prodigal.

"New arrived," Jarcey said and turned away from Jonathan's scrutiny.

"Can I be of sarvice?" he heard the other ask behind him lightly.

"It is kind of ye, sar," Jarcey said, without looking back. "I would admire to bind out to a printer. 'Tis my trade. I am a scholar, but prefer to work at the more physical trade than to be a schoolmaster."

"We have need of schoolmasters in Virginia," Jonathan interrupted. When Jarcey didn't answer, he went on. "Oh, of printers too, though we cling close to home for books and papers. Sometimes I think we cling too blasted close." He glanced over his shoulder at the officers who were by now nearly drunk at the bar, young Peregrine in the center of them, bleating with laughter like an excited calf.

Jarcey turned then, and met Jonathan's eyes. They began to talk as if they had taken up in the middle of some conversation long past, which both of them remembered.

Jamie Stuart listened to it, growing excited with boredom. " 'Tis said Newcastle hates Cumberland," he heard the little Englishman say.

"Dear God, what's it to do with me?" Jamie muttered and staggered up from the board. Behind him the voices lowered.

"Take a drink with us, Jamie," Lieutenant Halkett yelled.

"A hard life, from the pan to the fire," Jamie went on muttering to himself as he made his way with some care across the room.

Jonathan was easy; his hand lay cool against his tankard, his finger tapping it pleasantly, feeling the soft surface of the pewter. "I have never held the notion that the world spins on the fall of a leaf."

"Ye mean, had Caesar's horse fallen in Britain, there would still have been Philippi?" Jarcey was no longer nervous of the seeking wind. He leaned forward, sharp, inquisitive.

Jonathan's mind had jumped, though, away from old wars. His hand tightened on the tankard. "Mr. Hanbury is a friend of the governor here. He has the ear of Newcastle."

"I have heared tell of him."

" 'Tis common knowledge here; we go west through the wilderness to open it up with a new road, instead of through Pennsylvania, where it is settled to within thirty miles of the Ohio. Hanbury has the Ohio Company." Jonathan leaned close, too. "Ye're new arrived. Come and join us. The bounty for a soldier is four hundred acres. 'Tis a stake without goin to be bonded, and when 'tis settled where the bounties are to be, ye can have a vote."

Jarcey could not answer, and Jonathan went on.

"We go in a few weeks to Cumberland, then on across the mountains to the Great Meadows, where the French took poor little Fort Necessity last year; from there to Fort Duquesne on the Monongahela River where it flows into the Ohio. Ye'll see good Virginia country and can pick your land."

Jarcey found his voice. "Ye forget, Captain Lacey, I was bred up a Quaker," he said a little sadly. "I cannot in all conscience go for a soldier, though I have little of Quaker ways left."

Jonathan made a move, a jerk, and Jarcey added quickly, "I intend no insult to your profession, sar."

"I like to see a man abide by his conscience, sar," Jonathan murmured, far away, as if he were no longer talking to Jarcey at all. "As for my profession, 'tis that of a planter. A bad crop, a life too high on the hog—" He straightened up. "I have been to the west, surveyin. So there is use for me in the general's family. But I am no soldier, though that frank and generous fool the Virginian is a soldier by his life. Like Jamie there—as Virginian as tobacco; prodigal, wasteful; he loves the world as the philosopher yearns to and never can. Jamie! Jamie!" He got up as he called to the young man, who by now was showing his love for the world by getting Peregrine as drunk as the fiddler's bitch.

"But perhaps I can still assist ye." Jonathan glanced back at Jarcey. He drew a paper from his pocket and walked to a high slanted table covered with baroque initials cut by people trying to think in the persistent noise of the room. Quills and sand lay abandoned, thrown pell-mell over the table. Jonathan cleared a space, and Jarcey could hear first one quill and then another scratch slowly. In a minute Jonathan came back.

"Take this here to Mr. Hunter of Williamsburg. He is printer there."

"I am in your debt, sar." Jarcey was so pleased at the gesture that he could only retreat into formality.

"I would consider it amiss if I did not welcome ye to Virginia, sar." Jonathan bowed slightly. They had completely broken contact.

"Where is Williamsburg?" Jarcey was ashamed to ask.

Jonathan threw his head back and laughed. "South by the post road. Any drover will take ye there for your company, and damned good company it is, too. Come, Jamie, the ladies will be expectin us. Coz," he called to Peregrine, "I will see ye at supper; my wife expects ye." He had made contact with the points of his interest in the room all in one easy but slightly edged gesture, which, when he had completed it, had carried him out and away in the wind.

Peregrine said something to the still swinging door, and Lieutenant Halkett laughed and punched at his stomach.

Now that he was alone, Jarcey sat, dead tired, the paper in his hand. The wind intruded, grew stronger. He felt adrift, alien, a weak cat-gut stranger played by the continent. He could sense its hugeness, its hard back. From time to time, on the edge of his loneliness, he could hear the laughter of the soldiers. He was dimly aware that one of them had begun to sing. He dragged himself out from the City Inn to find his way to Williamsburg before the day was too far gone. Behind him the voices of the soldiers reached out.

> *"When my three years are over, my time it will be out.*
> *Come roll me in your arms, love, and blow the candles*
> *out."*

But Jarcey was so alone he paid no attention to the sweet song and didn't hear when Squire Raglan, who by now had already begun to ape the pride of his new soldier life, called and called from where he sat behind the carriage, at Jarcey's retreating back.

*   *

A month later, in the soft heat of April, blond Sally Lacey, aged sixteen, and her raven-haired sister Polly lay on the window-sill of their Aunt Stacy Mason's little town house in Alexandria and thoughtfully allowed the Virginia spring to touch their pretty bodies. Sal could feel the warmth through her thin shift. It lay like a soft hand on her stomach. She sighed, contented, and rubbed her own slim hands together in the air, letting them smooth each other, as if to give them pleasure.

Polly was sleepy. She had, in fact, been asleep for a minute without knowing it, and this gave her voice the quality of a dream.

"Jamie Stuart," she murmured, as if she had waited a long time to answer some question of Sal's that hung in the sweet air, "is my beau, but Mr. Brandon Crawford is my slave."

"Oh, Polly!" Sal's voice had a thrill in it. She leaned on her side and looked at Polly sadly. "Ma would tan your hide if she hyeared ye. She told Aunt Stacy ye was too amorous for a female and that she was damn tired sick of ye a-peartin Mr. Crawford nohow. What do ye intend doin?"

"Jamie Stuart is so damned poor it hurts," Polly said calmly and turned on her stomach to look out the window.

"There's other things," Sal said defensively.

"Listen to the fool gel," Polly told the pink-white apple blossoms, which had shot out new buds almost to the window ledge. " 'Tis better to marry than to burn! Dear God." She reached her white arm out farther and farther, then leaned her waist on the sill to stretch for the blossom. "Listen to her! Here y'are, Missy Priss, married to fine Mr. Johnny who ain't got a penny to bless himself with, and there's Sister off to Winchester above the fall-line, among a lot of Cohees and thieves and whores. What for, indeed?"

She had grasped the branch and now snapped a twig and brought her prize back to the window, pleased. "I'm settin my cap for Mr. Crawford."

"He's too old," Sal said with some spirit to hide the fact that the delicate feminine barbs of nap-time had hit her. "He still shaves his head. Thank God, my Johnny wears his own hair in the new fashion. You'll be damned sorry when his nightcap falls off," she jeered.

"Johnny Lacey can't afford a wig!" Polly flared.

"Captain Orme don't wear none." Sal scored her point. "And Mr. Shirley and Peregrine don't. Ye can't say they don't know the fashion!"

"Coz, coz, coz, coz," Polly chanted. "I'm damned sick and tired of leetle shirt-tail coz." She grinned and just caught her tongue to keep from sticking it out. "You and Ma make me laugh fit to kill myself with your showin off of the English coz. Dammit, he's the only thing Ma got off Johnny she ain't complained of since his Pa lost his fortune."

Sal was dead silent. She felt it was time just to look.

But Polly wasn't to be quieted that way. "Why, Ma went and give Betty to Peregrine for the campaign, when Johnny ain't even got a decent horse."

This did hurt. All Sal could think to say was, "Peregrine will bring her back."

"He'd better. She's the last good brood mare at Belmont." By now Polly was in full flood of enjoying her teasing, having waked up enough. She was beginning to feel the warmth, like wine, excite her for some action. She laughed, mostly because it was such a pretty day and she felt so good. "Your fine Johnny will have to put her to the plow after he quits bein a soldier. There ain't nothin else to use."

"He ain't never goin to run Belmont for Ma!" Sal's voice shook.

"What else, indeed?" Polly asked the now rubbed blossom which made her hands smell so fine that she buried her face in them.

"He's set for preferment, that's what, ye silly slut," Sal hollered at the surprised Polly, who looked up to see tears flowing down her sister's face. "He's goin to be a regular soldier and be

[87]

in a fine new British regiment along with Major Washington and not Provincial at all. Ma hyeared tell. She hyeared tell the whole thing. It all depends on this expedition," she said. "You just leave my Johnny be till ye can do as well for your silly self. Mr. Crawford! Huh! He's been to London and knows the *ton*. He won't get caught by a backwoods miss."

Polly unwound from the window-sill with great calm. She set boredom over her face like a mask. "If ye reckon the *ton* is all Mr. Crawford is a-lookin for, ye know even less than ye show." She was nearly at the door, having sailed sedately there as if the room were a ballroom and not Aunt Stacy's smallest bedroom.

Sal sat up, rigid against the window-sill, and delivered her last shot. "I suppose it is fashionable to affect indifference. I hope, my dearest, ye'll steer clear of such unnatural fashions. I have noticed that when a gel like you is too set on gettin married, she will get the fashion a leetle wrong and make herself a fool."

Polly clutched at the door.

"I reckon to tell ye, Polly, for, after all, 'tis the married folks ye have to look to for advice."

Polly slammed the door behind her in a rage that sent pleasure for a second to Sal's face.

Married folks. Sal was left alone with the words for company. She got up slowly from the window and threw herself across the bed, her blond hair tumbling along the high pillows and down the linen cover of the side. Married. The knowledge fell through Sal's mind like a cold stone and made her shoulders shiver once. She drifted after a little, suspended in the still heat of the afternoon, nearer and nearer sleep.

★   ★

It was almost dark when Jonathan met Philemon. She stepped aside at the turn of the shadowed stairs as he came trudging up them, the final staff-meeting before the move to Cumberland still possessing his mind and making him move, weighted, slowly up the stairs while the Negro woman leaned against the wall.

Once Jonathan had tried to tell Sal's mother that she had named Philemon and Baucis wrongly in her attempt to find genteel new names for the only two house Negroes she had left at Belmont. She had merely shrugged, using her feminine logic to plug up solidly the gaps in her knowledge. "Philemon's prettier for a wench."

Philemon whispered as Jonathan passed her. "She's still asleep. I went in and lit the candle, but she ain't waked up. 'Tis the spring fever." Jonathan had not answered when she added. " 'Tis best for the gal when she's a-carryin her first."

Jonathan nodded, and they smiled together for a second until Philemon slipped off down the stairs.

The bedroom was full of sleep. The evening dew had released the scent of the blossom outside the open window. The room seemed to float in it, mingled with the warm smell of wax from Philemon's candle. Its pale light caught Sal's hair where she had lain across the bed, not moving except to throw her hand up across a cascade of her hair in her sleep. Her fingers lay twined in it, still.

Jonathan tiptoed to the bed and sat down, moving as carefully as a hunter to watch the girl. She seemed to sense him even before she was awake, and she turned slightly on the pillow so that she could smile into the candlelight through a blond veil.

"I never meant to wake ye," Jonathan whispered.

"Is it over?" She swept the hair back and lay, pink with rest, watching him.

"We go tomorrow as we planned." Jonathan could only look at the floor, fearful of the shock of the news he had planned to break so gently to her.

When she kept on watching him without moving, he turned and leaned carefully toward her, his body losing the preoccupation of the final uneasy meeting of the general's family, the incessant

[89]

tearing at his mind of the thousand petty details of the march. He could feel them wash away, and sank hopefully toward peace.

"Johnny!" Sal sat upright, and her voice was shrill with delight. "Aunt Stacy give me a new green watered silk dress to wear to the ball tonight! 'Tis sprigged with blossoms, and the petticoat is quilted with French knots and shows my feet!"

Chapter Three

THERE WERE not even any birds. The men were quiet, their voices muted as voices mute at dusk, at first gently, then with a weight of silence they could not speak against; a weight crouched on the backs of the army, on the necks of the horses, dragging their heads down. The muzzles of the iron cannon glistened like wet snakes as they crawled, a long line on iron wheels. But no rain came down. The new road stretched away, a fresh white scar under the perpetual black trees.

At first there had been some solace in the road itself. At least it was a reminder that man makes miracles and had measured his way to some place through the dark, directionless woods, where the damp hung over the army, and the sun, high above the black pine roof, never penetrated.

To Peregrine these last three days, riding through the pine forest, no longer even feeling the movement of the horse under him, were the deadest days in his life of sixteen years. But he did not put this down to the weight of the woods, to the terrible defeat to the soul of penetration into the ignoring forest, which can only be killed and never wooed. He had no way of knowing these things; he could only experience them with his skin, his senses, as the least alive man in the slogging army did. A sound ahead, over the usual rumble of the long convoy, drew his eyes up from staring blindly between his nag's ears. One of the guns had jammed stubbornly against a rock. A tremor of delay, of dangerous piling up of the tired soldiers, the tumbrils, shuddered along the wagons as the shout to halt rolled back along the convoy. A red-faced sutler was swearing at his bass-horse; a blue-coated officer forced his horse's way through the snarl of men and bent down from the saddle. The sutler was now yelling at him; Peregrine could see that. Then the officer dismounted and bent down beyond sight. When he came up again a knot of men moved to the side of the road and dumped the rock into the woods. A woman climbed back into the wagon, and the sutler began to whip his horse.

The army, having used the halt like a sigh of relief, rolled again. When Peregrine passed where the trouble had been he saw that the rock was indeed a large one. It left a hole in the road where the carts stumbled and tipped drunkenly as they passed. The officer turned back toward him and smiled. It was Jonathan. Peregrine blushed as scarlet as his streaked, spotted coat, and retreated into a shell of his own embarrassment.

"I said"—a persistent voice below his worn nag's wither— "Captain Lacey spoke to ye, boy."

Peregrine realized that his man had been trying for some time to attract his attention. "I seen him," he answered sullenly, not looking down.

"Oh, I know that," Squire went on, but Peregrine still wouldn't look at him. "Ain't you the smart, though, with a fine grown-up cousin to keep watch over ye? 'Tain't the luck of all of us to have a nice Provincial cousin!"

"Oh, you let me be!" Peregrine was finally stung into looking down.

Of course, even in the sour and rainy woods, which the men had dubbed the Vale of Death, blasted Squire Raglan was reminded of something. He stretched up to the boy's saddle. "They do tell me," he whispered, not meaning to, in the quiet, "that if ye kill a rattlesnake they make ye a major in the Provincials. Two rattlesnakes for a colonel."

Peregrine couldn't help a weak giggle. It was one of the few jokes about the Provincials, the Yengees, he hadn't heard before. Then he remembered that, although Jonathan Lacey was a rattlesnake captain, he was his own cousin, while Squire was only his bought man. Peregrine clutched at some dignity, ashamed of himself. The man made him do it, had the quality of making him wonder if his boots were worn enough, if he'd said the right thing.

"See ye find a dry place for my tent tonight." He recalled Squire Raglan back to his position, and then, at Squire's quick, amused look and insolent pull of his well-dressed black hair, felt ashamed even of reminding the man that he was his servant.

Now silently, under the high black trees which blotted out the sun and made a world too pine-barren even for the nervous wild things, he moved without awareness, his saddle creaking under him; rhythmically, as he rocked, half conscious, the hollow clatter of iron wheels on the stones rose and then fell. From time to time they passed the sweet, sick smell of a dead horse. Somewhere in the distance a surprised order cut into the somnambulance and faded away among the ranks who moved beyond muttering—even almost beyond being afraid.

If Peregrine, huddled damp and cold astride his horse up above Squire Raglan's shoulder, had forgotten his newly bought man almost as he stopped speaking, Squire had as certainly forgotten him. He was a man in hell, and if there was any surprise left in him it was that hell was such a damned dismal place. He thought then of purgatory—the woods were more like that, the unredeemed, like gold watches in a pawnshop, lost in the dark shadows . . . or perhaps limbo—no, he rejected limbo; not even his father's God in all His mercy would leave the little unbaptized children to wander, crying, in black woods like these.

Squire thought of his father and stumbled, put up his hand and clutched the side of the tumbril beside him, and left it there, too tired any longer to carry his weight.

Purgatory, limbo—he looked upward. The terrible black trees rolled along the sky like a puritan army, miles high and cold with righteous indifference, blotting out the sun. The circling of their black, bare limbs made him dizzy, and he lurched his whole body into the moving tumbril and bruised his side and swore quietly.

No, he had died and was indeed condemned to the pine woods of hell. He groaned aloud in the sudden anguish of realization that hit him from time to time—groaned so loudly in the silence that he roused Peregrine, who called out quietly, "Squar! Squar! Ain't ye well?"

Squire looked at him and grinned—that insolent, careful grin by habit. "In the best of health, sar. I hope I may say the same of you." And he bowed, an elegant bow, still clutching the tumbril, which made the boy ashamed he'd been solicitous.

"Here. No leanin against them tumbrils." A busy sergeant was forcing his way between the file of men and the trees on the narrow road. "Oh, sorry, sar." He saw Peregrine watching him. "Is he yours?" He went on before Peregrine could answer.

Squire had stretched up from the thick wooden frame of the tumbril, conscious again for a minute, then blessedly unconscious with fatigue—until he was roused by the long drummed order to make camp for the night. The only thing he noticed about the last halt was that Hannah, in the sutler's wagon, had drawn up far away, under the trees to the left of the main camp. He groaned, damning the fact that he would have to walk so far for comfort.

Through the thick trees, shining in points of fire, in flicks of covered candlelight, here like a winking star, there making the canvas pyramid of a tent glow a little as if it were a screen with shadow puppets looming up, then disappearing, the first camp on the edge of the Little Meadows seemed huddled together, vulnerable and exposed, tiny under the great black sky.

Even huddled as it was, the camp had the relief of space after the fourteen-foot road running through the great trees. But space has its own fears. Peregrine, leaning his shoulder against a tree and watching the warm camp, muttering at having guard duty after such a day, felt the chill of that exposure, the chill of the night on him, the panic of feeling that the back of his head, the space between his shoulderblades, glowed, would lead them to him. He moved a little, casually, and leaned his whole back against the tree, watching where the men's shadows lurked around the pyramids of tents, all light now against the dark trees. Beyond them, along the road, the shapes of the tumbrils, the covered wagons, the carriages, the guns, loomed as huge bulks; against them the figures converged, separated, converged again, like fireflies. In the darkness he could hear the horses on long tether, munching and sighing among the trees, the cows free, identified when they moved by the watery sound of their square bells.

His twenty men huddled around their fire, most of them too tired to do more than move slowly, to throw on another dead log and lie down again under the spacious night together. Peregrine was tired of them. He was tired of their voices and their manners, tired of their smell and their complaints, tired of their ages (there were two men of over seventy who groaned from morning till night and ended the day with the terrible glazed faces of twins in age, too dumb with hardship even to make contact for sympathy's sake).

Most of all he was tired of their quarreling, and searched his deadened wishes for some dream to carry him beyond the trees, the gloomy valleys, the incredible sense of distance, across the sea to home, to order. But no dreams came; his fingers scratched at the bark of the tree, drummed, stopped even that. Peregrine sighed heavily, hardly knowing he did it.

[95]

But he could not escape their voices; after the noises of the forest had settled into his brain and become a background, the speech rang out, could not be ignored, a dripping pump of speech in English words that swept away dreams of past or future and replaced them with nightmares ever present, lurking in the trees.

A young Provincial soldier lay close to the fire, a braggart of eighteen they called Doggo, too big for his age, like a big pup. He rolled over once and caught with his heavy shoulder the foot, like a diseased root, which old Ted had undressed and now fondled, moaning as if it were a sick pet instead of part of his own body he cared for so much.

Doggo brought down his elbow on the foot, set his weight on it, and made himself more comfortable with a grin all round, which no one admitted to seeing. The old man's face went gray, but he said nothing, moved a little away from Doggo and the fire, and went on nursing himself. Doggo, when all else had failed, resorted to speech, hollered upward over his nose at the old man.

"Ye ain't got nary a chance, Ted, nohow," he told him, and slued his eyes down around the group for approval. "This Injun'll git ye afore ye can sneeze, you laggin back thar a-nursin thim feet of yourn. Yep," he told the trees, since after a month in the wilderness his voice—even that—sank into the ears of tired men and, as long as they ignored what he could say, touched no nerves. "Yep, thim heathens'll grab old Ted and give him the fiery death, paint his naked body black so Gawd'll think he's a Neegur when he finally dies. Thin thim heathens'll start in a-roastin old Ted like—"

"Ass-holes," old Ted said behind him.

Doggo rolled over and propped himself upon his elbow, pleased at having got some speech from the old man at last.

"Thin thim yaller dogs will start in a-tearin—"

"Shut up, ye goddam Yankee jailbird," one of the younger regulars interrupted casually.

[96]

"They ain't nobody goin to call me—" Doggo was on his feet, or almost.

"Set down and shut up, curse ye," came from the soldier again, backed by a murmur of, "Set down, Doggo," from the other men.

Doggo lay down again, sulking, having failed to affect his comrades, and was silent.

But minutes later, when the silence was broken by the gurgling hoot of an owl, to a man they looked over their shoulders, tensed their muscles to spring up, as neural as cats—even Doggo, who had started them thinking.

He had started Peregrine thinking as well.

Fear bores into the mind as an ache into the body bores, drills, is there, even when it is beginning to be forgotten, has become a part of living, negative as the missing leg that keeps on itching; but it bores, as being preoccupied, withdrawn, isolated by care becomes boring, deadening to the senses, a load to the mind, and arrives at last at the slow pace, the sterility of war.

So when his cousin, Captain Lacey, inspecting the pickets, stopped beside him, Peregrine was far gladder to see him than his behavior in front of Squire should have foretold. But when the older man, throwing an arm behind the boy where it felt secure, binding where there were no eyes, his cold, blind back, asked him how he was, Peregrine did not understand that he felt gray and tired with fear. He said, "I'm bored."

They both stood for a minute, watching the tents, saying nothing.

"Is't true we're to be split?" Peregrine whispered so the men wouldn't hear, conscious at the same time, with a twinge of jealousy, that he had to ask a Provincial for information, though part of him was proud at having a cousin on the staff.

"An order's drafted," Jonathan told him. "Thank God, too. The country's gettin even worse, though we won't have today again. St. Clair says they ain't no pine bogs, far as he's been

[97]

told. Boy"—his arm felt Peregrine's collar—"your coat's soaked through. Where's that sarvant of yours? There's agues in these woods'll make ye weak as water."

Peregrine shook away from Jonathan, annoyed. "I don't see why we have to split."

"Ye know when I rode back along the convoy today? I calculated it was four to five miles long." Peregrine's head snapped round toward his cousin. "That means stragglers can be picked off like ducks. There was a man today slipped off a little in the woods to relieve himself—just a young boy, ashamed in front of the others. I heared somethin there and went and found him. These were Shawnees—must have been—small-scalped him. Their rings are neat—not more than five inches or thereabouts across. They paint them up real pretty, once ye forget what they've been. I am kin to a lady who come with her husband west of Frederick Court House. She was the kind would go on duty almost as a soldier, though she was a lady. Cherokees scalped him and took her prisoner. Mind ye, they were out where they had no business to be. She said she sat by their campfire all night, lookin at Charley McAndrews' scalp, stretched on a ring and painted red inside, stuck on a pole on the other side of the fire to dry. She said it got to lookin so pretty 'twas all she could do to keep from stretchin her hand across and strokin it."

Jonathan felt Peregrine shiver under his protecting arm. "Listen, boy, I'm not bein cruel to ye. I'm tellin ye about Stacy McAndrews for a reason. She chawed her way through rawhide ropes that night and got away. Five months later she was married again to Mr. Mason of Princess Anne County. Five children by him and four by Mr. McAndrews. Listen, lad, ye've got to understand. Ye've got to." He knew he had lost contact with Peregrine, left him isolated by his clumsy attempt to warn. Warmly he told him, remembering, "Ye met her. Remember Aunt Stacy Mason ye supped with in Alexandria? A tiny lady, not more than five feet tall. I see her there, and women like her, and I think, if the Bard

[98]

had written in Virginia, he would have said of Lady Macbeth, 'Bring forth women-children only, For thy undaunted mettle should compose Nothin but females. . . .'"

They did not see the man beside them until he spoke. "I believe, sar, the scansion is as important as the sense. 'Tis in iambic pentameter"—he said this carefully—"or do ye know Latin?"

Now Peregrine had frozen, straight as a ramrod, throwing off Jonathan's kind arm. " 'Shun!" he called, his voice squeaking with nerves, and nineteen of the men shot to attention as if they had been flicked up. Doggo got up in several sections.

"These things are important, ye must see that, sar," the man finished gently, preoccupied, watching Doggo unfold.

Captain Robert Orme stepped into the circle of the fire.

At first look this man with the firelight flickering over him, as if it were pointing out his attributes to the men who watched him, seemed to need no name, Orme or otherwise. He seemed so much a product of the mold that had made him, so casual, so cared for, so poised. You imagined, seeing him, that if his mother had noticed one individual quirk in that perfection, one bump of personality, she would have had it buffed off early before it was painful, as a dog's tail is pinched at birth. He was tall, his figure not too perfect but good under the gold-laced red coat of the Coldstream Guards with its royal-blue velvet facings. A little fine lace fluttered at his throat as a breeze came up; it died again, and the lace was quiet. But the air had caught his long, fine, powdered hair as well, and as it moved too his face seemed incredibly still, watching Doggo. When the soldier was finally, sullenly, on his feet, Captain Orme's gentle, polite "Thank ye" rang so cool in the summer night that even Doggo looked down, remembering how big his feet were, how huge his rangy hands. Across the fire from him, Captain Orme's long gaiters shone like polished teak.

In a movement—lesser men would have pulled a lace cuff, touched their hair as the breeze caught it again and fluffed the side tufts forward on the cheeks for a second (most of the blond,

powdered halo was firmly held at the nape by a black ribbon)—
Captain Orme turned round to Peregrine and Jonathan, ignoring
himself as if he were his own statue, garlanded. If Peregrine had
dared look closer he would have seen that Orme's eyes were as
tentative as his own, but ringed dark with worries the boy had no
idea of. Jonathan saw something of this, and for the first time on
the six weeks' march felt some glimmer of kindness toward the
man whom all the Provincials and half the regular army hated
and damned.

It was indicative enough of Orme's powers of fascination, whatever emotion he might leave, that no one noticed, until he stepped
aside, that behind him stood four Indian warriors. Jonathan saw
them first.

"The Cuttaways—they've come," he said aloud, without waiting
to be spoken to. "But they ain't on the warpath."

"They've turned up—the four. One, I gather, is a prince of
some sort." Orme turned his back and said to Peregrine, "They
are to share your men's fire for tonight. Tomorrow mornin they
are to go back to their king with"—here he looked at the silent
four and smiled—"the usual presents.

"Men," he said to the fire, "these warriors are our allies. They
are of a friendly tribe, and have come to scout. Tonight they
must share your fire. By tomorrow their own arrangements for
campin will be made. See that they are fed. Good night, gentlemen." He turned with a sigh as he returned the men's salutes.

"Sar." Jonathan went after him. "May I walk with ye a way?"

Orme turned with a slight flicker of surprise. "I would be grate-
ful for your company," he said, not as automatically as he meant
to.

The moon had risen and cast shadows of the tents in the tall
buffalo grass. The forest had a rim of shadows. Around them the
summer air seemed to whir and gig already with the tiny insects
of summer. Jonathan's difficulty in speaking what was on his
mind came not so much then from Captain Orme as from the

pale night itself—cool, even in a droughty summer, because of the continent of breathing trees under the huge, impersonal dome of the sky.

★   ★

"I tried . . ." Those words, with no one to say them to, were being scratched onto paper by Jonathan an hour later. At the entrance of his bell tent, he sat on the ground, propped slantwise to catch the light of a candle. "I tried." He wrote the slow words, drawing them carefully on the paper, then crossed them out and began again with the sureness of a man writing to someone he loves and knows will understand.

> dr Sal, the army here is in a bad way. There is dissention among the officers and among the men. We are the strongest army which ever set foot into the wilderness and more equipment. We could—and I hope we can—run the French out of the Ohio basin. Even Maj. Washington is down with a bloody flux and may have to lay up at Gist's farm, which we hope to pass soon.

> The worst thing seems to be how the march has affected the officers, for they let wet ague and constant discomfort make dissention among them. They are pitiful and one can but pity and admire at the same time how in the wilderness they do with courage strut as if they were in a London park. Some take the campaign seriously. The two Cols. Halkett and Dunbar as well as Sinclair are old tried soldiers of many years, but they labour (at least Dunbar and Sinclair) under a burden of dislike by the more elegant officers which is that they must be fools because they are Scotch.

> The General himself is a genteel man, but he is lazy and I believe too old to stand the rigours of the Wilderness. Why you know he has not seen the Army but once since we left Cumberland. His eyes, ears, and some say his brains as

well are in his aide de camp, the fine Captain Orme. You will remember that very perfection of a gentleman. There ain't nothing you can say against him. Would I could understand a little of his ways. They is so much back-biting and talk of perferment and who has kissed hands of the King for his commission and who is what they call a rattle-snake Colonel (that is one who has gained his commission in the wilderness they say by killing a rattle-snake) you would think yourself in some comedy of London and in no Endless Mountains full of savages.

There are exceptions. You remember Shirley, the Massachusetts Governor's son, a gentle, London-bred boy; then Ralph Burton of Dunbar's Regiment, the finest kind of Englishman and Soldier. But the rest! I labour too much over these men who quote Horace but draw their behavior from Suetonius because I fear for us and for the men. We may carry over the mountains the greatest convoy since Caesar, and wheel and turn and strut like Guards and learn how fine gentlemen behave from the cool demeanor of such men as Captain Orme who grow up to believe that bravery is enough, but once we cannot trust or admire each other, how can we fight together?

This is melancholy, Sal, but if I pour out what is in my heart to my dear girl she will understand me. What are we, Sal, that because we live in the plantations of Virginia, far from what we have learned to call Home and look to for manners and sense, for the virtues that are not those hard gained ones of the Wilderness, to a place so *far away,* they who have not had to leave their fine homes and seek their fortunes abroad must treat us with mere polite contempt? It is not the behavior of gentlemen as I have been taught the true gentleman behaves.

You cannot imagine the fatigue of this march. We have picked a bad route and some of our own people have behaved toward us with shameful neglect, promising much and delivering in short measure both wagons and food. The horses is pitiful, more like stalking horses than brutes for war, aimless plodders dog lame and moon blind. Even these have to be belled and tethered from our own followers who find the march too perilous and steal them to desert us in the night. Of all the Indians who came to Wills Creek only six have stayed with us so far. One is Monocatootha, the Half-King—a Seneca of the Iroquois, whom we can depend on as a friend of George Washington. What has kept the rest of the Indians away I know not, but they are the greatest people on ceremony in the world and quick to take offence. You would think the Regular Officers who set such store by manners should see that.

Only tonight have arrived from the Carolinas four of those darlings of the Caroline Governor, the Cuttaways, who are among all Indians reckoned the best warriors. I tried to tell Captain Orme the reputation of these men and they should be carefully treated, but he said what I told him was stuff; he said he had treated them with all due courtesy and that they had to be got out from the General's Markey lest they got drunk and disturb his sleep with their great noise and smell for he is half sick from the jolting of the tilt in his carriage and sleeps ill. I hope all is well.

Our march has been slow and tedious, but so well guarded against surprise that no French or Indians, who we know watch our progress and would like to harry us, dares attack us. If this is regular discipline then I am a party to it. Orme has done well here for he is like a lash in the General's name. What these machines do when the TIME comes I dare hope is as good. With a solid enough basis in formal discipline dissention cannot snap the sinews which hold a great Army together.

Though I do despair for not many of the Regulars has ever fired a live shot at a target (for fear of scaring them is the reason) while we are like birds before the hunter to those who shoot through a bird's head so they will not hurt the food of its body. I can but hope, with the Regular's discipline of action, and our trained hunter's eyes, we are as two lame brothers who standing together make up a whole man—but we must think with kindred minds.

Oh Sal, the candle is long out, and I write by the light of the summer moon, as bright as early dawn. All round me the camp is quiet for the night, a little town of camp-fires where at each there is a picket as lonely as I. The land here—Oh Sal, this fine land—once the Savannahs a-top the mountains and the long valleys are reached is nine feet deep in soil. Chestnut trees and beech where good corn will grow; but despondent areas of Pine, too, some white oak which I mistrust although it grows buffalo grass and would make good grazing land if you had other. We crawl over it. Smoothing, rolling the road ahead. Some of the less patient thinks we should go faster. . . .

You will want to know about your Cousin Peregrine. He stands the march well and is no more or less despondent than a lad would be, picked up by a cruel and capricious choice and flung down in a world he does not understand and cannot learn to love, where he can but fear the night and hate the day. But battle and the gaining of the fort will cheer us all. I can understand now the yearning for action as the bird flushes from the bush—*anything* to end the deadly tread-mill of this march—which is a tour of fatigue to the teeth. . . .

Half a page was left, but Jonathan's eyes were dim and his quills dulled. He sat, holding the written pages in his hand, aware of the grumbling, the heavy movement of sleeping men nearby, of the animals moving in the night, dull shapes in the meadow under the nearly waning moon. Far down in a grove, the general's tent still glowed, an elegant pavilion shaped by its inner candlelight. By Jonathan a June bug whirred and startled him to action; he began to pack his writing equipment back into its leather box, and then to take his leaden, tired but wakeful body to try to sleep.

Besides the pickets now, only two men remained alert, not yet ready to admit the day was ended; Orme and the general's secretary, Shirley, sat in the outer room of the pavilion marquee. Orme's long, pale, sad face, still as it was, seemed to move in the light of the guttering candle; his over-fine hair, which not even powder could give much body to, seemed more wraithlike than ever, now that his hat was off. The muteness of the outside, with its familiar night noises, seemed here in the tent, broken only by the scratch of the men's quills and, from behind a curtain, the snoring and moving of an old man asleep.

Orme had turned the page; what thought he finished was hidden, but the words grew on under his fine white hand, in the square, impersonal script of a man whose passion is neatness and whose affection lies in order—and perhaps, for pleasure, small delicate objects to hold in his hands.

> . . . I am lonely. There are a few, a very few. The General is a most worthy man, whatever is said of him in London. I fear only that he is too lenient with the troops, for they, especially the Provincials and the wagoners (mostly Pennsylvanians), desert like flies, taking what they can. Desertion and drunkenness are the diseases of this Country; I would stop at nothing to cure them both, if I should stave every drop of liquor on it. The General wld do well to make an example, and I try to advise him so, but he says they do not hold desertion and drunkenness here for such serious crimes.
>
> There are others, Burton, Shirley, to talk to —most of the rest seem to me a wilderness of men in a wilderness of trees—more like Indians than like say Englishmen, although they think themselves as English as me. I notice though they have picked up Indian ways—not only in their constant eating of stuff called *hoggohominy* and their squatting in leather breeches by the fires, and their chaos which they call individual fighting; but also their blank faces when they do not know you, watching and quiet like the Indians, and their constant *brag* which passes

for conversation. Tonight we had to listen to it from Indians, by day on the march we listen to it from the Virginians.

This wilderness is the finest land I wld advise investing here. Right smart houses, right smart men—I must say they do raise pretty women—quite the ladies, some of them, though they say that the children of strumpets do inherit better looks by far than of uglier ladies. Though because they are so consciously du monde, manners demanded are quite *amusingly* courtly. Anything less is *infra dignitatem* (though some of their ancient and powerful dams *chew* or *rub* the weed in company and swear most charming).

By eight all conversation ceases; we are sick from the fatigues of the march; Oh God that I were back in England where order is, and kindness. I am embittered by the hostility and silence of these men.

As if that came from his heart, and all before had been only what he expected of his mind to amuse some friend at home, the last sentence was heavier on the paper; some sorrow had stretched to his fingers and leaped onto the page. Orme put his quill down, and his hand shook slightly when he did it. Carefully, his precision returned, he tore the letter across, across again, and set it to the candle flame, making, for long enough to cause Shirley to look up, a light as bright as day.

"Go to bed, Robert," Shirley said gently, when he saw how Orme looked. "Go to bed. There's no more ye can do."

Orme got up, moving as if he were a little drunk with tiredness, and leaned out of the marquee into the night. "Good night," Shirley heard him say.

And he said after him, "Good night."

Chapter Four

WITH THE firelight caressing his glistening skin, Witciktci the
Bald Eagle, nephew of the great Yanape Yalangway, a Raccoon of
the Catawba tribe, sat as silent as a stone, in a row with his
friends, and said nothing, waiting for the damned English to speak.
Across the fire, and behind the first lounging line of soldiers,
old Ted had finished caring for his feet and was ready, in his
labored way, to watch the world a little. It amused him mightily
to think that the younger soldiers considered themselves clever to
be so near the fire. Old Ted knew better. Don't sit too near, or in
the dead of night, when the fire dwindles, you get an ague and
will creak like a dry stick in the morning. Don't stare too much
into it, or when you have to turn into the dark suddenly you are
blinded long enough for those eyes to swoop—those eyes that
watch always, bore your back, that watch, even now. . . . But
from where he was the warmth was gentle; the fire lit a pale bowl
of yellow light that caught the faces of the men, here and there
caught and glistened on the reflection in an eye, the belly of a leaf,
the brass fittings of a musket, became a point as bright as the fire

itself, then, as the man turned or hitched for comfort, disappeared. Ted could hear the comforting hiss of caught sap in green branches, making a woody, sweet, strong incense in the night air; the flames leaped up and seemed to flick the tall trees out beyond the bowl of light with little touches of warm brightness, bringing the trees closer, making them intimate.

That point of comfort the campfire, the center of protection, of sleep, of food, of man-made light piercing the impersonal night —the soldiers were jealous of it and formal about its use. Ted realized that no one was saying a word, and he knew why. The damned captain, that Orme, who'd brought the smelly Indians and put them by the campfire of Ensign Cockburn's company, was still in the men's minds—especially in the minds of the Provincials, who were so sensitive to being thought "Indian" by the newly arrived, the disciplined, the bright boys. The flames seemed to grow beyond their faces, and Ted turned his eyes away into the trees beyond, knowing he'd been staring at the fire himself, like a fool.

When he let himself look back the fire seemed lower, and over it he watched the Indians, framed by its light. So these were the Cuttaways, the Catawba, the Ussheries—whatever they called them—the darlings of the South Caroline governor, who, people said, protected them more than he did some of his own people. Ted had seen Indians most of his grown life—spare-boned, hawk-like Iroquois, with their bald heads and scalplocks like long queues; Hurons, with their flat faces and wide noses, with eyes that seemed to shut from underneath; even the dark Nez Percé, padded with the skins of animals in winter; Delawares, who were still untamed, with their long, lank frames and their scalplocks like the clipped horse-mane on a Dragoon's helmet. These he knew how to kill. But he never had seen an Indian who looked like the strangers across the fire. Their fame! "He fights like a Catawba," he had heard one Indian say of another he admired.

But these! They looked like women! Especially the one with

[108]

stars tattooed on his cheek—like ladies' beauty spots. Old Ted knew better than that, knew that they were stars of death falling down Witciktci's satin cheek, just as the waves—four lines of them, tattooed on his right cheek—were honors of the dead, and the lines of dots festooned across his forehead said he could be called killer. Under the bangs of heavy, oiled, silky hair, the killer cat's eyes watched past old Ted's face, said nothing. Even as Ted looked he was seeing that these were no woman's eyes, whether the warrior's face was smooth as silk or not. The boy's face glistened with oil, and his black hair was iridescent with red dye; his long earrings, eight inches of blue-purple beetle's wings, clattered a little, caught by the wind. It whipped the fire, sent the light racing, rippling across the brightness of the face, the hair, the earrings. It made the light catch the great brass gorget where, against his white lawn English shirt below his red-brown throat, it shone like gold.

Ted had to admit to himself—he, who'd seen them all—that he'd never seen an Indian shine like that. Then he almost laughed when he saw that behind the high fanned egret feather of Witciktci's rank, held on the blackness of his hair with a diadem that seemed to be swan's-down like a cloud, sat a red turban of common trade banyan cloth. The young one probably valued it more than the whole match-coat of Indian-wrought hemp, covered with those compound purple-green dark mallard's feathers found only at the wingtips, which some squaw had taken years to make. It fell like the storm-dark wing of some huge bird, down from his shoulders, almost hiding his copperhead-skin belt, his buckskin leggings, as he sat, immobile, cross-legged.

Curiously, it was Peregrine who, out of politeness born of embarrassment before these strange, slight-looking red-brown men, made the only acceptable gesture. He offered Witciktci some tobacco. So the Indian rose, seemed to flow to his feet without the swelling of a muscle, took some, and solemnly offered Peregrine, in return, his buckskin pouch.

"Go on, sar." Doggo was watching, pleased at the joke. "Ye got to take some of the Injun's killinick and smoke it." He wanted to see the English boy gag over the tobacco.

So these two slight boys, the same height, both carrying the names of great birds—Peregrine the falcon trained to the hunter's wrist, Witciktci the bald eagle that ranges alone—stood, each taking in only the strangeness of the other, exchanged tobacco, turned away from contact, Peregrine with a slight shrug, having seen so close the kind of man he had been told he had to be afraid of and found him an eye-level boy as tentative as himself.

Already as Peregrine walked through them to his bell tent and disappeared inside, some of the men were asleep. Fatigue, the unconscious sounds of bodies slipped into or seeking comfort, seemed to creep across the company around the fire. Even fascinating as the Indians were, heavy sleep was possessing the exhausted soldiers as they watched, making the strange figures dissolve in color without detail, then disappear altogether, only to reappear, taller, wilder, here and there in troubled, fearful dreams that made teeth grind and gathered a kick in the backside from the nearest soldier, to stop the nerve-racking noise. Finally only Doggo, persistent in his passion to impress someone with himself as he saw them all drift out of his reach in sleep, and Ted, with the bleak wakefulness of the old, were left watching the Indians. Doggo, looking unhappily around the fire, finally turned and saw it glitter in old Ted's open eyes behind him.

"Oh, that's right," he whispered loudly at Ted. "Ye keep awake. Thim's the ones that come to git your hair." Even he was forced by the stealing, heavy quietness, to whisper. Then a twig snapped —a loud, triggered crack in the fire. Ted's voice, following the nervous sound, was louder, nervous itself.

"Ye don't know nuthin, kid, ye blasted little kid," he said viciously to Doggo. "I been fightin Injuns since afore ye was weaned—up the Mohawk, up Canady way, y'ain't niver seed nuthin or hyeared nuthin until ye've been in the North Wilderness in the dead of winter—dead, white and dead." Ted's mind wandered in the great snow, forgetting the boy, the Indians—only edging a little closer to the present fire as he felt, in memory, the terrible white cold.

"Thim black scalps is worth five pounds apiece." Doggo, not wanting to listen to Ted's wander-mouth, began to think aloud, strictly of business. "Governor Dinwiddie done said so. He said five pounds. And he didn't *specify* which kind of Injun."

"He didn't specify." Ted's voice was weighty with sarcasm. "He reckoned even a born fool'd know one of these hyar from thim sneakin Catholic Canucks. Ye young fool. Thim fellers is worth more'n any five pounds to usn. Ye thank the Lord they come, that's all."

"Thar ain't no difference between thim and any other damned Injun to me. Besides, the law'd specify efn it meant to," Doggo bragged. "All Injuns is alike. These are leetler, though. I could use me twenty pounds, I tell ye—more'n ye'd ever git a-wearin away in this hyar army, with nuthin to eat, and nuthin but people a-hollerin at ye." Doggo's gorge was rising. "Settin thim damned all-smelly Injuns right in with usn—right with usn as efn we was heathens. I hate 'em. Look at 'em thar, not sayin nuthin—jest settin thar, a-lookin at us like we was dirt—and us Christians. I hate Injuns," he went on, full of anger. "And don't call me kid. I ain't no kid, Ted. I'll kill ye efn ye call me that. I swear I'll kill ye."

Doggo was halfway to his feet in his anger. He roused the man sleeping beside him enough to make the soldier call out, "Shut up, ye goddam kid," to Doggo by habit, and roll to sleep again. An owl laughed in a farther tree, laughed again nearer, then nearer still, drawn toward the light. Now it sat in the tree nearly above them, laughing in the night.

Still the four young Indians across the fire never moved, only watched and said nothing.

Ted set himself to woo sleep, his head away from the fire and

[111]

the cats' eyes, feeling them watch him as the night watched, driving him out through terrible loneliness to sleep at last.

Doggo watched them as they watched, but with passion in his eyes, focusing at last on someone to pour out his bitter hate. "We don't need no damned Injuns. We can outshoot ye and outscalp ye. We-uns are the long knives, and don't ye forgit it, ye blasted black heathen deivals," he said for the last time to them now. Everyone else was asleep. There were only the glistening smooth dark faces, the black eyes, uncomprehending, only watching: it was like talking to a dog. Even Doggo gave up and slept at last.

Only the first picket of the night lounged against the tree, crept forward to set another log on the fire, crept back again to the tree, cursing the luck that had chosen him to go on watch, finally in his lonely watch forgetting even the Indians, who still sat, immobile.

Squire, coming back from seeing Hannah behind the sutler's wagon, saw a sleeping camp; around this local fire, by then, even the Indians, stretched in their match-coats, slept. He was fascinated by the central figure, wrapped in a cocoon of feathers, his egret feather spread in the darkness beside his head, his black hair pouring like water from a single point at his crown—a black medieval coif. The firelight, playing more dimly now over his sleeping face, made it rounder, gentler, slight and beautiful, now that the eyes were shut. Squire, who had seen only the civilized Indians slouching about the camp—some of them even let their whiskers grow—looking at the smooth skin, the half-inch-long nails of the narrow hand, watched at first as if he had found some savage princess asleep there; then, creeping closer, he knew from the tattooed stars, from the human hair fastened to the tomahawk pipe, from the weapons—he knew it was a strange warrior.

To try his skill, which was getting better now, he lifted up the cheap steel combined tomahawk, scalping knife, and pipe, of English make, that lay beside the man, just to see if the Indian would move out of his sleep. When Witciktci slept on, Squire grew bolder, bent down toward the fire, and examined the weapon by its light. It was a fine hatchet, on one side blazoned with an official English seal—Hanoverian horses in stiff heraldic attitude, the star etched on the polished metal, the waves below as rigid as those on Witciktci's cheek. On the other side of the blade an Indian artist had pricked a picture of an Indian with the hatchet raised high to strike a white man who looked, to Squire's trained eye, to be a preacher. The scalping blade was smooth, Sheffield-made, in a single piece with the hatchet blade. Both Indian and Christian had left it blank, its own flat spade-shape symbol enough.

But Squire knew, when he saw the preacher, that he had to have the hatchet as a joke, a souvenir. Still Witciktci had not moved. The picket lounged against the tree, too intent on keeping awake to notice movement so near the fire. Squire slipped the hatchet into his belt and crept away to hide it, then to stretch and sleep before Peregrine's tent, far enough from the fire to keep the stench of the men out of his fastidious sad nose. He went to sleep wondering how much Witciktci's feather coat would fetch in London.

The moon went on, paled, went down, leaving the dawn stars in the last blackness; a star swooped, fell in a long trail of light, blew out. The first gray dawn came; the first man woke. The Indians were gone. Not any of the pickets through the night could say they'd seen them go.

*   *

When Christopher Gist, the Indian agent, hunter, and expert scout for the Army, arrived back from the Catawba and the Cherokee four days later, he brought no Indians. Rumor said the South Carolina governor had persuaded them not to come, that unscrupulous traders had undermined Gist's authority and told the Indians they would starve with the English. But Gist himself, who knew them best, said the Indian mind could change as the angle of flight of migrating bird changes, for unfathomed reasons. He was not taken seriously. It was just "Indian" to come halfway, as the Catawba had done, and then go back. Who cared why? They hadn't come. All Indians were alike. The "Indian givers."

No one looked behind the bird-flight of their native minds to see the logic there—the unconscious insult of a bone-tired, wagon-sick general, too old to entertain four capricious young braves with rum; the silent soldiers who did not even give them food, the worst offense against friendship to a race whose manners demanded that they share even parched corn in famine time as if it were a feast; the setting of young men of the Raccoon down among common soldiers who were like slaves, who insulted and bragged and made war-talk, although the Indians came as friends, so could not answer; the young officer they had met, who had no battle honors, no scars, not even a weapon, yet had rank to lead men in an insane army shackled in heavy, brightly colored coats; the taking back of Witciktci's English tomahawk, which had been given to his uncle, the great Yanape Yalangway, the Young Warrior, at a solemn treaty. That was the whites; they gave and then took away, to cheat the Indian. No one could know that the army had been Indian-read as carefully as a broken twig is read—or the growth of moss or the bend of summer grass.

But beyond these reasons, worse than all of them, the barred owl had shrieked over and over in the night. As if that were not warning enough, the rope of a star was cut before dawn, and it fell, swooped down the sky, doomed. At this sign Witciktci and his braves had left; after those omens no sane man would have stayed among the already lost, for the strength of the army would be nothing once a god had warned, then turned his back.

Chapter Five

At FOUR O'CLOCK in the morning of the ninth of July, 1755, four horsemen in Provincial blue rode out of the black woods on the right bank of the Monongahela River.

Jonathan leaned down over his horse's right wither toward the water under the thin layer of mist, and through the mist saw a silken ripple of shallows where the drought had lowered the river. He could hear a whisper, the soft lapping of the shallows on the sand. He goaded the horse gently, balanced himself in the saddle, and let the animal step through the sandy bottom at a dead slow walk. Near him in the dark he could hear the three other horsemen putting their horses as delicately to the river—so delicately that the thin legs seemed to interrupt the winding ribbon-like flow of the water no more than the silted sand below, where the Yoxiogeny, pouring into the Monongahela, deposited the soil for a ford. The water, drawling up the horses' legs, was only three feet deep at the center of the wide river. The horsemen moved forward, making no sound, except that Jonathan's horse sighed and blew, then champed his bit. All of them stopped, frozen, listened in the

cold silence, and moved on. Downstream of them, and far upstream, soldiers, black-coated in the darkness, came out of the
woods. Jonathan looked back to see the two squads of Grenadiers,
with their high miters, slip toward the water.

The first horseman had gained the other bank and spat a quid
into the willows as his horse, with a spurt of desire for dry land,
clambered out of the water. Jonathan and the other two gained
the bank, fanned out, and began to climb toward the heights beyond. In the stillness, when Jonathan looked down, he could see
the Grenadier squads reach the bank below him and form to march
down the beach. Behind them, holding their muskets on their
heads, waded twenty infantry. A young subaltern, like a fool, was
making his horse whisk around in the water, charger fashion.
It was too far away for him to hear the splashing. Jonathan swore
and spat. He could just make out the Indian guide for the advance
guard, as Monocatootha, Half-King of the Senecas, and one of his
bucks slipped toward the water. It was still too dark for him to see
more than their forms, but he knew they would be nearly stripped
on such a day, painted black, and cleaned, body and soul, for war.
In the rear the squad of sailors and road-builders, marching in no
order, looked like dark apples bobbing over a wide space of the
river.

Below him the river mist was leaving the water, rising so that
the main troops of the advance guard could hardly be seen, their
officers silent ghosts, mist-shrouded, their wagons moving shapes
only in the water.

The last of the advance guard was over. They began to move
down the left side of the river to where, three miles away, they
would ford again below Turtle Creek and hold the northeast
heights, while the road was made for the main army up the steep
right bank. The double fording of the river, so close to Duquesne,
with the advance guard and then the main army, was dangerous
and necessary—Jonathan knew that. But he studied the river,

frowning quietly, wondering which ford the French would choose for their attack, wondering what it would be like to fight in a river. He shook his head to get his mind back to his present work. He set his horse sliding down from his lookout and came up in the rear of the men. Far to the front the other light horse took their places. To the east, ahead of them, the rim of the sky was turning faintly blue with dawn. Long after the last man had waded onto the near shore and shouldered his gun, the mist parted, the sun from down-river came up over the trees, and the brilliant morning had begun. But the misty river, now like silk riffling over the sand, was as empty, as undisturbed, as if it were the world's first morning.

By seven o'clock Jonathan had seen the advance guard safely make the lower crossing, and was back at his post above the upper ford again to wait for the main army. It was full day, and the high insect-and-bird jar of summer was all around him. He sat, beyond frowning, straining his ears above the noise, listening, entirely alone, to the river and the wilderness, asleep and inhuman. Below, a water rat rustling among the willows ignored him as it slid through the water. He could watch the rat, watch it move, hypnotized, finding it again among the willow branches, involved in its search, in the new-washed sun, in the river running—patiently waiting, warm after the clinging cold of the dawn, nodding a branch before his horse's mouth to keep away the huge deer flies, falling toward sleep.

He woke, jerked up so quickly that his horse plunged and recovered. Thin as a distant scream, he had heard through the noise of the birds the high hysteric fifes and a low rumble stronger than the river flow. The sound came nearer, defeated the birds, which whirred the air with frightened wings. The Grenadiers' march, on fife and drum, filled the new day with measure, seemed to burst through the slower mutters of the early sleepy morning.

Far on the other bank the great silk colors of the regiments, carried high, broke from the forest, were picked up by the down-river breeze, which fluttered them wide—great whipping patches of yellow, of buff, then of blue, the gold crowns whirling, the stripes alive. The fifes broke clear of the woods behind the colors; far up- and downstream the mounted flank guards rode out. The first fording for the main army had begun across the blue river.

The army that spread, as precisely placed as a ballet, out of the woods that morning was at first glance not the same one which had huddled, dim with fear and fatigue, around the forest at Little Meadows, dragged, deadened, and bitter, their uniforms dull, their eyes turned away from one another with boredom along the six weeks' march through the despondent wilderness, where men had knelt by the road and died of fatigue while no one watched.

As the turkey cock will strut and stretch, color and expand in front of his enemy or his mate, so had the army. The dangerous crossings, the promise that by evening they would reach the clearing around the fort, would surely fight before the day was gone, had brightened them. Since dawn, fear-quickened, they had hardly needed orders, had polished away the damp from their muskets, swords, and great seals, curried the sorry horses, dressed in full dress as on parade.

As it was, they were two hours late in getting to the river. Jonathan watched them spread, a hundred-yard-wide design of moving men, animals, guns, carts. Turkey-cock-noisy, turkey-cock-red, they rampaged through the water, brave and bright in the sun, which turned the spray into rainbows, caught the polished brass of a musket held level over a soldier's head, the sleek backs of the twelve-inch guns, which were like some great water beasts. Between the flank horsemen, who plunged at the water and spurned it, fan-shaped, and the main army, the cattle and spare horses struggled. Here and there a panicky head disappeared under water, recovered. The horses whinnied, white-eyed with fright. The dumb cattle plodded, horned heads surfaced, patient in their fear

[118]

as the water came deeper and deeper, until their horns lay back toward the water. Now the river was pale tan, beaten by thousands of plodding, slipping feet.

The fifes still struggled shrilly, the drums tried to pace sense into the switching rhythms of the ford. A fifer, a short boy, feeling the pressure of the water around his legs, slowed his music and seemed to waltz painfully, twisting through the heavy water. A tumbril stuck, a gun wedged sideways, and a rippling halt went through the army behind. The river ran quiet in a wide road made by the accident, the struggle over the righted gun. The tumbril moved again.

Already the first fife and the colors had reached the near bank, and the right flank the bottom of the steep slope below Jonathan's lookout. He reined his horse out of the way as the first horseman struggled his mount up the bank toward him.

" 'Tis a right fine sight, eh, Johnny?" Jamie Stuart called, full of joy.

"The finest sight I ever seen," Jonathan said, but not loud enough for the man to hear. He had never noticed until that morning what a handsome young animal Jamie Stuart was.

Half an hour later, down river, he could hear the first drummer beat a long halt. General Braddock's carriage was flanked by red-coated Grenadiers and Provincial horsemen, and on its right was Orme, gently urging forward a bay he had not ridden through the whole march. The colors, the Royal George, the yellow of the 44th Regiment of Halkett, the buff of the 48th of Dunbar, beat the strong breeze over their heads.

Jonathan did not see the Provincial blue again until the rear guard was crossing; he knew too well, to his shame, that most of the Provincial troops had been left with Dunbar, far behind with the heavy convoy. In front of the rear guard, high on the tumbrils, there seemed to be at least thirty women, lolling in the welcome sun. From time to time he could hear across the water their higher, nervous laughter, snatches of songs begun, then forgotten. But one seemed from far away to cling to his ears because it had a marching rhythm.

> *"With a ruffdom, ruffdom, fizzledom madge*
> *Under the sheets goes she . . ."*

The women were singing, nearer and nearer, now halting under him.

Jonathan spurred his horse down to report his reconnaissance to Captain Orme. If the army had seemed patterned from above on the ridge, now as he rode among the men they became instead a shouting, arranging, ordering rabble, in the flurry of preparation before they froze into the next rigid act of battle order. He passed Peregrine, who was shrilling out orders with an angry squeak in his voice, making his new mount dance. Below him Doggo and Ted, vainly trying to look the same size, were standing, right arms snapped to the shoulders of the men beside them, dancing their feet a little as they dressed ranks. Their brown leggings had been exchanged for white splatter-dashes; their red coats seemed to glow in the now bright nine-o'clock sun after the dimness of the woods. Even Doggo had polished himself and stood, concentrated on his pride to be part of the Army, his eyes blank, watching the man beside him, and listening hard for the beat of the long march. Ted looked as though he was thinking, far away, but his old clawed hand shook and made his bayonet catch and break the sunlight.

The long march rolled forward and backward, picked up by the drums from the general's wagon, away in front the high *whee* of the fifes. Rippling along the files, strained dry throats echoed a rasping shout. "By the right, quick march!"

Jonathan drew in beside Orme as the army shuddered into movement.

"The advance guard is over the second ford, sar. But the bank there looks a fair grade for the wagons. They'd started on it when I came back."

"Did *you* cross?" Captain Orme seemed hardly to hear Jonathan.

"I? No, sar. I thought—" Jonathan leaned close to the captain so he could hear over the noise.

"You are not to think. Do as ye're told." Orme wheeled his horse aside, a man temperamental with entrusted secrets, and trotted closer to the general's closed carriage.

His place was taken by Shirley, whose delicate hands seemed better for the pen than for the reins, though he held his horse's head high and strong. "He's been at the march since four. We're late. He's too busy to know . . ." He apologized to Jonathan for the slight.

"I wasn't supposed to cross. My orders were to bring the *avant garde* across this upper crossin, march three miles down the left side of the river to avoid that dangerous mouth of Turtle Creek, see that the *avant garde* recrossed far enough below it and started the pioneers to buildin that grade up the other side in time for the main army to use it. I did it, Shirley." Jonathan defended himself, then at once felt ashamed, hot in the sun.

"After the second crossin he'll be a different man."

Shirley looked after the captain, who was now bending from his horse toward the closed carriage.

"We all will," Jonathan admitted. "Mr. Shirley"—he paused and listened to his horse step for a minute—"if they don't attack us at the next crossin—" He left the optimistic question trailing, but Shirley didn't answer.

"They look a different army now," he said instead, satisfied at the furled flags, the new precision of line after line of red, with here and there a few double lines of blue, here near the general's guard a black-painted Seneca, his face covered with bright streaks of yellow, red, white. Even the four friendly Indians with the main army had taken step from the drums and the music, without knowing it. Only the grumbling of the civilian drovers, who drove with curses at the center of the lines of march, their whip cracks, and the thunder of the wheels and the horses' hoofs, created another din, which blended with the voices of the men—singing because it was brave to sing your way into battle, and each man gave full voice as well as full color to the day, singing no bawdy row but the British Army's cry, which was to them as the warwhoop to the Indians.

> *"But of all the world's great heroes, there's none who*
> *can compare*
> *With the tow, row, row, row, row, row of the British*
> *Grenadier."*

There was no one at the second ford when they reached it after a three-mile march—nothing, no crawling scouts discovered, not even those to warn the fort ahead.

"I don't understand it," Jonathan told Shirley. "We know we've been watched for weeks, every move we've made, and they haven't attacked. Now they don't even watch us! This here place—" He looked past Shirley's head down the easy-flowing river to where it bent south again from its westward course. "Virgin land!" he added, forgetting what he was about to say.

"Perhaps they've deserted the fort," Shirley said smiling. "That's what some of the men are sayin."

"By God, 'tis far from likely— Look!" Jonathan, watching the river still, saw the signal to begin the ford.

Sir Peter Halkett, sitting his mount, easy, patient with the warm morning, saw his son, Lieutenant Halkett, begin to move among the resting 44th detachment as he saw the signal. It was at that moment that Sir Peter had one of those terrible certainties, which rose out of the quietness like a bat to hover in his brain, that he would be dead by evening. He shivered, blamed it on his sweat and the down-river breeze, although the sun was hot. Pushing the bat out of his sensible soldier's mind—though he was Scotch and, some said, gifted with second sight—he rode down to take his place for the last act of danger before the siege.

[122]

Having halted in the sun, aware of their bright vulnerability for over two hours, they made the second crossing of the river, the whole twelve hundred men tense for the sound of a musket to split the lonely air of the hot, sleeping valley.

They were not attacked.

*   *

"Gentlemen, the king."

The toast was drunk from the general's crystal glasses in the clearing around a deserted house. Even the dog-day sun seemed to slow its course through the drowsy, hot hum of the noon hours. Where the sand had been churned in clouds, the river had settled and flowed uninterrupted, blue again. The dragonflies returned, gliding down to touch on the cool surface of the water. A ring of men stood in front of the deserted cabin, sheltered by a locust tree so full of leaves that it bent down toward them in the heat and made a dusky shade. Some lay down again after the toast and stretched their arms. One went away and spoke low to the stout old man, his face red with heat and his gray wig moistening his forehead, fanning himself in the privacy of a second locust tree, talking to Orme, who leaned against a log well-head, the wide scarlet ribbon of his rank so sleek it was like water. Jonathan, almost asleep himself between Ralph Burton and Shirley, saw that the man was Major Gage. When the major wheeled and spoke to Colonel Sinclair, who got up and followed him, Jonathan knew that the last short march to the fort was about to begin.

As they passed close, Gage caught his eye. "Dine with me tonight at Fort Kane, won't ye, Johnny?" And he laughed as a man would at a picnic in summer.

"I will, now." Jonathan turned and let his hat fall toward his eyes, not wanting to give up the last seconds of his rest.

He could hear beyond his half-nap the restless moving of the staff horses in a clearing off the narrow road below, when Gage and Sinclair mounted and rode off.

[123]

"It's strange to have it over, ain't it, Johnny?" Burton was asking him. "It looks like the Frenchman has missed his chance. If he didn't get at us on the march; if he missed the fords— Lord, I'll give ye there'll be some explainin among the Frogs!"

"I'll reckon." Jonathan sat up and began to flick the loose powder from his blue. Away in the distance he could hear a yelled order and knew that Gage's Grenadiers, with two six-inch guns, had marched on ahead.

It was as he got to his feet that he saw one of the scouts run into the clearing toward General Braddock and be intercepted by Orme.

"Mr. Shirley, Captain Lacey, Major Washington, come here." Captain Orme was laughing as the three men joined the group under the second tree. "It seems that the few monsieurs are a leetle late. This man has sighted a small force—not above two hundred, he says. They are ahead, comin this way. Late!" It was the first time Jonathan had seen Orme laugh aloud. Relief and laughter made him almost handsome.

"They can't mean to attack with so few," Shirley said, and, seeing that the general still had his napkin tucked in his gorget, felt to see that he had taken his own napkin down.

"Major Washington, ye look a damned scarecrow." The old man looked up, changing the subject. "Don't forget ye've had a bloody flux and we may have a warm half-hour or so before our boys run the others off. Don't exert yourself. I know you young-ins."

The very tall young man facing the general obviously didn't like being reminded of his illness—or his impatience—before the others. But he sensed the old man's tenderness and smiled. "Is that orders, General?"

"That's orders, buck!" The general heaved himself to his feet. "What's the lay of the land there?" he asked the scout.

"Half a mile of underbrush, and a dry crick bed, sar, but the advance Grenadiers under Major Gage have already passed that.

Thin up a hill and, after that, what ye might call a plateau, with only a few crick beds, white oak grove—big ones, sar; wide enough apart to drive a cart through any part. No underbrush, jest buffalo grass, sar. Hit goes pretty near as fur as Fort Kane that way, sar—like a fine park. I sighted thim Injuns, and French with them, way out beyond the fur one of thim dry cricks."

What the scout did not know was that two dry creek beds, with the high hill to the right and the river to the left, formed an indented horseshoe, a natural trench around the wide oak park. Neither did the French know. The deadly trap had lain there since the creeks were carved, waiting for men to use it. The French and their Indians were coming toward it, sore among themselves. Having missed the easier attack at the lower crossing, which had been their plan, they muttered blame at each other for being forced to fight in open, level park land. They stumbled on the first deep creek bed just as Gage's Grenadiers marched into the center of the oak park, their guns running easily now that there was no underbrush.

As the scout stopped speaking a single shot was heard, and the summer birds flew up, darkening the blue sky. It was a curious sound, a dry, hollow crack unlike the boom of a musket.

"That thar was a riffled barl!" The scout turned, startled, with the others, then back, expectant, to the general.

The old man was exuding practiced calm. "Now here, gentlemen, is your first lesson in real war—with your troops sober." He glanced at young Washington, who was not too pale from fever to blush. "The *avant garde* will clear the road, and we"—he turned away from them—"will proceed quietly to our places." He walked away down the overgrown path, setting an easy pace for the staff behind him; they could hear the shots increase as the steady shower replaces the first patter of rain. Somewhere between the locust tree and his horse the general's calm deserted him. He came to a slow trot at the last few steps and was helped into the saddle. The face they saw when he turned was almost purple.

[125]

"Get to your places—hurry!" he yelled. "Hurry! Halkett, goddam ye, get to your goddam place!" He wheeled his horse and dashed for the road.

To Peregrine, letting his horse graze beside the narrow road, the morning which had started with such a kind of frightened gaiety had now become only a series of waits, of fits and starts. The dawn promise had gone, and left him more depressed than ever.

He watched the same men in the same positions for the march —perpetually waiting—and knew that nothing was going to happen, nothing ever now. He had prepared, for one brief spell in the dawn, for a flag-shrouded death. Even carrying the colors was denied him. There was a younger ensign who sat his horse importantly, far up the narrow road. Peregrine, jealous as a girl would have been of another woman, picked him out by the flag, now drooping in the breathless, shaded road.

His horse reacted first to the shots. The mare trembled under his thighs, which tightened automatically as she moved—threw up her head, then, hearing nothing, nuzzled again at the roadside grass. By the third or fourth dry crack he had drawn her head up again. After the cracks a musket volley boomed and reverberated. Then quiet for five long minutes; then again the rattle of shots. Old Ted, below, looked around as if the woods themselves could tell him what it was, and then he seemed to slump back into waiting; even his gnarled hand relaxed on his musket, as if he realized it was too late—too late in the campaign, in the afternoon, too late in his life for surprise.

It was then that they saw the general's family canter past, looking so much what they were meant to be that they laid upon the army that kind of peace where illusion meets reality—for a minute, only a minute—and disappeared down the road.

From the front the drummed attack, growing in strength like a great warning, threw them into action, their feet obeying before anyone knew what they were running toward.

Peregrine, for his own company, couldn't remember one single

[126]

order that would have cut a dash in the Horse Guards Parade, or even in Mary Street, Limerick. What came to his throat was only the single sound "Ooooh," flung into the windstream of his own ride forward—carried, as the dam of waiting broke, by the narrow, yelling army.

Over the traditional "Huzzah!" trained from their throats as their feet were trained to hop to the drum, came the only command heard that day—from the last of the general's family, looking back with the smile of a boy in a game.

"March on, my lads, and keep up your fire!"

That gesture—for there was no such order—was all old Ted heard until evening.

Jonathan, in that race toward the now steady shooting, did not notice how fast he was going until he had outridden the other members of the staff. His horse hit the bottom of the first brush-covered creek bed and cantered up the other side to where the green-white oak park opened, sun-dappled, in front of him, before he reined in to wait.

Back of him the ravine seemed to lie for a second in a false, deserted peace.

In front there was a wall of smoke, the smell of sulphur. Jonathan could taste salt in his mouth as he drew in a sharp breath. The advance Grenadier company were running toward him down the narrow road, their faces blackened by powder. One man's white-rimmed, animal's eyes met his own in the distance. The man fell, as if he had been knocked down from the back; there were no more eyes. The rest raced over his body, stopped, as if they had remembered something they had forgotten in their running, and turned to re-form, the front rank kneeling out of his sight to fire again.

Through the fire, in the distance, he heard the heavy grunt of Gage's two cannon, their echoes slapping the trees, then a dead silence as if the angel of death passed low over the woods.

But after her, Jonathan more than heard; he was caught up,

[127]

buoyed, surrounded by a huge circle of a great gurgling animal shriek that swelled to a climax, stayed there, then ran along like fire down the hidden creek beds. It was as if the ear had split and there would never be any escape from that wild screaming.

His horse plunged, reared, ridden by the noise and not by him. Trying to control it, he hardly heard a light horseman ride past and call, "We're attacked, Johnny. We can't hold up yonder. Jamie Stuart's hit. Where the hell is the general?" He had gone past before Jonathan had quieted his horse, which had done a wild dance toward the Grenadiers as they fired a second time into the smoke. Jonathan turned as they turned, and to Orme and Morris, galloping up the slope and onto the level, it seemed as if he were leading a raggle-taggle charge of Grenadiers against the main army. He managed to turn again as he met them, and the three, without a word, waited until the soldiers were near enough to see them across the road, then drew their swords.

The soldiers stopped as water stops when diked. They turned and formed again. A corporal let his musket fall and ran back to Orme's stirrup.

"It ain't that we won't fight, sar. We can't see nobody up yonder. We can't see nobody." Several of the men heard him and were turning to say something when a sergeant at the end yelled the Ready. One, in snapping back, was hit in the stomach, and rolled, surprised and quiet, over to the side of the road, blood pouring gently from his mouth.

When Gates galloped up, the Grenadier was trying to crawl away from the others, to find some silence among the trees in the screams around them. They could hear the screaming behind them now, all the way along the creek beds on the army's flanks.

"This ain't my fault. Robert, listen," Gates called, and his horse flung him closer as if its back were afire. "Get the army back. Get it back. We can hold till you get back over the river . . ." He plunged around again and disappeared toward the smoke. As he passed the now distraught rabble of the Grenadier company in front of the horses, he switched his arm and drew them with him toward the right. For the first time Jonathan noticed the two-hundred-foot-high hill, sprouting puffs of smoke as if they were white blossoms.

"Oh Lord, Captain, do I go to the general?" Jonathan begged, waiting for the stone-quiet man, frozen still within that screaming, to move, to order.

Orme turned his head as slowly as if he were flirting and looked at Jonathan, surprised. "The general is back with the heavy guns, sar. I have had no orders to retreat."

"Tell him—" Jonathan was afraid to speak louder.

"Tell him yourself if ye're afraid." Orme smiled.

Jonathan, letting his horse dash toward the ravine, had no time to wonder at the man, but he heard somewhere in his galloping mind the silence of the forward guns, which no longer punctuated the high, gobbling screaming in the air with a bass note.

Halfway down the ravine his horse shied at Shirley, flung beside the road. He had been shot in the face and already scalped, but Jonathan knew who it was by the fine hands and the wide scarlet sash that came from London and made his blood look dull. Jonathan passed Shirley in seconds, but he kept the sight of him all through the day—that drop of silence where the deer flies gathered, between the wastes of noise.

He met the general galloping up the narrow road with Morris. How Morris had got there before him he had no time to find out. He did not remember seeing anyone pass him. The press of the army behind, the oxen, cows, spare horses rampaging around them, seemed to sweep the old man along in a current of panic; he passed by, his face distorted with that kind of rage that the unplanned brings to old men's and children's faces. Jonathan wheeled again to catch up with the general. It was at that moment his horse screamed, louder than a human being ever could, threw him, and went on screaming, dashed blindly against a tree, then lay still. Jonathan knew, without waiting, that it had been shot, Indian fashion, across its eyes.

In the time it took him to catch and mount one of the loose horses, to ride up into the oak park again, the trap had closed— its teeth surprise, the creek beds, a late meeting, and the relief of men relaxed after terrible long wariness; but its iron jaws the anger of an old man whose troops clogged up the only escape, that dead anger which is sometimes called bravery.

He saw suddenly, through the smoke, one of the colors flapping, then lost it again. The men, in ranks too wide for the narrow road, hunkered together under a bullet rain. A rear rank, in an insanity of order after panic, carefully let go a broadside into the trees. Thirty yards ahead of their sights, another rank of eight red coats began to split and wilt, shot in the back.

Orme was calling, "Halkett, Halkett!"

"Halkett's dead"—an answer came from the trees.

The general was off his horse. It lay huge in the garbled road. Jonathan rode forward, swinging out of the saddle as he rode, to give the old man his own mount. As he stopped he could make out the general's voice shouting, "Fight. We've got to fight. Get Halkett. Where is Halkett?" He had drawn his sword, but there was no enemy to engage; he began to use it broadside against the rumps of soldiers clogging the road in front of him. "The forward guns. Abandoned my forward guns, goddam ye!"

"Get the men out!" shouted Jonathan, but was swept away by Burton before he could say any more.

Burton yelled, "Buck up, my hardy. We're fairly caught, ain't we, by God?" and disappeared again.

★   ★

Far to the rear, within sight of the clearing, Squire lay watching, aware that most of the afternoon had gone in some hell to the front which filled the air. Farther down the road, in the lengthen-

[130]

ing shadows, he could see the rear guard, the only blue-coated Provincials engaged that day, skirting behind the trees. He could not tell whether they were fighting or had tried to run away, and he did not care. A Pennsylvania drover in a flat hat was trying to maneuver his wagon around to recross the river, but the driver in the wagon behind him was dead, and its wild horses had tangled it among the trees and blocked the road. The drover did not think to unhitch his team and lead them around the junked wagon. He just stood upright, cracking his whip over the trembling horses and yelling at the dead man. Squire saw him hit, but saw him still stand there, now silent, letting the reins drop. Then the big man began to wilt, surprised. He sat down on the seat, then fell across the buckboard and underneath the flailing hoofs of the panicking team.

It was while Squire watched him that a familiar object in the turmoil winged past his eye, and he darted forward, low, straightening only to catch the reins of the crazy horse. He had just time to still it and knock Peregrine's foot from the stirrup. The dead boy had been dragged for a long way, but, curiously, his face was only scratched. He still held his fine chased silver-handled crop. Wearily Squire pried it out with his fingers. He was trying to mount, wondering why his legs shook and refused to lift him to the saddle, when he heard the air split with sound rawer than the war yell—the pure scream of women gone crazy with fear. He thought of Hannah, then wouldn't let himself think as he shot trails of vomit down Peregrine's wet saddle, huddled, weak, against the horse's shuddering flank.

★   ★

Somewhere, while there was still dim light through the fog of sulphur smoke, Jonathan realized that at last the Retreat was being beaten—partly heard it, was partly dragged by the rhythm which made the men plunge like fire-crazed animals toward the river, allowed to find an exit at last; then that voice calling, as he was swept along, which made him fight backward against the current of running men.

"Sixty pounds! I'll give sixty pounds to the man who carries the general off the field!" The cry— "For God's sake, sixty pounds for your general!"—a weak voice, beyond anger, beyond the begging which came after. It was Orme's broken spirit, calling from beside a hill of a dead horse, trying to bribe the running remnants to carry General Braddock, who leaned against his arm, breathing out a fine pink froth. Orme no longer tried to lift him; his own right thigh was broken, his filthy white stocking soaked in dark arterial blood. Jonathan and another Provincial—he never knew who—reached them at the same minute and knelt down.

After that, time must have passed. They were in the river, weaving past the dead animals that made brown, moving tendrils in the water where they lay. He could only watch a strange man he had not noticed before, who seemed to wander in a half dance downstream and fell face-down in the water—he had already been scalped, but had got up and wandered there. After that, Jonathan saw young Burton standing like a cheap barker on a log on the bank, his red coat in rags and brown with blood, begging the men to reform around him, to attack the Indians as they settled like monster flies on the wounded and dead—scalping, scalping, unaware as the lion gorging on the entrails. But he could not stop them, only stand there and cry as they slipped past. Jonathan finally persuaded him to catch a horse and join them. Now he rode, as nearly unconscious as Jonathan, as the rest of the few who had escaped and dragged, unaware, unprotected, down the dank cold road in the woods.

It was night. Jonathan lay, half asleep, astride a huge cart horse, resting his arms on its hard neck, too tired to lift his head as the horse fought, step by step, its head in a dead up-and-down rhythm. Jonathan could hear, beyond the half-deadness of himself and the animal, the creaking sigh of one of the tumbrils. Once in a while, through it, he could hear the old man who lay across the straw turn and turn again to try to comfort himself, but mostly he was silent, and the dark figure of Orme, who slouched beside him, his head being bounced a little by the heavy log tumbril frame, was silent too.

Someone passed Jonathan so close that he caught a glimpse of the silver-handled crop, barely shining, and the sight flung him upright, sick with relief, to welcome young Peregrine.

It was Squire, too beaten to recognize the Provincial captain in the dark. He felt himself jerked by the coat, and threw himself forward to cling to the saddle. A voice mad with fury screamed, "Ye've stolen that horse. I'll kill ye . . ."

Jonathan could feel under his fingers a satin sash; he heard himself, as if it were another man, scream, "Ye've left him, stripped that boy naked . . ." But Squire's new horse had an edge of stamina, being the last pure-bred riding horse from Belmont, and it managed to obey as Squire urged it way from the yelling man.

He tried to ride beyond Jonathan's voice, which followed him, weaker and weaker, calling, "I'll kill ye. I'll kill ye if ye come to Virginia."

But the call meant nothing and went unnoticed by the men near enough to hear it but too sopped in what they had seen to lift their heads. Finally Jonathan realized that he had left off calling.

Now only one man, a Scotchman, was crying to no one, "We was a' beaten. We was a' beaten. I seen Donald McDonald up to his hunkers in mud, and a' the skeen off his haid." Then he began again to cry it, with no one listening.

Chapter Six

Bᴀᴄᴋ ᴀᴛ Dunbar's Camp at the Great Meadows, the men began
to drink—sodden, weary drinking, talking low among themselves.
Jonathan commandeered a tent from the main stores and put it up
himself, far enough from the log house to get some peace. Inside
the cabin, open to the wind, which some speculator had put up to
claim the land, the general was dying. Orme lay in the room,
watching, dictating sick explanations, attempting, while he cast
about for some position to give him ease, to catch and save in
hollow words some kind of reputation from the disaster.

"The sound will stay with me to the hour of my death," he dic-
tated to his clerk, forgetting it was a military report he was writing.

So each retreated to his private world: he to explain, some to
blot out the action, the general to die. There were rumors of what
the general said—the blame of the Provincials, blame of the soldiers who were filtering back to the deceptive safety of the camp—
but to Orme he muttered discordant words, and one sentence.
"Who would have thought it?" was what Orme remembered. From
someone in the room of the wounded, it was said, the order had

[134]

come to destroy all equipment, so for three days the detonations went on, and the fires burned green in the sunlight and red in the night, never stopping. They stayed three days to wait for stragglers, but on the fourth day—and yet the general had not died—they moved. Coming back, on the new fine road, they made the Great Crossing of the Yoxiogeny by evening.

Jonathan, surprised by himself, knowing that he ought to be of use, found nothing to do. What orders he thought of seemed so powerless against the whole disruption of the army into the sick isolation which he had caught that he could say nothing, only clutch sometimes during the day of his arrival at the letter Gist had brought him from Sally, thinking of her as a dream, but unable to settle his mind to read what she had written. He put it off, as a man holds medicine in his hand to cure his pain but is too involved with pain to take it.

Finally, by the fourth evening, straining his eyes against the falling night, he found spirit to open it.

The first word he saw was "Belmont," in her childish, pretty writing.

"My dear husband."

Darkness was silencing the camp. The damp croak of bullfrogs by the Yoxiogeny was the loudest noise, obsessively claiming, at the minute it began in the twilight, his whole brain. Jonathan moved the dear words closer to his small firelight and shivered. It was the first time she had ever written to him, and his half-finished letter, still against his chest, would have been his first to her; yet he could not read it because the peaceful words, more than the darkness, made his eyes wet and the words swim.

From the loghouse door Burton, coming to find him, saw him kneeling, so isolated, his head tipped to the fire, that he thought Jonathan might be praying, and stood watching without disturbing him.

"Belmont. My dear husband . . ." Jonathan began again, and this time he could read on, and almost hear her speak, hear the

[135]

reedlike precision of her voice, follow the careful movement of her thin, childish hand across the beginning of the letter. The house was there, the morning, and the sound of birds, and out the window from her desk a great flat stretch of hot sandy bottom-land, gone back to yellow sedge.

"As I seat myself to write to my der Man, my thoughts is with ye there, wherever ye might be, may the Lord watch over ye." All this was careful, round. But he could see where she had paused, relaxed—and thought how she must have smiled, for after that the pen had run faster, gayer, more her own self.

I said I was going to put down all for that is what ye would like best, but Ma says you do not care to hear my Rattling. Ma's headaches is not coming so frequent. I would have wrote before, but she has had the Hip so bad I have not set down for a Moment.

Mr. Cartwright says the farm is going pretty good, but to tell you the new field aint yielding the way he had hoped. For my part I think it is becuz he is a damned lazy Man and don't pay enough Attention to the Negrews. Lord I went down to the old Field tother day and seen that the Tobacco there had already began to sucker, so I told him out he ought to be Topping it long ago. So you see yr Sal is looking after things while y're away and I don't care a bit if he does not like to hear this from a Woman. The new field he blames on the Drout and I do think he is rite. It drains pretty fast there and we ain't had a bit of rain since early June. The dust blows up Awful and the plants are Dusty with the sand blowing and the heat.

We stirred ourselves to go up the river to Church last Sunday and you ought to see it shrunk down from its banks. All the talk there was Drout, Drout, Drout. They was a new Preacher from New Jersey (!) and he preached long and loud that the Drout was the Rebuke of God's Hand on us Virginians for wicked ways and we turned our backs and all that. Real Thunder, was what Mr. Stanhope said outside later if he couldn't bring Rain he could at least bring Thunder and Hot Air. Others said he was no better than a Presbyterian, at least Presbyterian inwardly in his Heart; and we had no use for Religion growed to Wildness and Enthusiasm. I don't think the new Preacher will last long!

Polly is in trouble for a Sassy Miss. We went to dinner at the Donnellys after Church and she pearted Mr. Crawford, you know what a fine gentleman he is. Well bless me he said to Miss Polly You're going on sixteen Child it's time you got married. And she said mighty fine—I'm waiting for you to grow up Mr. Crawford. He laid back his head and laughed and he said Dam me Miss Polly I'm old enough to be your Pa. 'Tis a good thing yr not, sir, says she, for I'm a-going to marry ye—and pranced by swinging them black sassy Curls she has took to wearing right down her back neck. Ma was fit to be hawg-tied and says Polly has set her Cap for Mr. Crawford who everybody knows won't marry a girl of No fortune and now ruint herself in the whole of Princess Ann County.

When Burton could wait no longer, and walked through the darkness up close to Jonathan and said his name, the man looked up from what he was reading with a younger, calmer face than Burton had seen in days. A smile stayed at the corner of Jonathan's lips, left over from whatever he had been reading, as sometimes a man will wake up with the expression of his dreams printed on his face.

Burton touched his arm. "Johnny, 'tis nine o'clock. The general's departed this troublesome life, God rest his soul!" And he fell forward and lay against Jonathan, crying on his shoulder, shaking like a leaf. His crying seemed to relieve him. Jonathan could feel Burton's back, going gentler under his arm. Then he muttered, "Dear God, Johnny, what will happen to us all?" He stopped for a minute, then straightened up.

"I went into the markey and there he was, layin at peace, the

[137]

pain gone from his face, and that suffusion of blood which had made his face so red and him look so angry had gone too, and he was nearly handsome. Orme had his back to me, and I never saw his face. There was just the pale line of his cheek, but when I looked toward him he turned his head away, and nobody could get near enough to comfort him."

It was just at dawn when Braddock was buried in full uniform with his watch and his sword and a silver snuffbox a famous actress had given him the night he left London. This was all he had left. His fine silver and his crystal glass and even his ivory toilet were left on the field. Jonathan spent the hours before dawn trying to find him linen, but nobody had a clean shirt. He was buried in his dirty linen and his fine uniform in the middle of the road named after him—Braddock's Road. George Washington read the service, and the whole army marched over the grave to blot out every mark of it from man so that the Indians would not dig up the body and divide it for spoils. There was no quick march, no slow march, and no stone to mark where he lay.

From the time of the death to the burial of the general, Jonathan seemed to move out of contact with the others, a man who had retreated into moving sleep. By the evening when he could read her letter again, Sal's voice already was singing in his ears, he seemed to have waited so long to get back to her dear ghost.

We et chicken and ham at dinner and the Men drunk Toddy a long time afterwards but 'twas a-growing late and Mr. Cartwright was a-waiting to row us Home. When we got to the River he was Drunk as every second Man in Virginia is by four o'clock on a Sunday so he rowed us home zig-zag.

Mr. Donnelly said that Colonel Innes, that tall Carolina man who ought to know Best had advised the General not to take too many smelly Indians as he really did not want their families cluttering up Ft. Cumberland till they returned. I am glad.

With a fine Army what do ye want with a crew of evil smelling savages ye might as well take yr own Negrews. I hyeared Jamie Stewart picked up with a SQUAW.

It is another day and lord lord what a day of all days. This morning who should come up a horse back on a fine roan and looking mighty rich and handsome too but Mr. Crawford to ask Ma for the hand of Miss Polly, so she brung it off like she said I'll be d—— she'll be a mighty rich lady and is fit to be tied. Here he has been educated in London and went and choose Poll! Ma bawled as she always does but in secret is pleased though she keeps reminding Polly Mr. Crawford is old enough to be her Pa.

So we are a planning a fine Ball thirty-seven people (all the Genteel folk in the County and some from as far as York River being Mr. Crawford's kin folk) to start at 3 with dinner for all at 4.30. Polly cried for a Barbeque which she dearly loves but Ma said the very idea twas no way for an Occasion. Next she'd be wanting negrew bangers instead of Mr. Temple to play the harpsichord and his son the gitter.

So Polly bawled but we've to expect that till her Widding Day I'm to have a new set of tamboured Ruffles of course the new dress goes to Polly and we are all starting with it tomorrow when Mr. Cartwright comes with *watered silk* from Williamsburg—a green to set off Polly's black angel's wings. That is what Mr. Crawford calls her eyebrows. Ain't it a sight him forty years old!

Of course Mr. Cartwright had to sell a negrew but Ma says go on for such an Occasion. We can't run up more against the Crop as it looks pretty bad owing to the Drout and as a result Credit is getting a *leetle* tight with the store keepers damn their Scotch Presbyterian Souls, they are no Gintleman.

How I wish you was going to be here but know not to disappoint myself by expecting you before the Spring. So we'll go to general Court then and step high my Love like we

did when all the fine officers was at Alexandria. My didn't Miss
Polly forgit Jamie Stewart as soon as he rid off, well serves him
right as he is a Scape-Grace, Jackanapes and a Flirt besides.

I prefer you my solum Love. Oh I cry to miss
you! You worrit Thing. How I miss Your handsome, Elegant face.
Ma says Polly got the Fortune, Sister got the Horse Sense, but I
won the Smartest and the Handsomest.

How is Pa's mare that Ma give young Pere-
grine, that little old Shirttail boy? I don't know why. She would
be our only brood of any blood if she comes back but Ma says
it was the Law of Hospitality. I reckon that Law has ruint more
Virginians than the Common Felonies! My love to Coz. Peregrine
and remember me to the Gentlemen I danced with. They are welcome at Belmont, though Taylor's drunk again and Lord knows it
ain't much here when ye think of them used to Whitehall and such
like.

I remain,
Your humble obedient and loving
Sally Lacey.

P.S.—Don't let Ma talk you out of the new
Commission if it comes. You know she has her eye on you to run
Belmont til Taylor is of age then where wld we be? She must be
Blind if she thinks you won't stay in the Army now, or at *least*
take the promised Bounty, and have a chance of land for yourself
of your very own so ye kin at least have a vote.

Jonathan put the now finished letter back to his shirt, his hand
shaking at the dream that flitted there and the dead that courted
and danced and rode through it. He could feel through the threadbare linen his letter to her, which he knew that he would never
send. For it was to another wife—a need of a wife, not to flighty,
blond Sal, who could possess and make the solemn, brave shadow
seem heavy, dull of understanding, and himself ashamed. It all

seemed out of place before Sal's neat, delicate spirit—his worry over the crop, his quick flush of anger over the sale of one of only six Negroes left out of ten at Belmont a few years before. He read the end of the letter again, but he was right. She had neglected to say which one.

But Sally, Sally, the sixteen-year-old stranger, blond and elusive wife, seemed closer to him that night than she had ever been, outside of dreams. He woke the next morning from his first deep sleep since the battle, his twenty-one-year-old body still heavy with longing for her.

BOOK TWO

August 15, 1763 – May 2, 1765

. . . and view the shining Glory Shore . . .

Chapter One

At four in the afternoon the sun sat burning. It threw down the quiet road the shadow of a man on horseback, who slumped forward over his sheepskin saddle, almost asleep, letting the horse amble. The shadow horse seemed to bulge wide at the sides with foal, but the real one, thin as a rake, carried no foals but two thick saddlebags and packets of skins thonged together and thrown across her, behind the man. Set like a knight's lance under his leg, and reaching high over the horse's head, were two long stakes, lashed together with chains, painted alternately red and white in a foot measure, dirt still clinging to their painted bases. Jonathan Lacey lifted up his head, and was not asleep but looking through the trees, intent, after his long ride, on the ford.

The years of war, and now the haunting problems of his own peace, had not changed him; rather they had drawn themselves more deeply in lines about his eyes and from his nose to each side of his straight mouth. His skin was harder, and the sun and wind had browned him nearly bark-color. When he got to the Fluvanna River he touched his horse gently on the flanks and trotted down to cross, so intent on the sight of the settlement that he never noticed another figure cantering down the other path which stretched toward the Roanoke River to the south. It was Squire Raglan, over whose good black broadcloth and ruffles lay a fine film of dust.

Jonathan, looking up at the splashing, saw the gentleman in black, watched him stop with a fine dash, throw his reins to a young Negro, and saunter, wide-legged, into the long log building, but he did not recognize him. After eight years the set of the figure only tugged at his brain, annoyed him, and by the time he dismounted in front of a small log office up the road his face was darkened by a kind of nervous worry at trying to remember.

Over the entrance to the office hung a painted sign, faded by the summer sun and streaked by rain. The lettering read dimly: FLUVANNA COUNTY REGISTER, and, under this, BRITANNI SEMPER LIBRI, and then, still smaller, *Jarcey Pentacost, editor, proprietor, and printer.* Jonathan dismounted slowly and leaned for a minute in the open doorway, watching the slight man in the leather apron delicately stroking tiny slugs of type into a typestick in his long left hand. For a minute Jonathan couldn't speak; the place buzzed with afternoon peace, the hollow flick of the type falling the only sound, the man concentrated over it. The small room was permeated with the smell of ink and soaking sheepskin. Jarcey Pentacost, having transferred the last of the type, and reaching for an ink-stained rag, raised his head.

"By God, Johnny!" He smiled, wiped his hands, threw off his apron, and took Jonathan by the arm to guide him across to the beaten yard to his one-roomed loghouse. "I'm damned glad to see ye back. Any luck?" When Jonathan didn't answer he went on. "By God, things are pretty hereabouts now. I got a might lot to tell ye of, but later. We'll take a drink."

The room was as neat as a monk's cell. In a few minutes Jarcey was mixing a bowl of toddy on a long bench, for the only table was covered with neat stacks of paper, books piled, an earthen Indian bowl full of pebbles with several turkey feathers stuck among them, and a bowl of sand.

While one silent man made the toddy, the other unloaded his tired horse, hobbled her in Jarcey's field, rubbed her patiently with a large sheepskin, brought his saddle and bags in, and flung them into a corner of the room. Jarcey prepared, Jonathan unpacked, as for a homecoming. At last Jonathan was finished. He brought in the long painted stakes and set them against the fireplace.

Jarcey looked up and saw the dirt. "Been doin a little stakin out, ain't ye, Johnny?" He handed him his toddy, and Jonathan sank with it onto the pallet. He smiled and took a drink. "That there is votin dirt," he answered, then wouldn't say any more but began to unwind his leggings and rub his bare legs while he thought.

"I'd admire to get into some genteel clothes." He sighed. " 'Tis strange what the touch of good broadcloth will do for a man."

Jarcey turned to his big chest without a word, lifted out a brown suit, a ruffled shirt, and Jonathan's cocked hat.

"I'll swear to my soul, Johnny, I do believe your clothes has spent more time in my trunk than on your ugly back for the last two years."

Half an hour later, washed and camouflaged in brown, Jonathan was at the door with a folded parchment under his arm. Jarcey watched him go while he drank.

"Ye're the very picture of the complete gentleman, Johnny. I hope Sanhedron's got his moccasins on. But he's a great fellow hereabouts now. You wait!"

Sanhedron Kregg's land office was right beside Jarcey's printing office. But it was an acre away, and set back from the dirt road. Jonathan had not noticed on first passing it that its logs were now covered with clapboard, painted white, and that Sanhedron's house had doubled in size and was clapboarded over too. Between the house and the road Sanhedron still planted corn as he had done for so long. Its silk tassels glistened among the soft green head-high plants.

Sanhedron had his moccasins on all right—but with them he wore a bought suit finer and with a shorter coat than Johnny's own. The moccasins were resting on a pine table. Sanhedron, behind them, was fast asleep, his face away from the sun, while his coat hung elegantly on a peg behind his head. His long face looked almost happy, but Jonathan had waited too many years to file his claim, to let Sanhedron have his nap out. He rapped loudly on the desk and watched the man fling his feet down and sit erect, assuming a face as solemn as an Indian's.

"Well, Johnny! Come to git your warrant, have ye? Ye been a mighty long time up-river."

"I been farther than up-river this time, Sanhedron," Jonathan explained and started to unfold the map. "The bottom's took up by now all the way to Jackson River." His forefinger traced gently as he talked. "Along here." His finger moved left; Sanhedron's chair creaked as the two men bent their heads low over the map. "Right here at the head of Carpenter's Crick, I want to enter a claim for about two hundred acres—it's nothin but scrub. Carpenter is settled up there with his family. He says he's sure nobody's claimed it, for there wouldn't anybody want it. He's already worked his four hundred and took up his pre-emption rights over this whole bottom here." He traced down the narrow line to the head of the Fluvanna from where he had put a red cross near the waved rows of penciled mounds that stood for the razorback of the Endless Mountains.

"Johnny, have ye gone out of your mind? What good would a little old passel of holler like that do ye?"

Jonathan's hand rose as if it were reclimbing the mountains. "Lookee." He pointed to a gap an inch from his cross, let his hand wander down a line marked Howard's Creek, across a thicker line that wandered south. "That's the crick"—he stopped at the next line west—"that Dr. Walker claims." The finger began to move on west.

"Damme, Johnny, you cain't git across thim mountains. I been down the New River myself." Sanhedron pushed Jonathan's hand away from the map in his excitement and pounded it with his own horny, long, thick thumbnail, his hand doubled up into a fist. "Thar's impassable falls down-river. Thar's a damned high cliff down to the water on both sides thar. Impenetrable barrier." He banged the table. "I don't mention nuthin about the Cherokees and the Shawnees who both hunt that bottom. The Iroquois let us have claim on all that land right down to Big Sandy five years ago, Johnny, claimin to speak for all the tribes. But thim yaller Shawnees wouldn't have none of it, Johnny. And all thim rivers a-flowin west right down to hell!" Sanhedron seemed to get tired now of banging the table. He sat back and sighed. Johnny waited until he was sure he had finished, and Sanhedron saw the finger rise again and hover westward over the map.

"I found a way down past the falls. The land I want to lay claim to is here." His hand fell to a square on the north side of the river, marked with the fine line of a creek.

"I reckon ye know what ye're doin, my Johnny! But damn my hide ye must of flew thar."

Sanhedron heaved himself up tall from the table. He turned and yelled out the window toward his house, "Tranquillity, git that lazy heinie up off the common dirt and bring Mr. Lacey and me some whisky." He turned back from the window. "Swear to Gawd, Johnny, thim youngins is a-growin up like wild Injuns. Sometimes I think thar ain't no use a-tryin, with Mame passed on."

"I noticed ye been makin some pretty improvements, San-hedron."

Sanhedron followed Jonathan's glance toward the main house, and his long face softened. "Hit looks mighty pretty, damme, but I need a woman. They ain't easy to come by when you git this fur up-river."

"I know where ye can get yourself one, Sanhedron." Jarcey had come to the office door and walked in. "Couple of families of German Dunkards just camped over to Brandon's across the river. They've got a whole passel of daughters—all blond."

"Well, by Gawd, I'll go and git me one soon as I enter Johnny's damned fool claim hyar, Jarcey."

Two dirty small hands waved above the window-sill, and a little girl's voice called, "Paw, I done brung the whisky!"

Sanhedron snatched it from her hands. "Brang, brang—ye brang the whisky and wipe your dirty nose. They're all over to Backwater's, eh? Well, by Gawd, I won't set foot on his land but I reckon I can holler across the Glory Ann. I can damn near spit across it." He handed the jug to Johnny. "But they're Germans. What'll I holler? Dammit, I wisht old Mame hadn't of passed over." He sat down sadly. "Ye know thim rivers all flow west, Johnny? That land ain't worth nuthin. Oh hell." He drew a large ledger toward him and began to flick through the pages.

"Claim entered for six months to await *cave*—ye been an officer so I reckon this is your bounty claim."

"Yes, my bounty claim."

"How much?"

"Four hundred acres with five thousand more pre-empted."

"It's way over your rightful claim but they ain't nobody else a-goin to want it." Sanhedron went on writing as he talked.

"Johnny's goin way out back whar they ain't nuthin but Injuns and Irish whores, Jarcey," Sanhedron said, closing the paper of specifications in the claim book. "Your wife ain't goin to take to hit. Why, thim Princess Anne County women think even Kregg's Crossin is the back of beyond and we ain't but eighty miles up the James. I'll copy it out in the mornin and give ye your warrant."

"Ye better think up some Dutch, Sanhedron," Jarcey called back as they walked down to the road from the office door, "if ye're goin to catch one of those Dutch gels."

"Dammit, that's true and no lie!" Sanhedron called back from inside, and they could hear him laugh.

It was the cool of the evening, and the whole of the tiny town had come out to wander about or stand nodding to passers-by from their doorways, drawn by custom as the breeze began to rise from the mountain up the Glory Ann, flutter the trees around the new courthouse, and ruffle the wider Fluvanna as it rolled down to the James.

"There, Johnny, don't it look elegant, now?" They had neared the courthouse and could see it through the trees, a new raw-red brick building. Jarcey bowed as they passed a few people on the wide lawn, now brown and hard with heat and the constant wearing of feet. The trees had been cut back level with the courthouse walls, so that, facing it, they could see the whole façade framed at the top and sides by branches. "It shows what ye can do, by God, Johnny. Twenty years ago the old dog-run down by the river was all there was, and old man Kregg was tradin with Indians and rulin his youngins with a rod of iron. They was all born there, the four boys. Sanhedron told me once they et nothing but corn and meal for years. His pa wouldn't even plant no melons or Indian beans. He said the prayin lasted longer than the dinner and then the old man would drive the four youngins back out. Now the four boys own close to twenty thousand acres, from the Glory Ann to the Audacity—a good deal of it frontin on the Fluvanna." Jarcey stood looking at the building proudly.

"Pretty fine." Jonathan dutifully admired the pointed pediment with its white dental molding, the neat rows of windows, and the cupola of white clapboard with its new blue-faced clock. "Went up pretty fast, didn't it, Jarcey?"

A man walked up close to his elbow and bowed. "Ain't it a fine sight, Mr. Lacey?"

"Howdee, Mr. Kregg." Jonathan smiled.

Moses Kregg had come across the road to walk among the trees. The tiny black-suited man was settling back on his heels, letting his head ride slowly back to take his evening look at the new building, when he saw a man trotting a big black gelding around from behind the trees, heading straight for them.

"Godamme, Johnny Lacey, welcome to Brandon's Landing! When did you come?" the man yelled.

Moses Kregg brought his head down again at the same speed he had raised it. "Ye'll have to pardon me, gintlemen. I ain't a-talkin to that blasphemious son of a Brandon bitch." He walked away.

"Howdee, Backwater." Johnny spoke up to a huge, red-faced man in clothes that looked as if he had worn them for a year of hard weather. Drink had swollen his face. Sun and air had creased it, so that it seemed like red stone, runneled.

"Ye come up-river, son?" He didn't wait for an answer but bowed low to Jarcey from the saddle. "Evenin to ye, Mr. Pentacost," he said coolly.

"No, down-river, sar," Jonathan told him.

"How far did ye git to?" Backwater Brandon asked, interested.

"A pretty far piece, sar, beyond the mountains."

"Lord," Backwater said vaguely. "When you goin to come up and let me kill the fatted calf? Tomorrow?"

"Thank you, sar."

"Very well, done then. Come any time. We dine at three." The big man rode through the fifteen or twenty grown people who by now constituted the usual evening crowd, and off toward the crossing of the Glory Ann.

Jarcey seemed to have withdrawn from Jonathan's company. "I see they are still at it." Jonathan tried to talk to him.

"Oh sure, and will be too till one of Mr. Brandon's kin marries a Kregg. Well, I'll be blasted and damned to hell," Jarcey said quietly.

Across the lawn, ignoring the watching men, went Sanhedron Kregg, dressed in a fine new suit with a ruffled shirt, his hair

[152]

powdered and his queue clubbed, holding a cowbell by the tongue.

"Look what he's takin as a present to court with!" Jarcey whispered.

Behind them a great voice was tuning up on the courthouse steps, and a scramble of Negroes and white children began to run toward it, as animals to feed, excited. "Oooo"—the voice rose from a low rumble to a hornlike note.

" *'O thou that dwellest among many waters, abundant in treasures, thine end is come!'* " The voice swelled. Sanhedron never faltered; intent on keeping the bell quiet, he went on.

" *'And the measure of thy covetousness. The Lord of Hosts hath swore by himself sayin, Surely I will fill thee with men as with caterpillars . . .'* "

Several men in the flat, black hats of German peasants, who had been standing a little apart, admiring the new courthouse, began to stroll toward the speaker.

"Caterpillars!" the man repeated ominously. The children began to snicker but didn't dare laugh.

"Oh Lord, Johnny, I've had enough. 'Tis Moses Kregg commencin his evenin duty." Jarcey began to walk back up the lawn faster, away from the range of the voice. "By God, in the day Moses Kregg is the meanest lawyer in Fluvanna County. He would skin a flint. As a storekeeper he would bargain your shirt to wad his shotgun. I'll swear to ye, one mornin the youngins sneaked to his window when he was sayin his prayers. They heared him whisper, 'O Lord, give me strength and cunnin to face the day.'

"Come cool of the evenin, he starts in on ryeligion. Ye ought to hear him, but not with me. He believes in givin the Kregg Negrews what he is pleased to call ryeligious instruction. He has took the courthouse so the Word can get to the Irish, and the town can count his Negrews, but he don't touch your real religion. 'Tis to keep them from runnin off to the Indians." He saw a man down the path, and veered through the trees to keep from passing him. Jonathan glanced up to see whom he was avoiding and saw Squire, looking cool and elegant in the summer evening. Now that Squire was walking, recognition flooded back.

"I pretty near killed that fellow once," he said quietly, following Jarcey, who answered without looking up, "Too bad ye didn't."

"It was the only time I ever wanted to kill. My hand itched for the uncomplicated whip. It don't seem important, except that I had that passion, uncontrolled. We was all tryin to get away . . ." Jonathan's voice trailed off, for Jarcey had walked well ahead and he was talking to himself.

In the dark cabin Jarcey was lighting a fire to dispel the evening dew, which had made a slight chill in the room. He talked as he did it, making points by throwing twigs onto the bright-blown punk. "That fellow calls his black self Charles Edward Montmorency and owns he was a Jacobite, which pleases the Irish and the Scotch down at the ordinary. A political prisoner. 'Tis strange how political common felony will grow with time, for I know him for a damned thief and scoundrel."

"Well, fine Mr. Montmorency was a plain sarvant when I seen him," Jonathan told Jarcey. "He belonged to my cousin. I think he got him off a convict ship." He saw Jarcey's face in the firelight seem to go quite still with disinterest. "What is it he does?"

Jarcey had turned away from him and was mixing toddy in a wooden bowl. The strong, sweet smell of rum blossomed like a night-plant.

"He calls himself a lawyer now, and indeed he must have had some learnin—he spouts bad Latin." Jarcey went on stirring. "As for what he does, he rides the back country hunting out squatters, who cannot be called settlers, for they've made no claim nor acquired any title under the King, and some for that part don't even know their tomahawk rights."

"I know. They conclude that God led them there like the ancient Jews." Jonathan paused. "A kind of water-veined heaven," he finished softly. Jarcey thought once again that Jonathan might be ready to tell him what he had found, but he seemed still withdrawn, drinking the toddy Jarcey handed him and watching the fire between his long stretched-out legs. So Jarcey went on, explaining.

"Well, up comes fine Mr. Montmorency, like as not on somebody else's horse, and he offers to file their four-hundred-acre claims for them for nothin if they just sign over to him their preemption rights to an added thousand as a fee for settlin. Most of them do it because they're afeared of law and titles. Some are from villages at home where there's been an enclosure, and got out to the border with their heads sore from bein dispossessed. Indeed who can blame them? Half the time it don't do them a bit of good, for the whole of western Virginia seems to be grabbed by one fine eastern company or another. He don't even tell them, for he cares nothin for them as clients—just for their blasted claims. They think they're safe but it don't keep them from gettin kicked off the land when the time comes." Jarcey said this so bitterly that it made him silent for a minute. He lit a stump of candle, then eased himself down in the other rocker and went on, the firelight flickering across his thin face and making his mild eyes seem sunk and witchlike. "Then there's the Pennsylvanians, all nonconformists, to say nothin of the nonconformists from hereabouts, who claim pre-emption rights to more than four hundred acres is a kind of sin."

"An Episcopalian, Tuckahoe, Tidewater sin. I know. I've heard them at it." Jonathan laughed and stretched, sighing. "The Kreggses seem not to think so."

"Oh, they been modified. We all get modified," Jarcey said sadly. He let the subject drop, and they sat quiet, drinking slowly.

A flick of cold wind blew out the candlestump. Jarcey got up and shut the door. Conversation had flickered like the candle.

They were content to make contact by voicing the edges of their thoughts from time to time.

"Ain't ye ever lonesome way out here? A man like you?" Jonathan broke the silence.

"Lonesome, but not for a woman. When the flesh overcomes the spirit I lie with Mary Martha. She's a fine, bloomin gel."

Later, as they smoked in the near-dark of the low fire, after Mary Martha had cooked their supper, Jarcey was finishing a story that seemed by his contented voice to comfort him. ". . . so Scipio, one of the greatest men that ever ruled the state, was seen often on the seashore with a friend, pickin up light pebbles and sailin them across the water."

There was a tap at the door, and it creaked open almost at the same time. The visitor was Sanhedron, who came in at Jarcey's call and stood by the fire. It seemed a long time before he said anything.

"I'm—uh—gittin married tomorry," he finally said down in his throat, confiding in his best shoes, which had curled up on his big feet as if to hear him better.

"Well, I'll be damned. Ye great blood!" Jarcey swung out of his chair and thumped Sanhedron's back, the expected gesture he seemed to stand waiting for. "We'll take a drink to the gel."

"She's mighty pretty," Sanhedron said sadly. "Hit sure will be fine to have me a woman around." Jarcey had already reached the toddy bowl. "A leetle, sar, then I got to tell my brothers." Sanhedron seemed to be better-spirited already.

"Can she speak English, Sanhedron?" Jarcey asked him.

"She'll larn," Sanhedron told him.

"Well, by God, sar—your health! Well done, my lad!"

But after Sanhedron had left, with Jarcey's toddy to aid him to face the rioting, the Black Betty, and the sport of next day's wedding, Jarcey said calmly, "I'll give ye six bits he bought her for the cowbell!"

"Done. If I know the Dutch it took a calf a-wearin it."

"Agin a Scotchman!"

"The pa was a Dutchman!"

Very late in the night the air stopped still. Jarcey, drowsing on his pallet, sensed it through the opened door, and it made him wider awake. Then he heard the tops of the trees begin to sway. He shifted as little as he could so he wouldn't disturb Jonathan, but saw that Jonathan was already wide awake, up on his elbow where he had lain on his blanket before the fire, staring into its last faint glow—or through it, rather, in a waking dream. His hair had loosened from its ribbon and hung like a dark wing along his brown cheek. His head came forward to his hand, and he leaned it and his hand against the chimney corner. In the faint light, his eyes bright from the fire, his face was more relaxed than he ever showed it by day, for he looked a mute dreamer usually, sometimes sad, always at some private ease, giving nothing away.

Far away up the Glory Ann, where it wound by Green Mountain, the thunder began softly, rumbled down through the river gap. For a minute it was black and still in the cabin; then the air flashed light as day and lit the faces of the men. Thunder cracked and rolled overhead.

"By God, that was a near one." Jarcey jumped up and ran to the door. There was nothing hit down the road, but up the road near Moses Kregg's a tree burned like Jehovah at night.

"I found somethin this trip, Jarcey." Jonathan spoke softly to the embers. "By God, at last I've found somethin."

The thunder cracked again, but there was no rain, only the smell of rain in the air.

"Summer-lightnin, I reckon it to be." Jarcey came in again.

"It's the prettiest stretch of bottomland ye ever did see," Jonathan went on, and Jarcey, startled, realized that he was going to talk about what he had found, as if the lightning had jarred him into speech at last, and that the waking darkness would protect the shy man and let him think aloud.

"It's seventeen miles or so down-river from the Great Falls of the Canona. I run a line along the up-river bluff, and around across a pretty little crick that waters it, and across another bluff and on down about three-quarters of a mile. There's five thousand acres of fine bottom layin there like the palm of your hand. Topsoil three-four feet deep. Beech trees and some chestnut, with a clump of cedars up on the eastern spur. There's pine aplenty for buildin, yet not near enough the bottom to sour the land. There's a right smart salt-lick there too, where the animals have been comin for so long ye can see great bones of awful ones that once came there stickin up out of the sand near the crick. They shine in the sun.

"Dear God, Jarcey, it's a lovely place, there for the takin up. The river flows west, but its headwaters are only a few miles from the head of Carpenter's Crick. Ye could build a canal someday, Jarcey, open it up over the mountains there. That's why I laid claim to a few acres up there—for an investment. Lord, ye know eight years ago my brother-in-law Tom Preston went up to Winchester. It was nothin then. He's damned near a rich man already."

"What about Indians? That's mighty far out," Jarcey asked him.

"I got a sanction for the land from Cornstalk, the nearest sachem of the Shawnees. The Iroquois give up claim to that land down to the Ohio a few years ago anyway."

"The Cherokee?"

" 'Tis not their huntin-ground. They're more to the south, a river the traders call the Big Sandy, and up around the Blue Stone—that way. Cornstalk wants a tradin post there for when they come to the lick in summer. So I'll go as a trader."

"How much does he reckon he can sanction?"

"It's not like that, Jarcey. Not like that. They don't bound their countries by lines, but by considerable extents of land. This is a bounding valley where they cross. The Six Nations give it up long ago," he said again to reassure himself.

What he did not tell Jarcey, and could hardly admit as a drawback to himself, was that the valley lay on the Great War

Path, and it was for that reason that no corn waved in the bottom-
land, and when the squaws were brought to boil brine there the
men of the tribe would patrol the bluffs, perpetually watching
beyond the yellow buffalo tracks. What came out from the
creaking thought, and the memory of Sal as he had last seen her,
twined together in the words.

"I've waited a mighty long time, Jarcey. Eight years. It ain't
as if I knowed what I could use for money to make a purchase.
There's all sold land the speculators have taken in the valleys
between here and there that ain't already settled . . ."

The dream of the future lay like a lid on the man's troubles,
and he was silent.

The thunder had receded up beyond the Glory Ann pass, and
now it whispered away in the distance.

"It ain't goin to rain after all," Jarcey said, then relented.
"Johnny, I'm glad. So ye're goin out to make the wilderness
flower with tobacco, are ye?"

"No, that I ain't." Jonathan sat up. The dream turned to
planning; he clasped his knee with a slim, large hand, balancing
himself, and watched out the door. "No. Not that. I've thought
for a long time and I've concluded to farm. That and the salt
trade, and for a while I intend public-house keepin, and a little
boat-buildin, for I see the day when they'll be plenty of settlers
and jobbers comin down the valley to the Ohio. There's more
in the way of business than tobacco. I reckon until Virginia gives
up her tobacco staple she'll be sold body and soul to England
for what she needs. When I was in the northern colonies in the
war, why I seen they could pretty well supply themselves with
what they needed—not like us, who I think depend too much.
We've got to stop thinkin in tobacco. It ties us to the apron-
strings of home. Of that I'm damned sure." The hand moved
down. Jarcey could see it, smoothing, smoothing the blanket. Then
it stopped still. "I knowed after Braddock we'd have to think
different—ye can't lose trust like that. Not with a shock like

that and have things be as they were, although I've wondered so many times why people drawed the conclusions they did from that day's trouble. I reckon people draw what they wish from a thing, Jarcey. I always reckoned it a sorry thing that the Virginians chose to lose trust in English discipline, which we have need of here with every Tom, Dick, and Harry with a wish for liberty that reaches to violence and chaos."

He said nothing more, but leaned his head nearer the waning fire and watched it until the room had gone pitch-black.

★   ★

Just after dawn Mary Martha hoisted a clothes basket up on her round firm hip and started swinging up the road. Even at that hour it was beginning to be hot, and the sky was too blue. Mary Martha, like an animal which grows fractious in a hot, waiting day, sensed something already in the air that early, and didn't like it. She reached the path that led down to the Glory Ann from the Courthouse Square, shifted the basket to the other hip and went on, her shadow thrown long before her, walking into it, annoyed. The sun caught her fine, dirty, tangled curly hair and played with it as she turned her head to look behind her suddenly. But the path and the road behind it were deserted as far as she could see.

The sun on her back was at last beginning to cheer Mary Martha up by the time she reached the bank above the Glory Ann; she was almost smiling and had shaken off her chill of wariness.

Then she saw the river. Sometime in the night a cloudburst up the gap had filled it violently. It had roared down through the pass, clutched at the topsoil of the bank, whirled round the trees. Now, at the mouth, the pale flood poured into the Fluvanna and made a wide, light, running road in the dark water. Below the bank where Mary Martha stood, the water was flat and swollen.

[160]

She could tell its current only by the white foam which rushed by in patches on its flat, tan back and slid away into the bigger river. Across the river, she watched Mr. Brandon's Negroes lashing the flatboats together again, for the flood had broken the bridge and sent them slapping across one another on the far bank. So far as she could see, he had lost several of the boats he usually tied up at the river mouth. Mary Martha squatted on the bank, fascinated, while five of Mr. Brandon's Negroes piled into a bateau, four to pull oars against the flood, while the fifth hung over the stern, hoisting the broken bridge chain to the near bank. From time to time she looked up to see how the Germans were getting on, trying to haul their heavy Conestoga wagons up from the lowland where Brandon had let them stay for the night. Now the thick wheels were nearly buried in the deep mud as the men swore and pushed, their mules strained, and rows of women and children stood solemnly under the trees.

Mary Martha, watching the excitement, almost forgot Jarcey's breakfast. As it was, she arrived panting, having run all the way, and had to bring the dirty laundry with her.

"Here, my gel, what's this?" Jarcey teased her, picking out a ruffled shirt.

" 'Tis that fine Mr. Montmorency's linen. I'd hate to think who he fastens on to make it so fine." She rolled her eyes upward, then, feeling for words, said, "Damn my blood and wounds efn I do!"

"Such language ill becomes a little gel, Mary." Jarcey sounded cool and turned his back.

So she babbled on to hide her embarrassed childish hurt while she fried grits for the two men, who were now squinting down the road toward the Fluvanna.

"Thar was a cloudburst up the Glory Ann last night, and she's flooded her banks, by Jesus. Old Mr. Brandon's lost some boats and the bridge is broke agin. Everybody tells him to move it up-river but he won't, he's too hardheaded . . ."

She realized the men weren't listening, and went on watching the little squares of grit sadly, then began to hum to show she didn't care.

The wedding party had already started, down at Sanhedron's house. The noise filtered through to Jarcey's cabin, and once in a while an individual yell split through on its own. Somebody had brought a banger, but the attempts to play it were obviously being squashed. As they watched, Sanhedron came from behind the offices, clutching a young yellow-haired German girl around the waist. They were both drunk.

"Come and drink to my fair young bride," he called out, and then forgot them and turned back again, the girl laughing softly.

"Pretty little gel," Jonathan said. "Who'll do the marryin?"

"Moses will, for he's the Justice of the Peace. There's no registered minister hereabouts. One comes in the spring on his way up the back-country circuit, but between spring and spring there's only a long chance of one droppin in. They say marriages are made in heaven, but I reckon up here they're made in Black Betty. These Presbyterians have to get drunker to face a marriage than they do to face a hangin. 'Tis because down deep they reckon the flesh to be so evil. What a terrible jest of God to lead them and their stern rocky souls to these lush green valleys where the very heat and flow of the water whets a man's senses. Anger, lust—they recognize the passions. Lookee there at Moses. The hard mouth, the clenched fist—his sweet senses are dead of shame."

Jarcey's subject was riding slowly by on his big black mare. The black clothes, the black animal, and what Moses wore for a wedding face, all seemed to strive against the too hot, dusty morning.

"Good mornin to ye, gintlemen. I hyear Mr. Brandon done lost some boats. Bad flood up-river," he said by way of greeting and rode on.

A man standing at the corner of the courthouse saw the wedding going on, watched the horseman turn in from the road and dismount, noticed the two men standing in the doorway of a cabin up the road, and made up his mind to go and speak to them. As he walked toward them they turned and disappeared into the house, and by the time he got to the open door both men were sitting at their breakfast. The first thing the man saw was that they both had napkins tucked at their chins like gentlemen, and, since he seldom came across such a fine sight, it drew him slowly inside. Jarcey heard him and looked up, and never again forgot what he saw.

One of the ugliest men he had ever seen was watching them, mouth open. His eyes drooped down like a bloodhound's; his cheeks were creased in vertical lines to an enormous chin, which was not supporting his pendulous lips because he was too surprised at the napkins.

"Sar?" Jarcey began to get up.

"Whar's the ordinary hyarabouts?" The man tore his eyes from the napkins.

"You'll git nuthin thar. They's all dead drunk last night. I got more hyar," Mary Martha told Jarcey calmly.

"You are welcome," Jarcey said, sitting down and motioning the man to a stool.

"Thank ye kindly," the man said, and when Jarcey forced himself to look at the face again the man was smiling and the ugliness had dissipated itself in his warm, shy look. He sat slowly, politely at the edge of his stool. He cleared his throat. "Since I come a-visitin I'll tell ye my name. 'Tis Solomon McKarkle. Solomon McKarkle. Now ain't that the damnedest name to live up to? I'll swear, if a baby don't have enough trouble in this vale of tears without his maw and paw a-callin of him Solomon."

"Come from down-river?" Jarcey asked him.

"Yes."

"Goin up-river?" Jonathan asked.

"Yes."

It was a ritual they all expected, this questioning—all business aired, all news, all rumor. It was the grapevine news source of the colonies above the fall-lines, and each traveler was expected to carry his part of it.

"Goin to settle?" Jarcey asked, chewing bacon.

"Yes. I concluded to try up around Jackson's River."

"It's all taken up—or it's sold land and not for settling," Jonathan told him.

"Lord God, is that true?" Solomon McKarkle seemed upset and put down his plate. "Whar'd ye hyear tell of sech a thing?"

"I just come from there."

"I don't know what a man can do. What the hell-far can a man do?" The poor man slapped the table. "I got me a wife and youngins waitin at Winchester for me—her a-doin chores for the sodjers. We tried up Pennsylvany way. That ain't no good. Cain't nobody decide up yonder whether that thar territory is Pennsylvany or Virginny and they're up thar a-fussin about it. Ye're jest as liable as not to git throwed off your claim by one side or tother afore ye've more'n built your cabin. Now I was a-goin up Jackson River or one of them cricks. I hyeared it was pretty good up thar. Hell and damnation. What's a man to do?" This great speech ran him out of words, and he stared down at his plate.

"Who's makin the trouble up Pennsylvania border way?" Jarcey asked him.

"Oh, land speculators. Lay claim and set on it and then sell high. Scratch a land fight and ye'll find yourself a land company." The man began again to eat, mouth to plate. "Thin thar's thim wild Scotch-Irish sidin up with first one thin tother, raisin hell-far. I'm a peaceful man. All I want is a leetle passel of land thar cain't nobody kick me off'n."

"Why don't ye go on further than Jackson's River?" Jonathan asked him. "I could—"

"Why don't I? Lord Gawd Amighty, man, ain't you all up hyar hyeared tell about the new Proclamation Line?"

The room seemed to die for a second.

"No. We never," Jonathan said quietly.

"Why, they've decided in London—that is the king's meenister has suggested—or p'raps has ordered. Everybody down-river is mighty het up about it. 'Tis some king's meenister. That is King George the Third, Gawd bless 'im. Ye knowed the old king was dead?" He looked up, questioning.

"We knowed that," Jarcey said.

"Well, this hyar meenister—I reckon 'twas that deival Boot. That deival—" The man pushed back his plate. "Thim was mighty fine grits, mawm." He craned around and bobbed his ugly head at Mary Martha. "Ye wouldn't happen to have a chaw of baccy, would ye now?"

"Ye're welcome to some. But what is the Proclamation Line?" Jarcey asked him, showing more impatience because Jonathan had gone so still.

"Up yonder mountains beyond Jackson's River, whar the river flows east. Now that's as fur west as a body's allowed to settle. 'Tis what's said. They're mighty het up about it down-river. That thar over the mountain they reckon is Injun land. Who ever hyeared tell?" Solomon was silent again, waiting for his tobacco. When he didn't get it he went on. "They reckon down yonder as thim Mingoes was our allies in the war. Thim and the Cherokee. Some say the king—that is George the Third, Gawd bless 'im—he reckoned to pertect as he said, and not take no land. Hell, what do they want with it—heathen deivals? Don't even farm more'n a leetle."

Jarcey handed him a tobacco plug, and he lodged a quid between his cheek and his teeth and started to ruminate thoughtfully.

"The way I look at it"—he expanded, and sat more comfortably on the stool—"the way I see it is thim meenisters don't want to waste nuthin pertectin too much border. Lookee, didn't thim Injuns show us thim sodjers wasn't no good back Braddock's

time? Why, the reg'lars ain't fit a fight with 'em yet they won."
He turned slowly and spat a long stream of brown liquid expertly
out the door. "What good are thim sodjers? What good are thim
sodjers? I ask ye. We don't need 'em. That's how I reckon it. Let
us pertect ourselves, I reckon. Hyar we went and won this damned
war, and we ain't gittin nary a thing out'n hit. That's the way I
figure it."

Jonathan was going to answer, but he could not even rouse his
spirit to defend the soldiers.

The man spat again. "Gawd Amighty, I ain't had a chaw since
up around the Rapidan. Mighty nice folks up around the Rapidan.
Y'ever been up thereabouts?"

"Will y'excuse me, Jarcey." Jonathan got slowly up, and
Jarcey saw that he didn't rise all the way but left the table still
slightly bent, never raising his head.

"Jonathan, wait. I'll go with ye for a spell." Jarcey jumped
up.

"Thank ye, Jarcey. I prefer to be alone a little," Jonathan
apologized and disappeared up the road.

"I wish ye could tell me more." Jarcey turned back. "Lookee,
I run a kind of newspaper when court's in session here. I print
the handbills and copies of deeds and all that. Then I reckon on
printin a sheet when news like this comes. I reckon this is liable
to get people pretty upset. There won't be an Indian safe when
the news gets out." By this time Jarcey was planning aloud.
"They need reason, a little reason on the subject. Lord." He sat
down again beside the man. " 'Tis a hard thing for all."

"Well, that's your business, are hit? Mighty fine leetle business.
I'm not much on that line of country. But I can read. Ye
wouldn't think a-lookin at me that I could read, now would ye?"
He presented himself for inspection as if reading were a third
ear. Jarcey waited patiently to wring the man's mind for facts. He
felt sure the general opinion would come almost pure from his
friendly mind, for he would be a man to agree with the majority,

echo the loud men in the ordinaries, parrot the drovers, the flatboat men, the immigrants he had passed on his lone journey down the valley, as a lonesome man will pick up bits and tags and store them as his own, sink them in his mind for company, pass them on to make contact wherever he goes.

"Now, ye wouldn't reckon in a month of Sundays what my business was, would ye? 'Tis more a trade. They ain't nary bit of use in your tryin. I laid that question to many a man—many a man." He spat a great stream out the door. "They ain't nary a one knowed. See thim thumbs?" He presented his two turned-back thumbs proudly. "That's a hint. No, ye cain't never tell." He didn't wait for Jarcey to answer but leaned forward, seeming surprised himself. "I'm a *hat-maker*. Now would ye ever reckon on such a thing? Would you, little gal?" He turned, as surprised as Mary Martha, who did look suitably startled, never having seen a hat-maker.

"Yessar. That's what I am. Ye can tell a baccy man by his thumbnail. Now he wears it long and hardens it in a candle. Ye know what for? Well, for toppin, that's what for. They do say 'tis for gougin and I hainta sayin hit don't come in handy for gougin, but 'tis really for toppin. My thumbs is for this." He made a quick, smooth, efficient circle with them to show. Then he was suddenly bitter, full of anger. "Leastways that's what I war. I war that. A hat-maker. Thin the law come and first they wouldn't let us sell no hats in no other colony. Well, damn near everybody in Philadelphy had a goddam hat. Good felt lasts a lifetime and ye can will a beaver to your youngins. Well, that there slowed us down, but niver stopped usn. No siree. Then along come another law sayin they warn't to be more'n two apprentices to a shop. I's the youngest of three, so I had to go. It was thim meenisters done hit—they wasn't buyin enough London hats here in Virginny to suit their fancy. Now ain't that a turble thing?" He relaxed again and smiled. "Ye wouldn't of knowed in a lifetime I's a hat-maker, now, would ye?"

[167]

The man was at least thirty, and Jarcey reckoned that, if he'd been an apprentice, the hat-making was a long time ago. Since then he had rolled, doing second-hand jobs, having second-hand opinions, but for his pride he could always say of one still point of being, "That is what I am. Whatever I look to ye, in my soul I am meant to make hats."

So Jarcey asked him gently, "What do ye aim to do now?"

"I reckon to farm. Dammit, I got to find a passel of land hain't tooken up. Ye wouldn't happen to know of nuthin, would ye, sar?"

⋆   ⋆

The sun beat down on Jonathan wandering up the valley path, raising dust with his shoes, walking dim with worry that beat at his head worse than the heat. He passed Moses' house without noticing it, wandered on up by a farm where the log cabin stood as yet unclapboarded. He passed it, then on along the dusty road, sensed rather than saw the dimmer woods, and let himself down slowly against a tree, picking up a handful of dry twigs as he settled himself. He began to break them, one by one, carefully, as he sat there; the heat made the air quake around him. He finished the first handful, then broke a second and a third, then a fourth, as he sat there silent, staring, breaking stick after stick in his shaking hands, where the sweat had matted the hair on their sun-brown backs. He went on breaking twigs until the sun was high and reached under the tree and weighed down on him, dumb with sorrow he could not tell to a living soul.

When he finally got up he stood straight and walked back more decisively. He had obviously made up his mind there under the tree, but walked on down past Jarcey's house and office, where he could see the printer in his leather apron, working. There was some difference in the wedding party as he passed. It had gone quieter; the men around the door were not smiling, not yelling. No one spoke around Solomon McKarkle, who had now been taken into the wedding treat and stood in the doorway, tipping back a stone jug, his big lips pursed as if he were waiting to kiss it. That Jonathan saw, but as he looked the circle broke, and Sanhedron loped out to catch him by the arm. His face was dark red from the heat, from the Black Betty, but, more than that, from a deep, frustrating anger. He gripped Jonathan's arm so hard that it hurt.

"Are ye married yet, Sanhedron?" Jonathan stepped back, trying to steer the drunken man off what he knew he was going to say.

"Yes, by Gawd, I'm goddam married. Have ye hyeared, Johnny? Have ye jest hyeared? They cain't do this to usn up hyar, Johnny. They cain't do this hyar!" He was out of words, and he shook Jonathan's arm.

"Yes, I heared." Jonathan was cool.

"Thim damned Injuns. I could go out right now and scalp the damned bunch."

" 'Tis hardly the Indian allies ye have to thank for this." Jonathan's voice was cold, withdrawn.

Sanhedron squinted at him, surprised, then turned as someone from the front stoop yelled, "Aw, San! Come back hyar and tune up your banger."

"Ye'll lose your piece of property, Johnny." Sanhedron looked over his shoulder, still a little wilted by Jonathan's quietness.

"I wouldn't worry, Sanhedron. We can all be lawyers or preachers. You'll make a pretty good preacher." Jonathan touched Sanhedron's shoulder and smiled and had already started down the road.

"Hell and damnation, he don't even seem to care none," Sanhedron said aloud, looking after him, then went on back to celebrate his wedding.

Jonathan walked faster, away from Sanhedron, away even from Jarcey. He didn't feel like talking; he didn't feel like calling up the reason Jarcey would demand, or the fate-cursing hate-bath that Sanhedron seemed ready for. He turned down the Glory Ann road, over the newly fixed bridge. The flood water swayed and twisted it under his feet as he crossed the flatboats to start up the slope to the big two-story dog-run cabin at the top. Numb as he was, he wanted only to talk to a man of his own background, to sit without thinking, watching down-river, while his mind went easy under a formal exchange of trusted, unimportant sayings, of expected calm, a kind of sensuous, false peace.

Backwater Brandon sat on his front porch and studied Jonathan's face as he toiled up the last of the bluff in the high noon heat.

"Howdee, Johnny. Jim Gold, bring Mr. Lacey out a leetle toddy," he bawled back through the shaded dog-run.

Jonathan eased himself down into the other rocker. Neither man mentioned the news; neither looked at the other. They sat in the peace of politeness.

A little dog ran out from around the house and under Backwater's chair, crouching under it and splitting the calm with its shrill yapping.

"Lyddy, come git this damned fiste." A honey-colored mulatto girl swung round the porch after the dog, squatted and hauled it out from under the chair, not taking her lazy eyes off of Jonathan any more than the animal had. He couldn't help staring back. She was beautiful. Her naked body pushed against her gunny shift. She walked away with all the dignity of the queen of Egypt, her brass earrings hanging calm against her perfectly still small head, slanted on her long neck, recalling her Yoruba blood—but her Yoruba black eyes were Brandon set.

When she had carried the dog away, Backwater mourned sadly. "I don't miss a blasted thing about my legs more than not bein able to kick that damned little old fiste. Lyddy just turned it loose so she could come look at ye." Then, because the silence had been broken, he went on. "How does pretty Cousin Sal keep these days, Johnny boy?"

"Oh, pretty peart, sar. I ain't seen her now for nine months or so." A small colored boy brought out the toddy bowl, and Jonathan dipped himself out a cup.

Now that he was talking to Backwater, Jonathan found himself watching him with some shock. If ever a man looked satisfied, his passions calm, his senses gratified, it was Backwater. Gratified— soaked, dulled. Jonathan realized suddenly that the man who sat there was dying, his own victim, and not caring, on the porch of sweet-smelling pine. How many rocks for a grown man to rock himself to death? The summer flies buzzed and swooped. Jonathan was startled to hear Backwater almost answer the question hung in the air with the flies.

"Damn my blood, Johnny. If I could just git off down that river any more. I git so mean settin up hyar with nary a soul to talk to. Maybe next year I'll go down-river and visit. It gits mighty lonesome for a man, I tell ye—nobody to talk to but Injuns and Neegurs. Them damned black-souled Scotchmen are nary a bit of good to a man. Damned cantankerous lot. All they aim to do is fight and argy. Cain't even set and take a drink with a gentleman. Why, Johnny, here I am an Episcopalian and a gentleman and I don't even git elected to no office in Fluvanna County. The Kreggses got ever' damned one—justice, burgesses, surveyor, and all. They've kissed every ass in the county don't owe 'em money. No sar, I'm pure Tuckahoe and they're pure Cohee, and the Lord made us to damn each other's ugly souls."

Jonathan laughed for the first time that day. It made Backwater expand. "They ain't a damned soul hyar for me to talk to but Scotch-Irish, Presbyterian blasted Cohees."

"There's Mr. Pentacost," Jonathan said because Backwater had stopped to be agreed with. "He's a pleasant, facetious man. Ye might call him a Tuckahoe."

"Oh Lord, nothin of the kind, the little scribbler! Scribblers and Quakers—I ain't got nothin to say to those milk-and-water men. Ye know what they do say—show me a poet, a painter, a

Quaker, and I will show ye three liars." Backwater's shocked amusement finished Jonathan. "Yes, I've concluded to go downriver. I aim to see me a cockfight and a horse-race afore I die," he added, stating his preference in a new, fine-fellow way, louder. "Go have a look at the new crop of pretty gels, bring me a wife home. Visit my kinfolk." Then he lapsed again into mumbling. "Maybe next year . . ."

His voice faded all the way to silence. There was only the sound of Lydia, the mulatto, suddenly laughing in a high, reedy giggle, then as suddenly silent again.

Down the hill, they could see the flatboats joggling the water as the older Germans and a few children came back from the wedding, and far away over the stillness came the sound of a banger and a flute, playing a fast wild jig for those from nine to fifty who had stayed to dance.

"God Amighty. Moses Kregg must be drunk. He's a-playin of his damned flute," Backwater said, and then said nothing more.

Back in the shade of his shop, Jarcey was working furiously. When he had started, the thought that he ought to go to the wedding festivities for politeness' sake had nagged at him a little. Now he had forgotten all that and leaned over his stone, composing fiercely. Once in a while there would be a pause in the tiny hollow rhythm while Jarcey looked up to watch sightlessly out of the window; then it would start again as he bent down. Here and there he changed a word, the tweezers pulling tiny type, returning it to the case as if they worked on their own while he stared.

Reading the broadsheet over when it was printed, Jarcey's spirits sank after the sensuous rhythm of throwing the devil's tail over and over, the balanced movement of the press, the growing strength, the faint sound of wood against wood. It seemed already, drying there, as if it were any other broadsheet he had read. Then his spirits rose a little. He had made it local, right to calm the blood of the people he served, make them think. He wanted badly to show it to someone, but there were only six men in the town who could read. Two sat on the opposite hill at Brandon's, and there he was not welcome; the other four were certain to be drunk. He had only printed fifteen copies—the extras with a hope that someone passing up the river might be able to read.

Sadly, after all the afternoon's lonely pleasure, he tacked it to the wooden board outside the shop, went back to his cabin, kicked off his shoes, and fell asleep in the cool, shadowy room.

In the deserted street the fuse of print flapped a little as the up-river breeze felt at a loose corner, flapped again, was still, pinned by the breeze to the weather-beaten board. It was nearly six o'clock before anyone saw it.

Up on Backwater's porch, the old man lay fast asleep in his chair; the bowls of toddy, the great dinner, had made him sleep as deeply and as noisily as if he were somewhere wrestling already with death. Jonathan was left to remember the day. But by now his hands were still, his face peaceful. He looked down-river, squinting far into the distance, his eyes long across his face and sunken with some greater fatigue than he had shown the day before after his long ride.

When he did move, the sky was streaked with sunset. Down near the narrow bottom the pale fires of the Dunkards were beginning to show up under the trees. Jonathan went downhill easily, and an old German looked up to see a leisurely gentleman strolling toward him, moving as if he owned the damned world.

By the time Backwater woke up for his evening toddy Jonathan was back again in the chair opposite, as if he had never moved. Backwater stretched and yawned, stiff with sleep. "I reckon I just dozed off for a leetle," he said, apologizing.

★   ★

Moses Kregg was the first to see the broadsheet. He read a few lines; then, without a word or a movement of his set face, he almost ran back to the wedding. Within a few minutes the four

[173]

Kregg brothers stood in front of the sign, the youngest, a boy of sixteen, tracing the words with a wavering forefinger until Moses brushed his hand away, without realizing he did it.

> Fluvanna Court House,
> Friday, August 16, 1763.

This morning arrived News from the Capital that a new Proclamation Line is to be established between Western Virginia and the Lands belonging to the Indian Nations of the Ohio Country. It is conjectured that such a line will run along the mountain chain which is a natural Divide between the Eastward flowing rivers, and those that find their Headwaters in the same Mountains, flowing Westward toward the Ohio.

This will close those Lands to the west for Settlement as being not under the Jurisdiction of His Majesty's Government of the Crown Colony of Virginia, nor under the Jurisdiction of the Proprietors of Pennsylvania. It has obviously been taken to quiet the Minds of the western Indians that the Intentions of His Majesty's Government are those of Honour with regard to the especial Treaties made during the late War with our Indian Allies, in return for their Help in fighting off the French Tyranny.

By many Treaties with them it was promised that people would be hindered from settling the Lands not Purchased of them; and if white people Squatted upon their lands, they should be removed. Those Promises have been without Effect before. Now it is time to show to the Indian Allies that they deal with an Honourable Government of free Men and with no false French Promises.

Who wishes the Lands of the Ohio Valley? Can we not take into our own growing Towns the Dispossessed who seek a Livelihood in Land? Would they not bring Industry and Husbandry to our own Gates, rather than expose themselves in a Wilderness without Safety, Government, or those peaceful pursuits that render us Civilized? Is Land the only Answer that is sought by those Homeless? Or is Land sought even more by those Insatiable Men in our Midst who because they can claim thousands upon thousands of acres of wilderness, think themselves as Rich as a South Sea Dream?

Those are the Questions we must ask ourselves. What are our real Rights? Have we mistaken *Right* for *Ambition,* Liberty for *Ruthless Licence.* We deem ourselves Gentlemen—even compleat Gentlemen in Virginia. *Are not the Acts of Gentlemen also the Acts of Honour in Government?*

It is true that there are many reasons behind our Hatred of the Savages here near the Borders that cannot be known in London, or even as far away as our own Williamsburg. But in the light of *Reason,* before we judge with too much dangerous *Enthusiasm* the Establishment of a Proclamation Line, should we not question ourselves whether it is Worse that a Savage who knows not Civilized Ways scalp a white Man, take his wife captive and kill his Children, or that a white Man in the name of Justice ruin the Lands for hunting the Red Man has roamed for Countless Centuries, take his scalp and that of his savage Widow and Orphan, and claim a Scalp Bounty of five pounds for his labour?

We have stolen their Lands in the Past, and imitated their Savagery, but that was necessary War. Was the Massacre of the peaceful Conestoga in Pennsylvania more justified than the Massacre at Jackson's River? The Savage Law is of Inexorable and Bloody Revenge. He knows no other way, *but is this also the Christian law?*

It is time for Peace. To move West on Broken Promises will mean more Bloodshed, more Revenge between the White man and the Red that can only be balanced by Death. Let us learn to govern Ourselves first. *Does it heal the Injustices of the Dispossessed that they Dispossess others as ruthlessly?*

It is here we must uncover false Reason, and

[175]

let true Compassion take its Place. It is Here we must learn to Dwell in Peace among the waters of the Fluvanna, the Gloryanna, the Outicity Rivers. It will be Easy for the Brutish Mind to lay Blame upon his Majesty's Government, or upon the Indians who are ready to be our faithful Children or our Deadly Enemies, however we decide to honour Them. In the Fire of *War* and *Unjust* Hatred, may ours be the waters of *Tolerance and Understanding.*

The writer of this Inquiry has spoken freely; because he has the Honour to be a *British Subject,* and under that glorious Character, to enjoy the *Privilidges* of an Englishman, one of which is to examine with *Freedom,* our public Measures, without being liable to the punishments of French *Tyranny,* which has so lately been our Real and Present *Danger.*

"Well, damn my blood for a cockeyed son of a bitch!" Sanhedron said softly.

Moses tore the paper off the board by the loose corner and crumpled and smashed it over and over in his hands, pounding it, saying nothing.

It was nearly dark, at the time of twilight when the sky has turned purple and the first stars are bright.

"The damned leetle Injun-lover!" The youngest Kregg had found his voice. "He ought git run out of town. Why damn his bloody leetle scribblin hide." His mouth went wide and slack as he gathered anger. He left it open when he finished speaking.

It was too dark to see Moses' face, but his voice was full of righteous fury when he did speak. "Yes. Yes." His words came clipped and breathless. "That's right." They could hear the spittle rattle in his throat. "What about thim drunken heathen Injuns lays down around the ordinary? They don't want usn. We don't want thim. Sinful ways—" He didn't go on, but choked instead, and there was only his coughing in the silence as the brothers moved by instinct closer together and found no more need to

[176]

speak, now that Moses had spoken with the voice of conscience.

When the four men walked on to the lean-to of Sanhedron's house the whole room stopped moving; the wedding guests were as still as Lot's wife, fear-frozen. Some of the men stared at one another, wondering who in the heat and drink of the wedding had insulted a Kregg, to make them stand together, close like that.

"You men." Moses spoke softly. "Come on outside. We got a leetle business." Then there was only the sound of Sunday shoes, heavy across the bare boards, and the men had gone.

Left there, the women began to whisper; then the whispering rose high in excited questions. "Oh Lord a-mercy thar's a-gonna be trouble. We women ought to stop it," somebody whined, still watching the door without daring to move. Only Sanhedron's new wife slept on in the corner, from the rigors of her wedding, unmindful of passion. It was her first Virginia party, and she had not spoken, only smiled and said *"Ja!"* excitedly through the day. Now she was still smiling, curled up, sleeping the sleep of a tired fifteen years.

Up on Backwater's porch in the cool of the evening, Jonathan was preparing in his mind to go home.

Backwater spoke out of the darkness. "Widdin must be over. I cain't hyear a thing. Sure do wish I's drunk with dancin instead of settin." Down far away, the row of white clapboarded houses seemed a ghost town under the risen harvest moon.

"Looks to me like you ought to get together with the Kreggses, Backwater. Their flesh and your spirit!"

"Oh, Johnny." Backwater laughed in the darkness. "Ye sound just like your pa."

Then they heard, blowing toward them, like a storm coming, the soft roar of trouble.

"Oh Lord, them Kreggses never could take whisky, women, and bad news at the same time." Backwater sounded quite peaceful still. "Lyddy. Oh Lyddy!" he suddenly called out. "I once knowed a Scotchman got killin drunk ever' time spring come. He couldn't stand the green, couldn't stand the feel of that old sap a-risin."

Lyddy's soft footfall sounded through the dog-run. He seemed to know when she was standing beside him. "Joe Gold in?" he asked.

"Yassar."

"Telemachus?"

"Yassar." She giggled.

"Succotash?"

"Yassar. They out back."

"What are they a-doin?"

"Jest settin thar." She giggled again softly.

"I cain't let none of my Neegurs run loose," he explained to Jonathan's back as he peered downhill. "I cain't afford to lose me a Neegur. What about Joe Little Fox?"

"Naw, sar, he ain't home."

"Where'd he go?"

"I don' know."

"You know all right. Where'd he go?"

Lyddy suddenly squatted, then sat cross-legged in front of the crippled man, formally suppliant.

"You give him money, Lyddy?" he shouted at her.

"Yassar," she mourned, beginning to cry.

"He's down to the ordinary, ain't he, damn ye?"

"Yassar." She was crying in earnest.

"Goddammit. I hope he ain't too drunk to git outa the way. Ye know what ye've done, child? The Kreggses are out. Jim Gold, Telemachus!" he yelled. "Git hyar quick!"

The girl let her slim hand steal up to his knee, and his own hand closed over it.

When the Negroes came he said, "Git down to the river and unchain the bridge. Now git!"

"Yassar." Telemachus, the oldest, rubbing sleep out of his eyes, wakened by the ordering voice, carried the command to the others.

"Come on, you Neegurs. Git!" he yelled and they faded away, running downhill.

"Wait, Backwater, for God's sake! There's something on fire down there!" Jonathan called. "It looks like Jarcey's shop! I got to go down."

"Go on then, if ye've a mind to. Ye can get back about four mile up-river. There's a tree fell across the narrows. Dammit to hell," he said to Jonathan's back. "I'm likely to lose my only boatbuilder. Lyddy, why ye have to go and steal my money for that no-count Injun?" But he said no more, just went on absently patting her hand, then her head as she leaned it forward on to his knees.

Down below, the fire grew higher, silhouetting the trees and then the tiny moving figures of his slaves as they wrestled with the great chains of the bridge. One figure ran across, and just as it reached the other side the bridge broke like a string of beads, and the floodwater swung the linked boats to the opposite bank.

*   *

For a while Jarcey thought he was still dreaming. He woke, or seemed to wake, in the dark, but fire shadows fluttered through the window and lit the room. Somebody had a hand, a small hand, over his mouth and was leaning close to him. He could smell Mary Martha's sweet body and could hear her whisper.

"Mista Pentacost. Mista Pentacost. Wake up. Don't make no noise. Jest lay thar still a minute."

The movement of his head showed Mary Martha he had waked up. The roar of men got nearer his consciousness, filled it. He could hear yells from outside the closed door.

"Whar's the leetle scribbler? Let's git 'im. Whar is 'e? Hey," somebody yelled, "gimme a hand hyar."

Then he heard another voice, yelling hysterically, "Mista Kregg! He ain't hyar! He's done gone up the hill with Mr. Lacey. Up to Brandon's."

"Well, he ain't a-gonna hide up thar. Le's go git 'im!" somebody yelled. "That Injun of Brandon's is down to the ordinary."

There was a little lull in the roaring. Jarcey could hear the crackle of fire.

"Injun." At the word the interest of the crowd outside had veered as the penned bull veers in its attack at the sight of a new flapped cape.

". . . go!"

He could hear running feet, moving down the road, could sense, as if they instead of Mary Martha were pressed against him, their movement away, with his whole body. He let out a shivering breath. Mary Martha's hand left his mouth and started stroking the cold sweat from his forehead.

"Now, listen hyar, Mr. Pentacost. They done gone for a minute. Ye got to foller me," she whispered. He staggered up from the bed, his legs weak, still too numbed to think. Mary Martha opened the door a crack, and the wild light from the flames filled the room.

"Come on," she whispered. They crept, low, out of the doorway. As they turned the corner of the house away from the road, they heard footsteps running, pounding up the road.

"Lay low," Mary Martha whispered and looked around the house.

Jonathan had got to the fire and stood for a second. Then a faint hope made him run toward Jarcey's house. Mary Martha caught him by the coat and pulled him around, away from the road.

"Dear God, Jarcey, we got to get ye out of here." Jonathan's voice shook, from running and from relief.

"We know of a way. Come on."

Mary Martha's light figure seemed to dance ahead of them. They could see her climbing the worm-fence of Jarcey's corn-patch. It was when they were huddled among the corn that they heard the men coming back. Down at the bottom of the field, away from the house, Jarcey had built a crib. They could only hear Mary Martha panting softly as she pulled at the men to make them crawl toward it.

Behind them, in the silence of the men back around the now raging fire, one voice called hopefully. "Me Pamunkey. Ye know me. Me Pamunkey. Good Injun. Ye know me!"

Then movement, and over the movement, a scream.

"Me Pamunkey. Good Injun. Me lest dunk. *Dunk!*" The word became itself a scream.

It was not until then that Jarcey seemed to realize what was happening, and that the now great funeral pyre that was flicking the lower branches of a tall tree was his own office. Jonathan, with his hand on Jarcey's shoulder, felt the man start a darting movement forward, and knew he knew. He gathered a handful of Jarcey's shirt and pulled him back. Mary Martha seemed to be crying.

But it was she who made them move on, over the next fence, and the next, the fire fading behind them. They reached the woods and were at the tree where Jonathan had sat so long that morning, before anyone said a word. Mary Martha's sobbing had turned to panting. They stopped long enough to turn round. The fire was lighting up the sky in a pink bowl. But there was no sound, no sound at all.

The first thing Jarcey said was, "They won't hurt the house none, Jonathan. Your surveyin kit will be all right." Then, to explain: "The house belongs to the Kreggses." And he began to laugh, and stopped laughing suddenly.

It took them three hours of walking, because of Mary Martha, who kept falling on the treacherous paths and had to be handed across the huge fallen tree where, in the darkness of the woods, they could hear the Glory Ann running wild below them. The moon had gone down by the time they got up the hill to Backwater's. He was still sitting on the porch. The fire was gone, and the town was dark and peaceful below them. He had had a bowl

[181]

of toddy and food waiting for them for two hours. Mary Martha fell asleep, after crawling on to Jarcey's lap without saying a word and starting to whimper in his arms like a puppy. He held her hand and rocked her gently, rubbing her arm above her elbow, where her skin smelled of summer leaves and cool sweat.

Over her dark head Jarcey told as much as he could remember of what he had said in his broadsheet. But the gist of it was all he remembered. The separate words which had dropped as type from his fingers were gone.

When he had finished, Backwater said angrily, "Mr. Pentacost, in my opeenion ye've been a damned fool, sar. A damned fool."

Jonathan said nothing.

Jarcey, moving the sleeping girl close, said coldly, " 'Tis your opinion, sar. I thank ye for your kindness. 'Tis time I went."

"Now y'ain't a-goin no place, sar. Ye're stayin here. Our opeenions may differ, but 'tis no reason for a man not to accept my hospitality. Let a man say what he thinks. We are all civilized gintlemen hyar." So for the first time in the nightmare, and from the man he least expected them, Jarcey heard words he recognized as kind.

He could only say, "Thankee, Mr. Brandon."

"Besides ye're a friend of young Johnny's hyar. So ye're welcome. Telemachus!" he yelled. "Come git me!" The call waked Mary Martha. She jumped up, embarrassed, and hung her head.

When two of the Negroes had lifted the old man from his chair and carried him in, they could hear him calling to Lydia, then giving her orders to lay pallets for them in his living room.

There in the darkness, when Mary Martha was asleep, Jonathan could finally bring himself to talk to Jarcey.

"Would ye come with me now, Jarcey?" He spoke quietly. "Or do ye intend to go back East?"

After a long time Jarcey's voice answered. "There's somethin ye ought to know about me. I come over on the ship with that thief Raglan. I'm no better than transported here."

"Well, I'll be damned. 'Tis your own business, ain't it?" Jonathan sounded casual, almost whispering.

"My pa is a physician in a market town. He prenticed me to a printer, for I had a flair for words. It's a lovely place, the town, with a fine wood, rich farmin country. There was trouble, for the woods and the commons where we all hunted game and grazed our cows was enclosed by the new squire—for improvement, 'twas said. He come back with an East India fortune and bought it up. Well, we'd all hunted that land since I could remember. All the village done it and considered it their right. 'Tis as if a piece of the wilderness here was fenced in, like fencin in something the Lord give ye. One morning they brought in a man to Pa. He was a farmer. One of his legs had been caught in a man-trap, set out to catch poachers in the woods. He still had the great iron teeth sunk together in his leg. His friends had brought him in. Pa had to take his leg off. I can still hear him, and hear the saw. 'Twas like cuttin a hard wood branch. The man was hollerin, and his friend was tryin to hold him down. After that I went wild with the injustice of it. I got caught poaching with a group of village lads. They hung one of them to stamp out the Intrusion—the judge called it Intrusion. I was let off with transportin, for they said I was an educated lad and had been led. I never was, Johnny. I never was led. Lord, how them people laughed at me for gettin caught." His voice rose a little, and Mary Martha turned and whined in her sleep.

"When there's wrongs . . ." Jarcey said after a minute. "Good God, Johnny. Pa sent a little money for me to get bought here by his cousin, a Mr. Pentacost of Philadelphia. He was ashamed of me and wouldn't take me there. But he did help me to buy my press and ship it up-river. I come to Fluvanna when they made a county of it, hopin to set up—I had great plans to carve me a place, seek my fortune."

"Ye set up with me, Jarcey," Jonathan interrupted.

"It's because of the fences, drivin people off what they believe to be theirs, I spoke so strong about the Indians. I—" But he said no more.

Both men lay in the darkness, waiting.

"The mulatto gel." Jarcey tried to clear the thoughts that bore in on him. "Does Brandon keep her for his wench?"

"Lord no, Jarcey." Jonathan sounded deeply shocked. "She's Backwater's daughter. I wish to God I could buy her. Backwater's liable to die up here and he wouldn't want to see her sold off to just anybody."

In one of the cabins at the back of the house Lydia lay in the darkness, listening for the sound of Joe Little Fox stumbling home, her body still full of hope.

In the main street of Fluvanna Court House only one man was left awake. Moses Kregg, the bachelor, under five feet tall, rolled back and forth as he knelt beside his empty bed, his black breeches soaked.

"O Gawd, look down on me"—he was groaning—"a pore weak worm that can stand scarce any affliction. Forgive me my sins. Forgive me my great sins, O merciful Gawd—my horrible temptations . . ."

But he could not pray the smell of Joe Little Fox and the burning out of his nostrils.

Jonathan knew that Jarcey was still awake. He could hear him moving on the cornshuck mattress. It crackled under his body.

"Where are ye aimin to go, Johnny?" Jarcey's voice finally came out of the darkness.

"West," Jonathan said. The word seemed to hover over them. "Jarcey, I'm goin on west. Damn the Proclamation Line." Then, without knowing it, he echoed Solomon McKarkle. "What the hell can a man do?"

Chapter Two

S QUIRE RAGLAN was lost. Or if he was not lost he felt a crawl of the same kind as the first hint of the fall evening seeped through his buckskins and touched between his shoulders, where panic and cold seemed fingered. The woods were hushed, vast; the night lurked beyond the trees. He had no choice but to ride on slowly, his two pack-mules, awkward under their high loads of pelts, straggling on long leads behind him. Only the rattle of an iron shoe on loose rock broke the clopped rhythm of their walk.

But at least that sound was some comfort against the indifference of the forest. The high Endless Mountains stretched to the sky above him, but Squire no longer wanted to raise his head. The hated trees dwarfed him enough. He rode on into the chill evening.

It had not been an easy business trip at first, the new one. He had heard about the Proclamation Line when he reached the fort at Looney's Ferry. There, among the jumbled crowded wagons of settlers, clogged by the news as logs are jammed in a stream, he had had to think quickly. The stop had been worth it. By the time he reached the new Fort Henry at Jackson's River, he was as impressive as ever, excited by his new scheme.

The scheme accounted for his being so far off the beaten track. It also accounted for the laden pack-mules. Squire was no longer demanding pay in pre-emption rights. He was demanding beaver pelts. Now he rode northwest of the main war trails to keep himself safe from the Indians, who were on the warpath again after the angry lynchings along the new border. All the way he had collected story after story of the refusal of settlers to move back from a place where every man was king of his own valley, and treaties were made too far away. The stories made him afraid—too afraid for comfort, even on the deserted path.

He had set his heart on sleeping in a cabin, although his fastidious nose disdained them. But the scent of the coming night was worse. The horror that grows of being too long alone drove him on, made him pray for the company of humans—any humans —to quell the sudden rage that sprang into his heart. He had known too often that God-cursing anger which could possess him, make him holler at the merciless wind for blowing too long until he wore himself out; or, worse, could rouse fantasies in the silence that forced him to be an unwilling pack-horse to his own heavy thoughts.

Most of the time Squire had learned to free himself of such slavery. In his eight years of exile to the world's end, he had taught himself to plan rather than dream. He had learned decision and coolness—not just the manner of coolness which was its fashionable imitation, but that of the soul, which comes from awareness of the individual steps of ambition.

He had long since weaned himself from the petty pleasures of stealing, and thought with contempt of the jimcrack he had been —that posturing, ridiculous boy who had stumbled into a transported hell for the price of a watch. In eight years the watch had grown into a fortune. Squire knew of many a transportee who rode a fine carriage in London on a Virginia fortune—even men he thought were fools. If he knew anything about himself, it was that he was not a fool.

He could see himself in his mind's eye, riding now not in the darkening woods but through the outskirts of the heavenly city his yearning made London, half expecting to see the lights of Twickenham at the next blind curve of the narrow trail. Homesickness possessed him in a dream: he straightened in the saddle and let himself, because he was so tired, tip his hat lightly to a neighbor tree. The gesture brought hot tears to his eyes, and in brushing them away he left a streak of dirt across his face, like a small child caught.

Now, the dream triumphant in the silence, he seemed to be riding toward a vicarage where a bent man stood, a hollow-faced saint, no longer full of righteous fury but stretching out his arms, not for the correcting switch but to enclose the Prodigal. This Prodigal, Squire Raglan, was no crawling, simpering failure like the fulfillment of an old man's wish in the damning jungle of the Bible. He was well mounted, and he wore gold lace, though not too much. His suit had been made in London. It was only by accident that he flicked the face of his father with his silver-handled crop as he dismounted, and then politely, gently, he apologized.

Well, at least he had got as far as the silver-handled crop. He ran his thumb lovingly down its pretty chasing, traced the crest, and smiled sadly. By day, and to help him in his business deals, the crest was his own. Charles Edward Montmorency, bar sinister. They liked the bar sinister, the clodhoppers, the sheep. If they understood nothing else, they understood a bastard. But as the night came on he was left stripped to himself, shrunk by the silence and the trees to ex-thief and backwoods lawyer—an educated failure with his living to earn—the crest stolen, the name stolen, even a stolen crop. He touched his mare behind her ear lightly with its white leather thong and brought her to a slow trot.

Clear across the still twilight the faraway bite of an ax chopping wood cut into his dream. His heart turned with terrible relief, and he kicked his horse to a faster trot, the dream blotted out. The sound gave point to his fear, distilled it, and he knew the same sickening urgency he had known as a child when, brave all along the dark corridors of the vicarage, he had broken into a terrified run when he saw the candle through the nursery door.

The driven ax was clearer, closer; he could hear the wood splinter and crack, then the log-end thud as it was heaved again on the chopper. He rode, tugging at the worn mules, for a quarter of a mile while the sound guided him.

In a tiny clearing, as he rounded a huge tree, he saw the man, bent, his arms rising and falling in unconscious rhythm. It was almost too dark to see him closely; the late light played tricks, made the figure seem huge, poised for a second above the ground.

"Halloo!" Squire called, and the trees caught his yell and echoed it.

The man turned slowly, the weight of a day's hard labor on his tired back. Squire was still a hundred feet away from him, but in the dusk he knew that he had come face to face at last with his father. He froze and pulled his horse up to wheel it and run, but the man walked nearer.

Of course it was not his father, only a man little older than himself. Still, from there it could have been—the same slow walk, the same sunken, saintly eyes, the murderous sadness. Squire stopped pulling at the reins, deadly ashamed of his panic. He found a voice the fright made almost natural.

"Ye scared me. Way out here. I had not expected—"

"Howdee, stranger." The man spoke shyly toward the ground and stared at him from under his heavy black eyebrows.

"Howdee, sar." Squire slipped into the safety of genteel politeness. "I got myself a mite lost. Ye wouldn't know of somewhere I could get some food and lodgin?"

"Ye're mighty welcome. Foller me."

As Squire walked his horse behind the tall, bent man, for once

[188]

in his life he found nothing to say. The shock and the cold made his fingers numb on his bridle, and he knew how near to exhaustion he was. Finally he told the retreating back, "I'm mighty glad to find ye. I'm dog-tired."

"Hit ain't much," the man muttered; the air was clear, and his words floated back. "But ye're mighty welcome."

"I'll pay," Squire told him. They walked on down the narrow path, and the darkness blotted out the man's shape. Far across a wide, waving meadow, glistening with frosty dew, Squire could see a tiny, winking, homely light.

" 'He that witholdeth corn, the people shall curse him!' " The man suddenly let loose his voice, and it reverberated over the meadow. " 'But blessing shall be upon the head of him that selleth it.' "

Squire's new-fledged spirit, revived with company, sank low again; the New Light of Baptism was not his favorite way of passing an evening.

It had been a long, cold day for Jeremiah Catlett, cutting wood to lay up for winter. But the stranger cheered him. He had at last, after a long tussle with his thoughts, found Guidance to welcome him, and Guidance cast out the animal fear he had caught from living so long in the woods, which nagged at him whenever he saw a stranger.

"We don't see many folks," he explained over his shoulder as they were crossing the nearly dry creek. "Last one was close on to six months—in the spring. I remember it. We give him poke greens. He et four helpins of poke greens. You like poke greens?" he stopped, worried, as Squire drew level with him, and looked up.

"Yessar. I like poke greens fine." Squire's back was hurting, and he spurred the mare a little past the man to keep him from stopping.

"We ain't got none now," Jeremiah said sadly, following Squire. " 'Tis fall. Ain't that too bad? I'd admire to have some

[189]

of thim myself." He walked on faster now, pleased at having got over his shyness and had conversation with the stranger.

"Hannah! Oh-h-h, Hannah!" he called. "We got company!"

The most longed-for words in the lonesome back country made Hannah fling the door wide. Four children hid against her, as still as frightened squirrels, and peeked at the stranger as he dismounted and strode up to the light of the doorway.

Hannah tottered, but the children clinging to her kept her still. She saw by Squire's gallant bow, and knew by his careful, "Evenin, mawm. Ye're mighty kind to welcome a stranger," that he did not recognize her, and she managed to move back against the opened door, holding two of the children tightly to keep from falling, as he strode past her into the firelit room. His nearness for a second in the doorway made her breath shake in her remembering body.

Squire dropped his saddlebags on the table. Dirty as they were, their finer leather was studded, elegant against the dead pine surface. He was pleased; the gesture stated his presence, and he looked around, now that he was placed again, with an eye to business. Stiff, dirty pelts, their bloodstains still brown, were piled up to the ceiling in the corner, but between the harsh skins there were glimpses of fine silk beaver hair. He could hardly keep himself from running a practiced hand over the soft fur, but he contented himself with indifference. He felt the woman brush past him, but before he could catch her eye for the first contact she had knelt at the fire with her back to him. She seemed to be trying to hide her face in the steaming caldron, where a rich, clinging smell of bear grease rose out into the tiny room. The children, after the first fear, stepped lightly, like inquisitive little animals, nearer. They stood staring, their bodies ready to scoot back to their mother if the stranger made a move.

Somewhere in the background the man had gone on talking without stopping. Squire found himself listening again.

". . . and ye can tether thim mules alongside the house and

put your horse in the shed. We got a shed, hain't we, Hannah? I reckon ye'll want bells for 'em in case they git loose in the night. We got bells—two bells—hain't we, Hannah?" Jeremiah said proudly. "We had ourselves a cow. I brung 'er back all the way from Carpenter's Crick but she up and died on us. That's whar I trade my pelts. You know Carpenter's Crick?"

Before Squire could do more than begin to nod, Jeremiah went on. "Mighty fine place down thar. Mighty fine gintleman that Mr. Carpenter. I been thar three-four times. He was pretty nice to me. He sold me that thar cow. Warn't nuthin ailin 'er when he sold 'er, though. I reckon she et somethin pizin. Thar's plenty pizin in the woods."

Squire got up to stop the flow. The children tried to bury themselves against their mother. "Watch what ye're a-doin thar," she said crossly.

"Ye'll want to be a-seein to thim critturs. I'll help ye . . ." Both men went out into the night, Jeremiah's voice going on. "I hain't been down in nigh over a year to Mr. Carpenter's. Got me a mighty fine lot of pelts."

"What kind?" Hannah could hear Squire's voice, cool, polite, as she remembered it.

One of the children tugged at her.

"Quit that, Ezekiel." She swatted back with one hand. "I'll whoop ye," she added fiercely, from habit, and went on stirring the pot.

All through the painful meal, with the wild children eating by handfuls out of their wooden bowls, Squire kept his eyes averted. He had been too long, he knew, in the woods this time, for the cold anger that he had let rise with the lonesome images out there had stayed with him, bit deeper as he could not keep out of his head the noise of these people eating like dogs. He hated them, hated and was a little afraid of their darkness and their staring, the intensity of their concern over whether he was getting enough to eat, where he'd been, where he was going. He answered shortly the

O BEULAH LAND

flow of questions, hardly aware that he did it. The woman said nothing; her concern was bearing in on him in a different way. She got up several times and moved around the table, touching his coat lightly as she passed to and fro on errands of her own. He never focused his eyes on her, but took in that she was thin and nut-brown, made by the life as like the other women of the border as nails which carry the same weight for years. The heat, the closeness, the compound of woodsmoke, cooking, and the sweat of years nearly choked him, stung his nostrils, even his eyes—the smell of animals, healthy but rancid, close, cloying. He shivered, chilled up his back, though the room was as hot as a den.

Squire realized that he had had enough of the frontier. He decided to get done what business he could with the gaunt man before he slept, and to set off at dawn toward the east at last, after his long business trip, on a rested horse, riding the whole lot of them gradually out of his memory. He could not stop shivering.

"The gintleman's tard, Hannah. Git thim youngins outn the way and come set him down a bed." Jeremiah examined him. Squire thought for one second that the man was going to reach out his dirty paw and feel his head.

"Thankee, sar." Squire looked up then and favored him with a smile. Then, remembering the New Light, "God bless ye, sar," he said simply.

Hannah disappeared, shooing the children up the ladder in the corner of the room to the loft. He was left alone with Jeremiah.

"We might be able to do a leetle business." Squire leaned back easily. "Would ye like a smoke, sar?" He was more at ease with the children's eyes and the presence of the woman no longer boring at him.

"Wal, now I don't mind." Jeremiah felt happy. "Ye can try some of my baccy. Wait hyar." He sprang up and started out the door.

"Don't bestir yourself, sar. Take a pipe of mine." Squire reached for a saddlebag and started to unload it onto the table.

But the man was already out the door. He called back politely, "I'm more partial to a chaw, thankee."

Squire felt the hand fall lightly on his sleeve and jumped. The chill came back. He hadn't heard the woman draw close to him.

"Squar, don't ye remember me?" she asked him sadly, knowing the answer.

At the sound of his right name his head shot round and he stared full at her. She had the shuck bedding hoisted onto her shoulder. Under it she looked emaciated, a woman made of brown roots; the weight of the pallet had hoicked her linsey bed-gown up and pulled it tight over a long, narrow dug.

"No, mawm. I can't say that I do," he answered truthfully. The woman's face was drawn over her cheekbones, her eyes sunk into her head. Her nose and chin were beginning to be pointed because she had lost most of her teeth. Hannah smiled, but he did not catch the sadness in the smile. To him it was terrible.

"Lord, honey, 'tis Hannah. Hannah that come over with ye so long ago."

For a minute he looked at the eight-years-older woman, hoping that by some miracle she lied. Even her once pert Billingsgate voice had flattened, like her body, into the deadened mutter of the backwoods, of people who spoke too little. The thin wet slit of her grinning mouth nearly made Squire retch, befouled that he had ever kissed it. He shuddered, then remembered in time that he had business to do.

"Why lord, Hannah, ye haven't changed a bit. How could I forget ye?" He managed to smile back, behind the safe façade of a gallant gentleman.

"Aw, Squar!" she said, pleased. When she had thrown the sack down she turned back. "Jeremiah don't know I come over like that." She spoke so low Squire could hardly hear her. "He knowed I was bound, and so was he. He don't know I was transported. He concludes me to be a redemptioner. I niver told him no different. Ye'll not tell him, will ye, Squar?" She seemed to poise for a minute on the edge of begging.

Her quick confession made him relax a little. "Why no, Hannah, why should I tell him?"

"Hit ain't right to keep things, but what can I do?" she asked, wondering.

Jeremiah called as he came to the door, "You try some of this hyar. 'Tis new-dried and fraish."

Squire picked up his pipe from the table. It was the tomahawk pipe he had stolen from the Catawba.

"Wal, efn ye don't look at that thar!" Jeremiah said, wondering. "That thar's a fine tomahawk. Whar'd ye git it?" He reached forward to hold it in his hand.

"I—won it," Squire told him simply, letting silence tell the rest.

"Wal, I reckon ye seed some sights, some sights!" Jeremiah handed it back, deeply impressed.

Squire felt more at home now, surer, but still too tired to brag, though usually a little bragging did him a power of good.

"Mighty fine tobacco, sar," he said instead when he had filled his pipe and held it casually by the hatchet-blade, though his eyes smarted because the tobacco had a black strength; Jeremiah had mixed it with sumac, and the killinick made Squire's head reel.

"Yep. I figure it's pretty good—Injun mix. Hit's what I'm a-used to. Hannah," Jeremiah called over to where she sat slumped, warming herself by the fire, her stool tilted a little forward.

"Umm?" she answered, not moving.

"Have a smoke." He had filled his jaw and now began to chew in a slow, comfortable rhythm.

"I reckon I will." She picked herself up and walked heavily away from her musing, feeling for her pipe in the pocket of her linsey bed-gown.

They smoked together, a ritual silence gathering around them. Outside in the dark an owl set up its long laugh.

Squire looked up, worried. The hollow noise made him sense the empty miles of black, raw silence around the tiny cabin. Hannah saw his weather-tanned face go a little gray, but it was not the owl. He could not have said what it was.

" 'Tain't nuthin," Hannah explained, relaxed, thinking she understood. "We niver got no Injuns up hyar all through the war. No war paths. 'Tis too cut-off."

"She knows a mighty lot about Injuns, the old woman hyar." Jeremiah started to brag. "Ye know what she done? She got took by the Shawnee up around Pennsylvany with the Braddock army and she got away from thim and come all the way back this fur from the Ohio Valley. Now ye wouldn't think a leetle old scrawny thing like her could do sech a thing, would ye? She was led." He couldn't think right off of a verse. "Why, when I found her she warn't a thing but rag and bone ye wouldn't of bought for two bits. If ye'd a-told me she could bear eight youngins, a-goin on nine—they hain't but four of 'em died neither. She couldn't remember nuthin what happened to her for a long time. But it gradually come back, didn't it, Hannah? Hit come back." Jeremiah finished, too proud of his story to take in a question shot from Squire before he realized what he was saying.

"What happened to the others?"

"The men was burnt, close on to a dozen of thim," she told him, both of them forgetting Jeremiah—the thing they remembered hung too strong between them. "I'll niver forgit it now. Niver. Lord, I wisht over and over it niver had of come back to me. Old Ted, from Ensign Cockburn's company, they took four hours to kill him. They thought up ways. Some of thim others— They made us all watch. They was all a-jumpin around the fires, yellin and shriekin, their legs was covered with blood from thim green scalps a-hung around their middles. Lord Gawd, some of thim had on cocked hats, and some parts of uniforms. Scarlet satin sashes around their ugly bodies. One deival had a pair of bloody britches hung around his neck—fine white London buckskins,

they was. Hit was like some turble dream of that fine army—all
the colors flung crazy like a wind had blowed thim at the Injuns
and they stuck thar. They brung the women down the Ohio. They
was only eight of us left alive. I niver seed that leetle ensign o'
yourn, sweetheart. I looked but I niver seed him. I reckoned you's
both dead. I was took to one of thim villages. I niver worked so
hard in all my born days. Lord Gawd, how thim women did work.
They done all the farmin—plenty pretty good farmin—and reared
all the youngins. Thim damn men don't do nuthin but set thar and
brag. They's pretty good to me, good as they was to their own
selves. But I couldn't stand it no longer. I couldn't stand it." She
begged Squire, by saying the words over, not to question her, not
to say it.

But he did say it. All the anger of the cold night, the squalor,
the scraggy, toothless woman who sat opposite him, and whose
thin arms shook even when she clasped her hands together to keep
them still, who forced him to remember that he had sunk so low—
he, Squire Raglan, with damn near a fortune to blot his shame
with.

"Where did ye bear the baby?" he teased her. "Or is it one of
these fine-lookin youngsters?"

"I come back alone, Squar. She was all right. They're good to
youngins. Ye ain't got no idea what it was like!"

Both of them realized what Jeremiah had heard and sat dumb,
but he only said, as mild as ever, "That's a mighty pretty book ye
got thar, mister."

Jeremiah seemed oblivious of what had happened. He picked
the book up. "I declar I believe 'tis a Bible."

"I would not be without it." Squire dragged his mind back to
the evening's business.

"Get to bed," Jeremiah ordered, without looking at Hannah,
and she moved softly toward the ladder. Squire could hear it crack
gently as she climbed up, and her footsteps creaking the wood
floor, then the rustle of shucks as she lay down.

The room had gone cold and lifeless; the fire was dying, shuddering with points of light in the dimness. Jeremiah went to put some logs on it and stayed, spitting into it, making it sizzle.

"Can ye read that thar Bible, sar?" he was asking softly into the fire.

"Indeed, yes," Squire assured him. He thought he had the measure of the stranger, who looked like one of his brown trees and was obviously too full of his own unspoken words to pay attention to what went on around him. It was easy for anger and shame to be turned to planning. Squire planned, at the man's back. First, the pelts. The fire sizzled as Jeremiah spat.

"I suppose, sar, ye're a pre-emption claimant under the law of filin claim, *caveat emptor qui ignorare non debuit quod jus alienum emit?*" Squire began his attack easily, sure of its result.

"How's that, sar?" Jeremiah wasn't reacting as he should. He showed no dumb surprise at the broadside of fine words, only seemed not to have heard Squire very well. He spat again, his mind out of touch.

If Squire could have seen his face he would have known Jeremiah was seeking Guidance, waiting a little impatiently for the ever-present help. "For a dream cometh through the multitude of business; and a fool's voice is known by the multitude of words." After a good five minutes that was all he could get. What that had to do with trouble and sin he couldn't figure, but he prepared to make the best of it.

The man had mentioned business. Jeremiah straightened and made ready to listen and find out whether he was also a fool— whether that was what the Guidance meant.

"Now what was that, sar?" He came back and sat down at the table, turning a little toward the fire so he could hit it when he had to spit.

"Ye see, 'tis like this. I might be able to be of sarvice to ye, bein back and forth to the county." Squire let the words drop soundly.

"We-uns is over the border. We hain't got nuthin to do with no county." Jeremiah missed the hearth and hit a stone, marbling it with brown stain.

"I think ye misunderstand me, sar," Squire explained. "I'm here to be of assistance. Ye see, I am a lawyer."

"A lawyer. Mighty fine thing to be, a lawyer," Jeremiah told him politely.

"Some of you people here beyond the border seem not to realize what protection they can claim. There are laws to help ye. Ye know, of course, the tomahawk rights, and the pre-emption laws . . ."

Jeremiah was obviously not clear. He looked at Squire, a little baffled. It was the sign Squire was waiting for, that the fish was nibbling.

Squire went on, easily now. "Ye may be across the border, but the border moves, and even beyond it ye have the right of your king's protection. *Qui abjurat regnum amittit regnum, sed non regem,*" he emphasized, rolling the words over Jeremiah's head. *"Patriam, sed non patrem patriae.* He who adjures the realm leaves the realm, but not the king; the country, but not the father of the country," he translated in a kind voice. The man's face had changed completely. He seemed cold with terror, like a caught coon.

"Y'ain't aimin to take me back, are ye?" Jeremiah begged. "Is that thar what ye come for?"

Squire laughed and leaned over to take the man's arm and shake him gently. He seemed too dumb with fear for a minute to talk to. "How would ye ever get such a fool idea, sar," he told him, and then let his hand slip round to pat Jeremiah's back. "I'm talkin about your land claims."

"Oh thim!" Jeremiah threw off his fear and was loud with relief and reassurance. "Lord. *They're* all right."

"Ye mean ye've *filed* your claim?" Squire let the friendly hand fall.

" 'Tain't thataway a-tall." Jeremiah hitched his chair closer, angled his quid into his other cheek, confident. "No, sar. I got no call to worry. Ye see, Gawd led me to this hyar valley. He meant it for me. Not that I deserve it," he explained humbly. "But Gawd seed fitten to watch over me. He give me this hyar green pretty valley. I call it Goshen—the Land o' Goshen. Led to it I was, as efn Gawd done had me a-haltered!" He was getting excited now.

Squire recognized the signs. "Render unto Caesar that which is Caesar's, and unto God that which is God's!" He snuffed the New Light in a loud voice.

It had never failed him on the border. It did not fail him now. Jeremiah sat completely still. He even forgot to spit.

"Now let's get back to your pre-emption claim. Ye have the rights to four hundred acres of land, *usque ad coelum et ad infernos.* That's your tomahawk rights. Over and above that, sar, ye have, if ye so claim, the rights to a thousand more acres—*provided, provided—*" Squire repeated the words, banging his forefinger on the table to drive his words into the dumb clodhopper's brain. "Provided ye show true intention to acquire the title to it, and have complied, or are proceedin to comply, in all good faith, with the requirements of the law to protect that right!"

Jeremiah moved the little Bible out of the way so the stranger wouldn't hit it.

"I hain't aimin for no more nor what the Lord give me," he explained, seeking for some sense in all the words.

"If ye don't—if ye *don't* make such a claim"—Squire was in full flood now, longing to get it over because his back was beginning to ache from the long ride—"No power on earth—I mean this in solemn truth—can protect ye if a land company gains a legal grant to this land. How long do ye think ye are safe? By accident few have yet penetrated this little paradise, but how do ye know that at this very moment some gentleman you have honored with your hospitality is not back there"—he pointed vaguely behind him—"layin *legal claim* to every stick and stone, every tree, every rill ye have on this God-given land? The very water—"

"I dug a well and it stunk turble." Jeremiah spoke from under a heavy load of trouble.

"That very stinking well probably contains some healing balm that will drive thousands of sufferers to your door! Why, rich people will drink that stuff, and pay for it. You can be a rich man. Think of your wife. Think of your children." The word slipped out, put Squire out of stride as he saw the man's eyes flick away from him. "Hell, man," he finished, disgusted. "Don't ye want to make any money?"

"I hain't after nuthin nor what I done got," Jeremiah told the fire.

"Then let me protect at least your own four hundred acres. God gave them to ye, and He expects ye to protect them in man's sight. I'll tell ye what I will do. . . ." And he went on to outline his services.

"But I hain't even got that many beaver pelts!"

"Half, then. It don't matter. I can't sit by and see ye done out of your rights."

"Thankee, sar, but—"

Squire had had enough. "Listen, man. You and the woman up there. Do ye know the law about ye? Both of ye can be returned to the colonies and ye know it. What ye don't know is that those four youngins, by the law, can be made to serve the master she run off from until they are twenty-one years old."

Jeremiah's face had gone sick.

"Are ye married?"

"Oh—yup. We are."

"Who married ye?"

"Why, she done, and I married her." Jeremiah looked amazed. "Gawd brung—"

"Men are harsh." Squire changed and became kind and not accusing. "They call such marriage *damnatus coitus*—unless," he added to make sure, "ye had a marriage at the fort by a preacher?"

"Why no, sar, we hain't niver reckoned on sech a thing. Hannah hain't niver been out'n the valley since she come. We couldn't take our youngins sech a way. I only been myself two-three times. Jest sold my pelts quick and come home with a leetle seed and a mite salt. I's aimin to buy me a hawg with these hyar. My hawg died," he said, crushed by all the trouble the man had flung at him. "We et all her pigs—"

"You need me, sar," Squire finished, seeing by the man's look and hearing by his voice that he had won the pelts. "Now you take your good woman next time ye go to the fort and marry her legal. Then we'll see what can be done about your sarvice. After all, it's been a long time. Unless your masters are told, ye are in no danger—and who's to tell them? But I would advise ye not to confide such a thing to anyone else. After all"—he got out a small leather notebook from his bag—"we can keep a secret. Name?" he asked, poising a pencil above the book.

"Jeremiah Catlett," the man said, exhausted. Then he knew, as Squire wrote the name, knew as if he had shouted it, that he was writing both their names, his and Hannah's; that it was the writing down, in words he couldn't read, that was the danger. A man could forget a thing, could even curb his tongue, but when he wrote it down the secret became black lines, as a crab draws itself across the sand and makes a trail that a man can follow. Jeremiah had never in his life seen his name written down except once, and that was when the sea captain had sold him for a piece of paper to that devil Mr. Oakley. He grew sick with fear.

"Ye can have my pelts," he said so dumbly that Squire could hardly hear him, close as he was. He looked up. The man's eyes were closed, or he was looking at the floor, Squire couldn't tell which. He shut the book and began to pull himself up from the table by his tired arms.

"Would ye do me a favor, sar?" The man looked at him then.

"Would ye read me a few bits of that thar Bible. I cain't git no guidance a-tall."

"Of course, sar."

"Thankee."

" 'Tis nothin," Squire said, conferring the favor, and sat down again.

Jeremiah picked up the Bible, shut his large eyes so tightly that the brows seemed to cover them. He opened the book and plonked down a finger.

"Thar!" he said loudly.

Squire took the Bible up, amused.

" 'I will call on the Lord, who is worthy to be praised; so shall I be saved from mine enemies.' " He could see the man relax with relief as he read the words.

"A beautiful thought, sar." Squire started to stretch, but Jeremiah had clutched for the book again.

"Thar!" he said, stronger now.

" 'Abraham begat Isaac, and Isaac begat Jacob,' " Squire read, bored.

Jeremiah took the book again, a little disappointed. He kept his eyes closed longer this time.

"Thar!" he gasped at last, nearly yelling.

" 'And when the Lord thy God shall deliver them before thee; thou shalt smite them, and utterly destroy them; thou shalt make no covenant with them, nor shew mercy unto them.' "

"Ah-h-h-h!" Jeremiah heaved a great sigh, walked calmly away from Squire, and climbed the ladder out of sight.

"Dammit, what a man has to go through to make a leetle money!" Squire muttered sadly to himself as he stuffed the Bible back into the saddlebag and prepared to go to bed.

He had completely forgotten that the man had first reminded him fearfully of his father—or, indeed, what he looked like at all —but the two of them still worried him, he couldn't tell why. He turned on the pallet and listened. Up above, in the loft, there was movement. He couldn't tell whether it was the noise of bodies moving on the shucks, or whether they were whispering. The sound seemed to go on and on, and once Hannah cried out—or he could hear a child start to whimper. The fire died, and the cold it had kept at bay filtered into the cabin. The whimpering faded after a while, then later the whispering or the turning—whichever it was. It was in the dead hour before dawn that Squire dropped off to needed sleep, overtired as he was.

He was awakened in the early morning by Hannah stirring the dead fire, but she didn't speak to him and seemed hardly to know he was there, she was so withdrawn.

It seemed hours, although the sun was still just above the trees as he walked his horse toward them over the meadow. He looked back for the last time, smiling now, satisfied with business well done. He could see, between the two trees that flanked the cabin, the curious children lined up watching him go. Jeremiah was striding down the creek toward the woods, carrying his long shotgun for a day's hunting.

"Good-by, my dear. Thankee." He couldn't resist rising in his saddle and tipping his hat, calling the words. "Goshen! Stuck between a bastard oak and a poverty elm. Lord!"

The children were too far away to hear, but they saw him tip his hat. The oldest found courage to wave, and the other three waved too.

Squire turned again and went at a walk toward the trail through the woods. After a mile or so he began to notice the brilliant, clear morning, to enjoy the comfortable clatter of the mules behind him as they struck small rocks along the hall-like trail. Only the warm clouds of his own breath, and, when his horse snorted, the twin puffs of vapor, disturbed the bright cold. There was no breeze, so that the few red and yellow leaves that fell settled calmly to the forest floor around him. Squire felt free and full of peace, drawing the dry smell of fall in deep breaths to drive away the fetid memory of the night.

[203]

Jeremiah rose up from a great tree in front of him, and he started to call hello. But his hello stuck in his throat.

To Jeremiah, standing steady, aiming, Squire's mouth seemed to hang open to take the necessary musket ball. He moved the barrel down and squeezed the trigger. The noise made him fling down the gun and catch the mules and the horse while they were still plunging, before they had started to run.

He tethered them and went back to Squire's body, fallen across a huge root. He turned it over. The man's cheek had a leaf sticking to it. Jeremiah reached down and brushed it away, as the fastidious white hand would have done if it had not lain, twisted, under the body. Then, for his impulse came not from hate but from dire necessity, he laid the body out beside the trail with great care, folded its arms in a becoming attitude, closed Squire's eyes with two of the shillings he found in his pocket, cleaned the bubbled blood from his mouth.

Jeremiah dug a pit in the woods and gently lowered the body into it. He saved the crop, the pipe, and the Bible. He could not bring himself to bury such valuable things. But money was stealing. He made himself throw it in the grave. Then he began to look for stones along the trail, to do what the Lord had told him.

"They took Absalom and cast him into a great pit in the wood, and cast a very great heap of stones upon him."

It took until nightfall to find enough stones so that he could say to himself that it was a great enough heap.

Late in the night, when the children had been asleep for a long time and Hannah had finally stopped crying, after she had told Jeremiah all her story and he knew that his preaching had made her repent at last her great sin of fornication, he asked her gently, "Tell me about the valley ye seed."

She watched him, saying nothing.

"We'll go thar come spring. The border's a-gittin too near, Hannah."

" 'Tis a right pretty little valley," she told him at last, remembering. "Thar's a crick, and some pretty good grass, and right smart trees. I only seed hit from across the river . . ." She apologized because she could remember so little. "Hit looked like about five thousand acres of bottomland, layin thar like the palm of your hand."

But she couldn't remember any more, and Jeremiah finally stopped questioning her because he had made her cry again. He told her, to make her feel better, "Look at it thisaway, how the Lord vouchsafed usn a couple of mules and a horse . . ."

Chapter Three

"BE READY in the early spring." That was what Jonathan's letter had told her, but he had told her the same thing before. Ten years now—ten years since Johnny Lacey had gone highhanded to join the Army for a vote and a bounty. A woman could just wilt inside, just give up. Sal read the letter, which had come to Belmont on Christmas, 1764, and looked out of the drawing-room window, where two Negro children were playing on a sandbank. It was already the middle of February. How many times she'd read the letter she wouldn't have admitted—to be caught again, after you'd lost hope (hope like a disease), entirely lost hope, and become calm again if not exactly happy.

"They ain't a one of our family but Polly knows the meanin of the word," Sal said to the empty small room where she was sure Philemon had forgotten to lay a duster for weeks. Then she realized she had spoken aloud, because the two children out the window looked up and grinned automatically at the sound of a human voice. She snapped her mouth tight and, slapping her cheek lightly with the letter while she considered the signs of early spring, she walked with quick, precise, small steps across the bare floor, planning (not hoping—but it didn't hurt to plan) all the way up the outside steps to her room.

There she planned aloud to Montague, who had been sent to the room to read his Latin, but who was really covering the exercise book with his signature: "Montague Lacey, Belmont; Montague Crawford Lacey, Belmont, Princess Ann County; Sir Montague Crawford Bacchus Lacey, Bart., Belmont, Princess Ann County, Crown Colony of Virginia, Great Britain, World; Lord Montague Crawford Bacchus Lacey, House of Burgesses, East India Company, West India. . . ." Then, tired of that dream, he marked his secret name—"Wilcat Lacey, Dismal Swamp." His mother came in, and he shut the book, murmuring aloud the page of his Latin lesson to show her he was studying, so she wouldn't fuss.

"*Usum si spectis Ferrum est pretiosius Auro*—though gold is unquestionably the most perfect of all metals," he read aloud, sing-song.

But Sal had other things on her mind. "Empty—the whole room empty," she interrupted him. "Lord knows what-all your uncle's sold. Let me tell ye, Montague Lacey, if I ever see you go like your Uncle Taylor, drunk as a sow and sellin up one piece of fine furniture after another, I'll tan your hide." Montague paid no attention. Between fussing and Latin, he preferred Latin.

"Mamma give me the English candlesticks afore she died, and Taylor went and sold them. Well, I've got title to Philemon and Baucis. He'll not sell them. And I've got my linen; that's hid, thank God—I'll just up and take what I've need of. There's ways."

She sat down in a rocker and went on planning, quietly now, while Montague turned the pages of the book.

The second letter came in the last week of February.

Sal, my dear, at long last the house is finished and I've settled some good people on my head-right. A family by name of Carver, good hard-working people, have settled. An old soldier from the Braddock wars turned up with his family, his brother and all, a wild fellow called Doggo Cutwright but a good shot, and his women work. When I come back last spring I found squatters already—a New Light preacher and his family calling theirselves Catlett. They have been a thorn in my side since they will not take a lease on the land and will not quit. So I am letting them stay for the time. You cannot persuade "Old Repent," as Jarcey calls him, he needs any sanction less than God Almighty.

I've got to go see Mr. Crawford and will see Montague there. I know there's no use to go on about Montague going to him. You know my mind—but well my dear if it makes you happy. After all he'll get a genteel education with Mr. Crawford and his Aunt Polly to prepare him for a gentleman of quality. But if you change your mind I've told ye there's a scholar on our land who's a gentleman will see he's taught well with the other children. I pray God you don't think of leaving Peregrine and Sara, too.

'Tis better we meet at Fluvanna as I've been able to git no white servants this far west, they being took up if they're worth the room they take, by the time they're got out this far. I tried for Dunkards in Fluvanna but they run into a war party up beyond Walker's Creek.

Solomon McKarkle, who I am sending to see you up-river, is a trustworthy man, though a little rough. He's hired out to me for a passel of land and is worth gold, a jack of all trades better here over the mountains than any master. If I try to come for ye from Hobb's Hole it will take valuable weeks and we must get west to git the first planting in.

Oh my pretty Sal—at long last we will have a home. You needn't to mind the tales you hear of the Indians now, as they're quite put down after Col. Boquet's affair and have a more peaceful attitude toward the settlements. What we have to fear now is the border ruffians stirring them up, but I hope to be able to call on the regular troops at Fort Pitt and down the Ohio a ways. I'm still arguing my claim which I have in fair deed with the Indians which I got from Cornstalk at Fort Pitt in the fall. I hear tell he has run off from there but believe he will keep his word with me as I have fairly bought not squatted. Lord knows the Indians sell cheaper than our own people.

               My bounty claim too, will hold the land until the Proclamation Line is extended. I never look upon that proclamation in any other light than as a temporary expedient to quiet the minds of the Indians. So I've hopes we won't be over the line into the King's part for long. . . .

    Jonathan had written then a list of things to bring, but Sal hardly paid any attention. She went on with her own planning, and for the next few weeks Taylor had as kind and convivial a sister as a man would want whose main ambition was to sit on the front porch and be friendly. He dimly sensed that there was packing going on. Philemon and Baucis moved back and forth like black ghosts. Sal, because she was going so far away, made him toddy whenever he wanted it and hardly fussed at all.

One day Montague was gone, gone with Polly in a chair to Mr. Crawford's. Sal cried and drank a little toddy with him that day. Then a man came, sent by Jonathan, but Taylor only passed a few pleasant words with him on the porch.

One day in March, with the wind whipping the sand and low gray clouds rolling in from the ocean, Taylor woke at noon to find them gone. The front door hung on its hinges, where Baucis, in a last effort to get the harpsichord out, had torn it back to make room. He had given it an extra wrench because Taylor had sold his two children. A piece of a letter scudded across the empty drawing-room floor. Taylor picked it up. It was the last page of Jonathan's list—"5 pounds horseshoe nails, 5 pounds building nails (buy from Norfolk at Mr. Blaines where I have credit) . . ."

He didn't bother to read on, crumbled the page and threw it into

[209]

a corner. He wandered from the drawing room across the wide hall made by his father when the cabin was clapboarded, to the elegant door put across the dog-run. It had been left open. The wind felt along the hall. Outside it grabbed at the field-bell and made it moan.

Taylor stopped in front of the six-foot-high mirror, the only thing left of his mamma's furniture. He examined the gilt, cracked by the salt air, and then went on to study his still handsome face in the mottled glass. His only movement was to pass his hand across his chin lightly.

Finally he went out and sat on the porch in his favorite chair, which, in a moment of softness, Sal had left for him. He said aloud to the beaten sand, "Dear God, I wish I was in heaven."

He was never heard to mention the matter again.

★   ★

Sal rode up to Brandon's Wharf in Polly's second-best hat, a summer leghorn with its ribbons knotted at her thin throat. It had been a restful trip up-river, and she stepped ashore like a queen.

Then she saw Jonathan's face as he looked at the loaded flatboat.

"Taylor gave it to me," she said flatly. "Nobody deserves it more than I do! Oh Lord God," she said suddenly, slapping her cheek, "I forgot the horseshoe nails!"

Moses Kregg was willing to swap the things Sal had forgotten for the harpsichord. In the meantime she sat on Backwater's porch, exchanging gossip and fanning with an Indian plaited fan.

They left Fluvanna to go over the mountains on the fifteenth of March. "The Ides of March," Backwater kept saying, not knowing why he said it but remembering the phrase from somewhere. "You take good care of this pretty leetle gel, Johnny."

Sal did look pretty again, too, that last day. At least from the look of her it was easy to see she had been a delicate beauty. Her slimness had turned to thinness, and the soft line from her ear to the tip of her shoulder was gone. Lightness had grown to nervous quickness. But as every woman who is loved carries the memory of herself, Sal carried her memory for Jonathan as he helped her onto the heavy wagon.

The two young Germans stood patiently beside their small wagon with their little boy beside them and never said a word, even when Jonathan motioned to them that it was time to start. Herr and Frau Mittelburger had said good-by to whomever they had on the other side of the world. They had ridden quietly behind Jonathan all the way to Fluvanna, and it was only when they were taken to see Sanhedron's wife, so that she could interpret some last orders to Herr Mittleburger from Jonathan, that he saw, for a little while, their faces lose their dullness. Frau Mittelburger was huge with a child.

"What brings them here? That's what I want to know," Jonathan asked Elsie Kregg.

"They tell me that a *Pfeifer*—piper—was, you know, at the fair. I seed thim many times, Neulander-Newlanders, with a pipe. *Lieber Gott,* like the Pied Piper from Hamelin! Promises, promises —*lieber Gott,* Mr. Lacey, ye niver have hyeared sech lies! Ever'-thin ye git for nuthin ye give but much shvet, *nicht wahr?"* She turned to Herr Mittelburger, laughing.

"Ja, ja!" Herr Mittelburger agreed happily. He had lost the thread of what they were saying, but everybody was smiling.

They rode March out and into April, slowly up the Fluvanna, past the Peaks of Otter, past Purgatory Mountain, past the Natural Bridge. They stopped at desolate cabins where naked children crawled, as shy as squirrels; went by chimneys standing like monoliths to mark the Shawnee massacres from the French war and from Pontiac's war.

Jonathan offered to rest at Fort Young, at the mouth of Jackson's River, but Sal would stay only an hour.

"Let me tell ye, Jonathan Lacey, I'll stay in the open air until I see my own home, but I'll not truck with a passel of whores," she told him, white-faced, on the captain's stoop, with the captain in hearing distance. She rounded up the two children and sat with them on the wagon, clutching their shirts, straight as a ramrod, never moving, until Jonathan made his apologies to the officer, who'd been his friend for years.

"Johnny lad, efn I'd knowed ye had your lady with ye I'd of cleared my squaw out," Captain Lewis told Jonathan contritely. "Hit would sure been nice to set down with a lady for a change. My squaw belches till I swear to God, Johnny, she can put a man off'n his food." The thought of a nice treat missed made him feel so sad that he almost forgot to answer the question Jonathan was asking when Sal laid eyes on the squaw.

"Oh, I reckon ye're pretty safe now that the treaty's signed, Johnny. 'Tis long past the time of spring for thim to start a-goin on the war path. We been lettin Shawnees and Mingos in here to trade all winter. Cain't do much tradin, though. They're pore as Job's turkey. You aimin to trade?"

Johnny was aiming to trade and, with all the rest of his troubles, didn't want to be depressed about it. "Did anythin happen when they come?" he asked.

"Ain't nuthin happened a-tall. Oh, a leetle thievin. Of course we have to watch these hyar Injun-hatin whites when they all git drunk. 'Tis thim renegades from both herds turns my hair gray. They're nuthin but damned powder-kegs out this fur. Maybe one day the riff-raff from both sides will fight it out atween 'em—with these hyar hell-far preachers in the middle.

"Oh, and listen hyar," he added, not looking at Jonathan. "I wouldn't let on I made no Injun pact about that land if I was you. These hyar people jest reckon to grab and set like the Jews did in the Land of Canaan, and not truck with no Canaanites. Thim damned preachers. Thim all damned hell-far preachers!"

Jonathan had said good-by and was out the door when Captain Lewis called him back.

"Now ye tell your lady, Johnny. Ye tell her us Lewises live

[212]

pretty good out in the Tidewater, will ye? Ye tell her that. We live as fine as anybody."

"I'll tell her," Jonathan said.

"Ye tell her what a sodger's life is like, Johnny. Ye tell her that."

"I'll be sure to tell her, Spotteswood. I'll tell her," Jonathan assured him.

"Little Doe, stop settin thar a-belchin. Git on outa here," Captain Lewis told the squaw when they had gone. "Damn and blast," he told the wall after she had slipped silently away.

★   ★

Frau Mittelburger began her labor at twilight on the fifteenth of April. She was rubbing wood to start a cooking fire when the first twinge grabbed her back. She went on rubbing the fire so she would have Herr Mittelburger's supper ready before the baby came on, but it took so long. Her hands were shaking, and she had not yet mastered the new way of making fire.

A hundred feet away, under the huge hanging rock that made a roof for Jonathan's train, Philemon had made another fire, which was already blazing. Sal sat beside it with Sara asleep across her lap. The little girl's mouth was slightly open, so that she dribbled a drop of spittle from time to time. Sal wiped the child's mouth automatically with a corner of her shawl, then drew it closer around her narrow shoulders, never taking her eyes off of a spot somewhere among the distant, new, green tree tops across the narrows. She pulled the child's head closer as it turned and slipped beyond her lap, held it in the hollow against her stomach and stroked back the dirty tendrils of blond hair, while the child smiled a little in her sleep to feel the hand and closed her mouth. But Sal, the whole time the fire was being built, never moved her tired eyes from the spot they stared at so blindly.

When Jonathan came back with Herr Mittelburger, Solomon McKarkle, and the Negro Baucis, both fires were going, and their

[213]

bright glow lit the deep cliff that stretched, like a long porch, for two hundred feet along the side of Limbo Gap. The stone floor was nearly all black with the stains of other campfires. On the rear wall, where it was not too sooted by smoke, little Peregrine Lacey was tracing with his forefinger along the legs of curious drawings on the stone—of pale men like huge grasshoppers, with deer heads, stalking skeletal deer. High above the boy's head, partly obliterating the dimmer drawings, were several bold strokes of red, and Jonathan lifted the child up so he could see them better.

"Eight Indians," Jonathan told him, pointing to the spidery drawings, "of the Shawnee Nation—ye see the long scalplock? They passed here on the warpath. See the red? They scalped two Virginians, for lookee at the long knives, and a Quaker with his round hat."

"Why did they write them pictures?" the child wanted to know.

"To tell the others they camped here and they were great fellows," Jonathan told him.

"When did they do that?"

"Oh, last year, in Pontiac's war," Jonathan told him, and changed the subject. "Ye know how to carve a heart on a tree, with your name and a gel's name, to tell the world."

"I don't."

"Ye will, son."

All the time the other child stood staring up at Jonathan while he talked. But he couldn't understand. He spoke little English, and that had been taught him in the six weeks' journey up the James and over the mountains, by Jonathan's son.

"*Ich kann* rattlesnake *sagen, und* damn my blood," he told his father.

"Johnny!" From the sound of Sal's voice, she had called more than once. But when Jonathan went up to the fire, carrying Peregrine, she had not turned round. She still stared out at the opposite hill. He stooped and set the boy down beside her.

[214]

"Johnny." She almost whispered the word again, her voice as thin as her face, fine and far-away like the whine of a breeze, although he was so close beside her. "I know ye're agin the two fires, but we got to learn them their place. 'Tis important to keep decorum, especially now." She had told him this so often, right from the beginning, that he knew she only said it because she was so tired.

"Sal, darlin, ye climb into the wagon and sleep with the young-ins tonight. Ye're wore out." He put his hand to her shoulder, but she never moved. "Sal," he said sharply, shaking her shoulder. She began to sob as if he had pushed her over the threshold into crying. The little girl stirred in her lap.

Jonathan lifted Sal's face up toward him and seemed to study it carefully while he brushed the tears away. "Ye'll be fine by the mornin, my dear. There's no harm in cryin." And he went on brushing the tears softly as they grew too big for her eyes and swelled over onto her lined face.

"Is it much farther, Johnny?" she asked, like a child herself.

"No, not much farther. A few days."

"How many days?"

"Just a few."

"Is there truly a house?"

"There's a fine house," he told her, as if he were chanting a litany of promise, wiping away a tear. "A house with—"

He looked at her mouth, and she said, "Four rooms . . ."

"And?" He wiped another tear.

"Two chimbleys."

"And?"

"A dog-run."

"And?"

"A stoop for settin on." Now she was smiling again. "I won't fret no more."

*   *

The fires had brightened and turned the twilight out beyond the rock porch dark; the cats' eyes gleamed. The evening wind died behind the skins McKarkle and Herr Mittelburger had stretched as screens between the fires and the night, so that the porch seemed more like a room than ever. Philemon had fed Jonathan and Sal and the children, and now the children were asleep in the front wagon. Sal was nearly asleep herself, on Jonathan's shoulder. Out beyond and below they could hear, faintly, the sound of bells where their hobbled mules and their two horses still fed. Solomon had brought the precious sow in and heaved her into his cart.

"What have ye done with the boar?" Jonathan called to him softly.

"I've tied that black fiend in a holler tree, may the Lord sind his soul to hell, Johnny," Solomon whispered. He wandered off and threw himself down by the other fire.

One scream reverberated and died down.

Herr Mittelburger jumped up from the far fire and ran over to the little wagon that stood nearest it. Sal jumped up to her feet before Jonathan could move.

"Philemon, come here," she called urgently into the shadows where the two Negroes had taken their food.

Mrs. Mittleburger screamed again.

"Oh dear God, she makes a noise," Sal fussed, worried.

"Anyone would think 'twas a painter," Jonathan said reassuringly.

"She'll have it easy. That class always do." Sal sighed because she was so tired and still had work to do.

Two hours later the child still had not come.

"She set on a rock. I told her not to set on a rock!" Philemon fumed.

The men had moved Frau Mittelburger out of the wagon and laid her close to the fire she'd built, so that Philemon could sit behind her, holding her up on her side, to push her back when the pains came. Between spasms Frau Mittelburger lay still against

Philemon's chest and stared, round-eyed, first at Sal's face and then, turning, at the Negress, as if they could do something about the pain but would not. Philemon pulled a rag from the woman's clenched teeth from time to time and dipped it in whisky for her to suck. It was all they could do between the spasms.

After four hours Sal caught Philemon looking sternly toward poor Herr Mittelburger, who sat huddled by the other fire.

"Oh Philemon, stop that." She had to giggle.

"He's been with another woman," Philemon said. "I know! Make this pore hard labor!"

"Dear God, Philemon, ye don't believe that."

"I say no more," Philemon announced over Frau Mittelburger's drooping head.

Toward the middle of the night the water broke and soaked the skins Frau Mittelburger lay on; her shoulder heaved up against Philemon's breast.

"Grüss Gott," she muttered and kept on turning her head back and forth. Across a gulf of silence the women watched each other. Sal could massage the top of Frau Mittelburger's belly but could say nothing because she did not speak her language.

"Change places with me, Miss Sal. I got to look." Philemon delivered her burden.

Philemon looked up from her inspection of the birthplace. "Hit's stayin wide." She grinned. "I can see hit's lil head."

"Come back here and push," Sal said, annoyed that the woman was so heavy against her. Her too close face was glossy with sweat and pain. "Quick, Philemon!" A spasm shook the whole woman and frightened Sal.

"Oh Lord." Philemon took Frau Mittelburger and sat rubbing her back as the labor grew. "Push her bottom, Miss Sal. Push her bottom," she yelled. Sal flung herself forward on her knees and pushed her weight against the back of the woman's heaving birthplace. "Hyar it come! Hyar come another damned lil outlander," the Negress crooned. She laid the woman gently down on the skins when the placenta had followed. Only then did she let herself inspect the baby Sal held. "Aw now, Miss Sally, 'tis a little gal." She nearly sang, as if it were the first baby she had ever seen.

Sal washed the baby while Philemon cut the cord and threw the afterbirth aside.

"Put it in the fire," Sal fussed.

"No mawm, I dassn't. I dassn't do that," Philemon said, frightened.

By Frau Mittelburger's head, her husband knelt and whispered to her. *"Wir haben ein kleines Mädchen."* He felt her forehead. *"Dir ist so kalt,"* he said to Sal.

"Oh don't jabber at me." Sal stood up and stretched her tired back. "Philemon, you stay and clean up. I'm goin to bed."

"Sweetheart." Jonathan wanted to put his arms around her and help her into the wagon, but she pushed him aside.

"Oh Lord, don't fuss me," she said, and lay down beside the children to draw their warmth as she slept.

The dawn in the mountains was cold, and a cloud of mist had settled in the gap. Jonathan's little train moved inch by inch down the narrow trail. Through the mist Sal could see dimly the figures in the front cart, could see that Frau Mittelburger sat straight with the new baby huddled in one arm, while she held on with the other against the jolting. There were only the sounds of an animal sighing, the cart chains clanking from time to time, and Solomon behind them, trying to drive the pigs with grunted, bad-tempered ho-hos as their bells sounded dully in the morning air. Baucis led the little cart, and Philemon sat in it with two chickens in rough cages. One began to gurgle and cackle a little, so she slapped the cage and raised a squawk. Then the hen went quiet, and Sal knew that Philemon would drop to sleep and sleep through the long morning as they wound up and down along the mountains, hardly minding where she was because she could do nothing about it.

Down below Sal, Jonathan drove the horses carefully, leaning against the wagon like a beast himself when the grade was too steep.

"Ye'll break your fool back," she fumed.

"No I won't, sweetheart. Anyway, Jenny there still ain't used to a wagon harness. I don't want to scare her. She might break a leg."

They began to roll out of the mist through level woods as the sun rose high. Suddenly in the clearing air, after so many days in the birdless wilderness, they heard a pure phrase of song. It was so pretty—then high in the trees some domestic quarrel made the bird change its tune to a shrill scream.

"That thar sounds jest like Miss Sal. One minute pretty, the next minute, fuss, fuss." Philemon, who had waked up in the sun and was enjoying her ride, whispered to Baucis. He grinned but didn't say a word.

"Mammy, you got peepee eyes, like a bird." Sara climbed over the tops of the boxes and bedding to her mother.

"Don't have time for any other kind. Set down and stop a-wigglin; don't say 'mammy,' say 'ma,'" Sal told her, too preoccupied to pay attention to what she said.

Jonathan came back and climbed up to drive from the wagon and rest himself. He set his gun handy between them and settled back to enjoy a few easy miles.

"Did ye hear the songbird, Sal? When ye hear that ye know there's humans built a farm somewheres. When ye see the honeybee and the wildflowers and the songbirds, ye know humans have come hereabouts and cleared the land for them."

"Ye mean Indians."

"No, I mean farmers of one kind or another. Indians reckon just to hunt this land."

They had come to a place in the road where the ground was churned to mud, left from the rains.

"There've been deer this way," Jonathan said. "Ye see them

[219]

stones." He pointed off the road to where stones were piled high in a great heap. " 'Tis the way the Indians bury their dead. I found an English shillin by that grave last year."

"Ye told me that." Sal bit, then said what had been on her mind all morning. "Sweetheart, for love I still don't see why ye didn't buy two more Negrews instead of these hyar whites."

"I've told you that, Sal, over and over. They cost too much. Even new Negrews was fetchin sixty pound at Hobb's Hole when I went up there. The outlanders cost four pounds apiece."

"But ye have Negrews for life. 'Tis valuable property. Could ye a-borrowed a leetle more from Mr. Crawford?"

Jonathan was quiet for a long time, but he knew Sally was rankling beside him, and that no matter how many times he explained, he'd have to go through the whole thing again for the sake of peace.

" 'Tis thisaway. We can't bring new Negrews this far out. They're not a bit of use. The Germans there are used to hard work. Even if we do only have them for four years, they make pretty good settlers."

"Ye're too soft with them, Johnny; 'tis your trouble all along—buyin a pregnant woman, lettin them bring their youngin."

"Put yourself in their place, Sal. How would ye like to be sold to work out your ship's passage away from your youngins?"

"There'd be no question of such a thing. No question at all. Remember who we are, Johnny Lacey."

There was no more to say. "Remember who we are, Johnny Lacey," was in the air, died down, and there was only the rattle of the wagon.

Jonathan thought it was over, but after another mile Sal said, "McKarkle drinks."

"Ye'd drink too, my dear, if ye had a wife like Solomon McKarkle's," Jonathan murmured, and was sorry the minute he'd said it.

[220]

But Solomon's habits had set Sal's mind off in another direction. She didn't hear. "Oh Lordy, I wish rum wasn't so dear. We'll have to use some of this seed corn to still some whisky."

"We can do that out of this year's crop, Sal."

" 'Tis medicine for the youngins. I won't have them go without medicine."

Jonathan jumped down from the wagon and threw the reins back to Sal. "I've got to go lead Herr Mittelburger for a while. Can ye manage, my dear, or shall I get Solomon?"

"I can manage." She took the reins.

"Lord have mercy, ye needn't to be mad at me," Sal muttered to herself. "I was only a-plannin. If ye just knowed how much plannin I have to do. Peregrine Lacey, come out of them woods. Them rocks are full of rattlesnakes," she yelled.

Peregrine wandered back beside the wagon.

"Jest like a bird, jest like a lil old mammy bird," Philemon told the caged hen. It clucked a little, then settled down.

Jonathan walked far ahead down the path to find the left trace that led away from the valley. He had passed that way the year before, in the fall of 1764, when he came back from the new settlement to gather his train and bring Sal out. It was where the Germans he'd persuaded to come out from Fluvanna had camped so they could use the deserted cabin; but they had been attacked there—the old man struck down a little apart from the others, as if he had gone out to talk in friendly signs with the Indian war party, not knowing that Pontiac had risen in the mist and set a trail of terrible fires. Now their bones lay bleached in the sun beside the creek; their hogs, gone wild, had eaten their flesh, and the remains of their wagons lay like some ancient animals' skeletons around them. Beyond them he had found the remains of a worm fence, the savannah grass grown almost over it, and the lonely, blackened chimney from a burned cabin. Its worn hearth with the fossil bones in it was no longer white but covered with

[221]

dirt and leaves. The beautiful valley was more desolate because human beings had lived there and gone away, and there were only the empty chimney and the white bones.

It was nothing for the scared outlanders or a wife and children to see, the dead valley Jeremiah Catlett had called Goshen, but which was now called Dunkard's Valley, because the bones were the bones of Dunkards.

After Dunkard's Valley there were no more names—only the wide buffalo traces, graded by flailing hooves; here and there a tree blazed with red streaks. They had passed beyond the world of words into the green heaven or hell of the keen senses and the watchful, warring eyes.

"How waste everything looks when ye can't fix a name to it," Sal mourned. They had stopped the wagons at a mountaintop, and, squinting through the blinding yellow evening sun, she could see the mountains stretching on and on endlessly.

"Only another few days," Jonathan said, watching her. He clucked at the horses, and the train wound slowly down to the lower plateau. "Sweetheart," he went on, "I've been thinkin of Peregrine and Sara. Out this far, they've got to know—" He tried again. "The children out here—"

"What have they got to know?"

"How to keep quiet, for all our sakes."

"I don't know what ye're talkin about, Johnny. Lord-a-mercy, feel this rain—we'll all get an ague, I know we'll get an ague, and then what will we do, sick way out here? Sara, keep your head under that skin like I told ye."

She had completely stopped listening.

An hour later the trace was too bogged for any of them to ride. Deer, passing along the track, had churned it deep in running mud. Sal and Frau Mittelburger waded through it, goading the cows. They thrashed knee deep, the heifer bellowing from time to time as Sal switched her. Ahead the men drove and pulled the horses through, heaving stones under the wagon wheels when they stuck deep in the mud. Jonathan pushed against the lead mule of his team, forcing it, talking it forward, the rain pouring over his face until he was blinded and had to pass his fist over his eyes to see again. That was why he couldn't see the back wheel skid over the side of the path until he felt the strain through the animal's muscles and fell back to see the wagon leaning crazily over the steep grade of the running mountainside, its cover half off, blown away from the struts. Sal was calling through the rain, but he couldn't hear what she was saying. He yelled for Solomon, who was driving the horses ahead of him—yelled and yelled, holding the heavy wagonside with his back until Solomon heard him and came splashing back, sending mud up to his sopping face and swearing to God Almighty for having made hell wet instead of hot.

The barrel had got loose and fallen out of the wagon before Jonathan left the mule-team, at the first deep lurch of the skidding wheel. He didn't know it until the wagon was righted and the train driven another hundred yards to where the rocky surface could hold the wheels. There they stopped, sweat- and rain-soaked, to rest. The children looked like mud images, their eyes white against their black masks. Philemon was trying to wipe their faces while they squirmed away, fighting, liking the rain. The heifer and the bullock stood, shivering and forlorn, with Frau Mittelburger crooning to them. Solomon was taking out the love-hate he felt for the valuable swine by cursing their caked bodies, driving them up under the trees to peel off some of the slowing mud from their short legs. Suddenly, in all the movement of preparing to go on, Jonathan missed Sal.

He started to run back through the mudhole, splashing mud high, lunging slowly through the morass, which sucked at his legs, holding him, the fear that had haunted him about Sal in the last days growing and bursting.

Where the wagon had tipped over there was a broad gap of mud left running down into the trees. The rain was still so heavy that he could see nothing for a second of stopping. Then he heard a small moaning cry, over and over, down the rain-soaked mountain. He crashed, without waiting to see her, down toward the thicket at the ravine bottom.

Jonathan found Sal fifty feet down the ravine, standing as still as stone, hugging something to her breast, her head bent over it, crying and crying. For one wild second Jonathan thought it was Frau Mittelburger's baby, but he saw that it was not, that whatever it was was small, clutched in her hands.

"Oh Sal, my dear Sal." The big man enveloped her, rain, mud, and all, stood holding her tight to his chest, feeling her small, wet body shake in his arms. She was covered with mud from her slide down the hill; her dress and the useless cloak she had insisted, like a child, on wearing instead of a hide cape clung to her body as close as flesh; her calash was gone, and her hair streamed down, plastered to her face and back. As if it were silk and not wet hair smelling of woodsmoke, sweat, and rain, Jonathan stroked it, kissed it over and over, and let her cry against him.

"Oh Johnny, my Johnny, 'tis all my plates. Dear God, my blue and white Cheeny plates, all sent from England. Oh Johnny, they're all gone, all broke to pieces. I hate it, Johnny. I hate this dead place. I hate these hyar trees that never wanted us. Johnny, please God, let me go home!" She lifted her face, muddy from his chest, and wailed, "Why have ye brung me hyar? Why have ye done this to me? Please, please, let me go home!"

"Now, darlin, now, sweet Sal. I'm takin ye home. And I'll buy ye more plates, the finest plates y'ever seen. I promise ye. Oh my lovely gel." He drew her face down again and leaned his head on hers. "I'll make it up to ye—oh my God, I swear I'll make all this up to ye. I'll make it up to ye, honey," he told her again, rubbing his face against her hair, not knowing that his own tears were hotter than the rain that still fell on her head.

All the way down the mountain through the heavy spring storm, and into the narrow valley that was more like a gorge beside the roaring river he had waited so long to see, she still clutched the one plate she had rescued from the broken barrel, and would not let it go, even to hold on to the side when the wagon pitched dangerously on the watersoaked trail. Up in the woods behind them, the barrel lay staved where it had crashed against a tree and exploded, scattering the broken china. Here a ladle handle, there a triangle of blue and white, lay consigned to the soft soaked ground, the runnels of water burying them slowly.

The rain stopped in the early afternoon, and they rested on a tiny grass plot by a creek that ran into the river. Sal had not noticed the river yet. She was still too intent on her plate, on the filth she was trying to switch from her clothes. The grass was already warm again from the spring sun, and the trees were green-gold, dropping water gently, as the train wound, cleaner, dryer, slowly beside the river. Jonathan, did not dare to tell Sal that, from the big bend where they stopped and looked on, every tree and every stone, every fallen trunk, was as familiar to him as the crook of her arm, the way her hair swirled against her neck; that from where they stopped and watched the great curve he could see the slight indent that was their own creek, far ahead down the glittering river, reflecting the sun. It was his moment of great triumph, but for some reason he could not tell her but could only watch her, hope as warm in him again as the sun was warm on his face, while she sat immobile, clutching the plate.

The sun made the Mittelburgers ahead begin to chatter to each other, as if they felt a new excitement in the air. Behind them Philemon and Baucis caught the moment and were laughing, hollering at the animals, the children helping them while they hindered, scaring the heifer up off the path from time to time. Solomon, passing the wagon, reached up and patted Jonathan's leg.

"We pretty near done it, hain't we, my Johnny?" he bellowed, not realizing Jonathan had said nothing to Sal. "Come on, honey." He poked the sow in her huge rump with his goad and made her squeal shrilly. "You and me's goin to take a drink pretty soon. A great big drink of bombo!"

"Honey, honey, honey," Sal said after him. "Why the Scotch have to call ever'thin honey, even a pig! And you by your Christian name! Lord, Johnny Lacey, what next indeed?" But her voice was light. Even she, after the sorrow of so many days, seemed to have caught the excitement.

But Jonathan had called her "honey" in the rainy wood. "I'll make it up to ye, honey," he had said.

"Men," Sal announced to the great river, "pick up every leetle thing." She leaned her head against Jonathan's arm. "Ain't it beautiful, Johnny?" The sun made her happy, that and being at last out of the mountains, and she enjoyed saying his name. "Ain't it a pity all that water don't flow eastward?"

"I've got hopes about that, my dear," Jonathan told her, meaning the tract of land he'd claimed at Carpenter's Creek, dreaming all the time of a canal—one day.

"Lord, the man's goin to turn the river around. Ye sound like a politician promisin to put the fall-line up-river!" She laughed aloud. Philemon was so surprised to hear her that she stumbled against the heifer and made it scuttle toward the woods again.

"How would ye like if I was to be a backwoods politician?" Jonathan caught the pleasure and teased her.

"Now it's a county! Will wonders never cease?"

"You wait, my gel. You wait. It won't be long before it's a county."

"Lacey County. My Lord!" Sal smoothed the glaze of the plate, feeling it satiny under her fingers.

"Ye just wait."

Jonathan jumped down and threw her the reins, without remembering that her hands were full, he had suddenly grown so excited. He ran ahead to motion the Mittelburgers' wagon to stop.

"What is it? What's happened?" Sal was worried as he ran back. "Have ye gone plumb crazy, Johnny Lacey?"

Without a word, Jonathan reached up and lifted her from the

[226]

wagon. "Baucis, come hold these mules," he called over her head.

"What are ye doin?" She knew it was something nice, not an accident, as he walked her up the path where it crossed over a spur of the low hill.

At the top of it they stopped, silent, just stood there.

Sara came running up after them. "Mammy, Mammy! Ma!" she called out.

"Oh look, child, oh just you look." Sal was crying so that the valley ahead swam like a vision before her eyes.

Whatever she said later, whatever she did, Jonathan swore to himself, watching her, that he would remember her like this, when she first set eyes on the valley, looking as a girl looks at her lover, with the sun glinting in her hair and her face transfixed and covered with tears.

"Didn't I tell ye, didn't I always tell ye?" He touched her face.

But habit is stronger than passion, and Sal answered without knowing what she said. "It needs a mighty lot o' doin to it"— and softened that by adding, "Oh, but 'tis pretty. Lord, what a pretty piece of property!"

The valley lay west of them; where they stood in the trees they saw down the broadening track to the creek. Except for cleared fields where at this time of year the black loam showed rich and damp, the savannah grass was already knee-high, blue in the evening light, a blue-green lake that the up-river breeze ruffled a little so that it seemed to breathe. On the other side of the valley, on a little knoll scarcely seeming to rise from the rest, a long loghouse stood. Even from across the valley Sal thought she could see the dog-run like a dark shadow at the middle. Beside it a worm fence meandered in a huge, lazy square around black earth. Sal could watch nothing else. She never looked to either side, as Jonathan did, studying the effects of winter on the desolate, girdled trees to the left of the knoll they stood on. He saw that the spring sap and the rain lay in deep pools around them, and that they had not leafed. Through the dead grove the yet

[227]

unseasoned upright logs of the stockade cast a long jagged shadow toward him. It was all right. He looked down at the wide river, but could not judge from there how high the spring rise had brought it up its banks. Down ahead, at the ford, the water of the creek was swollen. There was not a movement in the valley, human or animal. It seemed not deserted—it was too rich—but suspended in the evening, asleep in the long shadows of the farther conical green hills, the grass breathing, waiting.

Back in the lead wagon, Frau Mittelburger sat nearly asleep, suckling her baby. She only looked up for a minute as Jonathan and Sal walked back toward her, and smiled because it was so peaceful to be sitting after all the movement, letting the baby comfort her by taking the weight of her milk.

Solomon McKarkle had let his slow grin spread across his face, but all he said as he passed and Jonathan helped Sal up into the wagon was, "Eh Johnny, eh Johnny?"—wisely, nodding his head.

The wagon train rattled down toward the ford, on the left the girdled dead trees by the fort, on the right a rich grove of huge beeches dwarfing a one-room cabin that seemed to shrink into the ground below them.

"That thar's mine, eh. That thar!" Solomon touched the side of the wagon to draw Sal's attention, to show her, but she was still watching the big cabin ahead, never taking her eyes off it.

The train came out of the trees near the ford and rolled noisily across the creek, spuming the water high into the air. Sara, watching the pretty fans of water, pulled at Philemon and whined, "I'm thirsty."

The splashing waked the valley. Jonathan heard, over the noise of the wheels, someone call his name—wildly calling, "Johnny, Johnny!" Sal did not hear. From the nearer ford the loghouse seemed smaller. She squinted, judging it.

Jonathan had turned in the seat to see a slight figure, far down creek near the river, running half in the water, half on the bank, running and waving. Behind him in the square between the stockade and the creek, made by the creek mouth flowing into the river, Jonathan could make out several bent figures working in a huge cleared field.

"Lookee, Sal." He touched her arm. "Lookee here. 'Tis Jarcey Pentacost I told ye of. There's all the rest, sweetheart, workin the stockade field."

"Oh Lord, I do look a sight for meetin a gentleman!" Sal smoothed her hair a little and straightened her sun-dried wrinkled cape.

"He won't mind what ye wear, my love. He'll be too glad to see us."

"Well, *I* mind," she told him and pulled again at her cape. "Oh Lord, ain't it a sight? I am a fool gel!"

"I'm a-gonna drive the critturs up yonder, Johnny," Solomon called over his shoulder. "Come hyar, Baucis, ye drive thim beeves!"

Sal watched the figure run lightly nearer. She could see his small head, his shoulder-length brown hair winged back from his face as he ran, splashing the water. He had reached the ford, and, screwing herself about, she saw him race through it, sending water shoulder high.

"Lord God Almighty, Johnny, he's plumb naked!"

Jarcey was not naked. He had stripped his buckskin shirt for the hot work in the field. He wore a breechclout, Indian fashion, buckskin leggings and moccasins. The early spring sun had already browned him so that he looked weathered, his eyes white against his brown face. "Why, he's no more than a wild Indian," she said, too low for Jonathan to hear, and closed her mouth tight so that lines ran down from its corners.

Jonathan had leaped out of the wagon and was running to meet Jarcey. The two men met, hugging and slapping each other's backs. To Sal, watching, they seemed to be dancing around the wide buffalo road like two madmen buoyed up on a sea of undulating grass.

[229]

"Cincinnatus! By God, Cincinnatus!" Jonathan yelled.

"If it ain't the rattlesnake himself, well, by God! Let me see ye!" Jarcey stood back.

But when they looked at each other neither could find anything to say.

"Come see my lady." Jonathan took Jarcey's arm. They were both wet from the embrace.

"Oh Johnny, I ain't fitten to see a lady. Lordee, I forgot my shirt."

But they were too near the wagon for Jarcey to run away. He had gone so shy and quiet that his clothes sat strangely on him; he seemed to cross a mysterious line as he got to the wagon; before he had been like a wild boy, now a gentleman and a scholar came to the side of the wagon and bowed.

"Howdee, mawm. Ye're mighty welcome," were his first words to Sal.

"Howdee, sar." Sal bowed her head a little timidly, as she knew became her, as if she had just crossed the room instead of the Endless Mountains.

"I must apologize for my dress, mawm. 'Tis easier to work like this."

There was a dead silence.

Solomon could be heard then, shouting across the savannah. "Oh Johnny, come up hyar. Thim damned animals done broke your fencin. I've tethered the beeves, but I'll swear to God I don't know what I'm goin to do with these hyar damned hawgs!"

"Mrs. Lacey." Jonathan reached up to lift her down from the wagon. "May I see ye home?"

"Oh Lord, Johnny Lacey, listen to ye!" She clung to his arm, and they walked up the slight rise, across the meadow to the new cabin.

"Ye'd best drive the wagons up when they ain't so loaded, Johnny," Jarcey called, following. "This here land is spongy with the rains. Damn near a third of the stockade field is still under

[230]

creek-water. 'Twill be off from there in a few days, I reckon."
He seemed not to want to leave them, lingered behind, but
followed on. Solomon had stopped in the grass, and now he too
waited for them to pass. Philemon and the children had gone
ahead to the cabin, and Sal could hear them already in the house,
Sara's voice calling high above, "Come up here. Lookee what I
found."

Jarcey and Solomon walked close to each other as she got
nearer the house. She seemed to move faster than Jonathan, so
that by the time she reached the porch and had put a foot on the
step he too was following in the nervous, silent train of men. She
seemed to have forgotten they existed. She walked, trancelike,
across the lean-to porch and into the deep shade of the ten-foot-
wide dog-run, in which they could see her pause lightly, framed
by the flowering wild cherry tree which could be seen, through
the wide corridor, growing at the back of the cabin. She opened
the door to the right-hand room so slowly—they watched her
thin hand touch it lightly, heard the squeak of green wood that
seemed to go on and on echoing in the empty room as she pushed
the door wider. Then she disappeared, and the dog-run was
empty, a wide-open hall with only the flowering tree filling the
back opening now that Sal was gone.

Nothing happened. Two minutes passed, and still she did not
come back.

"I'll go and make myself more presentable," Jarcey murmured,
and almost ran away.

Solomon went on staring at the dog-run, watched Jonathan as
he bounded up the stairs and in the open door.

"Well, I'll be damned for a cockeyed son of a bitch," Solomon
said sadly to himself. "I always knowed we oughtn't to a brung
no women." He sat down, dejected, on the porch-side, waiting
for somebody to help him unload the wagons. Down the slope he
could see the Mittelburgers huddled beside the train, Herr Mittelburger holding his son up so he could see around him. Jarcey,

going off down the meadow, kept looking back, as if he thought something were going to burst behind him. Everybody seemed poised, but no one could have said why they waited.

Inside the nearly empty room Sal stood, her hand against her cheek, looking from one side of the big square space to the other, and back again, then back, sweeping the room with her eyes. She seemed to be pawing the floor with one foot, rubbing it without even looking down or knowing she did it.

"Sal?" Jonathan's voice broke gently into the silence.

Her hand moved slowly from her cheek across her eyes, and Sal burst into tears.

"Green, green. 'Tis all green—all green like something growed and not built at all," was all he could get her to say, her mouth square under her hand-blinded eyes. "I never knowed before how poor we was!"

Above her head the children had found the other loft and were bumping, shaking the roof, making the lichen of winter fall in pieces to the raw wood floor.

In her moment of despair and of coming face to face with some vision of herself as she was going to be across the mountains, in the empty room, Sal neither heard the children nor realized Jonathan was watching her, his face gone blank as an Indian's. She was completely alone in a limbo of poverty, her foot still, of its own accord, testing the rough floor that would never, never be smooth.

Jonathan saw, as if a sun glare had picked Sal out—saw for the first time, beyond rage, almost beyond caring, how set her head was, how thin her weak neck, how the tendons of it were stretching separately like a bundle of sticks and not like the slim, smooth column he had always remembered. Her face had gone red from the little burst of tears. Now she wiped her eyes and pulled her cape back from her shoulders.

"Anyhow, when it seasons a leetle 'twill be a mighty sight prettier than Mr. Brandon's." She had gone out of the room as quickly as ever, before Jonathan had even finished studying her. There had been no sun in the room. It didn't even have a window yet. Now, with her gone, it was cool and dim, an under-water room, peaceful as he had remembered it during his long trip. He went over and leaned against the stone fireplace, stared down at the ashes, where someone—Jarcey, he supposed—had kept a fire in from time to time to help to season the room. He stood for a minute, the whole fatigue of the day gathered on his bent back, then, hearing Sal calling the others, straightened and walked as surely as ever out to the porch, where Solomon and Herr Mittelburger were carrying the household up from the wagons.

Neither Sal—least of all she—nor anyone else knew that Jonathan Lacey had left something finished in the silent room. He stepped across the grass, passing her without noticing her at all, down to the forgotten German woman, who still waited, placid in the warm evening sun, to be told which of the few scattered cabins was to be her new home.

Sal called to him as he got down near the train. "Johnny—oh Johnny, do tell the Dutch woman to come help me red up!" But when he seemed not to hear she shrugged her shoulders, forgot him, and went on flapping quilts out to dry over the grass.

It was not until an hour later that Sal knew what it was to be rich.

The two bedsteads were set up in the left-hand room, and a fire was already piled high in its chimney. Sal stood frowning at them.

"I reckon they'll have to do for now," she said to Philemon, "but tomorrow mornin they go to the upstairs bedrooms."

"You goin to take the loft over this, Miss Sal, or tother one?"

"I don't mean any loft. I mean the upstairs bedroom. I don't care how 'tis done. I want them beds up there. Philemon, go get the quilts. Oh, I wish Taylor hadn't sold the good bedstead. Little old homemade things . . ."

"Lord-a-mercy, Miss Sal, lookee thar," Philemon stopped at the door and stared out across the grass. Around one of the spread-out quilts the women and children had settled like great birds, the children naked, the women stripped to the waist from their work in the field. None of them said a word, but from time to time one would pass a worn square hand out over the silk that had come from Polly's petticoat, or the piece of scarlet that had been Sal's father's sash. Here a finger pointed to a bright bit of satin—a cap ribbon from the time Sal went to Alexandria for the first time with Jonathan, a large piece of embroidered dark silk from Taylor's birthday suit when he'd gotten into a brawl on the way home from Norfolk and torn the coat so there was nothing else to do with it.

Sal saw the heavy fingers moving over the scraps of her whole life, laid out like a map for anyone to read, and she ran across the grass and snatched the quilt up into her arms.

"Get away!" she called, as she would have at birds. "Don't ye touch my only fine quilt with your dirty fingers! Philemon, come get the rest of the quilts. They'll trample all over them. Philemon!"

"I'm comin, Miss Sal."

Jonathan was strolling back to the house from the little one-roomed cabin across the spring branch where he'd been showing Herr and Frau Mittelburger their new home. Just the feel of his feet on his own land gave him peace beyond the bird-calls of women, and Moll, his bitch that Jarcey had been keeping for him, was walking to heel.

As he came around the corner of the house he heard Sal's words. The women were getting up; the children had scattered like frightened animals. Sal stood glaring in the astonished circle, rolling the big quilt over and over in her arms.

Jonathan came quietly up behind her and grasped her arm so tightly that she could feel his four fingers digging, pressing at her skin.

"Mistress Lacey is mighty tired from her long journey, ladies.

Ye'll have to forgive her." The pressure of his fingers hurt Sal so that she wanted to call out, twist away; but something in Jonathan's voice that she had never heard before—that and his anger, covered by gallantry, which she could feel strong because he stood so close—kept her quiet.

"Good evenin, Mother Carver." He bowed low. "Ye're in the field early. How's that rheumatism?"

The oldest woman's face broke into a toothless smile. "Lord, Mr. Lacey, hit's turble. Hit's plumb turble. Mag and Carver done got the cabin fever last winter, and they's laid up a-hoopin and a-hollerin. Y'aint never hyeared nuthin like hit. Sick as I was, I's on my feet morn and night. Wasn't I, Maggie? Wasn't I? I reckon a leetle hoein, hit hain't nary a hate to that!"

"Och, Mother, how ye go on!" Maggie, a big rawboned woman with red hair, grinned at Jonathan. "Hyear her tell we's damn near dead."

"Ye was, Maggie Carver. You's the sickest woman in Beulah!"

"Mrs. Cutwright, how's Doggo?" Jonathan turned to a black-headed woman, thin as kindling wood, who stood a little back from the others.

"Drunk," she told him, folding her arms across her bared chest and offering no more information.

"Why, Mary Martha, I didn't see ye there a-hidin. Did ye pass a pleasant winter? I'll swear ye're prettier than ever."

Mary Martha, who had once been O'Keefe and now was Mrs. Pentacost, laughed with her head back and her mouth wide open. "We had company, Mr. Lacey," she said, and stopped laughing suddenly. She stood quite still, watching the other women defiantly.

At the word "company" almost all the women turned and glanced at Mary Martha. Mother Carver's mouth folded into her gums. But Doggo's wife ignored them; she still surveyed Sal as if this were some new kind of animal she couldn't name but wasn't going to admit she'd never seen.

Under the fine quilt, hidden from the rest, Jonathan's knuckles were white from his tight hold on Sal's arm.

"What company, Mother Carver?" he asked quietly, but his voice seemed loud among the watchful women.

Several of the women started to tell him at once, their excited voices rising together, but Mother Carver won out over the gabble. The others began to listen.

". . . so they slept up hyar in your place, Johnny. Gawd Amighty, we was all settin thar all night with guns. Worsen Injuns. A sight worsen Injuns. Mr. Pentacost and Carver druv your beeves three-four miles up the holler and hid 'em. They took the preacher's hawg and et it!"

"Wait," Jonathan told her. "I did not follow. Were they jobbers?"

"Aw, listen to him, jobbers be damned." Mother Carver was growing angry in memory. "Dear Gawd, Jesus save us . . ."

Jonathan felt Sal's body stiffen, and tightened his fingers to shut her up.

"Listen hyar, Johnny, honey, they was no more nor border thieves. We'd eked out, eked out pretty good with the harvest, hadn't we, Maggie?"

Big rawboned Maggie Carver and several of the others nodded solemnly, now drawn close to Mother Carver as she told the story.

"Thim heartless souls come down from the north. I reckon they band up whin the huntin gits bad—come down like the locusts in the Bible."

"Like wolves," Maggie offered.

"Oh dear Gawd," somebody called from the back of the circle.

Mother Carver's voice rose to control the story. "Johnny darlin, I reckon thim to live in some mountain lean-tos with their women and jest live by huntin and thievin and Injun-killin. I reckon they got hongry." She shivered and her voice went low. "They wasn't nuthin safe afore thim deivals. We's a-feared they'd burn the place outa cussedness afore they left."

[236]

Jonathan never took his eyes from Mother Carver's wrinkled face, where easy tears of the old dropped unnoticed. But he did not loosen his grip on Sal's arm.

"What did they take?" he asked her.

"Ever'thin. They tooken ever'thin that wasn't nailed down. Aw, Johnny, thim wan't quite human, honey. They knowed they's leavin usn to starve, but they didn't give a damn. 'Twas dog eat dog, honey."

"Dear God, I took too long away," Jonathan murmured.

Mother Carver saw how troubled he was and put her gnarled hand on his arm. "Now Johnny, sweetheart, we-uns was all right. The poke greens come, and when Carver druv your beeves back we killed one o' your calves."

Sal jumped, and Jonathan's fingers bit into her arm so that she went a little sick from the pain and tears gathered behind her eyes.

"We'd a sight ruther a-had Injuns, I'll tell ye that," Mother Carver was saying.

Mary Martha had backed out of the circle and now wandered off down the meadow, her back brave. But no one saw her go.

"We sure Gawd would," Maggie was saying.

Jonathan looked over the heads of the women until he found the one he looked for. "Hannah," he said, "our sow's goin to litter. Ye can have a pig from her. In the meantime, ye better take home a flitch. Go fetch it from the smokehouse."

"Aw, Mr. Lacey, ain't that fine of ye." Hannah smiled, pleased at being singled out. "But y'ain't got no bacon yourself."

"We brung some—" Jonathan began.

But Sal, hurt arm and all, realized that the time had come for assertion. "You ladies come up for a visit after supper. I'll show ye my things," she interrupted, burning to get Jonathan into the house.

"Well, Miz Lacey, that's right pretty of ye," Mother Carver said, warm with pleasure and surprise. "Come on, let the pore

[237]

leetle thing git settled in. Any help ye want, ye just ask." Mother Carver began to steer the rest away. "Good evenin to ye, Mr. Lacey. Welcome home."

As Mother Carver and Maggie crossed the creek and turned up the other side to walk to their cabin, Mother Carver said to the ground, "She don't look much account, do she?"

"Hain't a mite of meat on her," Maggie agreed.

Jonathan marched Sal inside and set her down on one of the beds. Then he shut the door.

She sat, rubbing her arm, asking questions to stop his anger. "Lord, Johnny Lacey, is that what we've got to live with? If I hadn't a-brung ye in here, ye'd a-let them talk us out of house and home! Callin our place Beulah without so much as askin. Why, they're all Scotch! Or worse!"

"Yes, my dear Sal"—he turned from the door—"some are Scotch and Presbyterian too, and damned glad I am to have them, for they work like ye never saw. Some are nothin at all. Most of 'em can outride ye, outdig ye, and outbreed ye. Did nothin, *nothin* ye heared out there mean a thing to ye?"

He shook his head and looked at her. "Oh, dear God," he murmured to himself and tried again. "Now listen to me, you poor leetle gel. There's a mighty lot ye've got to leave behind ye, over the mountains. Ye can't help your ways and they can't help theirs. Back East there might be time for lickin your wounds with bein English-bred and high and mighty, but out here there's no time. There's work ahead, and there's gettin on with the rest, or there's sartain failure. Now ye're goin to do it, Sal. Tomorrow mornin ye're goin to take a hoe over your shoulder, and ye're goin down to the stockade field and ye're goin to work all day like a Negrew to show ye're one with the rest of us. There's laws out here, and ye're a-goin to obey them. The field for all gets planted first in case of attack. We might have to live in the stockade all summer if the Indians get stirred up. They all done

[238]

it last summer, and me with 'em. Doggo Cutwright's youngin was brained and scalped down by the ford last July, with us a-watchin and it all too far away for our guns to carry. 'Tis the kind of world ye've got to get used to. Maybe, if ye can't do nothin else, ye can remember ye're a lady and 'twill serve for all the rest."

Chapter Four

THE NIGHT had come down over Beulah, and the moon, risen high, cast thin shadows of the trees over the house, grown so small in the dark it seemed to sink into the ground.

Inside, with the fire banked up and three candles extravagantly lit, it seemed to the women crowded into the room more like a palace. Sal had set the one big plate she had left on the stone ledge of the chimney. Its glaze caught the light in deep reflections and drew the eyes of all the women back to it from time to time. No one, remembering the afternoon, dared to touch it, but they could look. Mrs. Lacey seemed to want them to look.

There was not a sound except a slight embarrassed cough from time to time. The eight of them sat, or stood, edgy with the new feel of cups in their hands; even the children had gone still against the wall. Sal was presiding over the little store of chocolate she'd brought from the East and planned to hoard so carefully. No one knew how to drink, so they waited for her to serve herself. The room was heavy with the fears of women. Finally Sal poured her chocolate daintily into her saucer and took a sip. Doggo

Cutwright's wife, her spare bones Scotch, but her flat face with its deep black eyes showing her to be half Cherokee, was trying to do what all the rest then did, as if it were some sort of follow-the-leader ceremony. She was so nervous that she spilled most of the chocolate on the front of her shift. She hardly seemed to notice that the hot liquid had stained and burned all the way to her skin, she was so intent on Sal. She just clutched at her shift and pulled it out from her sticky body until it cooled.

Sal sat bolt upright, like a queen, with a lace cap on, in the green silk gown Aunt Stacy Mason had given her.

"Now," she said, putting down the cup and saucer. There was a clatter as the other women did the same. A burst of laughter from the men across the dog-run in the other room seeped through the silence.

Mother Carver got up. "Will y'excuse me, mawm?" She curtsied to Sal and turned and walked out of the room. She shut the door behind her, crossed the dog-run, and knocked on the other door. Jonathan threw it wide.

"Ye wouldn't happen to have a dram, would ye, Johnny? That thar stuff hain't even laced."

Jonathan disappeared for a minute, and when he came back he held a steaming cup in his hand. "Here y'are, Mother. 'Tis hard going, eh?" He nodded across to the other door.

"Ye make a mighty good bombo, Mr. Lacey." The old woman grinned, ignoring the question. She handed the cup back. "I best go back now."

"We'll see ye in the mornin at the field, Mother." Jonathan straightened from leaning against the doorjamb. "If ye've need of another dram, just knock."

"Lord Gawd Amighty, Mr. Lacey, y'ain't a-goin to make that pore leetle mite work the field, are ye? Why, I ain't never hyeared sech a fool thing. Why, she's a right fine lady, Mr. Lacey, with all thim genteel ways. Y'ain't a-goin to git none of that kind of work outen her." She put her hand with its rough horny nails on his broadcloth arm. "Now ye listen to me. Let her garden. Let her raise a mite truck—'twon't hurt her none. She can milk, too. But listen, honey, field work she'd be broke in a week." She scuttled back across the dog-run and into the other room.

"Mother Carver." Sal said her name with relief, for in her absence something had happened to make the silence heavier. "I was sayin as how, there bein no church or prayers hereabouts, we might set up one for ourselves. I brung the Bible and the Prayer Book and the Hymns of Mr. Watts. We cannot have our children to grow up wild."

"We don't hold with none o' that." Mother Carver set her feet and glared at Sal, feeling a new bravery now that the bombo had warmed her. She didn't know about cups and saucers and suchlike things. "I know my religion, though," she said aloud. "We don't hold with no Popish ways out hyar. We're partial to a good sermonizin and we got ourselves a pretty good loud preacher. But we hain't a-havin none of that other. No, mawm."

Hannah, standing in a dark corner, looked up, relieved, the fear gone out of her face after Mother Carver's defense of Jeremiah.

Sal looked pretty confusion. "I just reckoned on a lesson or a hymn now and then."

"Well, we don't have nuthin like they." Mother Carver closed the subject and sat down in Sal's rocker. The creak of the runners being forced to a good speed was all the sound in the room.

Hannah smiled to herself.

"Well, we'll see," Sal said.

"Ye rear your youngins and we'll rear ourn," Mother Carver said to the fire.

Maggie's youngest child, asleep in the far corner, woke up and started to yell. "Quit that!" Maggie reached down and slapped him. He stopped.

Sal began to hum and drummed her fingers on the side of the table.

[242]

"I'm plumb wore out," Mary Martha said out of the shadows. "I got a crick in the neck, by Jesus. 'Tis time for me bed."

Her words started a general movement, the waking of children, and the room was a turmoil of women trying to get out.

Mother Carver, to soften her words about religion, told Sal before she left what she had said to Jonathan. "I done told him ye wasn't fitten. They hain't nary a one of us expectin nuthin like that from ye. Lord Gawd, look at thim sweet little hands!" She took one of Sal's hands and presented it to Maggie for inspection. Because they were going to leave so soon, and the movement had released them from the pall of unease, the rest of the women crowded around. They touched her lace cap, felt her dress.

"Feel that goddam weight!" Mrs. Cutwright said. "I reckon hit cost more'n a mule!"

Sal, in her new triumph, even let them pass the plate from hand to hand. "Now be keerful. Be mighty keerful," Mother Carver kept saying.

Sal, over their bent heads, smiled. " 'Tis all the way from England—Cheeny ware, like they make in Cheeny. See them blue figures? And the pretty leetle bridges? I had six of them but they got broke."

"Ye niver had six of thim!" Mary Martha was shocked.

"I did too. I'll swear." Sal was firm.

"Well, I'll be a cockeyed son of a bitch." Maggie Cutwright's sister-in-law, who had said nothing before, passed her leathery finger over and over the plate's surface.

"How many youngins have ye bore?" Mother Carver was studying Sal's waist.

"I've bore six and reared three," Sal told her proudly.

"Now would ye believe hit? A leetle old skinny thing like that!" Mother Carver said.

A new sound and smell drew their attention to the fire. Maggie's youngest had decided to pee into it.

"Quit that!" Maggie yelled. "For shame of yourself, Jedediah!"

The child remained calm, even though she called him Jedediah instead of plain Jed.

"I do it to home," he said as he finished.

"Only when hit's goddam cold out, and ye know hit. Come on home, ye leetle heathen!" She drove him ahead of her out into the night.

Sal, finally alone, found it easier to speak to the fire than she had to the women. "Cohees!" she told it, disgusted. "I'm out here with the Cohees and away from my own kind, and I might as well get used to it. But the chocolate was worth it; ye can be polite and friendly but 'tis as well to show the lower class of the people right off the ways ye're used to. Lordy, there's some reddin up to do, and me in my one silk gown." She straightened up from gathering the cups and told Jonathan through the two closed doors, "And ye needn't to reckon on me field workin like a convict or a Negrew, Johnny Lacey. I showed ye. By God, I showed ye." She set the cups down more sharply than she meant to. "Well, indeed." She sighed, inspecting them carefully to see that none was cracked. "It takes a woman to understand these things." She was so tired that she didn't notice until the next morning that one of the cups was gone.

Later in the night, when she had gone to bed in the loft, where she'd already made Baucis and Herr Mittelburger move the bed, she lay listening to Jonathan and Jarcey murmuring, and was pleased that they'd moved to the room below to let the children in the other loft sleep.

She heard Jarcey say something about the whore of Babylon and smiled. At least Mr. Pentacost had the right idea about the Irish Catholics.

Down in the room below, Jonathan turned from building up the fire, motioned upward, and put his finger against his lips. Jarcey lowered his voice. Sal heard no more and began to drift toward sleep.

[244]

"Yes, my sweet Johnny," Jarcey almost whispered now, comfortable in Sal's rocker. "I must admit Mary Martha is the whore of Babylon herself. I'll wake one bright morning and find her gone off with some mule-driver. But never ye mind. She's as good a wife as I could find in the wilderness. . . ." His voice was so low that a great crackle of the log catching drowned what else he said.

They said nothing for a long time, staring at the growing fire. Jonathan broke the late night silence that lulled them in the warm room. "Mother Carver told me what happened."

"Did she tell ye Jacob Cutwright went off with them?"

Jonathan stopped rocking.

"I was certain Doggo would go too," Jarcey went on, whispering to the fire. "Him listenin to the wild with an ear cocked as he does all the time. But he stayed. I couldn't let the lady know, but he's got both the women with child now. That comes from Mother Carver, who never misses a pregnancy from the day 'tis conceived. The Carvers was gold all the winter. Maggie come down like a fallen tree with the cabin fever, her and Carver, but the old woman pulled them through it and kept things going. I come on her the first day of the spring, rootin out the new pokeweed and a-cryin fitten to kill. She kept on tellin me the poke greens had come just in time, how good the Lord was, and all that. 'Tis ones like that revives me when I conclude the world around me to have turned into a pack of wild dogs."

"Jarcey, ye—" Jonathan started to interrupt.

But Jarcey had sprung up out of the rocker. "Johnny, Johnny, what I seen was beyond reason! Oh Lord." He remembered to lower his voice again and passed his hand across his eyes; the empty rocker seemed loud on the bare boards as it went on rocking. "The inhumanity of them! They're worse than the savages, for at least the savages keep to the ways they know, if we would but learn them. But these! They're like wild animals that have been cooped up in cages, turned out along the borders,

[245]

cavortin around full of hate. I used to pity them, for I knew what dregs they come from, without a chance or hope in the world. But they ain't fitten for compassion."

He sat back down in the rocker and rested his head in his hands. Jonathan watched the firelight on his hair and knew to wait for him to go on. When he did he sounded exhausted. "Ye don't know the worst. They took Mary Martha at gun point and kept her up here with them—to cook, they said. I thought she'd gone for good. There wasn't a body to help, but Doggo and Jacob drunk with them and Carver laid up and half out of his mind. Jeremiah Catlett, Old Repent himself, as much as he hates me, he tried to help. He come up here in the mornin, shoutin out, 'Repent, for the day of the Lord is at hand!' like he always does. They took him and threw him off the stoop and broke his leg. They let me come pick him up and carry him home. I stayed up there and nursed him with Hannah. Two of their youngins died about January of the cabin fever, and she was weak with it herself. The poor man kept on tellin her, 'We ought to have moved on west, Hannah.' 'Twas heartbreaking to hear him, and her sayin nothin back. Mary Martha come back three days later, all smiles and full of stolen food. At least 'twas the first good meal she'd had in quite a time. The huntin got pretty bad with the deep snow. When it went, even the wild critturs was as starved as we was."

All this he had told the floor. Now he raised his head so that the firelight caught his eyes as he stared at it. "To be able to do nothin in the face of that scum. What could I have done, Johnny?"

"Why there was nothin ye could have done."

"If only the soldiers patrolled down this far. Did ye see about the soldiers? Did ye find out?"

"Yes, I found out." Jonathan said it so low that Jarcey had to lean forward to hear him.

"Well, will they come out this far?"

"No." The word hung in the room. " 'Tis hopeless, Jarcey. We'll just have to hope for more settlers comin in the later spring and bandin up with us. There's so much trouble roused up back East over the soldiers." Jonathan sighed out the next words. "The old question of the Parliament layin a tax on us to pay for the soldiers has come up again. This time 'tis to be a Stamp Tax, a pure internal tax thought up by the Parliament. Now ye know the people back East won't stand for it. The whole thing has turned to that unhealthy phrase, 'a question of principle.' Bute and his Tory cronies are stuck on the Colonies recognizin the Parliament's rights, and the colonies are stuck on Parliament recognizin their rights. 'Tis now beyond a question of money. Lord, I distrust any government that hangs on abstract definitions of principle! Dear God, it all seems so far away now!"

Jarcey interrupted, furious, "And in the meantime we set out here, havin no representation even in the Burgesses, and get eaten by border ruffians, the scum of Europe run loose. By God, I—"

"Jarcey, be reasonable—even now be reasonable." Jonathan's heat when he used the word made Jarcey, as angry as he was, smile. "We're in the King's Part. We've little right to be here, accordin to the treaty. No one would listen. Back there, I'm one in hundreds, just comin out here and squattin, like Jeremiah Catlett. Ye talk to his like about treaties!"

"Now who's standin on rights, Jonathan?"

"Listen. The people back east of the mountains are safe. They hate the soldiers anyway and see little reason in payin for them. I saw it begin. Lord, I saw it begin back in Braddock's time. Down here they've distrusted the soldiers ever since, and even built up a great passel of lies about what happened. They reckon on the militia defendin them, and reckon they've no need of the soldiers, now that the French have gone. Most of them, except for a few who have property out at the Blue Ridge, count the border land as more trouble than 'tis worth."

"We need the soldiers now."

"We need them for a little while, but they've need no longer in the Tidewater and even in the Piedmont. The war done that

[247]

for us. When a man no longer needs a thing he sloughs it off like a snake sheds in the spring, but, bein a man and full of words, he'll comfort his conscience with causes and rights and suchlike baggage."

"And what of us?"

"What of us? Jarcey, in ten years we won't have need of them neither. Up in the north the liberty mob leaders already talk of leavin the king! It's gone that far."

"As far as treason?"

"As far as that. Of course, there's no question of that in Virginia, for we depend too much on England, havin but the one main crop, but up there they depend on commerce. All the time we fought the French they kept up trade with them, free as birds. My God, this is the time for men of sense—men like Pitt. In the meantime fools will try to force authority down our throats for the sake of authority. Pure damned stubbornness, I call it." Jonathan still remembered to talk so low he might have been murmuring pleasantries by the fire. In the loft, he could hear the bed creak, and his voice seemed to catch the interruption. "Look at the way we English entertain the Chinese notion that all are fools and beggars but ourselves!"

Jarcey was going to protest, but even as he started to speak he realized that Jonathan was coming as near as he ever would let himself to talking about Sal, and that he included them, too, to make what he had to say easier.

Jonathan got up and kicked the log, sending a shower of sparks up the chimney. He leaned on the rock ledge, watching the sparks. "Do ye think the skillful and industrious people we need will come to be looked down on and spurned because their ways are not ours? Back a man to the wall with arrogance and contempt, and he strikes out blind in his roused pride. We're proud to be English, Jarcey, but we are Virginians and Americans, too. Parliament will force us to define it, Jarcey, mark my words, they'll force us to define it, and when we do—" Jonathan brought his hand flat down on the rock ledge, and the plate began to roll. He caught it just in time and set it carefully in its place.

"Poor Sal," he said softly. "All the plates she was so proud of was broke but this one." He couldn't help drawing his finger over it as the others had, to feel its smoothness. "After all, what are we, Jarcey? You and I educated men; poor little Sal up there, who sees herself a fine lady; to the East we are no more than those scum who infest the border. They don't care about us any more than the Parliament cares about them. But we'll make ourselves felt, my Jarcey. We'll make ourselves felt. If I thought I'd brought my children out here to rear them up wild, without grace or a genteel background—"

"So we still look to England," Jarcey told him.

"We still look there for the sensible virtues we've brought across the mountains. Oh Jarcey, what do I mean? What can we become out here? We may have brought the virtues, but we've brought a cancer, too." Jonathan sat down again and put his head in his hands.

"And the plate," Jarcey interrupted mildly.

"Yes, by God, the plate!" Jonathan lifted his head and smiled, trying to shake off the despair that had gathered in him. "Let's take a drink."

After he had made the toddy and they had settled by the fire, Jonathan asked, "Did ye have a chance to hold school this winter?"

"Well, ye know, I did." Jarcey's brown slim face had lost its strain, and now he sipped, contented, rocking. "But I still can't make headway with the Cutwright clan. Ye know, the ignorant are so violent about learnin. They reckon it to be some kind of secret. Jeremiah is afeared, but the Cutwrights hate it, hate it because they equate learnin to bein a gentleman, as if words and gentlemen were some sort of talisman to be rooted out and destroyed. 'Tis as if it was witchcraft—it fills them full of hate. The lower orders have brought that fear from home and turned it loose in the woods."

"Ye've been having trouble with them, Jarcey."

"Jacob Cutwright got drunk one day and broke into our cabin when I was to hunting, and Mary Martha off to help out with the Carvers. I come back and found two of my books all scattered and tore, around the floor. He'd gotten hold of *The Pilgrim's Progress* and *The Arts of Government*. He'd even fouled them, Johnny. What excess of bitterness in a man will make him foul Locke, who champions him, just because 'tis wrote down in a book? Lord, the unleashin of vices and virtues we've found out here! But I kept my Horace safe. 'Tis a lucky thing. I never hunt without him," Jarcey said a little primly, and added carefully, as if the new thought weighed more by word than anything he'd said before, "I find out here a growing weakness for Horace. 'Tis a need for me, that kindness in the midst of all this. Ye know I once distrusted— Oh Johnny, understand. I admire Virgil more. I admire him more." He sipped his bombo and smiled a little to himself, having confessed.

Jonathan looked for a long time at the man he had brought to the wilderness, though Jarcey never noticed, thinking of his lost, precious books. The broken plates, the fouled books, the sad remnants, the terrible stripping down of the new life—now Jonathan no longer watched Jarcey but sat immobile, dreaming, too.

The sound of Jarcey's getting up roused him.

"I'll say good night to ye, my Johnny. Thank God ye've all come back home safe."

From the lost world over the mountains they had come, with their memories for a crutch—or a weapon; it was Jarcey, after all, who had come farther than any of them, who could use the word "home" without even thinking.

Jonathan leaned for a while against a joist on the porch, watching Jarcey cross the gray, whispering grass in the moonlight. The moon was at its highest and seemed to race through wind-driven clouds, quickening the night. A breeze cooled his forehead from the heat of the room.

Hannah, hiding in the shadow of the porch, waited to see the white ruffle of his sleeve against his face before she was sure enough that it was Jonathan to dare to speak. She moved forward even then so quietly that he didn't turn until she touched his arm, as timid as a cat.

" 'Tis me, Hannah Catlett, sar," she whispered, still holding his arm, before he could do more than start a little with surprise. "Can we have a mite words together?"

"At your sarvice, mawm." Jonathan bowed a little, but whispered too, without knowing he did. "I thought all ye ladies had gone."

"I waited."

"Why didn't ye knock? I'd have seen ye any time."

" 'Tis between us. I knowed ye'd come out. Ye always come out to measure, like, with your eyes over the ground, afore ye go to your bed. I seed ye plenty times." Hannah, now more at ease, told him his habits pleasantly. "We-uns could walk down the bottom. We won't wake up the lady." She pulled at him to make him go down the step. "I seed her goin to her bed. She has a separate gown for nights. She'll catch her death cold one of these nights, strippin down bar like she do."

By this time she had managed to lead him down the steps, and he fell in beside her to walk up-creek across the deep grass. As they looked toward the Catlett cabin, almost in the far trees up the two hill spurs from where they stood, they saw a tiny glow of light.

" 'Tis Jeremiah with the door opened, a-waitin for me. See thar!" Hannah pointed, pleased.

Now she could think of no more to say, and a shyness caught her at what she had been nerving herself, out on the shadowy porch, to do.

"Mr. Lacey," she finally asked, "have we yet been took into the county?" She seemed to be holding her breath beside him. The moon slid behind a cloud, and it was pitch dark.

"No, mawm, we ain't become a county yet." He heard her sigh and took it to be disappointment. "Never mind. 'Twon't be long. The government concludes to keep on a-treatin with the Six Nations."

"How long?" Her voice was so small he thought she had moved away, but the moon rode out, and he found her, shrunk there, with her arms crossed against the cool breeze, looking up at him, and he saw she was afraid.

"Mrs. Catlett, your husband and me don't see eye to eye, but I'd like to help ye if I can."

"They hain't a hate nobody can do." She stared past him, unseeing, withdrawn.

"How would it be if ye leased that land proper from me? Would ye feel safer then?" He tried to probe into the blank sadness.

"Hit hain't that thar, Mr. Lacey. Jeremiah reckons that passel up thar to be hisn nohow. Ye know how he reckons he was led to it."

"But don't he understand I'd laid claim in the county and bought it from the Indians before you come?"

"He jest concludes Gawd wouldn't a-played sech a damned low trick. I keep a-tryin to tell him. He says I seed hit first, but I done told him 'twas only from across the river. But he won't listen, he won't listen, Mr. Lacey. He jest says Moses niver done nuthin but see the Land of Canaan from afur, but hit still went to his youngins. Once I made him dip for Guidance when Mr. Pentacost was a-readin him the Bible. What come to him he's been a-sayin ever since whenever hit come up." Hannah's voice

[252]

rose in an unconscious imitation of Jeremiah as she called over the dark, empty valley. " 'Thou shalt no more be termed forsaken; neither shall thy land any more be termed desolate; but thou shalt be called Hephzibah, and thy land Beulah, for the Lord delighteth in thee, and thy land shall be married.' 'Tis no use to argue with him." She had retreated again into looking past him, and he saw her shiver a little under her thin shift.

"Here, put my coat about ye as we talk." He took it off and threw it over her shoulders.

It seemed as if that was what she couldn't stand, the little kindness about the coat. She clutched at it with both hands. "Oh Lord, hain't hit the prettiest thing to be on a man!" She looked again at him, and her face had gone so full of pleasure that he could see she had once been pretty in her youth.

"Now hain't that like ye, Captain Lacey? Y'always was one to think of people, not like thim others that called theyselves fine gintlemen and spit in your eye. Lord, when I seed 'twas you, the first time ye rid out of thim trees a-horseback with Mr. Pentacost and that ugly Solomon, I just said to Jeremiah, 'Now put that thar gun away.' He's aimin to shoot ye. He would of, too, the Lord bein on his side and guidin him—he's a-hit ye, too, Gawd in his sights even efn that damned old musket hain't nary a bit of good no more." She had come so close now that her eager, thin face seemed suspended in the air, gleaming white under the moon. "I said, 'Jeremiah, efn they's a man livin ain't no man's sartain enemy till he's crossed, 'tis Captain Johnny from the Braddock wars.' "

"Why, Hannah Catlett, was ye there? Why did ye never tell me?"

"Well, ye and Jeremiah wasn't seein eye to eye on the land question, so I bided my time. Now with the county comin closer— Ye remember the mornin. By Gawd and by Jesus, what a sight! 'With a ruffdom, ruffdom fizzledom madge.' " Hannah let go of the coat and pushed Jonathan's chest to share the joke. "By Gawd—oh by Gawd, what a sight!" She seemed to have rollicked backward over years; the sight of the women full of a frenzied, frightened pleasure, singing as they crossed the sun-drenched river, was between them.

"How did ye get here?"

"Here" brought them both back into the darkness and the present.

She didn't answer. "I said to him when I seed ye, 'Jeremiah Catlett, we cain't go on and on a-runnin jest when we got settled and planted. We got to stop sometime.' Thar we was, both of us a-wrastlin over that gun, me arguin fit to kill and thim youngins settin up a wail. Ye have to know Jeremiah, Captain Johnny; he's a good man but he don't know nuthin of the ways of the world. Now me, I's teethed on the ways of the world.

"A man"—her voice went thin, and she didn't say what man— "come by when we was a-settled back yonder. He said we-uns could git tuk back and sold up—and he said our youngins could too. 'Tis the law," she said simply, accepting it as one of the burdens of mankind.

"Hannah," Jonathan interrupted and touched her shoulder to quiet her. "We've no care here about the past. I'll protect ye. A man," he said, but not to her, "has got to look after his own. I don't want to know how ye got here. Don't tell me none of that."

"Thar's one thing," Hannah told the crushed grass by his foot. "Efn we-uns was freeholders, nuthin could touch usn. Freeholders," she told it, full of a sad dream, "has ever'thin their way."

"Ye want to buy your passel off me." Jonathan said it somewhere above her head so she wouldn't have to.

"I hain't got nary a thing to pay ye with, sar." She was hopeless again. "I's kind of hopin your missus—she likes things pretty fine." She had hoisted her skirt up to her waist and drew out from beside her white, thin leg an object that shone dull under the moon. "I reckoned on this hyar crop we-uns found once, and thin this hyar." The skirt had dropped again, and she fumbled awkwardly in her pocket and drew out an egg-shaped object that was black in the night. " 'Tis a mighty pretty stone I picked up once. 'Tis the prettiest thing when ye put it in the light." When he didn't answer at once, she went on, persuading. " 'Tis a good stone. I reckon it to have value. Ye wouldn't think I knowed sech things, but I did. I did once, Mr. Lacey."

The pressure of the woman's almost hopeless wishing made him speak finally.

"All right, Hannah. I'll sell ye forty acres."

"That would be mighty fine. Jeremiah cain't work more'n that now nohow. Captain Lacey, when ye give me the deed, ye won't let Jeremiah know, will ye? He'd feel better jest goin on thinkin it's Gawd. He'd feel better thataway."

"A secret between us, Hannah," Jonathan promised. "And no more about the past."

"I knowed ye'd do that, Captain Johnny. I jest knowed ye'd do that. Will ye really give me a deed? A deed with our names on hit?" She held out his coat to him and started away to where the dim light still glowed in the dark valley. "That's why I wouldn't let Jeremiah shoot ye, honey. I know'd 'twould be all right." She stopped formally about ten feet away. He only saw her stop, and the moon hid again, and she was out of sight.

"I hain't very good on thankin, Captain Johnny," was all the voice said out of the dark. "I'll tell Jeremiah that ye'll see us right," she added in complete faith.

She was far away when the moon came out. From that moment she never called him Captain Johnny again, being a woman who had learned how to root out the past like a weed when it grew again.

When Jonathan got into his own kitchen he knelt down by the almost dead fire to examine the crop. There was enough light to see, even through the brown tarnish of years, what it was. The last time he had seen the crop it had glowed in Squire Raglan's hand. He knew then who that man was Hannah had talked about. "Why I wouldn't see a dog hung for killin that damned scoundrel." He said to himself what he would never have a chance to say to Hannah Catlett.

Before he climbed up to bed he hid the crop from Sal, to give to Peregrine, his cousin's namesake, when he came of age. The ruby, which Hannah's hand had polished over the years to a dull red, he put away for Sara, as a pretty jewel when she grew up.

"It's no value, I reckon," he whispered as he knelt over his deed box and thrust the stone down into a corner. "Johnny Lacey, ye've sold up forty acres for a stolen crop and a pebble, but a secret's a secret to a man of honor." He shut the box carefully so that the click wouldn't wake Sal upstairs. "That poor leetle woman. Lord God, some has hard lives!"

When Jonathan woke up the dawn was sifting white through the open door of the loft. Sal was already up. He could hear her below, calling to the children, picking at Philemon, as if she'd been in the house all her life instead of for the first morning. She had put his good broadcloth away, and he saw his buckskins laid out and scoured neatly.

When he climbed down the steep outside stairs and opened the door, the children were already at breakfast, but Sal was not there.

"She's already across in that other room, a-workin like she was a-killin rattlesnakes," Philemon told him. "I told her to come on in. I told her to, but she wouldn't mind me."

Jonathan found her by the sound before he opened the other door—the sound of rhythmic scraping. He found her down on her knees, rubbing, rubbing the damp wood floor with sand.

"I've got to get it polished!" She looked up, blind-eyed with worry. "Don't ye see, Johnny, it's got to be polished. Else how are folks to know 'tis the parlor?" Her hands were cut and raw from the sand.

"How long have ye been at this, Sal?" He tried to help her up from the floor, but she shook away and went on rubbing, her rump to him, hardly knowing he was there.

"I woke up thinkin and plannin. I planned on doin it thisaway. And somethin else I planned. I've concluded to have everybody as they pass down valley bring a rock home. A big one. That way we can collect enough to have a stone house. I always reckoned to live in brick or stone so folks'll know we're quality. Mind ye, this is good for now. 'Tis all right for now. Oh Lord-a-mercy"—she sat back on her heels—"will this wood never come smooth?"

"Won't ye have your breakfast, my dear?"

"Oh ye men! Get along, my Johnny, and let me alone."

None of the Cutwrights turned up at the stockade field. All morning the others worked, hoeing the delicate new plants, trying to put out of their minds the loss of needed hands. Only Mother Carver voiced once what they were thinking, and that with a loud yell.

"Mr. Lacey, I reckon usn to be quit of this hyar by tomorry, no matter. We all reckoned on today, but no matter. Plenty of time to git to work on our own truck, hain't it?"

"Plenty of time," Jonathan called back, lifting his head, but standing to stretch his work-weary back.

It was then that he saw a small two-wheeled tumbril in the distance, drawn by one sorry horse. "Well, I'll be damned." His voice made the others look up.

Jonathan was already running to his mare Nelly, which was grazing below the field, where he'd ridden her in the early morning.

As he rode nearer the wagon, across the creek and up the buffalo trail, he could see that it was Doggo, flogging the horse forward, while the two women hung on to the sides. They had no children with them.

[257]

"Halloo, Doggo, where the devil are ye going?" Jonathan drew Nelly in ahead of the wagon.

"Ye let me by, damn ye," Doggo yelled.

"Talk to me like that and I'll drag ye off that thing and horse-whip ye."

Doggo made a move for his rifle.

"Put that fool thing away and talk civil."

Doggo's anger, which had switched from the horse to Jonathan, changed to sullenness. "We jest reckoned on goin a leetle further west." He looked at the road, far away.

"Why? Ye've got a fair lease from me. Your family is safer here in numbers."

"Hit's a-gittin a mite too crowded hyarabouts."

"We don't hold with no Dutchmen and Neegurs." Doggo's sister-in-law shrieked.

"Now you shut up," Doggo growled at her low, but her words had unleashed his own bitterness. "We-uns come out hyar to git away from ruffle shirts and Whigs, a-bringin their Neegurs and cups and saucers and fancy ways and settin up like back East. We-uns hain't got nuthin to do with sechlike."

"Doggo, talk some reason." Jonathan, sitting on his horse, trying to keep calm with the man, didn't realize that the very look of him there, so at ease, only strengthened Doggo's hatred. "Ye ought to keep your women here. It ain't safe further west with no fort built."

"I hain't afeared of no damned yaller Injun. We-uns is better than thim."

"I hardly think 'twill be a question of the virtues if ye meet up with a war party," Jonathan told him lightly. "And what about your young?" He looked back and saw that they had not brought their children.

"Keep thim brats and send thim to school," Doggo yelled, furious at last. He flicked Nelly with his rawhide whip and made

[258]

her shy out of the way. "Ye try and make thim wildcats into Tuckahoes! Git out'n the way, Ruffle-Shirt," he called as his own frightened horse started past. He kept on flogging it as the tumbril rolled away up the road.

His half-Indian wife, still with the brown stain of the chocolate down her shift, kept hoping the rattle of the cart wouldn't break the cup she'd stolen from Sal, but she didn't dare say anything. Doggo was too furious for her to dare.

"Injun-lovin son of a bitch!" Doggo called back—the final insult, but Jonathan was too busy getting Nelly under control to pay any attention.

The exertion of quieting the horse took the energy for anger, and left Jonathan staring at the road until the tumbril disappeared around the down-river spur.

"I don't know," he told Nelly, patting her wither still, from habit. "Oh, little Sal," he went on, now that he was alone in the middle of the huge meadow. "Poor little Sal, ye're a mighty dangerous woman."

He rode slowly down the creek side. The day's hands were lined up, resting, watching the hanging head, the delicately walking horse get nearer.

"He's a-thinkin," Mother Carver read from the figure. "Wouldn't ye say he's a-thinkin, Jarcey, honey?"

"He hain't happy in what he's a-thinkin," Solomon told them, from where he leaned on his elbows on the worm fence, spitting from time to time. "I can read that thar man."

"Oh, you know so much," his wife argued beside him.

"Shut your mouth," Solomon said casually.

Now Jonathan was near enough so that the hollow *clop* of Nelly's shoes was loud on the creek rocks below.

"Hey, my Jarcey," he called up to them, and when he raised his head they saw that he was smiling. "I've got ye a passel of youngins if ye'll have them.

[259]

"So ye've won," he said too quietly for Jarcey up at the fence to hear, "and ye don't even know it." But Jarcey couldn't have heard anyway, because Mother Carver had already started to cackle furiously and gather Maggie and Mary Martha up to go see to the lonesome little wildcats.

BOOK THREE

March 16, 1769 – July 20, 1774

My Heaven, my Home, forevermore.

Chapter One

THE HOUSE was alive at last; the doors were all opened to the veering warmer wind which had made the vines scratch their bare fingers against the rough log walls. Philemon flapped the quilts wide out over the stairs by the chimney. The first pale sun of the spring of 1769 had finally come, and she let it kiss her black, heavy face while she stood, her eyes closed, letting the quilt settle over the banister like a tired flag. It crawled a little with the wind, but that had not the strength of Philemon's solid arms. How long she stood there she didn't know, long enough to enjoy the slight warmth and then be scared that Miss Sal would find her. Way off down the creek, she could see the smoke rising from the one-roomed cabin of Mr. Pentacost's house, and she knew with some jealousy that the children were at their last lessons, just sitting there not doing a thing but reading and writing, before plowing time would shut the school. She'd heard Mr. Johnny and Mr. Pentacost talking about it, reckoning on keeping them in till the last moment. Philemon grinned at the smoke, knowing that, however much the men planned, the youngins in another few weeks would be hard to hold as fish in the spring freshets. She leaned back for a minute against the outside wall and hitched up her shift over her swollen body to rub herself a little bit. Far up the creek she could see Old Repent, out smelling the strong, melted earth. She could tell it was Mr. Catlett by his stick.

Philemon sighed and started to shake the bedding again, looking, sleepy-eyed, around the valley, feeling too lazy to do more than flap gently, almost not flap at all, just let it air easy, as she was airing—easy.

Suddenly she went rigid. The quilt dropped from her excited hands. She pounded down the steep stairs, her weight shaking them, her huge breasts jigging wildly under her loose shift. The noise of her feet warned Jonathan and Sal, inside the kitchen, before they heard her voice, screaming.

"Miss Sal, oh Miss Sal, Mr. Johnny, come quick. Come out hyar."

They both ran to the door. "It's her baby come," Sal gasped. "Go git Lyddy!" She rushed past Johnny.

Lyddy, the Yoruba mulatto who had belonged to Mr. Brandon, lifted her sweating face from the hot tallow caldron in the back washhouse, listened for a minute, and then wiped the rolling sweat with her arm and went back to work, disinterested and sad. It was not the baby.

"Oh Miss Sal, git upstairs and dress in your good gown. Go on, now, you mind me. Thar's company a-comin. I done seed him. He jest rid out'n the woods."

Sal hesitated for a second, and Philemon pushed her on toward the stairs. "Go on now, ye don't want to git caught in your shift. I'll red up the parlor."

"There ain't a fire in the parlor! What'll we do?"

"I'll git some out'n the kitchen. Now go on!"

Sal ran. "Philemon," she screamed back, "the quilt! Don't let him see the quilt."

"I'll git it. Go on! He's pretty near at the crick!"

Jonathan, watching the rider pass the deserted stockade, saw him hesitate at the swollen creek, where the new-melted snow and the pouring raw hillsides had filled it so that it was already up over half the stockade field. Then Jonathan saw the rider flip his feet out of his stirrups and lie flat along the horse's back to force it to the creek. He saw him glance down-creek toward the new log ordinary, Jarcey's house, and the schoolroom, which, with several new cabins and a boathouse, had grown in four years into the beginnings of a main street. The rider paused, then turned his horse uphill. Jonathan began to wave.

"Johnny!" Sal's voice came from above a muffled scream under her gown. "Clout your hair back. Y'ain't got time for powder. He'll think ye're an Indian! Take off your moccasins and put on your shoes. Johnny!" Her voice came clear and sharp, her head free of the gown. "D'you hyear me?"

"Yes, sweetheart." Jonathan laughed. " 'Tis all right."

"The first company since way last fall, and he says 'tis all right. Indeed to goodness!" Sal complained loudly.

Ten minutes later the watersoaked, filthy traveler had led his tired horse up to the front porch.

"By God, sar! 'Tis Captain Lewis." Jonathan ran down the steps, his arms outstretched to hug the man. "Ye're a blessin to the lonesome. Baucis!" he called round the house. "Come get Captain Lewis's horse." He clasped Captain Lewis's wet body by the shoulders, then drew him up to the porch. "Come right in, sar!"

"I ain't fitten to meet a lady," Captain Lewis said shyly, trying to brush the mud from his coat, which was so dirty it seemed brown instead of blue—remembering too vividly his disastrous meeting with Sal at Fort Henry.

It was too late. A calm, poised Sal had walked out of the parlor. "Howdee, Captain Lewis." She curtsied low. "Welcome

[265]

to Cicero. There's some water on for ye, if ye care to red up a mite after your journey."

"Well, that's mighty kind of ye, mawm." The mud-splashed figure bowed in turn. Philemon, in the kitchen door, looked on to make certain that he was a gentleman before she put out Mr. Johnny's razor and his good ivory brushes. When she saw the bow she disappeared inside, satisfied.

Later in the morning Captain Lewis slumped over a toddy in the now glowing parlor, in Jonathan's best shirt. He was fighting to keep from going to sleep, now that warmth and ease were running through his veins with the whisky, after the cold, the rain, the automatic half-dead jogging of his all-night ride. His blue Provincial coat, with the silver lace rubbed bright by Sal, lay near the fire, drying.

"We've plenty of time for conversation," he said to Jonathan and Sal who both sat clutching the closed packets of the first news they had had in six months. "Now ye'll want news of your families. Go ahead. Ye go on ahead. One of the letters is a mite old. It come in the late fall. But there's some ain't more than a month or so." He sat back, peaceful, the rustle of paper the only sound in the room. It would have put him to sleep, except from time to time Mrs. Lacey, behind him, would slap her cheek and talk a little to herself as she read her thick letter.

"Well, indeed!" she said. Then: "Lord-a-mercy, how can they *breathe?*" There was a short silence. "The silly, vain thing." She giggled. "Lord's love!" she said solemnly. After a long pause, there was a resounding "Huh!" full of contempt.

Jonathan, reading the news he had waited for so long, sprang up so that his rocker skidded behind him.

"Sal, Sal, we've settled with the Six Nations. We're to be taken into the county! By God, at last!"

"Shhh!" She put her finger to her lips and began to make the words silently with her mouth to show she was concentrating.

Jonathan asked Spotteswood Lewis quietly, "Does it mean we'll get regular soldiers?" Lewis had gone to sleep at last, his head cradled in his arm and his toddy beginning to dip dangerously toward the floor. Jonathan tiptoed over and took the cup gently from his hand; he smiled to himself and retreated back into his letter from Brandon Crawford.

As more than my brother-in-law, Johnny, as one on whom we depend in the King's Part, I reckon you should know all.

Along with certain other gentlemen of your acquaintance, Mr. Lee, Colonel Washington, Mr. Burden, among others who have interests beyond the old Proclamation Line (Forgive me if I set down what you already know but I must write all this in some order) I have been bringing steady pressure to bear, both through the Burgesses, and by private means, to effect a satisfactory settlement to the Line question.

The County seat should be a reasonable distance from you; this is merely my Conjecture, for I have neither data nor postulata to reason upon as yet, there being contending interests. I paid off the Land Office with the Money you left for that purpose, so your Grant is clear, and accompanies this letter.

I have succeeded in getting a substantial Grant myself, something above fifty thousand acres, though some of it is still questioned due to the border Dispute with Pennsylvania. One Grant includes a place called Dunkard's Valley, which I have concluded to turn into a summer home for myself, since I am informed that there is an excellent medicinal spring upon it, which might help the rheumatic pains that have troubled me of late, so that I can scarce stand. The rest I propose to settle with tenants, for I believe Money to lie now more in the Land itself through Quit rents than ever in the Wasteful Crop of Tobacco, and also in the Iron Mines which I have opened beyond Carpenter's Creek.

The service you have done me in surveying Land more than overpays any debt you owe me for helping you to locate over the Mountains, and I confess myself your debtor. It would honour me if you spoke no more of it.

I have hopes that you and I can serve together in representing the new County. To make this more certain I have proposed, and have reason to suppose that I will be obliged, to see you appointed as a Justice of the Peace in the new County. From that office it should be easy to become known to the Freeholders, and we can but hope a place in the Burgesses will follow, without our having to Electioneer and kiss the A——s of the District. Your presence in the Burgesses would be a welcome one to myself and my friends who prefer a backwoods Gentleman to a backwoods Ranter. The Freeholders who have had business with us over the Land will be more obliged to us without our Ranting and Raving as ill becomes Gentlemen. I propose to sell a *judicious* amount of my Land holdings.

As for the news from Home it could hardly be worse. We have put our dependence on a Colossus of glass. Pitt has fallen, and after all the hopes we set upon his Ministry it was a Chaos. I heard gossip there that all that could be glimpsed of the man who held the British Empire together was that great profile passing the window of a darkened room in Hampstead, where some say he sat for days in blackest melancholy, and that his Mood was so deep that no one went near him; his only contact with the world being a roasted chicken pushed through a hole in his door each day to keep him from dying. So he lay in Gloom while that brilliant intractable Charles Townshend rode the Empire like Phaeton with the Chariot of the Sun. God save us, I distrust Genius in Administration as much as I distrust Fools. We seem to be served with one or t'other!

The result of Townshend's attempts to collect Revenue here is a disastrous fomenting of Crises with us. The Northern Colonies, and now Virginia too, are boycotting all the

[268]

Articles named in the Revenue Acts, which is a particular loss to British Trade.

"Oh dear Lord, listen to this." Sal looked up brightly. When she saw that Jonathan was concentrating so, she looked down again, a little hurt, and went on reading.

Jonathan did not hear her. He was trying to make sense of news that presupposed a contact he had lost.

Added to this they have had a killing Spring, and the common sort of people is in great suffering. Great pains are being taken for the sake of Office to irritate the people against America, especially the Freeholders, and to persuade them that they are to pay great Taxes and we none; they are to be burdened that we may be eased; in a word that the interests of Britain are to be sacrificed to those of America. This is partly to counter the popularity of that rabble-rouser Wilkes and take the mob hatred from the King who is hooted by the People when he goes forth.

Jonathan understood at last. He said aloud, "Spotteswood, he says here some fool in Commons did demand that every gentleman who bore office here should be compelled to declare his loyalty aloud to the king and the right of Parliament to place taxes. This is the deepest insult."

This did wake Spotteswood for a minute. He tried unsuccessfully to suppress a yawn.

This time Jonathan spoke only to himself. "What will come of it I do not know." And as if the letter answered him, he read on:

I can only fear the spread of the Northern turmoil. Let the tobacco crop but fail again here, and we will have the poorer planters (who are wildly extravagant in keeping up the genteel appearance of little Nabobs and are deep in debt as always to English merchants and therefore welcome the fashionable Boycotts to save money anyway) risen beyond Control. Why in God's name have they insisted on using the Curb with us before they but tried a Snaffle? Thank heavens we Gentlemen of Fortune have learned the adaptability of good business here and are not now so sunk in tobacco that we will see the Colony ruined.

But enough of Sound and Fury. Let me tell you about your son Montague. I take as much Pride in him as if he was my own Son, since God had only blessed us with a Daughter. He has grown into a fine handsome fellow, and is good at his Studies, though not unbecomingly so for a Gentleman. He is long in the leg, has good hands, is right well-spoken for a boy of his age, although sometimes inclined to rashness which I take mostly to be his youth. But he can hold his Liquor as becomes a Gentleman. I think he will do well in Politics.

Polly is well and is still as beautiful as a fine work of Art, but has no more children. We are most anxious to hear that you and Sal will visit us soon, when you feel well settled enough to leave the Back Country. Let me know whatever you want done. I am always Obliged to serve you.

I remain,

Your humble Obed. Servant,

Brandon Crawford, Esquire.

"Lord, she says here," Sal interrupted before he could speak, as she saw the letter he had been reading drop onto the table, "she says, 'Stays is gettin ever longer and higher with what they call a "fishu" to top it off like a pouter pigeon.' Now what to my soul is a fishu, Captain Lewis?"

"I don't know, mawm." Spotteswood, realizing at last that he had been asleep, pulled himself awake, embarrassed, said humbly, "I ain't been East now for two years."

"Oh." Sal looked back at the letter, disappointed. "She says 'tis unfashionable to have any article that is on the boycott, and that ladies have stopped sendin handkerchiefs and fans when anybody dies, since they are English made. What would they send, indeed? I never hyeared the like.

"My, it does sound fine, the way they live at Crawford's Grove. Hyar's a mighty funny thing. She says their Neegrew postillion has took to runnin off. They have two coaches and a chair," she explained to Captain Lewis, as if that was nothing at all. "So Mr. Crawford makes him get dressed up and then he fast chains him to the driver's seat when they go abroad, to insure their ever gettin home again!"

"Sal, my dear, I think Captain Lewis and I would welcome a leetle more toddy." Jonathan glanced at her from the letter, which he had picked up again.

"I know," Sal was arch. She curtsied to Captain Lewis. "His mind is on great matters and he is bored with my frivol!"

"Will ye send down to Jarcey and ask him to dine with us?" The question caught her at the door.

"Yes, my dear." She walked out of the door in a dream, already setting her head high for new stays and a fichu. All the way to the loft the mood carried her, but once there she sank into a chair and screwed up the letter in her hand. "Polly's just a-flauntin her riches, the hateful thing." She pounded the knot of paper against her leg. Then she smoothed it out carefully to read again.

*   *

"Johnny." Her voice came out of the dark when they had gone to bed.

He was almost asleep.

"Do ye think Mr. Crawford will make Montague his heir? Johnny!"

"Yes, my dear."

"I said do ye think Mr. Crawford—"

"I heared ye, Sal. I don't know."

"Well, ye seem mighty uninterested. Goodness, look at all he's doin for us!"

But he didn't answer, so she supposed he'd gone to sleep.

So when Jonathan answered Brandon Crawford's letter more hands than his own held the pens. If he had struggled to reconcile himself to patronage, if he had let ambition fight a certain twinge of new pride in his land beyond the mountains, if the wishful question over Montague had affected him, all these things were settled and at peace when he handed the packets with two solid letters, from himself and from Sal, to Captain Lewis to take with him until, in time, he would meet a soldier or a scout going back across the mountains.

Beulah
March 18, 1769

My Dear Brother,

I am eternally obliged to you for the interest you have shown in me, and in this part of Virginia. The new county will settle many Problems that have plagued us, and have kept the industrious from settling here. The people have cried long and loud for some Authority to defy the lawless thieves which infest this Section. The rich and honest are far from safe from their own blood—though you must understand that a Fortune in the eyes of most here is reckoned by the possession of a Sow and a Mule!

I am most desirous to know what form the authority you have told me to expect will take. We seem from your letter farther from the East than you are from England and I must ask Questions you who live in settled parts can afford to take for granted. Will there be some form of circuit-court, and if so will I as a Justice be required to ride Circuit? I have no Objection to this, and indeed would welcome the chance to bring some Order to this chaotic Frontier, but it is necessary for me to settle my affairs and leave my family safely in charge I can trust before I undertake such a Task.

May I suggest that a show of Law be backed

at once by the raising of a Militia here? We have great Need of authority to protect our lives and property, indeed even our wives and young girls, from roving bands of Cattle and Horse Thieves who are our greatest Danger and Problem. I would be obliged if you would send me some such book as Blackstone's Commentaries or such another useful work on the Law.

We have not had trouble with the Indians at Beulah since the Pontiac wars, although we have had threatening drunken Indians from time to time who can foment trouble by quarrelling with the lower sort of whites, who hate them, lie with them, live like them, and murder them because they are thought an inferior Breed of Man. Indeed, where it is tantamount to a gouging bout to call a man a Scotchman or an Irishman in the East, here you can shed a right smart chance of blood over the word Mustee or Yellow-belly as they term half-Indians and Indians here.

I have wrote to you some notion of what our real Problems are, for we fear that the East thinks of us as Riff-raff who stand a kind of Border Bluff between the Piedmont and the Six Nations, and have no internal troubles to call our own.

That is why I receive with such relief and joy the news that Gentlemen of Fortune such as yourself are indeed still concerned with investing beyond the mountains and turning the Territory into a County instead of letting the troubles to the East take your interest from us. I am in great agreement with your conclusion to sell up some of your Grants in hundreds (that is how I reckon it to be easiest). Sold land such as yours, Mr. Lee's, etc. should fetch along about eight pounds an hundred. I doubt you will get more as it is general knowledge here that the Government price is three pounds.

I must warn that there will be some tumult when the poorer classes of settlers find all the good bottom-land to be already spoke for in large Grants. They had hoped for much of it for the taking up. Indeed there will be thousands of acres for that, but 'tis Pine Barren or hilly land. I must admit to you my whole heart in this matter if we are to understand each other as Gentlemen should in the Event of our standing a Poll together in the future.

I am sorry for the people here to see the new land go in such large Grants. Some of them have waited long and patiently without squatting (as the meaner sort have done) and they seem to be poorly paid for their Patience. I have a family here who have taken short lease on my land in hopes that they can lay a legal claim and become Freeholders when the law allows. Now there is little chance. With their children being taught lessons here, and the safety of numbers, they had hoped to locate within a few Miles, but Captain Lewis brings me the news that all the Bottom Land over the River has been included in some huge Claim. He does not know which but suspects it is one of the claims of Colonel Washington. As a result I have no choice as a Christian, knowing the virtues of the Carver family, but to sell them an hundred of my own land and let them farm the other three as tenants.

I put this attitude and opinion down because it is necessary to be absolutely open-hearted with you in view of our Connection and to show you how living here has changed my point of view of necessity to that most in sympathy with the people among whom I live. On the other hand, I admit freely that one aspect of these large Grants is of the *greatest* relief to me. That is that the control of immigrants will be, to a certain measure, in the hands of Gentlemen of Breeding, Interest, and Sense. I hope you will be sensible to some Advice I will set down here from my Experience.

For hard work and standing on their own feet, the lowland Dutch and the highland Scotch seem to make the best settlers. They bring with them the self-reliance of people who are used to fending for themselves, which is what we have great need of here. Beware of too many settlers from the more tyrannical small kingdoms of Central Germany as they are too used to the Whip to be able to do without it. I have an excellent lowland couple here who are worth gold, but the Prussians I tried last year were like dumb animals and the woman died of grief for her chains like an old horse taken from the tread-mill. The man works like a dog who must always be ordered. Such people do not have the tenacity required in this hard unbending Wilderness.

On the other hand many of the Irish who come raggle taggle, poverty ridden and too much ordered (what the Germans call *bossed*) are mostly as useless in the other extreme. They are like hound-dogs kept leashed too long, who turn to brainless cavorting beasts when they slip their lead. They can stand scarce any Constraint—which here is not human but the constraint of constant war with the Elements which are a harder enemy than any over-lord. They drag down the frail structures of civilization we try to build by rash irresponsibility. Indeed many have gone over to the Indians, seeming to have no such blood-hate of them, having been counted so long an inferior Breed themselves by the English, I suppose. Of course this is not true of all but can serve as a useful Generality for the course you propose to take.

The Protestant Irish (they call themselves the Scotch-Irish) from the north of that island, on the other hand, are tough and self-reliant to the point of blind stubbornness. They carry a chip on their shoulders from having been a minority in religious thinking at home, and from having suffered, as they reckon unduly, by English laws restricting their former employment in weaving wool. This they count in their Passion to be a punishment for their being Roundheads in the great Revolution, though I see no sense in such thinking and am bound to look, as always, for *Interest* rather than *Passion* for any English measures against them in the past. I must admit I have never yet seen the spirit of violence plow a straight furrow, nor proud ignorance fell a tree.

I know you will not welcome greatly my suggestion about the Scotch (and for that matter the northernmost and westerly English who are fine settlers, being used to small farms until forced out by so much enclosure) since the first are Presbyterian and the second tend to the new enthusiastic religions such as the New Lights, the Baptist and the followers of Whitfield. Indeed I cannot even try to acquaint you with the thousand different sects that grow like weeds here among them. They will follow any new ranter who preaches the wild ignorant way to God, and the Divine Right of White people, like ancient kings, to swallow up Indian lands. You will think them unsound politically unless they are tempered with enough settlers of the established Church. You have reason there, but *I can foresee the time when the interests of common problems will outway religious scruple.*

However they make fine settlers, their religion makes them straight-laced and solemn but also preaches a virtue of great industry which we had better to have *with* us than *against* us. Also in their favour, too great a class sensibility as among the English has not sapped their pride and turned it to Jealousy and Pretention (I have also counted the unbounded extravagance which you mention and which you know I suffered from in my youth to be but a mirror of that apish pride of place so many brought with them to the Colonies). Oh why are the English virtues so great they can rule the world, and their vices of Arrogance so vicious they can lose it again!

I had a curious happening here when we first come back. One tenant who though not good was the best I could find at the time, a man named Cutwright who had married with a Mustee—or at any rate called her his wife as there is little chance for the forms of marriage this far out—left me and went on westward. This troubled me as I had been good to him and patient beyond my usual way, since the man had fought with me in the wars. I found then that otherwise good God-fearing women had bound to *hate them out* since the woman was of Indian blood

[276]

and that she carried an added grievance that no one came to see their baby buried the winter before because of the blood, though I suspect it was really the cabin-fever which raged here and kept them all away, for I hesitate to judge them as heartless as that. The strange part was that they left their other children behind them seeming at the time to care nothing. I see now 'twas to give them a chance to have learning as we have the only school within an hundred miles at least. One of the six took the way of his father last spring, being wild, wretched, and unteachable as a savage in confinement, but the others turn into useful, pretty children in their new life.

The schoolmaster and I watch them bloom, fond as fools, and it revives our hopes, which sometimes seem so foolish at more melancholy times, that we may make a damned fine civilized place here yet, though Miss Sal sometimes moans at our own children being reared up with the little breech-clouts as she calls them. It is hard for her here, though, and I wish heartily it were possible to send her and my daughter Sara who is now eleven and a wild rose in beauty, back to you for a spell of the genteel living she hankers after.

As I have wrote before, locating out here and improving the land forces us to take up a new Economy, more primitive Barter than ready exchange of notes or tobacco as in the East. The Barter here is Ginseng, which I accept as payment in the Mill and the new Ordinary—also for Seed, Machinery, stores. I do in turn exchange this (which fetches a high price) for more acceptable Currency in the East—it is the *only* product we have worth taking over the mountains. I hope to see more money soon for I intend Public House keeping in company with Mr. Pentacost, and I am preparing for it now. We will take upwards of three pounds each day during the spring when the Land Jobbers come through.

I have kept 'til last my thanks for your great generosity and feel myself your constant debtor in spirit for the

[277]

confidence and support you have given me. I can only accept your generous offer, for my family's sake, in the humility and Christian spirit you have offered it. A man tugs many ways like a horse in the traces to ease his shoulders of his conflicting pulls of loyalty. If I have caught a spell of regional pride, I confess it is weak, compared to the real debt of honour and friendship I owe you. What's done is done about the great Grants, and for practical expediency I can but accept my place in the Scheme of things. I could only as a man of honour, temper the thanks I owe you with honesty as you would wish and respect.

In reading over my news, I see I have left so much unsaid. There is so much time to cover in our infrequent letters! Thank you for seeing to the buying of Brandon's two neegurs for me when he died. I reckoned the inheritance to be in the hands of his Tidewater brother. They arrived here by wagon-train last fall. You see by the rest of my news why I am forced to have more neegurs and also why it is expedient for you to sell when you can rather than conclude to have too many tenants. Any tenants are whetted by the idea brought from too long without land at Home, that of one day being lords of their own domain. I think it is cherished by our people to an excess which frequently injures them and exposes them to useless danger. They bring out here an iron pot, a hog, a memory of jail, enclosure, or bending to landlords, and a fear of gentlemanly learning and the law as their natural enemies, which is one bit of plunder for settling we could do without.

Give my fondest love to my pretty sister, your daughter, and of course, my Montague. Tell him that from your reports I am mighty proud of him. The English news affects us little here as the cash we get cannot go to imported goods, but it is much appreciated and I wish you would keep me informed. I reckon to indulge myself in the luxury of interest to keep my mind alert, for I confess too regional a Mind on such matters, tending to think as the rivers flow, away from the Tidewater and Tobacco.

Since we cannot *roll* hogsheads east we tend to think away from Home. Many of the people, I confess sadly for their own happiness since it breeds unhealthy Resentment, wish to forget because of their own failure there. I mention this because it is as well to have Incite if we are to have ambitions as Politicians.

I remain,
Your humble, obedient servant,
Jonathan Lacey

Chapter Two

IT TOOK four days of reading over and over the few copies of
The Virginia Gazette and the precious *Gentleman's Magazine*
which Captain Lewis had been able to bring. Jonathan and Jarcey
ate them, argued them, memorized them, a little bewildered by all
the changes, then calming at the realization that so much was the
same in the world. Solomon came once and stood by the fire, reading slowly and spitting from time to time over the paper into the
fire, and arguing with the news in a steady mumble. When he had
talked them to a standstill he lit out to carry the titbits he had
digested. It was his version of the tags of news of the winter that
Carver heard. Solomon could pitch news with the same verve he
pitched hay, with much passion and only fair accuracy.

"No, we hain't a-buyin nary glass and tea and—oh, all kinds of
truck." He stood, having forgotten the rest, in Carver's door. "Oh
I tell ye, Mr. Carver, I tell ye 'tis pretty serious."

"Oh Solomon, what good are thim things to us, nohow?"
Mother Carver called from her wheel, which hummed in the room
behind Carver like a swarm of bees in a hive. "Don't fash your-

selves. Etty, turn that wheel faster, ye lazy slut." A girl of eight roused herself from a sleep of boredom and began again to whirl the big wheel.

"This is a mighty important to-do, let me tell ye, mawm. I been in Philydelphy and a lot of places—"

"We-uns have hyeared all that thar, Solomon. All this hyar taxin is not to do with usn. Lord God, what could we-uns reckon on a-buyin, nohow?"

"You wait, Mother Carver, you wait," Solomon told her fiercely over the sound of the wheel.

It never faltered, and the distaff stick she played as delicately as if it were a cello moved a little in rhythm between her knees as she sat akimbo, calm.

"I'm a-waitin." She snorted with laughter and never faltered in the measure of her spinning.

Solomon yearned for an ordinary where he could find a little argument. He wandered off, disgusted, down the valley, and even, in his lonesome fit, collared Jeremiah to tell him. It was like talking to Aaron the priest about the Gentiles, Jeremiah was so uninterested. He poked his stick into the soft ground three times, watching the mud ease back into the holes he made. Then he found something to say to Solomon, who stood with his worried face thrust forward to aid conviction, so intent that he forgot the tobacco spittle down the cleft of his huge mouth.

" 'Render unto Caesar that which is Caesar's, and unto God that which is God's,' " Jeremiah finally said to the third hole, because Solomon had mentioned taxes and he thought he ought to say something helpful.

"Well, now that's a mighty pretty sentiment, a mighty pretty sentiment. Thank ye, Preacher," Solomon said, baffled, as Jeremiah limped away from him, lost to a nice little talk, still watching his stick enter the ground.

"He walks slower ever day." Hannah, coming around the corner of their cabin with sticks for the fire, had caught sight of Jeremiah and murmured to the tall young boy who sat cross-legged in the sun, patiently cutting a piece of rawhide into strips. "I'll swear to Gawd, I don't know what we're a-goin to do," she went on, looking almost angry with worry at Jeremiah, who was toiling up the last of the hill.

Ezekiel, the eldest son, now fourteen and already gone thin as a sapling, looked up slowly from his work, and watched downhill, under his eyebrows, frowning a little at the light. For a second he looked so like his father that Hannah found herself surprised, as she always was when she noticed it. Then he lowered his head and went on driving the knife slowly through the rawhide.

"We-uns will manage. Jest don't let on to him, Maw," he told the rawhide calmly.

"I wasn't about to let on, honey," Hannah said low, because Jeremiah was so near now. She hoisted the sticks she'd been gathering to her other hip and disappeared into the cabin. "Thim two is alike as peas in a pod. I cain't say nothin." She threw the bundle down so hard it scattered over the floor.

"Oh Lord, Becky honey, pile thim sticks. I'm wore out."

"Yes, mawm." A small girl of six put the huge broom she was wielding up against the wall and turned to the scattered sticks. She bent down, sighing a little hopelessly, a grown woman's sigh.

Hannah sat, rubbing her tired arms. She yawned widely. "I got spring fever," she said through the yawn and pulled herself up again to the never-ending work as if she carried a heavy load on her back.

Ezekiel moved his eyes from the knife for just long enough to see Jeremiah's feet and the stick as a tripod standing between him and the sun. Mud had splashed above Jeremiah's winter moccasins onto his leggings. Ezekiel lowered his eyes, and the knife began to move again slowly through the hide.

"Hain't ye finished thim straps yet?" Jeremiah demanded.

"Jest about," the boy answered.

The weight went onto one foot, and he could see the stick sink slowly under it. He could feel Jeremiah's impatience growing over his head.

"Oh, hyar, give hit to me." Jeremiah sat slowly down beside the boy, who handed over the knife and the rest of the hide without a word.

"See you git thim staves chopped afore tonight, Zeke. Ye're so damned slow y'hain't worth a hate no more."

Ezekiel wandered off down toward the woodpile without a word. By the time he got there he seemed to have forgotten why he'd been sent, for he lifted the ax and just drove it softly, over and over, into the ground, his face dark with trouble of his own.

"Why don't ye leave the boy alone?" Hannah, who'd heard Jeremiah from the door, called over to him.

"He's bone lazy."

"He hain't bone lazy. He's a-growin too fast. Lord Gawd!" She picked up one of the cut straps and started to chew it.

"Mr. Lacey and Mr. Pentacost are a-settin down thar readin," Jeremiah said sadly.

Hannah went on chewing the hide.

"They been settin thar four days." The knife came free of the hide and flashed loose. "Don't git much done, settin thar readin. Ye'd think they hadn't no more to do." The knife lay by him while he remembered the secret look of the papers.

"Zeke hain't a-going to pick up thim notions, I'll tell ye that." He started another strap. Hannah wandered back into the house, paying no attention, still chewing the strap.

"Hain't no son of mine goin to pick up fool notions," Jeremiah went on, without knowing she'd gone until he heard her furious voice.

"Rebecca, git up from thar, ye lazy idle thing!"

"Yes, mawm," the little girl's voice floated back.

Down by the new-cut window, Sara and Peregrine watched their father's back, still, hardly breathing, waiting for him to put the paper down. Peregrine, grown as tall as Ezekiel, lounged against the wall, taking it all casually, aware of his thirteen years, but eleven-year-old Sara clutched the window, a suppressed whirlwind of excitement, trying to attract her father's attention by staring hard at his ear.

"Come on, Sara, Ma'll catch us and put us to work," Peregrine whispered. Even the light whisper made Jonathan move the paper a little.

"Sh-h-h't!" Sara motioned quickly to him to shut up.

They needn't have worried about their mother. She, waiting at the door in the dog-run, was intent on business of her own. Finally she could stand it no longer. Sara saw her come into the room, and dropped out of sight below the window.

"Johnny, ain't ye read them yet?" She heard Sal's voice, demanding.

"Yes, honey. I reckon we're about finished." Jonathan put the paper down, smiling at Jarcey. "We were wonderin how long everybody would hold out."

"I've got a thousand uses for that paper." Sal began to gather the precious *Virginia Gazettes* as if she were harvesting. "I don't reckon," she said with little hope, "ye'll let me have the *Gentleman's Magazine*. 'Tis so good and thick—"

"Now, honey—" Jonathan began.

Sara had released the whirlwind. She ran past her mother and threw herself at her father's lap. "Pa," she yelled. "Ye promised! Oh, Pa!" She burst into tears.

"Quit that, Sara." Sal stood with the papers clutched victoriously in her hands.

"Pa, please, please." Sara kicked the floor.

"Shut that up, miss, or I'll tan your hide," Sal yelled over the crying, trying to grab at the girl's dress, but the legs were like flails and kept her away.

"Now, sweetheart, don't take on so." Jonathan smoothed Sara's soft hair, and Sal's knuckles went white against the papers.

[284]

"Ye promised!" The girl's voice came, muffled, from his lap.

"So I did. So I did. Sal, my dear, a promise is a promise. Don't ye think we could spare one of the papers?"

Sara caught her breath and waited for the answer.

"Ye just spoil the gel, Johnny. 'Tis all ye do. Lord knows when we'll git more. If ye only knew the uses for it. I've run out of poultice paper. I ain't got nothin to line the chests, nor to cut patterns."

Sara stayed still as a mouse, but she raised her head to watch her father.

"I think we can spare one. 'Tis little enough pleasure for the child."

"Pleasure!" Sal snorted, still clutching the prize.

"Oh Sal, my dear. Let the children have a paper!"

Sara looked at her mother. It was a look of pure triumph. But when her mother looked down at her she knew that, sweet as it was, the triumph would be short-lived.

Sal drew one of the precious papers from the thin bundle and slammed it down on the table. She turned and left the room without another word.

Sara had turned from triumph to joy. She hugged her father, grabbed the paper, and ran from the room, the prize flapping behind her.

"Perry! Perry! I got one. Come on!" she called as she passed the porch.

The lounging boy, with one look at the paper, turned from bored man to racing child again. They were off over the meadow.

"By God, 'tis leetle enough pleasure," Jonathan said again, now that the room was quiet. "Jarcey, that leetle gel is growin up. She's turned pretty as a yearlin doe. She's goin to be a beauty."

What hung between the two men they didn't say. Instead Jarcey went on to the next thing that sprang to mind.

"Peregrine is smart as a tack, Johnny, but I'll swear to God, if I had the books I could turn young Zeke into a scholar. But what's the use! Why turn him to chop logic when he'll have to chop logs all his life?"

"He's the livin image of his pa." Jonathan got up. "Well, our feast is over. Let's get back to work."

"I have a dream about him." Jarcey followed Jonathan out onto the porch. "I like to think he's what his pa might have been if he'd a-been taught the Roman virtues instead of the Jews'!"

Jonathan laughed. "I confess I can see Old Repent preachin a fine sermon over the Sabines instead of Jezebel."

"He's pretty fierce on Jezebel, ain't he?"

"Fierce? He loves the woman as I suspect John Knox of lovin Mary, Queen of the Scotch."

"How much longer do ye reckon we can keep the youngins in school?"

"A few more weeks—in the evenin anyway. By God, 'tis spring, Jarcey. I don't envy ye tryin to hold 'em!"

"I still cannot see what the Parliament can hope to gain . . ." Jarcey's voice was interested in the discussion, as he had been interested in the article on conch-shells. "By God," he said, "if I could go to Italy once . . ."

Jonathan had ceased to listen. "I reckon we ought to open the ordinary, Jarcey, as soon as we can. Now that the county's open and the trails is a-clearin, we'll get more people through here all the time. I wish to God we had some rum to sell . . ."

★   ★

Sal straightened up from smoothing the papers on the kitchen table. "Dear God I'm tired. Tired! Tired! Ye'd think he'd under-stand. He don't care nothin about me. These Cohees all laughin because I ain't got no babies." She leaned back and let herself rest against the wall for a minute and closed her eyes. When she opened them again the first thing she saw was the fireplace. She uncoiled and shot to the door.

"Lyddy! Lyddy! Come here at once!"

"Yes, mawm," Lyddy's languid voice came from the outhouse. She walked slowly up onto the back of the dog-run.

"Ye was just lettin on to clear that fireplace this mornin. Get in there and do it agin, ye lazy slut."

"Yes, mawm." The insolent Brandon eyes raked at her as the Negress passed. Sal struck out and slapped her across the shoulder, hard, meaning to hit her face and missing, to her shame.

"Git, now," she yelled.

She might as well have hit the river to make it flow faster. Lyddy flowed in and knelt by the fireplace, paying no attention.

"Oh Lordy me!" Sal beat her fist against her thin petticoat. "I'm up against brick walls! Walls all around me. Little they know." She stopped and surveyed her rock pile. The sun, the fine great pile, made her happier and fed her pride. There it lay, by now six feet high, in the hill field. Jonathan had insisted that it should not be set too near the house because the snakes gathered dangerously. But he could not stop her from having it. He couldn't stop that.

"Well, at least I made them do it. And I'm going to keep right on makin them do it," she said so loudly that Lyddy grinned as she knelt by the fire and slowly swept with a witch's broom while she rubbed a little snuff she'd sneaked, happily.

*   *

"Zeke! Zeke!" Sara called through the trees as they scouted him out, standing by the wood-pile, pegging the ax to the ground. She didn't call loudly enough for anyone else to hear, lest he be stopped, out of habit, by a grown-up.

He dropped the ax when he saw the tall, thin girl running through the trees.

"We got it. Come on!"

Now there were three of them, running in a ragged line, escaped from the stockade of constant children's work, down the hill—

[287]

now five as they passed Carvers', now six as a flaxen-haired boy looked up from the creek and saw the paper. Sara stopped only for a second to slap a tiny child away. They were moving too fast to be bored with the littler children.

Solomon sat in his only chair, tipped against the wall, enjoying a bit of peace while his wife was out of the house, calmly watching them run toward him like piglets to a trough. He saw the paper in Sara's hand and slowly rolled his quid across his tongue and lodged it in the pouch of his other cheek.

"We got it, Solomon." Sara was in front of him now, shy with hope, while the others waited.

"Well, I don't know as I got the time right now." Solomon waved a path between the children and spat, dignified and slow. "I got a right lot things to do right now."

"Oh Solomon, please." Sara begged for all of them.

"I got a right lot on my mind right now."

Nobody said a word.

"Oh, all right, give hit hyar," he said at last, wearily in charge of the situation.

They watched the paper go into his hands. He folded it and began to tear it to pieces, the white bits flying, some straight to the hard-packed ground that made his porch. Some, caught by the wind, fluttered away, caught against the children's shirts; one lodged in Sara's silky hair, but she didn't notice it. She was too fascinated by watching the blunt fingers, now moving quicker and quicker, tearing and flipping the pieces away, now as light as woman's fingers, tearing, tearing . . .

"Thar!" Solomon gave a yank to a secret place at the top of a fold. Slowly he raised it, and the worn-out copy of *The Virginia Gazette* had become a tree, as shapely as a cedar, its paper branches lifting in the wind as he held it up for them to see.

"Oh, Solomon, can I have it?" Sara whispered.

" 'Twouldn't do ye a mite good. 'Tis magic. Efn I hain't a-holt of it, 'tain't nuthin a-tall." He kept the tree raised up, and then began to lower it.

"Don't let go yet!" The flaxen-haired boy found a small voice. He swallowed loudly, embarrassed at having spoken.

The moment had reached its climax. Solomon, from old practice, knew it. He let the top go, and the paper collapsed to nothing but a worn scrap, sadly settling on the ground.

It had had the moment of beauty, and then death, of a firework.

Peregrine moved to Solomon's shoulder. "Please, Solomon, next time show us how," he begged, pulling at the man's sleeve to persuade him.

"No," Solomon announced finally. "That I cannot. 'Tis a star in the head, and y'ain't got hit. So say no more. Say no more," he finished, a man important with knowledge.

But, having had his pleasure, he relented a little at the disappointed faces around him.

"Ye see, 'tis thisaway. Some has stars in the head for one thing, some for another. That thar is mine. That and hat-makin. Ye wouldn't believe your eyes, that ye would not, efn ye could a-seed me makin hats. Slip, twirl, cut, flip. By Gawd, sar." He suited the action to the words and twirled an imaginary hat before their eyes. "No goddam coonskin with a tail, that thar is a vulgar thing when ye've seed this hyar beaver hat, made by Solomon McKarkle." But his empty finger waving in the air made him sad. "Nope. Now I hain't a-sayin ye hain't got stars of your own. Take the little towhead thar." He pointed to a squirrel collared with a rawhide string, which rested, round-backed and tame, on the German boy's shoulder. "He's got one with critturs. They hain't a crittur he cain't tame, from a leetle shy scawmed doe to a snake. But efn ye try tamin another snake I'll take on myself to whup ye!"

The boy looked at the ground. The squirrel chirruped by his ear because everybody was watching.

"It weren't his fault it got loose," Sara said kindly.

[289]

"Now you, Miss Priss, ye got one, too. I hain't a-sayin what hit are. But I been a-watchin ye. I seed." He looked over at Ezekiel, who stood a little away from the others. "Mr. Pentacost says ye got one for larnin. Why ye don't know—ye might git to be a fine gintleman, with a ruffle shirt and a hoss of your own."

"He will, too." Sara watched him coolly. She leaned against Solomon and whispered wetly into his ear, "He's my sweetheart."

"Oh, ye sassy slut!" Solomon crowed. "Hark at her! Ye've turned him red as a fall leaf!"

"Have I got one?" Peregrine interrupted, hoping but remembering not to care, whatever Solomon said.

"You?" Solomon surveyed him. "I'll reckon a shootin star more like. 'Tis a pity y'ain't got your pappy's. Now him." Solomon settled himself firmly against the wall again, so that Sara's weight wouldn't tip him over. "He's got one about the land. I seed folks like that. Lookee out thar." He swept his hand around their heads toward the valley. "Ye youngins don't see nothin but a few clearins and a mighty lot of weeds, and a bunch of damn trees. I know that man. He don't see none of that. He looks right over hit—right over hit, and sees himself a right fine town, with carriages and— Oh Gawd, they hain't no use tellin you leetle heathens—hain't none of ye been no place."

"I'm a-goin," Sara bragged. "I'm a-goin down-river and I don't know where-all."

"Oh y'are, are ye? When are ye aimin to set out?" Solomon leaned his head against the wall and laughed; the others caught the joke and began to laugh with him.

Sara stamped her foot. "I am too!" She began to cry. "Oh, I hate ye all. Ye don't know nothin. Y'ain't got no manners and ye don't know nothin." She began to run up-creek, through the harsh new buffalo grass, which rippled and tossed in the strengthening wind and seemed to fright her as she stumbled and struggled, blind-eyed with tears.

She turned up into the wet, cold woods, hot and panting, and found a tree to lean against.

She knew whose hands were on her shoulders, gentle, turning her to bury her head against him.

"I will too," she cried at Ezekiel. "I will. My ma said so. I don't have to stay in this hateful place if I ain't a mind to."

Away in the woods, where no one could see them and break the silence with strange grown-up hands pointing and faces saying terrible things, it was so easy to hold her closer to him and kiss her face and her hair to make her feel better.

"Ye will, Sary honey, ye'll do what ye want. So will I. I'm aimin to do right smart things my own self."

"Zeke, don't tell nobody, but ye're my sweetheart," Sara whispered, forgetting at once about going wherever she wanted to.

"I won't tell nobody." He didn't dare to touch her body, though he wanted to explore it, but felt a new shame, like a current through him.

Sara felt it from him and thought he was cold. "Y'ain't got enough clothes on, Zeke. Here, snuggle up with me. I don't want to go back yet—Ma'll get after me. I seen ye naked in the crick yesterday. I watched," she confessed.

"I don't keer none."

"Ma says I can't come swimmin no more. The hateful thing! She says I have to go by myself."

"I'll watch from the bank and see ye don't come to no harm."

They sank down, snug against the tree, their arms around each other tentatively, almost asleep, curled round like animals seeking warmth.

Sara's arm was wrenched up, held like a thin white branch in Sal's hand. In her other hand she held a hickory switch.

"I found ye, I followed ye, ye dirty little slut!" The thin face was gray with anger, and her hair had straggled down from battling through the woods. To Sara, starting up, her mother's face seemed to fill the whole sky over her.

[291]

"Don't, Ma, ye hurt me!" she screamed as the woman jerked her arm again to make her struggle to her feet faster.

Zeke sat up, frozen with fear of the woman. The switch came down across his face again and again. He tried to twist away, put up his arm to protect himself, and the switch fell against it. It seemed an hour of the switch falling on him, like fire, before he could twist away.

He could hear Sara screaming behind him as he ran off through the woods, his hands still over his face, protecting it from the switch. When he took his hands down finally, still running, they were bloody from the broken welts across his face.

"Ye let him be! I'll kill ye!" Sara's voice faded behind him. "Ye she-devil. She-devil!" The switch came down on her legs, and she screamed again from anger.

"I'll larn ye to talk like that to me." Sal was whispering with fury. "I'll larn ye. That'll larn ye." She still held the girl's arm, but Sara's body danced and twitched under the whirring switch. "No daughter of mine is a-goin to lay out in the woods like a filthy whore. I'll tell your pa. Ye'll git sent where ye can get a proper rearin."

They both were silent. Only the switch, swishing and slapping against the girl's legs, broke the cold spring silence.

Sara, now that her panic was gone, wouldn't let herself cry out or move. She only flinched as the switch landed, her face filthy with tears and dirt.

Finally she heard herself say, "Please, Ma, oh please, Ma, please quit," and was ashamed, broken. Her mother let go her arm then, and she fell back against the tree.

Sal was worn out. Only her eyes still showed any anger; her thin chest pulled in air and stretched her shift over her low, flat bosom. The switch dropped from her hand. Wearily she leaned forward and gathered the back of Sara's shift in her fist. The girl had started to cry again, but she didn't sob. The tears ran down in runnels through the dirt. Sal marched her ahead across the meadow, home. She stopped only once to pick up a rock at the creek. Sara's body flinched again as Sal handed it to her, thinking her mother was going to hit her again, but when she saw what it was she only cradled it in her sore arms to carry it up the slope without a word.

Peregrine was leaning in his old place against the porch wall when he saw them coming. The bitter boy, who longed for a star in his head like the others', was satisfied and ran round the house.

He ran slap into Lyddy and knocked the logs she was carrying out of her arms. She grabbed his shoulders to shake him before she remembered herself. Then she looked over his shoulder and saw the two coming onto the porch.

"Ye tattled. I hyeared ye, always a-runnin to your mammy." She looked at the boy, the barrier of her race too strong to let her say what she wanted to.

"I only told Ma where she was. She asked me," the boy said, not daring to look straight at Lyddy. "I never meant nothin." He pushed on by her, and, far enough away, turned back.

"What business is't of yours nohow, Neegur?" he said quietly to her back as she bent to pick up the logs.

Sal, on the porch, pushed Sara toward the stairs. "Get up there and clean yourself up," she called after the girl, who was pulling her sore, red-streaked legs up the stairs. "Put down that rock, ye leetle fool. Ye can take it out to the pile later. Lord God, what am I goin to do to keep her from runnin hog wild?" She pushed open the kitchen door and sat down at her wheel and set it whirling. "Well, one thing," she told the whirring spindle, " 'tis the end of that riff-raff's school days if I know my mind. Takin advantage of his betters . . ." The distaff whirled under her competent fingers, and she licked and fed, licked and fed the spindle, her foot making the wheel whirl faster and faster, feeling peaceful at last.

Sara sat alone on the bed in the nearly dark room that huddled under the pitched roof. All that was left to her was complete bewilderment at why her mother had whipped her. But it was too much to figure, so she crept downstairs again, tiptoeing to cover Lyddy, who'd forgotten to put any water in the upstairs bucket, and, hearing the wheel going in the kitchen, knew her mother wouldn't see her as she crept back to the outhouse to wash and find Lyddy to steal some vinegar to ease her sores.

Lyddy told her the whole thing, told her in whispers in the dark outhouse while she bathed her legs.

"I know ye niver meant nuthin, my honey-pie," she crooned, happy to set Sara right. "But 'tis the way the world are. You a-growin up."

What she told Sara made her hang her head and run away from Ezekiel when they came out of school the next day.

But the story that Sal told Jonathan of the terrible thing she had seen meant that it was Ezekiel's last school day.

"I only half believe it, Jarcey," Jonathan told the despondent teacher, "but 'tis as well for now. In the fall 'twill be forgotten. 'Tis only the way of children."

He did not reckon on Jeremiah's saintly anger, which made him beat the boy so badly for his sin that Ezekiel ran away to the woods for two weeks, and came back half-starved, because now that he was a fourteen-year-old man he knew that they couldn't run the farm without him.

Chapter Three

A LITTLE dry dust fanned up from the hard-beaten path to Jeremiah Catlett's cabin. Here it settled on fine, pounded yellow dirt, there on bare rocks which through the years of scuffing up the path, had been exposed, the ground packed hard around them.

Jeremiah's dragging left foot no longer quite left the ground when he walked. It made a thin, indented trail in the summer dust. Three o'clock on a hot summer day was no time for a man to be trudging along between the sleek cornfields, now so high that he could not be seen, except from the hills, as he walked between them. But they gave no shade; they drooped their flaxen tassles and their leaves under the heavy weight of the sun.

That there was something on Jeremiah's mind heavier even than the sun on his head was evident in the way he gazed at the ground, in the negligent way he carried the precious ginseng he had gathered in the faraway woods. The years had made him frailer. Like the weathered cabins and the widening fields in the ninth year of Beulah, Jeremiah had settled, nearer the dusty ground.

He looked up at his cabin. No one stirred there. All Beulah

was asleep, or driven to the woods. Jeremiah, now that he had gained the rise, could see a Negro working far off in a cornfield beyond Jonathan's farm buildings. But outside of one bent back, the barn, the smokehouse, the milkhouse, the new paddock, the little row of slave cabins all seemed deserted, given in to the heat.

Jeremiah looked back at his own place. Nothing new built there; nothing added but the pain of sickness slowly fading the life out of a man, and the pain of growing up added too quickly to a black-eyed boy of seventeen who had had too soon to become a man.

He had reached the cabin; its green coolness after the heat was like a sigh. But Jeremiah did not stop to sit down and rest. He heaved the ginseng onto the table and turned slowly, inspecting the room to see if there were any signs of Hannah.

When he saw that the room was empty he stood for a minute, thinking, then hobbled over to the ladder. It took so long getting up it, dragging his leg, that he stopped halfway and started to look around for someone to help him up. But after he had rested a bit he went on, snail-slow and twisted with awkwardness, up into the loft. Once there, he never stood quite upright. The roof was too low for him, even in the center. So he walked as quietly as he could across the creaking boards, his head thrust down as if he were praying.

He heard a sigh below, through the open boards, and stopped, still as a hunter.

But Hannah, seeing the ginseng on the table, stopped too and listened.

"Jeremiah," she called out. "Where are ye?"

There was no answer. The house had its own sounds of high summer—the steady hum of flies, the gentle scraping of heavy vines that by 1773 almost covered it to the roof in summer, light green and watery against the pine boards.

Jeremiah knelt down carefully by the cedar chest he'd made for his coffin, but not carefully enough.

[296]

It wasn't the sound that had given him away, but his presence up there. Hannah sensed at once the feel of emptiness, the feel of presence, even of a chipmunk or a snake under the roof, because she was a woman and it was her house.

"Jeremiah!" she called again. "Are y'up thar?" The empty room buzzed while she waited, poised, listening.

He didn't bother to answer, just opened the chest lid and let the wood screech.

"Efn hit's one of thim youngins . . ." Hannah made for the ladder.

"Jeremiah Catlett!" Her head appeared at the top of the ladder. From where he knelt sideways to ease his leg, her head looked presented to him on a platter, peering there across the loft floor. "Whatever are ye a-doin of?"

"Nuthin." He laid out his best buckskins she had taken so long to make, and on top of them his linsey shirt.

"Ye're a-goin up thar," she told him.

"I hain't a-goin to do no sech thing, Hannah."

"How'd ye git up hyar anyhow?" she fussed. "I'll declare, ye're a-gittin worse than the youngins—sneakin around."

"I niver done no sech thing," he said calmly, beginning to undress.

"Well, leastways ye can warsh efn ye're a-puttin on them Sunday clothes." Her head disappeared, but her voice went on steadily as she went to dip water from the rain barrel. "Lord Gawd, though why ye'd want to go whar ye hain't welcome . . ." She sounded bitter, and Jeremiah's face went blank, even by himself, to hide what he might be thinking.

"Thar, now don't slop the pail. Hit runs through the floor," she said with a habitual angry warning as she set it on the floor beside him. Then, seeing him so bent there, staring at the wall, cast down, she relented. "Don't ye fash yourself." She patted his shoulder. " 'Tis damned fard mean, but we-uns hain't a-goin to show nuthin."

" 'Tis my own son," Jeremiah said hoarsely, and cleared his throat. "I niver knowed Johnny Lacey would do sech a thing."

"Now listen hyar, honey. 'Twarn't him done hit, 'twar her. You know that."

"Sure I know that. We-uns jest always done hit our way, him a-doin the county marryin and me a-doin the holy part. I niver reckoned on no furrin preacher like that. That are a damned sight more'n a man can swaller." He couldn't say any more, but sat numb with his disappointment, looking at the clothes he'd laid out.

"I'll help ye, honey." Hannah, to lighten his mood, sprang up, and hit her head on the roof. "Jesus," she said sternly. "I damn near butted my brains out. I know why ye're a-goin. Ye jest got to lay eyes on that preacher."

" 'Tain't as if—" But what he was going to say was lost in his sadness. He cracked his knuckles instead to watch them go white and jump. "I hain't niver seed a real preacher but Mr. Stone."

"Ye got a mighty sight sang down thar." Hannah changed the subject as she had for years when Mr. Stone's name was mentioned. It was like pulling the bung out of Jeremiah's memory. The whole story flowed out if it wasn't stopped, and Jeremiah looked sad enough to do a lot of talking just to brighten himself up, remind himself who he was. "Hit ought to fetch pretty good price."

"Hain't hit strange how the Lord provides—"

"Considerin," she said calmly, "hit's been pretty near famine through the winter, 'tis damned strange."

"Hannah!"

"Go on. Git your clothes on." She disappeared down the ladder, holding her head.

When Jeremiah limped out of the house, looking neat as he could be, she watched after him proudly. "He's bent and he's broke, but he's still a nice, proud man," she said aloud.

"Did ye want me, Maw?" Her daughter, now ten, and begin-

[298]

ning to be round and pretty as Hannah remembered herself, ran around the house at the sound of her mother's voice.

"Oh, I don't know. Go tote up some taters." Hannah searched for a chore for the girl to do, now she was there.

"I done dug some."

"Well, dig some more," Hannah told her crossly. "Don't sass me."

The girl went off down to the patch beside the cabin and bent low in the hot sun.

"Next thing we know ye'll be out thar a-bringin back a woods-colt. As efn we hain't got trouble enough!"

Jeremiah, now that his mind was made up, was no longer sneaking. He was striding out as well as he could with his limp, and to anyone who saw him he was at peace with the world, just having a nice walk.

Mother Carver caught up with him down by the creek, where their two families had long since worn a packed path. She caught up with him, and they walked on, slow, scudding the dust.

"Brother Catlett," she told him flat, "I'm a-tellin ye flat. We-uns hain't happy about the way ye been treated. They hain't nary a one of usn a-goin to the widdin."

"Sister Carver"—he looked straight ahead and made his voice good and strong—"we-uns can turn tother cheek. 'Tis my youngin, and I don't want him sad at his own widdin."

"Ye're a fine man. They hain't nary another man would take what you done." He was obviously in no mood to talk, and the sun was too hot for Mother Carver to walk far, old as she was. Finally she gave it up and stood panting in the pressing heat.

"Leastways," she promised after him, "they ain't nobody a-goin to kneel and carry on."

But he never answered. She put her hand up against the western sun and squinted after him as he crossed the nearly dry creek and started off up the slope.

[299]

"He went up thar—he's a-goin up right this minute!" She couldn't wait to get back and tell Mamie.

"The only ones showed any sense was thim youngins." Mamie came to the door to look.

Mother Carver laughed. Her toothless mouth spread like a pumpkin slit. "Oh before God, Mamie, they sure done that. They's more ways to kill a dawg than choke hit to death on butter!"

"I coulda told Miss High and Mighty, Miss Clatna litty!" Mamie spat tobacco on the truck-patch carefully so as not to waste good manure.

"We all coulda told her, but ye know what the Bible says. Thim as has years . . ."

"I'd like to see her face right now."

⋆   ⋆

"Whatever they can say about me," Sal told her stays as Philemon laced her into them, "they can't say I never did what was right."

"Now, Miss Sal," Philemon fussed, "stop bein so fidgety and don't git all het up agin. I've had enough trouble with ye."

Sal held the bottom of the stays and took her last deep breath, to stretch her body into some comfort. "Where's the gel?"

"Miss Sara's across in her room."

"What's she doin?"

"Jest a-layin thar a-thinkin."

"Huh! I reckon she's got herself plenty to think over." Sal raised her thin arms against the gown Philemon held.

"Aw, Miss Sal, why don't ye let bygones be bygones. She's your own—"

"She's no daughter of mine, Philemon. Ye mind your business. I'll go through this because 'tis right to keep up some decent ways —but don't ye talk of the gel to me."

"All right, Miss Sal. All right." Philemon sighed. "Now don't ye look fine?"

[300]

" 'Tis nothin but Miss Polly's old clothes, but 'tis better'n any of these Cohees. I wish I had a mirror."

"Oh Lord. I knowed when Lyddy broken that mirror 'twas seven years' bad luck." Philemon went back to an old moan. "I wisht ye'da let me throw hit in the crick!"

"Oh, Philemon, don't ye ever forget nothin? Is ever'thin ready? Has Mr. Cory washed himself? Did ye look after him?"

"I looked after him, Miss Sal, now ye know that. Quit wigglin. I washed him myself. He's so damned saddle-sore he couldn't no more bend over. I washed—"

"Don't tell me, Philemon. I don't want to know."

"He's having himself a mite toddy with Mr. Johnny."

That was the first thing Jeremiah saw when he came up to the porch, the toddy in the preacher's hand. As if that wasn't enough, there wasn't one thing about him that said "preacher" to Jeremiah. He didn't look a bit like Mr. Stone. He didn't look holy at all. In the first place he was fat—pretty hard fat, but still huge. In the second place he had on a brown coat and ruffled shirt with a fine-looking black stock. His hair was powdered, and he wore it cut short as a pig's ridge on top and sticking straight up, with sausage curls at the sides, and a black bow. In the third place he was laughing, laughing with Johnny Lacey up there, damn near fit to kill.

"No, by God, if I'd known I was goin to ride two thousand miles a circuit in a year I never would have set foot in Botetourt County, I'll lay ye that, Johnny Lacey. But I figured on pickin up a mite property, same as the rest. Oh, poverty is a sore trial!"

"It was mighty good of ye to come out this far." Johnny reached forward to take his cup.

"There's nothin I like better than a widdin." The man laughed again. "Makes me feel some use in the world. I tell you it's a fine rest to be conductin a gentleman's sarvice in a gentleman's home. I spend my whole time marryin whores and baptizing bastards. Do ye know"—he didn't notice that Jonathan had stopped still, for-

[301]

getting to fill the cup—"out of the last hundred gels I've married, ninety-five of 'em was with child?"

"What do y'expect, sar, when the church ignores us and expects one man to ride circuit and stop two-three times a year at the most."

Mr. Cory looked up at him then, soberly. "I beg a thousand pardons, sar. I never knowed. Would ye care to talk with me about it?"

"There ain't nothin to say, Mr. Cory. Poor leetle gel."

"What's the man like?"

"Man!" Jonathan set the cup down so hard it cracked. "He's no more than a boy. They was drove to hide under my very eyes. No, I don't hold nothin against the boy. God Almighty, Mr. Cory, ye know what 'tis like out here. Ye turn a leetle savage to survive. 'Tis the ways of nature warrin with the ways of us feeble men. Nature is a strong enemy. We live closer to the body out here. I'm sorry. I'll get ye another cup." He disappeared into the kitchen instead of calling Lyddy, to get out of the man's sight for a minute.

She was in the kitchen, her brown arms deep in creamy white dough. When he sank for a minute into the chair by the fire, she came over, wiping her arms, and put her pink palms against his temples. She knew better than to say a word, but when he got up and took the cup out he was calmer from the pressure of her palms against his throbbing veins. He hadn't even looked at her. He had only paused, as a runner pauses and becomes centered in the comfort and peace of himself, before he sharpens power to run again.

Jeremiah had reached the porch, and now stood arrow-straight, watching Jonathan as he came back out of the dog-run. The preacher's politenesses had obviously fallen like spent arrows from this stern presence. Mr. Cory had already lapsed into the apprehensive silence of a friendly pup that gets no reaction.

He was even more surprised when his host ran past him, boyish with pleasure and relief, and clapped his hands against the man's straight arms over and over, and he saw a shy smile slowly transform the solemn face.

"By God, Jeremiah, by God, sar, I'm glad to see you," Jonathan said. "Come and set a spell with us. Mr. Cory, here's a man of your own complexion, a preacher as well. Come, draw up a cheer and talk with the passen!"

"I's jest a-walkin by and I reckoned I might as well." Jeremiah sat down carefully on the edge of a chair.

"Ye'll take a drink with us, won't ye?" Jonathan called out, "Lyddy, come bring another cup!"

"What persuasion would ye be, sar?" Mr. Cory rocked back.

"Oh, nuthin like that," Jeremiah told him. "I jest seed the Light."

"The New Light?" Mr. Cory teased gently.

"Jest the Light." Having not been allowed to tell Hannah what had flooded his memory for the day, he began to talk.

"I's a-layin out thar in that cornfield . . ." The excited voice caught Sal as she stepped out onto her stairs. Jeremiah heard the rustle of her silks before he saw her, and the story flagged. By the time she turned on to the porch, he was dead silent.

"Mr. Catlett has come to take a drink and meet the passen," Jonathan said and helped her down the last step.

"Indeed," Sal said coolly. Her voice made the last of Jeremiah's fire go out.

There was nothing to say. Jeremiah got up. "I got to go now," he told Jonathan.

"Let me walk a leetle way with ye." The two men went together off of the porch.

"Will ye come tomorrow, Jeremiah?" Jonathan stopped, down the slope. "The youngsters and I would miss ye."

"I'd admire to come, Colonel Lacey, but—"

"Now, let's have no buts." Jonathan could say no more, but they watched each other for a minute.

"That thar's a pretty nice man—looks larned and lets a man say what he thinks," Jeremiah went on. Mr. Cory had hardly said a word to Jeremiah, but his own spate of talk had been to him sweet conversation.

"I'll be hyar in the mornin." He hesitated for a minute. "I reckon hit would be right nice if Hannah come up and helped git things ready."

"She's mighty welcome, sar." Jonathan said good-by and went back to the porch.

"Well, I'll declare, Johnny Lacey, what will ye do next indeed? After all our trouble with them Catletts I find ye hobnobbin as if they was quality. God Almighty, if I never watched he'd have the hound-dogs in, a-settin on my best cheers a-talking politics."

"Mr. Cory"—Jonathan ignored her—"that's Mr. Catlett, my new son-in-law's father. Since he's soon to be a connection of ours, I think the least we can do is make him welcome."

Mr. Cory, who liked nothing better than a little ease and quiet entertainment, seemed to turn on a spit between the two fires of their anger, under their light words aimed at him.

"I always believe in a good welcome," he said judiciously, and plunged into compliments. "I wish I could tell ye what a fine thing 'tis to find a gentleman's establishment away out here. I don't consider it blasphemous to say 'tis like the Holy City to a tard traveler. If ye could see some of the places I've had to sleep, saddle-sore and weary—nothin but lard and pone day after day. Well, Mrs. Lacey, ye keep a fine house. Makes a man feel to home agin." He left room for a remark, and when none came he sailed on. "There's a mite danger sometimes, I can tell ye. I'm the last man to want trouble. I reckon on it being a peaceful world if we let it be. But I'll tell ye, there's time more'n my cloth was in danger—'twas my life too."

"Indeed to goodness!" Sal finally was impressed enough to speak.

"Yes, mawm, I've had my horse stole and the dogs set on me and insults from the backwoods Presbyterians and Seventh Day Baptists would sicken a soul stronger than mine. But 'tis my callin, and the Lord gives me grace and courage."

"What do you *do?*" Sal's eyes were wide. "I've hyeared some things but not attackin a man of the cloth."

"Well"—Mr. Cory sat back peacefully—"I try to pass over it with that Christian meekness and compassion I've larned in my callin"—he folded his hands—"and of course the contempt and derision befittin a gentleman," he went on to explain.

"Oh, of course." Sal pursed her mouth and touched her best fichu lightly with her fingertips. "I know too well what ye go through, Mr. Cory. Oh Lord, there's been times—I'll tell you, surrounded by people that has been brought up so differently from myself that when sick and low-spirited their company only disgusts me. Oh let me tell you"—she fingered the fichu—" 'tis a ray of light to have a gentleman like ye for company. I just wish ye'd come in less—unfortunate circumstances."

"Now, mawm"—Mr. Cory leaned forward and tapped her knee—" 'tis a widdin, and there ain't nothin finer than a widdin! Ye must make the best of it as becomes a lady of quality."

"I am makin the best of it," Sal said in all humility. "There's not a woman livin who tries as I do."

"I'm sure of that, Mrs. Lacey, I'm right sure of that." Mr. Cory's eyes wandered over her head to see if Jonathan had forgotten the drink, but he had gone out of sight. Mr. Cory sat back with a sigh.

*   *

Up in her loft room Sara sat on the bed and watched a ladybug move across the floorboards. She bent forward slowly and laid her long, slim, sunbrowned hand in front of it, hoping it would crawl on her and give her good luck. When it did she raised her hand

[305]

slowly and watched the ladybug move importantly along the length of her finger. It reached the round fingernail, split its sleek spotted shell into wings, and flew away.

Sara lay slowly back on the bed then and gazed at the roof, where one or two tendrils of creeper had forced thin, naked, pale fingers in between the bark shingles and seemed to be feeling for a better hold as a slight breeze caught them. She closed her eyes and tried to sleep, to shut out the fingers and the day itself, which crept so slightly through the few niches between the logs that the room was dim. But she couldn't sleep; she could only lie there, smoothing her stomach under her white shift. Something brought a smile to her drowsy face, but it was wiped away as something else chased it, and she lay as sad again as ever, beyond even tears, watching the vines. She turned her head to keep from staring and noticed that a small patch of light had moved across the floor. She sat up suddenly, aware of time, listening. The light drone of voices on the porch below told her where her mother was.

She got up, smoothed down her shift, and tiptoed to the door. Barefooted, she had learned to make no sound at all. She got the door open enough to ease her slim, now tall body through it and stand waiting on the little outside landing. The sun was blinding after the dim room.

Down below, she could hear Sal's voice. "Times is pretty bad, as bad as they can be. Mr. Lacey fed one poor soul after another. . . ." And the strong carrying preacher's tones, answering, " 'Tis a true thing. Back East the lower class of people are in a tumult on account of the reports from Boston; some expect to be pressed and compelled to go and fight the Britons! But 'twill never come to that. Nobody wants that but a few radical republicans who rouse the mob to dangerous extremes. . . ."

Sara went down the stairs as soon as she was used to the light, at first slowly—then, as she felt the bottom step, she began to run, as fast as she could, down the slope.

"Wherever is that sassy gel off to now? I told her—Sara! Sara, you come back hyar!" Sal ran to the porch edge and yelled. The girl didn't stop. "Lookee there. Barefooted too. I just can't make her mind. Oh Mr. Cory, if ye knew what I went through. Her gone wild out hyar in the wilderness. 'Tis the least I could hope . . ." even Sal had reached the place where she had to recognize that she was beaten.

"She looks a right pretty leetle gal, mawm." Mr. Cory tried to pour his habitual drop of oil.

"The number of times I told her, 'Sara,' I told her, 'now ye mind Mr. Pentacost and pick up some larnin from him, and some manners from me; if ye can't have beauty ye can have brains and good breedin, and we'll send ye back East to be reared up proper by your relations, the Crawfords.' But she wouldn't listen, went barefooted and rid a-straddle, swimmin in the crick naked as an Indian. Oh Lord! The ugly, pesky thing!" She couldn't keep the tears from her eyes, but cried and rocked a little because it was all right to rest for a minute in front of the parson.

"I done the best I could." Sal took a deep breath and leaned back in the rocker. "In all Christian humility, Mr. Cory."

"Now I'm sure ye did, mawm. Ye wouldn't happen to know when Colonel Lacey returns, would ye?"

Sal wasn't paying him any attention. "Do ye know the Crawfords, Mr. Cory?" she asked lightly.

Mr. Cory said he did and they were as fine as Virginia had to offer, but his eyes swept the slope for Jonathan because he was getting as dry as a Baptist.

"Of course, the Crawfords are no finer breed than my own side. My sister married a Crawford, but we were Sawyers from England. My husband's uncle is a man of great fortune, a Member of Parliament he is, too—Sir Miles Cockburn." She stopped to figure. "A Cockburn married a Lacey. Now *my* father—well, my father . . ." The rocker rolled sympathetically as Sal recited to life her frightened spirits.

[307]

★   ★

The evening star hung low in the sky, although it was still light enough to see the ripening white flax fields, when Jarcey left the ordinary to go home for his supper. On the way he stopped at the empty schoolhouse as usual—just put his head in to see if everything was all right.

Sara sat all alone in her white shift, one bare leg curled around the leg of the long bench, the other jack-knifed along the bench with the long, grass-stained sole showing. She had her mother's hair, that's what Jonathan had always said. It lay, a thick blond column, tied back like an Indian girl's, soft against her back. She looked so concentrated on what she was doing, leaning low over a piece of slate as she had always done in school, that Jarcey stood still in the doorway, shy of disturbing her. The slim, light girl seemed left over at her trestle table, still studying while the other children had gone out to grow up, as if she had remained to haunt her own childhood. On such an evening, before her wedding, a girl did not sit like a child drawing at her slate.

"Sara," he said quietly, not to surprise her too much, "what are ye doin here?"

She turned coolly, completely unsurprised. "Howdee, Mr. Pentacost. I just reckoned I'd draw a little." She went back to her picture. The only sound was of the hard chalk stone scratching on the slate.

"Will ye let me see?" He came on into the room and stood beside her and looked over her shoulder. On the dark, uneven slate were many attempts, blotted by tears, and one small, nearly finished drawing of a house—a castle with two round turrets which Jarcey had told them about once. She saw the wet splashes and tried to wipe the whole thing away with her slim, long forearm before he noticed them.

"It ain't nothin," she muttered, "nothin at all."

[308]

"Honey, whatever is the matter?" Jarcey put his hand against her back, and she was shivering. "Ye're shakin like an aspen."

She didn't answer but made one last attempt to draw, the chalk clutched tight in her hand as if it held her secrets and so long as she could keep concentrated on its movement they were safe.

"Move over a leetle, my dear. Let me sit down."

She unwound her leg and moved, put both feet together formally, her whole body withdrawn from him, and, as he sat down, moved the slate over to begin her desperate scratching again. Now she held herself upright, poised, still as a listening animal, her delicate shoulders drawn in so that she looked thin and gawky; her fine collarbone was sharp against her skin. She had not quite succeeded in lifting her head, though; it drooped, hiding her small lovely features from him, down toward the slate where she could no longer make herself draw. He could not see her eyes; she had turned a little away; but one tear glistened against her round child's cheek and rolled, unchecked, onto the slate again.

"Tell me, my little sweetheart, tell me what's the matter." Jarcey put his arm around her shoulders.

"I've been hidin here so long a-waitin for ye." She choked and cleared her throat, as if the waiting had been what was wrong all along.

"Why did ye never come and find me? Ye knowed where I kept afternoons."

"I knowed ye'd come here. I seen ye come here and just walk around, a-touchin things. I thought ye'd never come this time." She spoke so low he had to lean close to hear her. It was easy to hear her heart thumping, caged in her narrow chest.

"Tell me, honey, if ye want to, tell me." He was as patient as a woman holding her hand out to lure a pullet to the safety of its coop.

She sat so long he thought she would slip away any second, without speaking at all.

"What if a person—" she finally began slowly. "If this person—"

"Yes." Jarcey helped.

"Well, this person never knowed things was wrong, and this person loved this other person and they played together always and he was nicer to her than anybody else and wouldn't let nobody tease her 'cause she never said her r's like her ma taught her, and called them Ma and Pa instead of Mammy and Pappy." She seemed to be chasing words wilder and faster. "Well, this person loved this other person more than anybody else in the whole world and he loved her best his own self." The tears were falling now as fast as her words, blurring the bare pine room, blurring her voice. "And they never thought they done nothin wrong and they had a house, a playhouse out in the woods where there weren't nary a body to holler and fuss at them and they had a secret and this secret was important."

She climbed into Jarcey's arms and lay against him, sobbing, clutching tight to his shirt, trying to burrow for safety.

"And everybody found out and said I was mean and low and bad and I never done nothin ugly but what was natural to me. They said I was bad and sinful out of the Bible and would go to hell and he was bad and we never done nothin low but love each other more than anybody in the world ever did before and I couldn't help it Lyddy done said it was natural and Ma said 'twas a dirty common thing I done I wish I had died and then they'd be sorry."

The last words were more sobs than words, and now there were only sobs. She lay against Jarcey's chest, and he hugged her as if she were a lost hound-pup he'd once whistled all night for in the alien woods. The evening star was bright now in the purple sky; the bare room and the slow, dark river outside were still, as if the whole valley waited through the in-between time for the girl to stop her crying and the night to plunge down and bring out the pattern of the little settlement in winking supper lights.

Finally she was quiet enough for him to talk to her; he cradled her head to one side so she could hear him and gave his sleeve for her to wipe her nose and eyes.

"Now, Sara, listen to me. This is a secret between us and your Ezekiel. Ye understand that?"

He could feel the silk of her hair against his chest, and she nodded, shuddering to stop the last sobs.

"What you done in love was never a sin, child"—Jarcey's voice dropped peacefully in the near-dark—"for love cannot be a sin; it can only be dirtied from outside by them that go cold from their cradle to their grave and never felt love. 'Tis only for a few people." He wiped her fine hair back where it clung to the sweat of her forehead. "Don't ye see, for them that's never felt love but only fear, they've got to call it a sin, lessn they holler like Job at God for having chained them in cold bodies like prisons so they dassn't fly out to each other. 'Tis a secret from them, and they see the secret shine out of another face and want to destroy the face along with the secret so it can't hant them with what they never had. 'Tis so with the poets and the saints and the lovers."

She was so still he thought she had cried herself to sleep. But when he stopped to listen to her breathing, she whispered, "Go on."

"Now ye know the story in the Bible?" She stiffened against him. "No, no, they ain't all stories of hell and damnation in the Bible. Folks just pick those out to explain why they're so afeared, and to scare each other. This is a better story. Do you remember when the people brought the woman taken in sin for Jesus to judge her? They stood around waitin with stones in their hands to blot out her face so they wouldn't have to look at her carryin that secret couldn't any of them share. Well, Jesus stooped down, and with his finger wrote on the ground—'as though He heard them not,' it says—and then He lifted up Himself and said unto unto them, 'He that is without sin among you, let him first cast a stone at her.' And again He stooped down and wrote on the ground."

Her head turned, and she looked out at the bright star shining in the deep purple night. She leaned against him still, but now relaxed, cool and almost weightless, quickening with her growing up and with her child at the same time, as if all the blessings and curses of womanhood plunged over her at once.

"What did He write on the ground?"

"Well, the Bible never said, and a man can only reckon to himself. I always reckoned He done it to keep from lookin at them, as a man whittles a stick of wood, or you drew on your slate, holdin of Himself in to keep from bawlin at the sight of those people who never understood about love, because He was so sorry for them."

"Mr. Pentacost"—after a little while.

"Yes, sweetheart."

"Did Ma love Pa?" The question fell heavy on him.

"Well, honey, she did as much as she could—that's all ye can reckon on, people's best. But your pa, he loved her as I hardly ever saw a man love a woman."

"He don't any more," Sara said firmly.

"Well, he does now. 'Tis different, though. Have ye ever tried to pour a whole jug of water into a little glass? It slops over and runs every place. That's the way with your pa. He's got so much over to love his land and his friends and his family."

"He loves Lyddy. I love Lyddy too, because she's soft and pretty. I don't care if she's black. Perry says if I kiss her the black will come off on me."

She whirled her whole body around against him and planted a dry, warm kiss on his cheek. "I love you, Mr. Pentacost, and I

[312]

love Pa, and I even love Ma when she's workin real quiet and don't think nobody's a-lookin at her. But I love Zeke the most. Don't ye?" she asked, worried.

"Zeke's my favorite pupil, and ye're my favorite leetle gel." She could see his face above her, and she read its familiar lines and shadows. It was more solemn than what he'd just said so lightly.

"Are ye mad at me?" she asked anxiously.

"No, leetle gel, I'm not mad at ye. But Sara, Sara, why did ye never go and talk to your pa? He wanted ye to. He never would have let ye go on, sad like I found ye. He could have explained it's not the killin nor the clearin only but leetle gels like you will settle the country."

She turned away from him again and leaned back. "I wanted to lots of times. But 'tweren't right to. He'da told me anythin I done was all right because I'm his leetle gel."

The unconscious imitation of Jonathan's voice made Jarcey smile in the darkness.

"Ye see, when they said all them things to me—when Ma done about my being Cohee and riff-raff and low, and Mother Carver, she laughed and poked me in the ribs and said I was sassy and Old Repent—I mean Zeke's pappy—well, he stood in the way in the path one day and rolled his head back and forth like Ma's clock, and said I was shapen in iniquity—Lord God, whatever is that anyway? Well, I knowed none of them *knowed* to tell me, so I figured for a long time and I always believed what you said, so I come to ye." She settled herself more comfortably against him. "I had to find out from somebody that could whup me. By God, ye sure could do that."

" 'Tis the business of a teacher to keep order—"

"Oh, Mr. Pentacost, ye sound just like ye was in school!" She laughed. The soft easy laugh made Jarcey feel successful, and suddenly almost tired to death.

[313]

"Why did ye never marry, Mr. Pentacost? I reckon ye'd make a mighty fine husband." Her voice came out of the darkness after a few minutes.

"Why, I did marry, honey, ye know that. Don't ye remember? But my wife didn't take to the life out here. She went off."

"I remember now." Sara rattled on, now that she was happy, with the unconscious cruelty of fourteen years. "Mother Carver told me. She went off with a land-jobber and she wasn't a damn bit of good." She jumped up and stood tall beside him, then leaned down a little to hug him. "You's much too good for her!" She made this pronouncement, so like her mother that Jarcey was startled into saying what was on his mind, without shielding her.

" 'Twas not all Mary Martha, poor ignorant leetle beast she was. I kept myself apart from her like a man does in his pride. I thought 'twas youngins, but she never stayed, even when the leetle Cutwrights come, so the Carvers had to take them to rear with their own. I was a man of reason and I had an ideal to love all equal. Well, I have it still, but that ain't what a woman fancies. A calm man sittin nights in a hollow room, with a tame dog, a tame deer, and a tame squirrel skitterin in the rafters, throwin nutshells down on my head!" He laughed and turned, finding a kind of self-pity he didn't know he had, embarrassed. "But sometimes it gets damned lonesome."

The girl was gone. She had not even heard him. He saw the tow-linen shift, a narrow white slip in the dark doorway, and he heard Ezekiel saying, "What for did ye run away, Sary, all barefooted? Your paw's searched all over for ye. He finally come to me." The last was muffled in her hair as he kissed her.

"I knowed whar she'd be, Mr. Pentacost, sar." Ezekiel had his arm tight around her waist, and Jarcey could see them moving toward him. Ezekiel towered over the girl. Now, at seventeen, he seemed to have stretched to his full growth, but his youth still made him move tentatively, between lankiness and grace. In the darkness he was a large, substantial form; only his great eyes, black and sunk in his bony face, shone out for Jarcey to see clearly.

"We just had a leetle talk, son," Jarcey told him. The two of them, like a single figure, seemed to cling together against the darkness.

"Oh, Mr. Pentacost, don't he smell nice—like smoke!" Sara murmured proudly against him.

"She's barefooted, sar. I reckon on carryin her home now." The boy's new manly voice was hoarse and timid. "I brung your book back, sar." He bent down to put it on the table.

"Now ye'll have a home of your own, Zeke, what's mine is yours to read."

"Thankee kindly, Mr. Pentacost, thankee kindly for that. Come on, leetle gal, I'm goin to carry ye home." He lifted her up into his arms, and they were gone as silently as Ezekiel had come.

Jarcey, left alone, picked up the book and fluttered the pages idly. He sank down again on the bench, moving like an old man, and put his head down in his arms.

"Where the hell's the scholar?" he heard somebody yell through the new night from the door of the ordinary, and someone's voice answering, "Yes, by Gawd, whar are he? I do like me bombo sarved by a gintleman and a scholar!"

Ezekiel carried Sara close to him, slow across the flax field, which shone like mist moving over water. Neither of them said a word, forgetting even Sal, standing with a candle shaded in her hand to watch for them. Only the yellow hound at Ezekiel's heels whined a little as it followed.

Chapter Four

EZEKIEL woke the next morning at false dawn, so early that the loft was full of sleep. He stepped over his sister's arm, flung trustingly out onto the floor from her mattress. The other children were huddled together, the quilt kicked off; a faint smell came from the warm pallet, where the youngest had wet it in the night. Jeremiah groaned a little in his sleep and gnashed his teeth, making Hannah turn over, but not waking her. Ezekiel bent down to cover the children again, then went on tiptoe to the ladder and down into the kitchen, where the fire had almost died. He blew at it and put a new log on the glow he'd uncovered.

In the dim light he ran to the rain barrel, as if there were urgency in the air, stripped off his buckskin of the night before, plunged head-first to his waist into the ice-cold water, and rubbed himself with his bare hands until he was warm again. Inside the kitchen Hannah had laid out the new clothes that it had taken nearly the winter to make fine enough. The skins were tanned nearly white. The thick tow-linen shirt had lain so many times in the sun to bleach that he could still smell the warmth and grass in it when he put it on. He took his new pants out with him to the rain barrel again and splashed water from it over his legs and his naked thighs, then drew the pants slowly, carefully over his wet skin so they would set right to his body. The feel of pants, instead of leggings and breech-clout, was uncomfortable and strange. He walked back stiff-legged and stood by the fire, moving his legs up and down until the wet of his skin worked the pants enough for him to sit down. Finally he got his gun and his scalping knife and placed them on the table in front of him, close to hand, to wait for the ordeal by wedding to begin.

It was lonesome, waiting, and Ezekiel was scared. All the stories of being a groom stiffened his back as he waited—the time young Jacob Cutwright, just his age, brought back the mustee girl to marry her proper, and they had stripped him in the woods and painted his billy-cock red so the girl wouldn't be yearning after the Indians; the time they cut Bogie Carver's hair close to his head with their knives to make him pretty for his wedding; the time . . .

Ezekiel reached out for his knife and waited, watching the full, pure blue dawn come. Far down the creek, he could see the rope of summer mist that hid the river and remembered that he had not set his seine the evening before.

Hannah found him there when she groped her way down, still half asleep. He was so intent on the open door that he didn't hear her, so she could stand a minute watching him, enjoying how handsome he'd become, tall and lean without an extra ounce of flesh on him, looking so fine in his new clothes that she wanted to snivel. Hannah had never seen Jeremiah at Ezekiel's age, but she liked to think that that was how he might have looked, with his dark hair heavy on his shoulders and his face strong, but still with the delicate skin and features recalling the child, before he had to shave himself leathery like a man and the angles of his thin face sharpened into their final mold.

But what she said was, "Lord Gawd Amighty ye forgot to

comb your hair. Hit's shaggy as a pony." And she moved to do it herself with the thick wooden comb Jeremiah had carved, so it would be done right.

It was done right, too, although the boy squalled at her pulling.

"Dear Gawd, ye sound like a baby," she fussed, "and you already a-gittin married."

He didn't know that she had come down early too, so as to protect him as best she could.

She stood, a sentinel, to greet the men with whisky when they poured into the cabin an hour later. Because she was there they only made Ezekiel drink; what other wedding jokes they had planned were forgotten.

From her front porch Sal could hear them singing and roaring as they left the cabin and rode down the valley, racing for the bottle for good luck.

"Whoopin and hollerin like a bunch of Indians," she told Jonathan, who was waiting by the barrel of whisky he'd had brought around to the front yard of the house so they wouldn't muss up Sal's rooms.

"Now talk to the boy, take him back and talk to him." She disappeared into the kitchen, where Sara sat, not daring to move and dirty her new white linen dress, which Sal had trimmed with the best lace from England, which came from her own father's shirt, as a wedding present.

"Linen! Common linen. Never mind, 'tis only hundred linen, fine as a kerchie. I pulled it through my ring when it was wove." Sal bent down and fingered it. Sara, watching her head, was afraid to speak to her mother in her new mood, for she had never seen it. Sal seemed determined to make the best of it if that was what they all wanted. "The least I can do," she told Jonathan when he promised to bring the parson, "is make it a decent, genteel widdin!"

She seemed now to move through the hubbub outside, and the chatter of the women who thronged her kitchen, as if she could walk a fine line through the treat, making a single snail-track of good behavior. She, too, had heard and seen what could happen at a wedding. She moved stiffly, afraid of the laughter, the wild sense of acceptance of the results of love that these people had, afraid that it would turn on her, as it had on others they considered high and mighty—the lessons taught for putting on too many airs, the horses' tails and manes cropped and carried wildly waving on long poles, to mark their joking fury. So she walked with care, as formally as she could before the constant critical eyes.

The day, the wedding itself, seemed to pass like a dream for her. She even managed to exclaim politely over the presents, the crude kindnesses, the linen quilts, the blue and white linsey counterpane woven by Mother Carver, even a bed that Solomon had carved—and kept following her around, drunk, to describe.

"I cain't whittle no sparl. 'Tis crooked as a dog's hind leg—nor yet no spools for they come out all different. But thar hain't a man better for making of a thimble bed. Now hain't hit the prettiest thimble bed y'ever seed, mawm?"

Sal said it was—every time he asked her she said it was, keeping her head away from his stinking breath. In the middle of the presents she had set her own, two of the last Delft cups and saucers, a single silver spoon, a pair of shoebuckles she had thrown down in an ecstasy of generosity that had affected her like a twitch of nerves.

Solomon kept on following her, pleased that she liked the bed, and happy, as he told everybody who would listen, that Mrs. Lacey had more to her than he reckoned.

Her mind lodged on one failure, stuck as a hook on river weeds, but no one knew. The dratted boy, standing there like a half-drunk Indian in his buckskin breeches, had refused to wear her present—Jonathan's second-best suit of broadcloth and a ruffled shirt she'd made herself so he'd look a little better when he got married. She had only wanted him to look a little like her

Peregrine, who'd dressed up fine, the way she wanted, and whispered to her, "There, ain't I the macaroni!" making her giggle, and had stood, looking as contemptuous as she felt, in the background. But lank, ugly Ezekiel Catlett couldn't do it for her, not he.

"No, sar," Ezekiel had explained to Jonathan. "I shot these hyar, and Maw made thim. I reckon they're fine enough. Why, sar," he had said simply, "Maw would take hit hard."

Jonathan had laughed it off and slapped the boy on the back and said he looked mighty fine.

"The dirty drunken thing!" Sal bit her lip and stood for a minute in the smokehouse alone, rigid with disappointment, her small hands clenched.

Ezekiel was not drunk; no liquor on earth could have roused him from the island of shyness that he and Sara were isolated on together all through the day—the wedding party as dim to them as it was to Sal.

The dinner was over and the night down. In its warmth they crowded out of doors and danced reels and jigs to Carver's banger, sending up shouts like sparks in the night, and stamping so that the hard ground boomed like a drum.

Sal, standing in the doorway with the parson, who looked so pleased she found herself wanting to slap him, heard Mother Carver yell, "Give usn a song, Carver, a pretty love-song about murder."

The dancers flung themselves down, sweating and hot, in the grass. The Negroes moved among them with gourds of toddy. She could see Lyddy's dark form, and Philemon, now grown massive —wandering black shadows. The lightning bugs and the stars seemed to gather and dance, filling, hurting her eyes.

Sal went inside to enjoy the last bright, constant light of the spermaceti candles she'd saved for eight years, and they'd hardly noticed. She rocked and tried to shut out the words from her head, but gradually, as the song conquered the noise, she had to listen.

"Neither ride to the east, neither ride to the west," Carver's voice lifted thin and quavering with sorrow in the hot night.

"Nor nowhar under the sun,
For thar's no man but God's own hand
Can cure this wounded one."

Sal tried to shut out the sound with her hands. The spermaceti candles, now low, smelling so fine, flung their last light as if they too laughed at her for trying to make a wedding out of a few objects in the jungle of common roistering.

"She took him by the yaller locks,
And also around his feet,
She plunged him in that doleful well
Some sixty fathoms deep."

Even through the sobbing voice she could imagine their ridiculing laughter.

Sal closed her eyes, as if now that the sound had caught her she could shut out the sight of love and summer that was trying to get at her. Somebody touched her arm, and she jumped, frightened.

"Oh, Johnny, ye scared me."

"I'm mighty proud of ye today, my dear. 'Twas hard for ye, and ye've not let it spoil the treat."

"Oh, Johnny Lacey, I don't know what ye're prattlin about." She got up and sighed, exhausted. "That common lanky boy with them mountain eyes—wouldn't even dress himself proper for the widdin—"

"Come back to the others, my dear. They'll miss ye."

"What do I care for that? Now 'tis time for supper. Eat us out of house and home!" She shook her shoulder away from him. "All them Cohees, common as dirt, entertained like they was

[321]

quality. To think a daughter of mine should fetch up with such dirt as that." Sal had said the old refrain again, what she really thought, and Jonathan saw that it was only her pride that had carried her through the day.

"That will be enough, my dear. Someone will hear ye," he said coolly, beyond any surprise.

"What do I care for that?" She went to the door. "Haven't I done my best, my very best?" she whispered back to him.

But it was too late to whisper. Solomon had blundered into the dog-run to find his new lady friend and bring her out to hear the singing. He had seen Jonathan go in, and stopped politely. So he heard all she said.

Solomon felt betrayed. He stood stock-still in the shadows as they passed to go out on the porch again. He remembered how he'd told everybody all day what a fine woman she was, not a high and mighty Tuckahoe trying to shame them all, a right fine woman. It wasn't right. Solomon slipped behind them off the porch and tapped his son Ben sternly. It was hard to tap him, for Ben had Till Carver in his arms, her head against his shoulder, listening to the pretty music. All Solomon did was tell him, a little tearfully, what he'd heard. He never even saw the young boys gather, whispering, ripe for a joke, for he went to sleep soon after on the grass.

After supper, at the time for toasting, Sal leaned against the porch edge in the dark. She had found the parson again and tried to stay close to him for anchor. But he was a bad anchor; he kept turning away from her, mixing and jollying, joking with Mother Carver, and solemn old Jeremiah stuck like a leech, never taking his hollow eyes off Mr. Cory.

"Here, my dear." Jonathan found her in the shadow. "Take a drink. 'Tis the time for toasting."

Jarcey gave the bride, looking fine in his ruffled shirt; he had even powdered his hair and wore black shoes with buckles, as if he understood and was trying to help Sal. The guests roared.

Jonathan gave the groom and said, "God bless him." The roar was louder at that, the atmosphere breathless with approval.

The parson gave the king, and cheers rang out and bounced against the porch roof.

"It should have come first," Sal muttered, but no one minded her.

Peregrine gave the queen as elegantly as he could, and Mother Carver yelled, "Hyear, hyear!" It made the cheerers rock with laughter. Peregrine flushed and stared at the porch boards, thinking the laughter was at him.

Carver gave Virginia, and the laughter turned to a tidal roar of joy again.

Sanhedron's turn came. He gave in a loud voice "The Sons of America!" This time a scream swept over the close-packed crowd. Someone began stamping his feet. A Liberty Song wavered on the edge of the crowd, and the rest took it up, bawling the words and stamping to the rhythm.

"Well, I never thought I'd hear the like of that in my house. 'Tis fair treason!" Sal said, furious, plucking the parson's arm to apologize.

"Mawm, the last time I heard that song was in Mr. Lee's house in the Tidewater," Mr. Cory told her calmly. "Times change, mawm," he went on, for fear his remark might seem insulting to a lady. "There's no disloyalty, I think, in growin up." He leaned toward her, to see her better. "The Whig gentlemen are standin bluff, mawm, in the trouble with home, and there's many at home who agrees. There ain't no treason in a matter of honest pride."

She could hardly hear him, the song was so loud, but she had heard enough to turn her hot with shame at no longer even knowing the ways of genteel people. Sal backed to the edge of the porch, lost in her own wilderness. The parson turned his back as Mother Carver jogged his arm with her elbow and said something—Sal couldn't hear what. It was the last she knew. A hand

[323]

swept across her mouth. She could feel the salt taste of its sweat as she was swept back into a flood of darkness.

Jonathan couldn't find her when his guests were leaving, and Jarcey could see he was angry. They stood together, watching the last of them spread out across the valley under the moon. The parson came up into the dim light of the porch, where the candle-stumps swam in their pools of tallow in the hanging lanterns and the night moths banged dully against the heavy glass.

"It was a mighty fine widdin, sar," he puffed, "mighty fine. Ye do things proud. Lud, I just been to see if my horse got his tail cropped. The Presbyterian boys do it sometimes for a joke, in an excess of spirits. Well, he's safe and his hair's on, thank God for his mercies."

"Oh, these boys wouldn't do that!" Jonathan joked with him. "We're pretty civilized people hereabouts."

"An established passen ain't safe nowhere in the backwoods, sar, but in his bed—when he's old and fat as I am, anyhow! I'll say good night to ye, gentlemen. Mighty fine widdin." He disappeared up the stairs to the loft where Philemon had put him now that Sara had gone, making the bed ready in a veil of tears. Peregrine found her there and kicked her out. His thin face was flushed from drink, and his hair, which his mother had powdered for him for the first time, hung in thick, caked locks from sweat. He rolled onto his pallet, fully dressed, and fell asleep at once, forgetting or not caring that the parson was sharing his room.

Mr. Cory found him there and covered him over so his cooling sweat wouldn't give him a chill in the night. He unloosened the boy's shirt and left him. Now, in sleep, Peregrine's face was erased of the watchful disdain that seemed to plague it by day. He murmured a little, but Mr. Cory couldn't make out what he said. He smiled at the boy's pretty sleeping face and took himself to bed.

Both the men on the porch were watching the candlelight from the new cabin, built down-river on the next slope to where they stood. They saw it go out, and stood longer, not saying a word. After supper a ragged procession of waving lanterns had seen the children to their new home, felt the bed, made their formal jokes, and finally left them. Now they were alone, the valley quiet, here and there a dim yell in the distance of someone faintly blowing the last of the celebration alive.

"Johnny, y'ought to be a proud man this night. Ye've begun a dynasty in Beulah."

"I wish it had happened without pain." Jonathan's head was turned away.

"There ain't nothin happens without pain, my Johnny. 'Tis how we're born and how we come to be here, both of us. But somethin's come out of it. Dear God, do ye remember when we first come, and lived on fear and lard? Even the trees seemed tryin to push us out. I used to dream that I was bein hacked down by the trees, or girdled and bled to death. 'Tis a strange thing, I never dreamed of Indians, only the trees."

"I reckon Sal has gone to her bed," Jonathan said.

"She done ye proud today. Give her just due, Johnny, she don't bend easy. 'Tis her way."

"She don't bend a-tall. She still calls this place Cicero, like old Backwater back at Fluvanna—won't give an inch," Jonathan said wearily. "I sometimes think I done her a great wrong, bringin her from what she was used to. But there was nothin there—there was nothin left for us. I've made here what she wanted, but she don't see it. She clings to a dream instead. Her mother did for home in England in her late years—I never seen it, but I knew 'twas an England in her own mind." Jarcey felt Jonathan shake a little beside him, as if he were pushing away his thoughts. "There ain't a hole deep enough to bury the past. I used to think there was."

"Go to your bed, Johnny. Ye're dog-tired."

Jonathan was tired, aching and bleak, as he pulled himself up to his room.

He sat on his side of the bed in the dark to take his shoes off carefully, so he wouldn't wake Sal. Then he realized that she was not there; the rocker was going slowly in the corner. The room was full of a smell he couldn't identify, but it wrapped round him like the smell of death and filled him with terror.

"Sal," he called gently, but there was no answer, only the runners, hollow against the floor.

It took time, too much time, to light a flint for the bedside candle. Finally its light grew slowly, too dim to reach the corner, though he could see her shape, moving slowly as she rocked. At first he thought she had gone to sleep there. He lifted the candle high to see her better, and walked near her slowly so he wouldn't frighten her. Her eyes were open; the candlelight glittered in them as he brought it closer.

"Sal, Sal." He tried to make the eyes focus on him.

She smiled, and the smile turned to a little giggle, but she never looked at him.

"Johnny," she said carefully, "I know a secret. Our Sara's a-courtin. She's a-courtin a fine young man, a right pretty beau. He must larn Latin, though. I won't have Sal marry a beau who hasn't the graces. Lordy, Lord, ain't it a thing? Our little old Sara. I reckon to make her a fine widdin—no jigs and bangers. Ma says 'tis not seemly." She giggled again, and the giggle grew, began to shake her.

He brought the candle closer, saw her eyes focus on it at last. Her thin mouth opened, wider and wider so that it seemed to fill the room, a wet red hole; the spittle and snuff lodged between her few teeth glistened in the light. Her mouth was a cave where the candle lit its walls, and the remains of her hair hung like close-eaten grass over her forehead. Jonathan jerked off her cap and saw her naked head as the mouth began to scream, a scream that never seemed to stop.

The boys had had their wedding joke. They had cropped the mare.

[326]

Chapter Five

For once in his life Solomon knew he was first with a piece of news. He rode through the rain, forcing the last speed out of his worn jade, his rawhide cape sailing behind him; man, horse, cape soaked and running with water. He hit the swollen creek, not even stopping to see if the ford was too flooded, swimming through rain so heavy and blinding he couldn't tell where the rain stopped and the creek began, forced the blown animal down-creek to the warm lights of the ordinary.

As he threw himself off his horse and tied it to the rail fence, the door of the ordinary opened and a blast of noise and warm steam hit the pall of rain. Mother Carver poked her head out.

"He's hyar!" she screamed. "Take off thim wet things. Hit stinks of men and wet skins in hyar already!"

Solomon pushed by her and stood, raining a storm of water from his cape, savoring the waiting silence, and began a slow grin which spread across his face like warmth itself.

Jarcey knew then, before Solomon said a word, and ran forward through the crowd of men to throw his arms around him.

"By Gawd," Solomon spoke at last. "By Gawd and the shores of hell, what an election!"

"He carried it!" Jarcey ran for the jug.

"He carried that election by Gawd like hit war a leetle child. Carried it? Ye niver saw the like!"

"Make him a place by the far," Mother Carver yelled. "The man's half drownded."

Solomon made his way, dignified with knowledge, through the path the men made for him, and stood with his back to the fire. He took the gourd Jarcey handed him and drank in one gulp. They all waited and watched him stand and steam, as if he were the devil popped up from the floor in a cloud.

"Now, lemme tell ye. Lemme tell ye right from the beginnin," he began, and made himself more comfortable by throwing his rawhide cape off his back to let his buckskins steam instead. The smell of wet animal almost drowned the smell of hot whisky and winter-long sweat which clogged the little room.

"We rid up to Fincastle Courthouse by dawn that mornin. Mr. Crawford had placed horses for usn. We niver stopped only to eat and git breath, for two days. Mr. Crawford had took a room for Colonel Johnny and he went in thar, saddle-sprung and filthy as a hawg. He come out from thar, gintlemen, as long-tailed a lookin candidate as any of usn are like to see this side of blue blazes. I'll swear afore Gawd he looked the prettiest fellow I ever seed. All dressed up fitten to kill and eat—ruffles, him hair-powdered, and Mr. Crawford in a wig like a triffit. Oh, Lord, what a sight! Thim two gintlemen sashayed through the courthouse lot slow and easy, shakin hands and a-sayin good mornin to all thim people, friendly to poor men and all. We had a fine treat for breakfast—Lord ye should have seed Mr. Crawford. That man does his friend proud. No electioneering, nuthin common, mind ye. 'Gintlemen, would ye care for a mite salt shad, can I help ye to a leetle warm toast and butter, would ye give me leave to lace your chocolate with a leetle spirit?' Jest a fine treat for the friends in his and Johnny's interest afore they went up to the poll. I niver seed sech a sight."

One of the men started to speak, but Jarcey shushed him, knowing that the only way to get the story was to let Solomon roll like a river with the facts floating with him.

"By the time we rid up the courthouse square agin, 'twas the prettiest April shiner y'ever seed. Gawd, I niver seed so many fine boys, they's court in session and sale day and election day all together. I seed gintlemen swappin horses and watches and stories. 'Twas a real press of people. Well thim two walked through hit like 'twas a church meetin, through hollerin and fightin and Lord knows what all by nine o'clock in the mornin. They hain't much of a courthouse yet, 'twas only log. The sheriff was a-settin outside between a couple of trees at this hyar big long table. Somebody yelled at Johnny, 'Hey there, Colonel Johnny, d'ye aim to stand bluff?' He come back, cool as a melon, 'I aim to abide by my conscience, sar.' They's a fine cheer for that, and a couple of blasts from the back, but me and another gintleman took care of thim. They's drunk anyhow.

"Thin, by Gawd, hit begun—a real good election. The two up-country gintlemen that was runnin together, they come and stood one side the table and Johnny and Mr. Crawford, they fetched up tother side. Thar 'twas, plain as your nose, New Light riff-raff to one side, gintlemen tother. Real simple to vote your ruthers. The sheriff, he got up. Ye know who he are—one of thim Brandons— and he hollered out, 'Gintlemen freeholders, come into court. I declare the poll opened.'

"Only of course nobody went into court, for 'twas right outside under the trees. Thim other two gintlemen had been a-stumpin up and down the county, a-promisin and a-kissin asses and a-treatin for all they was worth, which warn't much nohow. Up-county they was—up-county New Lights. They seemed to have right smart chance of friends too. I's right worrit. I can tell ye, hit skeered me thar for a while.

"One after another thim freeholders come up to the table and said out real loud who they's a-votin for. That would raise a holler.

"When 'twas Colonel Johnny, he'd step out and shake hands and say somethin like 'Your vote is pershated, Mr. Jones.' He niver went wrong on a name, nor niver said the same thing twice. But that Mr. Crawford—I niver seed sech a sweet-tongued gintleman in my life; afore Gawd that man shined like a light with breedin and money. 'Twas as good as a play. Ever' time a gintleman voted one side would bawl, 'Huzza!' and tother side would cuss. But Mr. Crawford—oh Lord-a-mercy!"

Solomon bowed, carried away by his story. " 'Mr. Sawyer, I shall treasure that vote to my dyin day,' or, 'Mr. Cyarter, your support will be regarded as a feather in my cap forever,' or, 'Mr. Sawbuck, may ye live a thousand years.'

"One man come up, drunk as a sow, and sprawled all over the votin table and said he'd vote for whoever give him a drink, but somebody carted him off. Ever once in a while the sheriff would look up and tell a gintleman he had no right to vote for he had no land or was under age—but not often. They let most of thim vote, though some got throwed out. Hit made the up-county candidates mighty sore. I reckon they'd combed this hyar county of all the riff-raff had a horse to ride. Them Cutwrights was thar to vote agin Colonel Johnny. Ye could tell right off they wasn't votin for, they's votin *agin*. They couldn't be throwed out though, for they've got claims down Big Sandy.

"Along about three o'clock, I reckon hit war. Yep. I's gittin mighty hongry so hit musta been along about three o'clock; they's right smart jugs a-passin back and forth, but— Yep, I'd say hit was long about three o'clock, the sheriff he got up and hollered, 'Gintlemen freeholders, come into court and give your votes, or the poll will be closed.' They's only a few left. By thin we all knowed 'twas all right.

"Thin I hyeared the sheriff call, 'The poll is closed. Mr. Crawford and Colonel Lacey have carried the poll!'

"I couldn't see nuthin, but this hyar yell went up. They's a fight goin on in front of me, and gintlemen a-clamberin over each other to collect bets. They was a mighty sight money changing hands, I can tell ye. I seed Colonel Johnny thin, histed up in the air along with Mr. Crawford. They was carried all over that courthouse lot, everybody whoopin and a-hollerin and shootin in the trees. I thought they's goin to shoot thim both out of pure lovin joy. Of course they'd been treatin with whisky all day—only after the gintlemen voted, not before. They done hit right.

"But the real treat come after. Lord Gawd, Mr. Crawford done proud by all—a couple of roasted hawgs and barls of whisky, I tell ye that Mr. Crawford knows how to give an election treat. He ain't one to turn his back and despise pore folks. Well, as soon as I sobered up I rid back ahead with the news. Colonel Johnny will come a few days after me, for he's business to attend to with Mr. Crawford."

"Gentlemen," Jarcey yelled through the rising roar of talk as Solomon turned, his story over, to warm his front, "take a drink with me!"

Sanhedron Kregg strode up to the counter, grinning. "So the Tuckahoes carried it, did they?"

Jarcey smiled back as he handed Sanhedron a drink. "Howdee, Sanhedron, glad ye come through for the celebration. Now Johnny ain't no Tuckahoe. Ye know as well as I do his interest lies here in the west, but he likes to look at both sides of a question."

"He's a damned Tuckahoe Neegur-owner and he carried another in on his back!" a tall man yelled from the fire. "Ain't ye fools got no notion what they's up to?" The room went still, waiting for a fight. "No damned long-tailed Tuckahoe like Crawford woulda carried a new county, without Johnny Lacey run with him. He's a turncoat, by Gawd."

[331]

Nobody moved.

"We've done let the Tidewater and the Piedmont buy our county votes. They own most of the land already, ye poor fools." Jarcey leaned down quietly and laid his gun on the counter. Solomon crouched forward, his thumbs stretched straight out from his fists. The tall man didn't see Jarcey's gun, but crouched to spring as the floor cleared between the two men. He jutted his thumbs and started catwalking toward Solomon.

"Lacey is a diehard Tuckahoe Episcopal ruffle-shirt Tory king-lover who lies with a Neegur," the man told Solomon, quiet with the room.

"He's a Whig Cohee and a right fine gintleman, and ye're a pox-ridden kid who cain't afford no Neegur and too all-fard ugly to git a white," Solomon whispered as they began to circle.

"Gentlemen"—Jarcey lifted his gun and pointed it between them toward the fire—"among my many talents, I'm the best shot in this county," he said gently. "The first one of ye crosses that floor gets a year shot off."

The tall man crouched lower. Solomon's thumbs began to waver.

"Hey, Azariah, the scholar hyar means what he says. Now put thim thumbs down and behave yourself. The election's over," Sanhedron called, laughing. "Oh Gawd, Jarcey, I sure am glad I's stoppin through in time for this hyar; ye're a beautiful man! To think I nearly had ye to a hangin party once!"

Azariah and Solomon straightened up slowly, still watching each other.

The gun moved over to Azariah. "I think the gentleman wishes to apologize for what he said in heat," Jarcey said.

"I reckon I's pretty warm after all," Azariah told the gun-barrel.

"Now, gentlemen, step to the counter, and we'll celebrate this election with some good spirit." Jarcey laid the gun down, the tension over, the room tuning up again.

[332]

" 'Tis right full hyar for April," Solomon whispered below the noise.

Jarcey handed him a copy of *The Virginia Gazette.* "Lookee." Solomon read it slowly, not daring to use his finger to point the words in front of Jarcey.

Fincastle County, Virginia,
January 27, 1774

Notice is hereby given to the gentlemen, officers and soldiers, who claim land under his Majesty's Proclamation of the 7th of October, 1763, who have obtained warrants from his Excellency the right honorable Earl of Dunmore, directed to the surveyor of Fincastle County, and intend to locate their land on or near the Ohio, below the mouth of the Great Kanawka or New River, that several assistants will attend at the mouth of the New River on Thursday, the 14th of April next, to survey, for such only as have or may obtain his Lordship's warrant for that purpose.

"Oh, my Gawd, Jarcey." Solomon looked up, all the election joy wiped from his long face. "They hain't a-takin this bunch down thar?" He nodded back at the crowded room.

"Ye read on." Jarcey saw where Solomon's finger had come up unconsciously to mark his place. " 'Tain't the worst yet."

Solomon's sad head went back, close to the paper.

What Solomon had said, *The Virginia Gazette* twitching slightly in his hand as he concentrated, shook Jarcey's memory back to another frail paper long ago, where the pen had not been mightier, but a pathetic instrument wielded in a high wind of hate. He watched Sanhedron, the friendly man, lean down to slap a friend as they laughed at something, and a shiver went down his back.

I would therefore request that the claimants or their agents will be very punctual in meeting at the time and place

[333]

above mentioned, properly provided with chain carriers and other necessaries, to proceed on the business without delay. Several gentlemen acquainted with that part of the country are of the opinion that to prevent insults from strolling parties of Indians, there ought to be at least fifty men on the river below the Great Kanawka to attend to the business as the gentlemen present may judge most proper until it is done, or the season prevent them from surveying any more.

"Oh Lord, oh dear Lord," Solomon kept muttering and shaking his head, not knowing he did it.

Should the gentlemen concerned be of the same opinion, they will, doubtless, furnish that or any less number that may be necessary. It is hoped the officers or their agents who may have land surveyed, particularly such as do not reside in the colonies, will be careful to send the surveying fee when the certificates are demanded.

William Preston
Surveyor of Fincastle County.

Sanhedron's hand clapped down on Solomon's back. "Readin of the invitation to the Injun fight, are ye? Come on with usn."

Solomon's face was mule-like with trouble. "I don't like this hyar a-tall. Ye hain't got no woman and children settled out this fur. Why, takin all thim quick-fingered Injun-haters down thar'll start a damned war!"

" 'Tis the way I see it," Jarcey said low. "Sanhedron, are ye goin to be able to keep this mob in line?"

"Oh hell, Jarcey, ye old Injun-lover. They won't nuthin happen. We might meet up with a few parties, but they won't attack. We're too many."

"That ain't what I said. I just hope to God y'ain't set on crossin the Ohio, that's a fact."

"Nobody ever said nuthin about crossin no Ohio. Keep your

hair on, Jarcey, and take a drink with me. This hyar's government business. I'll say that for the Tuckahoes, they finally made the governor settle thim claims."

"You keep *your* hair on, more like it."

"We hain't had no real trouble out hyar since 'sixty-four,'" Solomon interrupted. "Thar's youngins half-growed niver spent a summer forted in. We even cut winders in our shacks. Ye don't reckon what ye'd start. They's been leetle bits of trouble off'n on already."

"Hell, I ain't got enough hair for a Shawnee baby's bottom!" Sanhedron answered Jarcey over Solomon's head. "Two of your own boys want to come along with usn."

"Who?" Jarcey's head went up.

"Why, young Peregrine Lacey and his brother-in-law, Zeke Catlett. I'm takin thim on as chain-carriers." He read the surprise in Jarcey's face. "Now they hain't a-goin to—what does that goddamn thing say?—prevent insults. I like that. 'Tis a damn neat turn of phrase. They're a-goin to chain-carry, that's all."

"I've got to find them youngsters. Mother Carver, here's my gun; watch the liquor." Jarcey had crawled from behind the bar and was out of the door into the rain, hatless, coatless, almost as soon as he had finished speaking.

"Whatever's stuck in his craw?" Sanhedron asked after him, surprised.

Jarcey had gone so quickly that he forgot, until he got halfway up the valley through the pelting rain, that Peregrine had been in the ordinary all evening; but he sloshed on up the pouring slope, his eyes screwed up to see, through the black, wet blankets of water, the dim shape of Ezekiel's and Sara's cabin.

Ezekiel opened the door to his knock and saw the bent man, his gray hair plastered down his face, his clothes awash.

"Come in, sar. Ye're like a drownded rat. Sary, git Mr. Pentacost a mite toddy."

Sara got up, still nursing her baby.

[335]

"Sit down, sweetheart. I don't want no toddy. Zeke, I've come to have a little talk with ye."

"Ye can speak afore Sary. She knows."

Sara's face was glowing from the fire, from the weak toddy she had drunk to help the baby sleep, now that he was teething, and from the pleasure of nursing. She sat down again with her feet tucked up and her toes curling and wiggling at the fire. Her face had grown a little rounder since the baby's birth, but this was the only change. She rocked back, cuddling the baby against her bare, small breast.

"Ouch!" She giggled. "The leetle darlin bites!" Then her eyes lost light as she tried to explain. "I'm in full approval, Mr. Pentacost. I know what Pa will say, but 'tis no use ye say it for him. We ain't aimin to be beholden to nobody. Zeke reckons on havin a look down Kaintuck way, now 'tis openin up."

Jarcey's surprise made him say what he thought. "Zeke, ye know damned well your pa-in-law wants ye to have this here land. Peregrine—" He realized he had said too much.

"Peregrine ain't fit to run nothin," Sara interrupted, "and Montague's courtin Cissy Crawford for her fortune, though I hyear she's ugly as a mud fence." Sara pulled her teat from the baby's mouth and shifted him to her other breast before he could do more than gasp, sucking the air. She kissed his head. "Ye know we've took right much from Ma, and been mighty patient, her bein like she is, but we aim to take our youngin out'n her sight."

"We ain't aimin on bein beholden to Peregrine," Ezekiel said behind Jarcey. "Efn Colonel Lacey was to die afore he done nuthin about hit, usn and my maw and paw and the youngins would git kicked off this land. I always knowed they's hyar on the colonel's kindness—Paw not signin on as tenant nor nuthin. Sary, put your feet down in front of Mr. Pentacost."

The boy's trouble was so clear to himself that Jarcey had nothing to say. He stood watching the fire, dripping on the bare floor, so sad that Sara saw for the first time with a shock that he was getting old.

"I don't know what to say. I just don't know."

"Now sit down and warm yourself, Mr. Pentacost. Have a mite samp if ye won't take a drink. I know you." She tried to tease him as she settled the baby back into his cradle. "Ye forget to eat unless ye're watched."

"Your father—"

"Don't ye fuss about Pa. He'll understand. He done the same his own self."

"Your father," Jarcey said to the fire, "has just been elected to the House of Burgesses."

★   ★

Back in the ordinary, Azariah Keel sat nursing his gourd, still furious, but the fight gone out of him. A tall, loose-bodied young man, with one lock of sandy blond hair hanging over his forehead, forced his way through the mob. His eyes seemed to focus slowly on the people he pushed aside, registering them only as obstacles. He stopped in front of Azariah, who, when he looked up, thought he had another fight on his hands, from the boy's look. Azariah put his gourd slowly down on the bench beside him. But the young man only made an elegant low bow; Azariah stiffened to take his body if it fell in his lap. The young man recovered balance.

"Sar, I would like to shake you by the hand," he said and grasped Azariah's rough paw before he had had time to straighten out his fingers. "Ye'll shake me by the hand, won't ye? I don't hold with your politics, but by God I love your sentiments." Before Azariah could answer, the boy was gone, and the door of the ordinary had slammed behind him.

"Who the hell was that?" he asked Sanhedron.

"The colonel's son, Peregrine Lacey, the Tuckahoe throwback son of a bitch." Sanhedron spat at the fire.

"Now let the youngster alone," Mother Carver told him. "He's born sad and wild like Ishmael in the Bible. He's et bitter fruit ever since his maw broke. He cain't help himself."

"Hell, he's jest born cussed, from the looks of him," Azariah grumbled.

"What happened to his maw?" Sanhedron asked.

But for once Mother Carver was unwilling to gossip. "Oh, she jest broke," she said vaguely. "Azariah, if ye got to spit, aim at the far, ye dirty thing."

"I'm sorry, mawm," the contrite man tried to wipe the tobacco juice away with his jackboot.

Chapter Six

IT WAS May. The sun beat hot, drying the new grass. For days the children had felt it and searched the sky for unwelcome rain. Now the grass was ready. They didn't have to feel it; they could hear its dry shuffle. They stood in a huge circle around Sal's rock pile and watched Baucis whirl the old dry hay wide around the rocks.

"Make hit big! Make hit bigger," one of the children yelled.

"Hell and damnation, I'm a-makin hit big as I can!" the old Negro called back. He finished the circle and threw more hay against the rocks with a long, pointed pole.

"Lord, I hope none of thim youngins gits hurt." Philemon watched from the porch.

"Who's out there?" Sal's voice behind her was thin and disinterested, but Philemon told her anyway, making the recital as exciting as she could, to cheer Miss Sal up, because she hadn't even bothered to pull herself out of her rocker and look, even at her precious rock pile, which usually held her interest when nothing else did. Philemon remembered many a time being sent back

[339]

through the sucking mud and the rain if she'd forgotten to bring
a rock up when she went on an errand to the creek.

"Thar's thim five Middleburg towheads. I'll swear to Gawd, two
of thim are barefooted. I told the Dutch woman not to leave thim
out in the grass this late thataway. She won't mind nuthin. She still
don't understand nuthin. Thar's Carver's four; that oldest one of
his are totin a mighty mean slingshot. He'll git one of thim
youngins in the eye. Thar's McKarkle's three youngest and his
six growed chillun; thim others is a-gittin too big, I reckon. The
preacher's is all thar. I'll swear to Gawd chillun grows scrawny
out hyar. They don't look like no Tidewater youngins. They's all
lard and hominy, fever and whisky and runnin hawg-wild. Hit
makes for lean meat but it sure don't put on no fat. Lemme see,
thar's thim two youngest Cutwrights. Colonel Johnny said he seed
their paw at the court and he niver even asked after thim."
Philemon snorted. "Reckon thar's a sight more whar they come
from, but ye'd reckon he'd come git thim now they's big enough
to work."

"Philemon, I'm thirsty." Sal whined a little, bored with Philemon.

"Ye jest wait right thar. I'll git ye somethin cool."

Up outside the circle, some of the small children jerked with
impatience. The older boys stood looking blank, showing nothing,
being hunters. They could smell the snake den, the acrid-green
dungeon smell the sun brought out, the reminder of dead cold
danger that could warn in the woods and make a horse shy
before a man could even get the scent.

"I seed one. I seed one," thirteen-year-old Tad McKarkle
yelled, forgetting his calm and raising his slingshot.

"Quit that, Tad, ye'll have thim snakes slitherin out all over
ye," Baucis ordered.

"Ye niver seed one!" Elsie Carver sassed. Tad wanted to
push her down. His whole self itched to whip her, hold her down
with his body until she cried, "King's cruse!"

[340]

Baucis told Rouge Carver he could light the circle. It made Tad madder than ever.

They stood watching the blue and yellow fire lick slowly around the hay, until it made a huge ring—crackling, lifting tongues. The boys ran, beating it, forcing it in toward the rocks, driving the flames in an ever narrower circle. The fire began to nibble at the hay on the rock pile.

"Git ready! Hyar they come!" Baucis called. "You big boys come in hyar." A rattlesnake had crawled up onto the highest rocks. Baucis lifted it with his pointed stick and threw it into the flames. The children shrieked. Rouge Carver took careful aim with his slingshot, sighted along the rawhide, and whipped an accurate pebble. Another snake cracked high into the air and fell into the fire, writhing. There were more and more, creeping up the rocks away from the flames, their delicate tongues vibrating wildly but their bodies dragging. The boys circled, shooting stone after stone and yelling when a snake flipped up. The flames were so high it was hard to see the snakes unless they whirled up from the heat. Some, still alive, crawled blindly around the hot rocks where the hay smoldered. They made easy shots. Even the little children could poke them back into the flames with sticks—snakes of all sizes, from the new-hatched to the big ones that could later part the high grass when they crawled through it.

"Thar! Thar. Git him. Quick!" Becky Catlett screamed, jumping up and down, her horsetail of hair flapping on her neck.

"Don't look at thim eyes. They charm ye. They'll charm ye and ye'll burn up!" Elsie Carver kept calling over and over.

But it was hard to stay too close. Snake-oil boiled and made the fire hotter. The children scampered, black-faced and demon-eyed from the smoke, in and out from the heat and the cloying, pungent smell.

Finally the fire was out; the mass of twitching reptiles lay across the tops of the rocks, thick, reeking smoke rising from them in heavy coils, like their own ghosts.

"Now, git on home," Baucis ordered. "They ain't a-goin to die till sundown. Snakes don't niver die till the sun goes down. Don't jest gawk around watchin thim twitch. Go warsh yourselves." There were a few parting flicks from the slingshots. Even the stubborn had to admit that the snake-killing was over. They wandered off to try to swim the smell away in the creek.

Tad McKarkle caught up with Elsie Carver halfway down the slope. They rolled over and over. "I told ye, Tad McKarkle," she kept whispering when he pinned her down. She looked like a raccoon with the rings of dirt around her eyes. But he couldn't make her say, "King's cruse."

Jonathan, in his office on the other side of the house, tried to ignore the noise the children made. He worked slowly at his account book, but his pen stopped too often for a man who was concentrating on what he was doing. He rubbed his tired eyes with his thumb and forefinger as if that were the matter. Finally he threw the pen down and got up to shut the door against the sickening smell.

Ezekiel stood there. He looked blank with fatigue. "I come back."

"I can see that." Jonathan was cold.

"Colonel Johnny—can I set down?" the boy asked weakly. "I been a-runnin for the last three days."

Jonathan caught him as he tried to walk. All the anger left him as he put his arms around the boy's skinny, hot body.

"What's happened, son?" he asked gently. He set the boy down at his table, and Ezekiel put his head down on the ledger, across his arms.

"I'm sorry, sar. I'm kind of tard." The boy tried to apologize. "Colonel Johnny, somethin turble's happened."

Jonathan had to lean close to the boy's shoulder to hear him, but the dim urgency had been put out by exhaustion again. Ezekiel said nothing more.

"What happened to your horse?" Jonathan asked him to break the silence.

"He got rid out and started to bleed. I shot him. I had to shoot him. I'm sorry, Colonel Johnny; you give him to me. I—" Ezekiel clenched his fists on the table, leaving dirty sweat on the ledger, and his face began to pucker, but he didn't cry. He sat frozen, but he didn't cry.

"Never mind, son." Jonathan held his back. "Never mind."

"Colonel Johnny, I done mussed up your account book." Ezekiel tried to scrub out the marks with his fist.

"That's all right, son. I was just doin a leetle last-minute business before I go East."

"Ye got to take thim with ye. Ye got to take Sary and the baby. Ye got to tell thim." The boy staggered up.

"Ye better tell me what's happened. Now calm yourself down and tell me."

"We went down the Ohio River." Ezekiel sank down again. His voice was so dead Jonathan could hardly hear him. "We done a right lot stakin out on the way. We met a few Shawnees—jest peaceful families a-mindin their own business. Some of thim was a-headed up hyar to trade for salt. I talked to thim. They's skeered of the men, ye could tell that. But we let thim be, only give thim a leetle rum for to watch them cavort. Did they git hyar?"

"We had a few through. They done a mite tradin and biled some brine and went off. They were friendly."

"I knowed somethin was a-goin to break. I could smell hit and so could Mr. Kregg. But we still reckoned 'twould pass off all right. Hit niver got no worse than one of thim jobbers takin aim at a canoe passin up-river. Mr. Kregg knocked his gun down, though, so 'twas all right. He's drunk anyhow." Ezekiel sighed, shaking, as if he hadn't had a deep breath since he started to run. "Mr. Kregg and Colonel Preston seemed to have things in hand.

"We got down-river thar about the mouth of the Scioto when we run into a big party of Shawnees with their families. They had thirty horseloads of skins with thim, a-reckonin to go up-river on the Ohio side to Fort Pitt to trade. 'Twas the whole winter kill for the tribe. They's some others with thim, some Mingoes and one of thim wild renegade Catawba. Mr. Kregg and Colonel Preston told the men they wasn't to start in to drinkin with so many, but ye cain't stop that kind of thing. Colonel Johnny, thim Injuns had a goddam fortune in skins. Thim jobbers reckoned they could swap for liquor if they started thim a-drinkin.

"I don't know how hit started. They started in to powwow and gamble. Some of our men got the idea 'twould be a fine sight to set a couple Injuns a-fightin and make bets. They reckoned they could set the Catawba on one of the Shawnees, 'twould make a right smart fight, thim bein natural enemies—like a bear and a dog. They started bettin among theyselves and makin Injun jokes. I could smell it. I could smell the fight warn't a-goin the right way. The more jokes thim men would make about a Catawba bein better'n a Shawnee and a Shawnee being better'n a Catawba — They's jest jokin to rile thim up a leetle. Well, the more they egged on, the stiller thim Injuns went. Ye know how they can go. Finally the Catawba stood up for minute and started to Injun brag. I couldn't git what he said; he's talkin his own tongue, but ye could tell hit was big talk. Not even the Shawnees could git what he said. Then he come over to me and lifted that pipe tomyhawk Paw give me out'n my belt. I figured he wanted to do a swap, but Paw give hit to me and I niver wanted to. He jest stuck hit in his belt and walked off. About halfway across the circle he reached back and slapped his heinie. Ye know 'tis the worst insult an Injun can do. Thim Injuns laughed fit to kill, jest bellered. A couple of our men started eggin me on to Injun-fight him for hit. I's pretty mad, but I warn't a-goin to start no fight. Mr. Kregg, he went up to the Catawba and took the tomyhawk

[344]

out'n his belt. They jest stood thar a-lookin at each other. He walked back and give hit to me. I thought 'twas all over.

"Thin I seed one of thim half-breed Cutwrights rear up and take aim. Afore me and Mr. Kregg could stop him, he shot the first Shawnee got in his sight in the belly, shot him mean.

"Well, hit started. Thar was only me and Colonel Preston and Mr. Kregg tryin to stop hit. Thim Injuns was too drunk to fight back. We couldn't stop hit, Colonel Lacey. We couldn't stop hit. Why, thim deivals had planned hit all along; they's jest a-waitin for a sign so they could start shootin and steal thim skins. One of thim had gone round and spiked thim Injun's guns while they was drinkin.

"Hit was awful, Colonel Johnny, 'twas like a big snake-killin. The jobbers scalped every one they could lay hands on. For the love of Gawd, Colonel Lacey, ye got to take the women with ye. Ye got to. Thim thieves stole that whole winter kill. The powwow was on the Ohio side of the river."

"I can't go now," Jonathan said. "I can't go after this."

"Ye got to, Colonel Johnny. Me and Mr. Pentacost can take over hyar. But ye got to git thim women out."

"Where's Peregrine? Why didn't he come back with ye?" Jonathan's face had gone white.

"Colonel Lacey, if Perry comes back hyar I'll kill him."

"What did he do?"

"I hain't a-tellin."

"Tell me," Jonathan walked over to the table, looking like a man trying to hold his drink. "Ye tell me, or I'll—"

"I hain't a-tellin." Ezekiel couldn't look at him, but he got up to face him. He could see Jonathan's fist raised, the knuckles white.

Jonathan pushed Ezekiel out of his way clumsily and sat down. "Oh dear God, my own boy."

Ezekiel could say nothing. They could hear the deer flies buzz and the children yelling, far away, down at the creek.

[345]

"Tell me, son." Jonathan seemed to beg. He slumped, defeated, on the chair.

Ezekiel turned away from him, withdrew from watching him shrink, the sun and age lines going deeper in his face, the news stripping him naked. He stood at the door, watching the children, white bodies jumping and disappearing into the swimming hole, where the huge sycamore spread its low branches like a protecting tabernacle. He suddenly wanted desperately, more than anything in the world, to go swimming, down below the sycamore where the sun made dappled patterns on the cool water—holding on to a solid root and floating with the current like a waterweed.

"I've got to go and take my seat in the Burgesses." Jonathan talked behind him but seemed to be talking to himself. "It's what I've been a-waitin for all my life."

Ezekiel tried to drag himself back from watching the creek. He could almost feel the insistent water carrying his hot, naked body.

"Zeke, son. Tell me how he could do it—go along with them riff-raff. Ye're young as he is. Tell me."

A deer fly lit on the account book and washed itself. It buzzed away again, its whine filling the room.

"Don't make me tell, sar," Ezekiel muttered at the floor. The deer fly buzzed at his head, attracted by his sweat. He slapped at it savagely.

It seemed an hour before he heard Jonathan say, "All right, son. Go on and see Sara and get some food."

Ezekiel muttered something, too low for Jonathan to hear, and disappeared out the door.

He had not gone a hundred feet before he heard Jonathan call him.

"Bring her and come to the house as soon as ye can. I'll round up the others." His voice was strong again, commanding.

★   ★

Baucis was trying to harness the mule-team in the shivering dawn, but he was having trouble. The trouble didn't come from the mules themselves but from the whole settlement, children and all, which milled around the wagon, yelling at one another, the children getting under his feet and too close to the off-lead mule. He kept hollering that the mule was mean, but nobody paid any attention to him.

He watched for the office door to open, trying to will Colonel Johnny into coming before somebody got hurt. The lead mule's long ears flattened back, and Baucis gave a sharp shove to one of the preacher's youngins before it got kicked. He didn't notice which one. The child started in to bawl, but nobody heard it. They were all making too much noise, hollering orders and advice at one another, as if they were all going on the long trip East instead of just him and the Colonel and Philemon and Miss Sal.

Another small body pushed too near the mule. Baucis saw that it was one of his own children. He gave it a sharp slap to get it out of the way, and leaned against the mule's head, whispering honey to it sweetly, to calm it, stroking the thick ridge of its backbone until the ears began to lift again.

Sal sat above the racket, bright with pleasure. "Philemon, have ye got ever'thin? Are ye sure ye've got ever'thin?" She twittered at Philemon whenever the Negro woman lumbered up into the wagon.

"Yes, mawm. I got ever'thin," Philemon told her patiently every time.

"Where's Sara? Don't she want to say good-by to her ma?"

"She's in the office with Colonel Johnny. They comin right out."

Down below, Mother Carver was saying something to Sal, but she paid no attention, trying to shut out the noise, stop the impatience that was killing her, her eyes pinned to the eastern spur where the road, cut deep by heavy wagon wheels, was ridged with mud. The sun, just rising over the up-river mountain, made her squint until she remembered not to because Philemon had told her it made common sun-lines, like a field-hand's. At least they'd have a last sight of her looking fine in a linen ruffled cap that hid her short, thin hair, and a white shawl thrown over it, ballooning around her head, as Polly had shown her, drawing a picture ("we sport heads like Montgolfier's *balloon.*")

"Miss Sal, I done told ye thim ain't good clothes to wear yet." Philemon had climbed up again and breathed heavily against her. "Ye done got your pretty leetle white mittens dirty already."

"I told ye once and I'll tell ye again. I'll put somethin else on when we get over out of sight. I ain't goin to go off all draggle-tail," Sal said calmly.

"Lord Gawd, all dolled up like that, ye'd think ye's goin to church in Williamsburg instead of ridin a mule-train for three weeks!" Philemon fumed impotently. "Put down thim hands, ye dirty thing," she screamed at one of the children who had managed to climb up the wagon side and now peeped over, wide-eyed, at the loaded floor. She swatted at the hands, and the child dropped out of sight again.

"I *am* goin to church in Williamsburg," Sal said happily to the distant road.

The hubbub increased as Carver and Solomon heaved a huge sack over the hanging tail-board onto the wagon floor.

"I don't know why we have to take all that sang." Sal turned, annoyed at being interrupted in her dreaming. "Philemon, go tell your master to come on, before everything gets ruint."

The wagon shook as a second sack was swung up and loaded on the floor. Sal wedged her feet against the buckboard to keep from falling out.

"Go on—get him," she screamed at Philemon. Somebody was tugging at her skirt. "Quit that," she bit, slapping at the hand. But it was Mother Carver. She was climbing up onto the seat. She started to talk but, even so close, Sal could shut out her voice

[348]

because of the noise and her own series of thrills that went through her. The wagon shuddered as some of Jeremiah's ginseng was hoisted aboard.

". . . and don't ye fash your pore self account your youngins and usn." Sal looked at the old woman, amazed, wondering what she meant. Before she had a chance to answer, Mother Carver had clambered down again.

"Ye didn't tell her about the Indian trouble?" Jarcey caught Mother Carver and helped her down.

"Lord no, Mr. Pentacost. I niver told her nuthin like that." Her voice dropped sadly. "I's jest tryin to be a mite neighborly."

"What?" Jarcey yelled.

"She looks fine, don't she, today? Like somebody's jest woke up," Mother Carver said loudly.

"Oh yes, that she does." Jarcey turned away, waiting, too, for Jonathan's office door to open.

Inside the closed office Sara and Jonathan stood, isolated in embarrassed calm, the noise of wagon-loading dim outside. They were both obviously empty of words. Sara had been crying, but by now she had stopped, her face flushed but still, her hands locked behind her, as Jonathan knew she always stood when he had to punish her.

He turned away and fumbled awkwardly in the big deed chest. "Now that I've told ye about the Catletts' deed, sweetheart, ye'll understand my will—if anything happens."

Sara lowered her head. She seemed to be trying to batter against the shyness between them.

"Don't take on, my honey." Jonathan managed to smile. "I'll be back here before ye know it. Listen," he explained carefully, pulling one hand from behind her and holding it, "I'm aimin to go to Williamsburg with your mother and leave her at your Aunt Polly's. She can't stay out here now—she'd be more trouble than help. Though 'tis not her fault. Ye must understand that, Sara. Please, honey."

[349]

She tried to take her hand away, but he held it tight until the pulling stopped.

"Now, when I've done that I aim to get Mr. Crawford and other gentlemen with interests out here to make the governor call out the militia. I reckon it to take a leetle time. Then I'm a-comin back to settle this business."

"Oh, Pa." Sara's hand turned in his and clutched it. "What's happenin there is your business. Ezekiel says we a-goin to fight the British."

"Oh, he does?" Jonathan smiled. "What about?"

"Oh, taxises or somethin. I don't know." Sara looked at the floor again and blushed.

"Honey, honey, I'm not teasin ye," Jonathan told her.

Somebody was pounding on the door. "All right," Jonathan called shortly. "We'll be out in a minute."

Philemon trudged down the path again, feeling between the devil and the deep, with Miss Sal nagging and Mr. Johnny gone stubborn. Her five children detached themselves from the frenzy around the wagon and ran toward her. They fell against her huge thighs in a bunch, all trying to talk at once.

"You all mind Lyddy," she told them. "Mind Lyddy good. Your mammy's comin back in no time a-tall." She caught Lyddy's eye. "Ye'll look after 'em, won't ye, Lyddy?"

Lyddy nodded absently, her eyes only for the shut door.

"I'll come back afore ye know hit." Philemon waddled through her family and made for the wagon.

"Oh Philemon, is he a-comin?" Sal called impatiently. In a quick burst of excitement she added, "Philemon, ye and me's goin to Miss Polly's for a long time, and live off the fat of the land!"

Philemon's heart sank, but she brushed trouble aside as she brushed the children, because she had so much to do.

"Sara, ye won't change your mind, will ye?" Jonathan took the answer for granted as he asked the question for the twentieth time time since the day before.

Sara no longer answered.

"I don't blame ye." He turned and picked up a paper from the others. "By God, child, I don't blame ye. I'm damned proud of your vinegar. Women like you—" He didn't go on, but tapped the table with the folded paper instead. "I wrote this last night after everybody had gone and 'twas all decided ye stubborn women would abide here. Ye don't need to read it until the time comes. "I've cut Perry out," he said harshly. "He ain't worth leavin a hog-pen to. Montague's bein left five-six thousand acres up Greenbriar way at Dunkard's Valley. Mr. Crawford told me at the election. This here's yours—yours and Zeke's—if anythin happens to me."

Sara couldn't say anything, so she kissed his lined cheek and rubbed her own soft one against it, gulping to keep from crying again.

"Oh, honey, my dear." Jonathan at last let his head fall toward her shoulder. "Tell me what Perry done. Dear God, I've got to know I ain't wronged him. I've got to know that."

"Pa, he went blood-crazy." Sara knew then that she had to tell him. "Zeke said he was drunk with killin, like Injuns gits drunk on rum. That's all he told me. He wouldn't tell me no more."

He seemed to be hoisting himself away from her and down to the table, moving as if unused to his own weight. When he finally answered, it was not to her, although he said her name.

"Sara, I can't understand it. Is it that we can't rub up against the Indian ways without it drivin some of us crazy?" What else he said was in snatches, the oral tip of some far deeper trial in his mind. "A cruel white once he's caught the Indian ways is far worse than any Indian. . . . 'Tis as if their dark and bloody practices don't hurt them because it's what they take for granted. . . . But with us 'tis a disease, like our rum is a disease with them. So the wild ones don't know war from sport no more. They start it, and we fight it—fight and fight with good men among the Indians, because of the wild ones. We could have settled this country without so much killin. We could have, Sara. Ye Gods, have we always got to carry the weak and wild like Christ's Cross on our backs?" He seemed to be begging an answer, not from her, but from the valley, the narrow rim of his world set like a hand in the mountains. Then he set the seal of responsibility on his own shoulders. "Sal," he asked her, still not seeing her, "do we rear the wild ones to dare our worst desires? Once I nearly—your own father nearly—" He never realized that he had called her by her mother's name.

"Please come on, Mr. Johnny," Philemon's voice yelled through the door. "Miss Sal's about to whup me!"

Jonathan lifted his head again and looked at Sara. "Watch your youngins, darlin, watch your youngins for it."

Philemon knocked, wondering if he'd heard her call.

"Sara"—Jonathan asked the final terrible question of the parent —"honey, what did I do wrong?"

But, like another troubled, frightened human being who turned away from Pilate, Sara turned numbly, her head heavy with tears.

The office door opened at last. Half a dozen people raced to get to Jonathan.

"You stand bluff for usn, Johnny. Stand bluff to the governor. Larn him how stubborn Virginians can git!" Solomon yelled happily.

Someone kept trying to grab Jonathan's hand.

"You stand bluff for new Virginia agin the damned Tidewater. That's what ye stand bluff fer. What's taxises to do with us? We ain't got no money," Carver argued loudly.

It was Jarcey who was trying to grab his hand. Jonathan stopped.

"Take this letter for me, Johnny. 'Tis to my father. I wrote it last night after we talked."

"I'll take it for you, Jarcey, of course."

"I just want him to know why I'm taking a republican stand, though the very word would be treason to him. I want him to see

our side. 'Tis nothin to do with treason, but a bigger thing."
Jarcey ran on quickly as if Jonathan himself were his father, somewhere in England, who had to understand.

"Damn it, Johnny, this here's my home," Jarcey said and recovered himself as Mother Carver tried to buffet him out of her way.

"Good-by, rattlesnake Colonel." Jarcey grinned. "We'll take care of things till ye get back."

"Goddammit," Carver argued with nobody in particular, "I sure do wish we-uns would settle with the British so we could git back to hatin the Tidewater."

"McKarkle, Carver!" Jonathan called. His voice quieted them all, and they listened in a short calm after the roar of loading.

"Captain Pentacost here is in charge. Don't forget that."

"Yessar," Solomon half-saluted awkwardly.

Mother Carver cackled like a hen. "Gawd love ye, Colonel Johnny!" She threw her old arms around his chest; it was as high as she could reach. "We're mighty proud of ye, son! You argue with 'em. Argue fierce!"

Lyddy stood in the porch shadow, the Negro children huddled against her, all hope gone that he would remember to look her way.

What had seemed a jostling mob a few minutes before as they called good-by, looked now a ragged, too small knot of people muffled against the wet dawn in the huge, engulfing forest—the clearing of the valley pitiful after all their pride and work against the endless alien green, as Jonathan looked back from the eastern spur. He waved a last time, but they were too far away to see the movement. He wheeled his horse and trotted up beside Sal. She didn't hear or pay attention, so he could watch her face. Her illness had left her cheeks almost transparent, they were so pale. The skin stretched white over her small nose so that the bone was like a naked bird's wing. But her eyes glittered, as if a light had been lit behind them again at last.

[353]

After a while she was aware of Jonathan, walking the horse beside the wagon.

"Johnny, my dear"—her face puckered with worry—"are ye sure we will go to the governor's ball if ye're in the Burgesses?"

Jonathan said he was sure they would.

"Oh dear. The Countess of Dunmore herself will be there. I *must* get Polly to larn me the *ton*. If the pesky gel will do it. She's as selfish as a pig. Honey"—she turned to Jonathan—"don't ye think me mean, please, for bein so happy. I know ye got things on your mind. Ye think I haven't knowed what was a-goin on—how pushed we are. *I* understand it all. I been pushed myself, God knows." She smoothed her lap with her lace mittens. "I just didn't let on. No lady would." She said nothing for a while; then, with more shy apology in her voice than Jonathan could remember for years, she said, "Honey, I've so *long* admired to go East where a gel knows who she is."

"Ye better not say 'honey'—ye'll be took for a Scotch Cohee," Jonathan teased, relieved at her lifted spirits. "Whup up them mules, Baucis," he ordered. "I want to go some ways before nightfall."

They trotted away faster up through the wet woods, Sal singing to herself, now that Jonathan had forgotten her again, a snatch of song she'd picked up from the children.

" 'With a ruffdom, ruffdom fizzledom madge,' " she sang over and over to herself in rhythm with the rattling wheels; she didn't remember any more of the words.

Chapter Seven

Aᴏᴛᴇʀ eight years fear came back to squat in the valley of
Beulah. At first its presence froze them, sucking the strength from
their voices, slowing their movements. The children caught it,
exposed as carefully as they would be to a disease, to get it over
with and make them immune. They picked up danger from their
parents, shed their summer spirits, and learned to stop dead still
in mid-movement, anywhere, when the owl hooted, or the snake
parted, rolling through the grass, or a dead branch dislodged in
the woods and shuffled the leaves as it dropped. Their bodies were
forted, confined by it, their sense sentinels, watching, listening,
smelling the fear that squatted, always just out of the eye corner,
somewhere hidden, somewhere behind them.

Striving for urgency against the deep inertia that the fear
brought, the whole settlement prepared for its defense. They
seemed to get excitement from action, any action that transformed
the fear into protection, into a new way of living. They had long
since grown out of the old fort, as a child kicks out the boards
of its cradle. The fort had become a place to play, to hide in,

later to court in away from the scheming wit of parents, but it could no longer hold them for defense. It had lain unneeded, taken for granted, deserted on the hillside, the vines growing over it until they formed thick pockets for animals, curled stubbornly around the rotten gate hinges, made strong cats'-cradles across the sentry and firing holes, turned the old fort into a folly, a ruined summer-house to grace a garden and whisper in. Inside, the underbrush had tangled around the tiny cabins and the animal stalls. The field before it no longer grew corn but more luxurious flax—a huge white summer field with the breeze to comb its silky surface, showing blue flowers.

So Jonathan's house, with the smokehouse, the milkhouse, the big cellar under the hill behind it, the one-room office, the smithy, the slave quarters of six cabins, the big new log barn, the corncrib, became the fort. Carver's family, McKarkle's, the German's, Jeremiah's and Hannah's, the five young couples, drove their children and animals into the buildings. The new living made urgent noises among the outhouses where the hounds fought and the children got in the way, and the heifers bawled at night, all of them straining at the hated tether.

Sal's rock pile diminished, spread in a big square fence around the farm. The men and women, and children old enough to carry the weight, built the wall against fear; it grew quickly, urgency deepening into elation when the dawn brought no screams, which grew by midday with the frenzied party of jostling, joking people.

Sara, heaving a rock on the new three-foot fence, called out to Zeke as he passed by with another. "Wouldn't it beat Ma? Wouldn't it just beat her?" She stood back and inspected the wall. "Lord God, how I always hated them pesky rocks!"

"Ever'thin comes in handy, honey." Mother Carver came and stood beside her. They turned together to get another load.

Outside the wall the boys sharpened staves with their jackknives and planted them thick along the ground, acres of dragons' teeth for naked feet.

[356]

So the new fort grew; the log sentry boxes lifted at its corners. Guarding one another, they harvested everything they could. In two weeks the fort was finished.

June dragged along, and July crept after it. Still the fear was silent. They got used to it, learned to live with it, hardly noticing any more. It was harder every day for Jarcey to keep them confined. First the newlyweds, Tad McKarkle and Elsie Carver, sneaked out to sleep alone in their own cabin; then even Solomon drove his and Johnny's beeves so far to graze that he didn't get back until sundown.

"They've et ever'thin down hyarabouts," he told Jarcey sullenly, ashamed.

Mother Carver and Hannah got into a fight over a shoat that wandered from its litter. They both counted their pigs over and over loudly, shedding the stultifying fear in righteous name-calling.

Jarcey killed the shoat himself. It screamed worse than the two women when he cut its throat, but they shared the fresh meat, and the dogs snarled over the bloody yard.

Monotony. It was the new face of the fear. It fell on the children like a whip.

"Goddam it to hell, Mame, git out'n thim blackberries afore I whup ye!"

Jarcey heard the tight frenzy of the woman's voice, from where he sat at Jonathan's table in the office.

"I wisht somethin would happen. Anythin's better'n this hyar," Ezekiel muttered, pegging his knife at the wall.

"Shut up, ye fool boy. Ye don't know what ye're talkin about." Jarcey was shorter with the boy because he voiced his own unconscious wish.

"Carver's been sayin they hain't no use in all this." Ezekiel stopped pegging because he was sick to death of everything he did.

"Ye know that ain't true," Jarcey told him. "Carver knows better than that."

"When the hell is Colonel Johnny a-comin?"

[357]

"I don't know no more than ye do, Zeke. That scout brought news the militia was formin. They ought to come through any day. Johnny will come with them."

"That was nigh on three weeks ago," Ezekiel said sulkily. "This hyar time crawls like a wounded snake." He started pegging at the wall again.

"Quit that, Zeke. I'm tryin to think," Jarcey snapped.

"Hell," the boy said and wandered out into the yard. "I hain't got nuthin to do." He sounded like a sulky child.

"Zeke, come back here." Jarcey shook off his depression to think of a hard enough job for the boy to lift his spirit. "I got a job for ye."

The boy almost ran back into the office.

"Go see them calves is branded. They're gettin mixed up."

"Oh hell, Captain, I done that already." Zeke slumped with disappointment and started pegging the wall again, forgetting he wasn't supposed to.

On the nineteenth of July, Hannah and Jeremiah drove their pigs up into the woods to feed on mast. "I know Cap'n Jarcey told us we wasn't to, but they're a-gittin too skinny," Hannah said as they turned up into the woods behind their own cabin.

Jeremiah limped along on the other side of the litter, keeping them together. "They hain't a-goin nuthin happen nohow," he said, and expanded in the familiar shelter of the woods. " 'Tis more'n hit's worth, a-stayin cooped up like that. They ain't his hawgs nohow."

The litter felt the new freedom and scampered, after weeks of the filthy confinement of the pig-pen. They scattered under the chestnut-trees, nuzzled among deep mast, streaked off a few yards when leaves hit their backs, and stopped as suddenly, poised still and listening, and nosed delicately for chestnuts.

By late afternoon it was time to drive them back. Hannah and Jeremiah made themselves move again, out of the big, free silence that had calmed them after weeks. They spread out to round up the litter.

But the scent of wildness had caught the little pigs, triggered their nerves. They posed, using their stillness as camouflage, until Hannah or Jeremiah were nearly up to them, then slipped away like lightning in all directions to pose again, tantalizing, among the underbrush. It was like trying to herd bugs in a water-barrel.

Hannah and Jeremiah were still running them, concentrating by now in a panic of losing their winter meat, when the sun went down.

"Dear Gawd, Jeremiah." Hannah slipped up to him in the twilight. "We've got to abide out hyar till the dawn."

"Don't git worried now." He studied her face where the brambles had scratched it and combed her hair crazily down over her puckered forehead. "Thim critturs will herd their own selves when 'tis dark, and once 'tis dawn we can drive 'em afore they scatter."

"Gawd, I'm hongry." Hannah yawned, leaning, worn out, against a tree.

"I'll git usn somethin. 'Tain't the first night we-uns spent in the woods." Jeremiah started off.

"Ye hain't a-goin to use your gun?" she whispered.

"Naw, honey, I passed a blackberry thicket back a ways."

As they sat together, eating the berries, Hannah said, "Cap'n Jarcey's going to be mighty riled up."

"They hain't his hawgs." Jeremiah settled that. It was, after the long familiarity of trouble, the only thing they mentioned to each other about being caught out—the annoying small new authority set up in the fort.

In the dead, still time before dawn, Hannah was ripped out of sleep by the owl hoot. She listened for the answer without daring to move a muscle. It came, from across the valley. It came again from down-river. A hoot rippled in the up-river distance. The nearest hoot began again; then the woods were so still she could

[359]

hear the thump of Jeremiah's heart—or her own. The fear was back, breathing close in the woods; it smothered her body, reached in and froze her mind. She could smell it, like the warning smell of the snake.

"Jeremiah," she whispered, close to his ear.

He was awake, posed beside her as the pigs had posed, listening.

"Sh-h-h-t," he whispered.

The near owl laughed, and the pin-point answers laughed back, now five, now six, in place around the valley.

"Listen, Hannah." Jeremiah's voice was a breath in her hair. "We can cut up across the ridge and down behind the fort. We got to git thar and warn—"

"Listen." Hannah stopped him. But it was only one of the pigs, turning a delicate hoof in the leaves.

"We have to wait for a leetle more light. Thim youngsters will shoot anythin movin."

"Listen!" Hannah whispered again. They hid against the ground, trapped by fear, while the endless night slowly lifted.

Ezekiel, on watch in the sentry box, counted the owl hoots as they came again. He lowered himself down the ladder, aware as a hunter. They came again. He stopped, counted, waited. He ran across the sleeping yard among the animals, too lightly to wake them, through the open door of the office where Jarcey slept, and knelt beside him.

When he touched him, and the man's body tensed under his fingers, he knew that Jarcey was already awake, and that there was nothing to tell him.

"How long before dawn?" Jarcey whispered.

"An hour, sar."

"Wake the men. Get them down to the yard and to their posts. I'll get the women."

By the first light of the true dawn, every man and boy over twelve years old leaned on a gun at one of the openings, where the logs had been driven upright against the stone. The valley was as still as a tomb. Behind the men the women and girls fingered the linen wadding, counted the lead bullets they had been molding for six weeks, waited. Inside the main house the little children huddled, black and white, as quiet as the grown-ups, waiting, wide-eyed, poised, as if the familiar room were some strange station in a never-ending dim journey.

The fear was no longer a blanket. It had formed into a sharp star the size of Beulah, its points spread out to the owl hoots, its center a chill of horror, the time before action, the knife still cold in the belt, the gunmetal still dead against the cheek, the body huge with sensed exposure, under the coming, indifferent dawn. The men lay on their arms; the figures behind them in the icy river mist stood like shrunken shades, clutching their shawls against the invasion of daylight.

The birds began; the creatures inside the barn and in the fenced-in corner of the yard stumbled to their feet, began to low and whinny. Some woman, running past the hogpen, made the awakened hogs start their dry, frenzied squeal for food. The human beings shook off their dead silence and talked low, protected by the noise; the cold changed to excitement growing to the trigger-point of release.

Jarcey stood at the center of the yard, where they could all hear him, and gave his last command.

"Now ye all know," he said, "to watch for fires. You women, if ye see a lit arrow comin your way, take your buckets and follow it. These yellow fellows are monstrous handy at startin fires. When ye run your bullets, if ye've need to, cut off the necks close like I showed ye, and scrape them, so as to make them less like to jam. When ye lift patches, see that they're an hundred finer than those ye ordinarily use. Have them well oiled. If a rifle gets choked when the attack is on, there is one gun and one man lost. Ye will have no time to unbreech a gun and get a plug to drive out a bullet. See that your locks are well oiled and your flints sharp, so as not to miss fire." His voice rose, and they clung to it for calm.

"The enemy ye are fightin is the most cool, logical warrior in the world. He don't do nothin outside his trainin, and he don't lose his temper. He kills only men prisoners and children too little to work. If he gets in, don't you women be fools. Fight him till he grabs ye, but once he grabs ye, go still. Ye stand a good chance of not gettin hurt thataway, unless the Indian is a renegade that's picked up poor-white habits. Now his logic is the most dangerous thing about him, and 'tis his Achilles heel as well; he works to pattern once he starts to fight. It's a hard pattern to make out, but once ye do ye can whup him. *Don't get sore.* Keep cool, and run 'em off. Once they've found out we're well forted, they won't come again. Ye know Colonel Johnny has sent word that two thousand militia, mostly hunters and Indian-fighters, are a-headed this way. Cornstalk of the Shawnees is not a fool. He will keep his warriors around him once he knows the militia are a-comin, to protect the Indian country.

"Ye fight them fellows off today, and I reckon our troubles to be over for a while." Jarcey must have heard something, for his voice seemed to break, become gentle. "God bless—"

"Hyar they come." Zeke's mutter from the corner firing-hole was louder than Jarcey's voice because for days they had listened for those words. He had not once mentioned the fact that his parents were still out, but he had changed places with the youngest Carver so that his rifle would cover their cabin. He knew, they all knew, that the cabin was far out of range, but no one said a word.

Jarcey ran to his post. Solomon rolled over his rifle and grinned. "Thim bloodthirsty women are as merry as if they was havin a corn-husk." He licked his thumb.

"They were just damned sick and tired of waitin." Jarcey cradled his rifle against his cheek. *"Despueter, virgo: numero deus impare gaudat,"* he murmured.

"Oh shut up, scholar, afore I shoot ye in the tail." Solomon grinned at the open meadow and laid his cheek to his gun.

[362]

Zeke kept his eye on the creek, where he had seen a shape move in the high grass. Now it was gone again. Here and there over the meadow the grass moved, quieted again, seemed to roll toward them in flicks of patters that were gone as soon as they saw them. The quiet valley breathed movement in the sun, movement that came nearer, as if the valley itself were rolling toward them.

"Hold your fire." The whisper went from Jarcey along the stockade to the twitching fingers of the boys and quieted them.

"They hain't enough of thim," Solomon whispered, worried. "I don't like it."

"Wait." Jarcey had half risen, concentrated on the puzzle the movement made.

A shot cracked from the back of the house, then a volley.

"By God!" Jarcey crouched and ran. "Solomon, Carver, follow me. The main attack is from the woods uphill."

A shot whizzed out from Ezekiel's corner.

"I've got the pattern! They're attacking downhill, the goddam fools," Jarcey yelled, elated, over the rifle patter. "Every second man here cover the woods. Leave nine of ye for the valley side." They ran, bent low, around the house toward the shooting.

Carver belched sadly and fell. Mother Carver grabbed his gun and loaded it as she ran.

"Bring back my gun, ye damned interferin old woman!" he yelled. "I'm only hit in the leg. Goddam it, Jarcey, they're in the trees!"

"I'll attend to ye later, Carver, talkin thataway to your pore old maw." Mother Carver took aim.

Jeremiah and Hannah must have seen the Indian pattern when they tried to creep back over the hill-path to warn the fort and reach shelter. Ezekiel saw them first, Hannah in front, Jeremiah trying to keep up, with his game leg, as they appeared, crouching as they ran out of the up-creek woods, cutting a wide circle to try to get to the front gate.

Hannah stopped and screamed. She had flushed two Indians,

[363]

crawling in the grass. They lifted, as quail lift, from her feet. Ezekiel saw Jeremiah raise his gun. He and Jeremiah shot at the same time, but the boy's shot was spent, pitifully, too far away. He thrust his rifle back to Sara. "Oh Jesus," he kept whispering. "Holy Jesus, look down on thim. Holy Jesus, help thim. Holy Jesus." His hand clutched for the rifle. "Hurry, Sary." He fired again and handed it back.

Neither of them heard the fighting behind them any longer. They could only watch the terrible dumb-show, too far away. Hannah twisted and ran toward the fort. Jeremiah tried to reload. It was too late. Ezekiel saw his gun rise to bludgeon the naked figure that closed in on him. They seemed to stand like statues for a second, hugging each other, long-lost kin. Then Jeremiah's gun dropped from the air, backward, and he crumbled out of sight. The other figure knelt over him, only his shining naked back visible above the grass. He could have been an animal, calmly feeding there.

Hannah was nearer, within gunshot. "Oh Gawd, Sary, hurry," Ezekiel screamed and clutched for his reloaded gun. He missed the man, afraid to shoot too near his mother. He saw them close. "Keep still, Maw, keep still," he whispered. "Keep still, Maw. Oh pray Gawd make her keep still. Turn him, Maw, I'll git him if ye turn him." The shot whistled near the Indian's head. He ducked a little, annoyed.

But Hannah had seen Jeremiah behind her in the grass. She had been running with her knife out. She drove it into the wall of brown that closed in on her; Ezekiel saw the wound open like a surprised mouth and pour blood, saw her try to drive the knife again, saw it fall from her loosened fingers.

The Indians pulled the bodies toward the creek, out of range, as a panther pulls a deer to safety, its legs flapping awkwardly. Ezekiel could see that the Indian with Hannah's body dragged with one hand, the other holding his side.

"Jest pull her dress down, pull down her dress," Ezekiel was whispering without knowing he said a word.

To him the rest of the fight was dim. They won; somebody said they won with two wounded, and the youngest Carver dead. He had got overexcited and straightened up for a good shot. Jarcey and Solomon had taken an Indian prisoner, who had crawled too close and tried to reach over the stone wall to fire the logs. But he had lost too much blood from a wound in his side, and fainted as he stretched up to touch the brand. Jarcey and Solomon used him as bait, kept their guns trained over him when the others tried to drag him back.

Long after the firing had stopped, and they watched, dumb with sorrow, at the walls while the Indians, in their retreat, made another terrible pattern in the valley as they fired the cabins. Cabins and chairs, the long winter work of slow men whittling, of women spinning, weaving, the woof and warp, the endless hours, the spirals, the thimbles and the spools, grew to red bonfires in the evening light. So long to build, so little time to destroy, like the trees before them—an age to grow, a winter to bleed to death, an hour to fell.

It was Jarcey who lifted Ezekiel down from the wall and took his gun. He led the boy and Sara into the house, from where they had stood, loading and firing numbly into the empty air.

The boys were already out, scalping what bodies they could find, hallooing, wild with victory, before the light went.

Ezekiel sat in the office, not moving, not crying, stroking Sara's head as she lay against his lap. Someone came in—Jarcey never remembered who it was—and said something about the prisoner. Then Ezekiel stood up, let Sara drop away from him. Jarcey took his arm, but he shook it off.

"Let him go." Jarcey heard Sara's voice behind him.

The Indian was tied to the post in the yard where Jarcey had tied the shoat. He sat, his body still, his eyes raging like a baited cat's, while the children screamed around him and dared one another to go up close. He focused on Ezekiel as the boy walked through them, pushing the children away. If there was a glimmer of recognition between the two men, Ezekiel never knew afterward. Witcitki, the Bald Eagle, saw his own tomahawk that his uncle, the great Young Warrior of the Catawba, had given him, at the same time that Ezekiel saw the knife-wound in the Indian's side.

Witcitki tried to rise, but could only straighten proudly. "Mine, white thief," he said loudly to the Sheffield blade.

"Have it, then." Ezekiel spoke the first words since he had seen what he had seen, his voice as tired as a judge's, and drove the tomahawk into Witcitki's skull. Then, as carefully as he would have skinned a panther, he drew the scalping knife around Witcitki's head and tore off his scalp.

The children didn't dare go too near the body for a while after Ezekiel had gone. They closed in slowly, curiously. Finally Becky Catlett reached down and pointed out Witcitki's tattooed stars that fell across his cheek.

"Pappy, pappy," the youngest McKarkle called, excited. "He's got stars in his head, like you have. I can see thim. Pappy!"

They found Jeremiah's body lodged against the sycamore roots in the swimming hole the next morning. His legs floated gently in the lapping water, and the blood had congealed and clung to his scalped head like water weeds. Hannah lay abandoned, as she had once, long ago, fallen in the meadow, her petticoat torn to shreds, fluttering a little as the grass fluttered under the hot sun. The deer flies rose in a cloud as Solomon came near, and buzzed around his eyes.

Up behind the field where the rock pile had been, where now the settlement graveyard grew, Jarcey threw up the earth for the three graves, until they stood, two deep beds together in the black earth, and one in the Carvers' lot. Ezekiel brought down buckets of earth from farther up in the woods.

[366]

"Get plenty, son. We don't want these a-sinkin." Jarcey leaned against the grave wall and wiped his sweating face. "This soil is too good for graves.

"Dig a pit." He held the boy's ankle; Ezekiel turned and listened to his teacher's grave, factual voice. "Dig a pit deep in solid ground. If the earth that was took out don't fill up the pit when ye throw it back lightly and walk on it, the soil is fruitful; but if ye more than fill it, the soil is heavy. Remember that, son. 'Tis from Virgil's *Georgics*—useful to a farmer." Jarcey bent down again into the grave. "Some says *spissus* means barren, but 'tis not. 'Tis what we call heavy soil—the thick Canona grapevines grow in it . . ."

Ezekiel could hardly hear him now that the spade shuffled the earth up and clashed against small stones. "Yessar," he said dutifully and went back to the woods.

★   ★

Inside Sal's parlor two rough coffins stood on quilting trestles. All the fine-honed coffins they used as chests were gone in the fires that had lit the valley all night and died with the dawn. Sara's eyes burned from old smoke and old tears, but she couldn't cry any longer; she could only watch the still faces of Hannah and Jeremiah, shrouded and prepared by the women, clean and shrunken a little— "Peaceful at last after the perils of this wicked world," Mother Carver had said, examining her work, "though who'll bury 'em I can't think. Carver and McKarkle got mouths like hawg-pens. 'Twill have to be Captain Jarcey." She went off to help her daughter prepare her grandson. "He's a sweet talker."

The room was dead still; the fly whisk flagged in Sara's hand. She strained to keep her stinging eyes opened, after a night without sleep—now beyond feeling, beyond even listening to the noise in the yard. As her head fell she saw the coffins, reflected perfectly in the glassy surface of Sal's polished, genteel floor. Sal's gut-work, the skin of her hands, her unbending will to conquer the only

[367]

enemy she knew, even her sanity, seemed to mock now from the reflection of the Cohee Catletts' coffins, mock as the rocks had mocked that protected them, that there were more kinds of conquerors for a new heaven and a new earth than one fool gel could reckon.

Sara could almost hear her say so, and listen to the stamp of her small, bony foot.